THE

FIFTH

LETTER

A NOVEL

VIVIAN L. CARPENTER

Vivian L. Carpenter

Supreme Communications Group, L.L.C.

This book is a work of fiction.
The Fifth Letter. Copyright © *2015* by the Vivian Carpenter Trust.
All rights reserved.
Published in the United States by Supreme Communications Group, LLC
www.The FifthLetter.com

Book Cover Design by Michael Nowosatko
Interior design by Kathryn F. Galán

Cataloging-in-Publication Data is on file with the Library of Congress

ISBN: 978-0-69236-453-6

PRINTED IN THE UNITED STATES OF AMERICA

FIRST EDITION

In Loving Memory of My Ancestors

Hattie Thomas, My Muse, Related In Many Ways
Washington Thomas, My Great-Grandfather
George Washington Thomas, My Grandfather's Brother
Dr. Charles Lincoln Thomas, A Motivating Uncle
Doyal Wilson Thomas, My Demanding Father
Clarence Thomas, My Restrained Grandfather

John Galt was a famous Scottish author writing at the end of the enlightenment period—the early 1800s. He is not just a character of fiction. Galt created a Blackamoor character named Sambo in one of his once-popular works of fiction, *The Annals of the Parrish*. The author John Galt influenced many writers, even if they didn't realize it.

Some of his words are used in this story.

The Fifth Letter was inspired by the author's efforts to uncover her family history. She was compelled to explore the possibility of a family tie to Supreme Court Justice Clarence Thomas by her uncle, Charles Lincoln Thomas, who shared family stories. But she could not authenticate a direct bloodline to the sitting justice and claims no relationship. Given the nature of her family history, she does not believe anyone could uncover her family's secrets at this point in time—because they were buried long ago.

Hence, this is a work of fiction inspired by historical events and oral Thomas family history. Names, characters, organizations, businesses, places, events, and incidents are either a product of the author's imagination or are used fictitiously. The author told herself stories to create multiple points of views and lots of food for thought.

Enjoy.

"One day something happens—and things will never be the same again."

—*Hattie Mae Cobb*

Chapter One

Wednesday, July 10

Katherine Helena Ross waited on a vintage brocade settee in the West Wing of the White House. She was studying Norman Rockwell's painting, *The Problem We All Live With*, which depicted a young Black girl in a white dress on her way to school flanked by four U.S. marshals. The controversial painting's prime placement reminded all who waited to see this Democratic president that race had been a problem for the people, and suggested it was a problem that we all still lived with today.

Katherine studied the painting for an hour, waiting and wondering exactly what high-level appointment the President had in mind for her. She had filled out FBI paperwork months ago for a federal court appointment. *Was it the D.C. Circuit? Maybe.*

The President's chief of staff poked his head through the doorway. "He's ready for you."

Her heartbeat thudded against her chest and her hands went cold. *Nerves*, she thought, standing straight, marching through the opened door.

The chief of staff spoke as they made their way down the hallway. "Let me warn you. The President only has about thirty minutes. We've been vetting you and a few other candidates for months. If you decide to accept, we're prepared to make an immediate announcement. For reasons the President will explain, we decided not to confirm press speculation on the candidates under consideration until a final decision was reached."

A Secret Service agent opened the door to the Oval Office.

This was good.

President Nathaniel Greene rose to greet Katherine from the Resolute Desk, a nineteenth century wooden partner's desk with an eagle motif on its center panel. She noticed two speaker-telephone systems on the desktop, three neat stacks of documents, and family pictures on display. Red draperies with a cornice board framed the three ceiling-high windows. Rockwell's *Statue of Liberty* maintained its position on a prominent wall.

It had hung there for years.

Her gaze shifted to the President as he moved toward her. His speckled hair reminded her of the stress that aged all who occupied this office. Normally his gray eyes twinkled with excitement, but not on this day. He looked hollow-eyed. Tired. Grave.

His reelection campaign was not going well.

"I'll leave you two alone," the chief of staff said, closing the door as he left.

"It's good to see you again, Katherine," the President said, and gave her a hug. "Have a seat." He pointed to one of two facing sofas, then sat next to her. "I wanted you to be the first to know who my next Supreme Court nominee is—That is, if you decide to accept my nomination to be the next associate justice."

For a moment she thought she'd heard wrong. *Not the D.C. Circuit? He'd said associate justice.* Stunned, at first she could say nothing. Her mouth dropped open as a torrent of emotions flooded her. Elation. Then doubt. Could she handle the job? Then her confidence rose. "I didn't expect a nomination to the Supreme Court. It's been my dream, so yes. You know the answer is yes. But why pick me?"

"First, you're one of the best constitutional appellate lawyers in the country. Plus, you've got political support in both parties and you have a solid business background. Second, I believe the appointment of the first African American female to the Supreme Court can help unify our nation. Your academic credentials are above challenge— editor-in-chief of The University of Michigan Law Review. We believe you can make it through the process."

"Can *anybody* make it through now, with the dysfunction in the senate?"

The President looked away. "It will be tough, but you've got friends in this town."

"There were others under consideration with good legal pedigree—Harvard and Yale graduates. I heard someone else had been selected. What happened?"

"To be honest, everybody else I considered had red flags or couldn't get a blue slip of approval from one of their senators. You were the most qualified, all things considered. The confirmation process is brutal. But that's not the end of it. I need to level with you."

The President leaned forward, arms on his knees, his shoulders hunched. "A fierce battle has been raging since the birth of the country between two factions for control of the government. They operate in both political parties, working through invisible fraternities and associations—and powerful families. Most of the time, it's a battle of words, but the property rights debate is reaching a tipping point. There'll be winners and losers with billions at stake, if the Supreme Court takes on certain unsettled property issues. Sometimes these factions use violence to get their way."

"But that's not going on now, is it?"

"Justice Bands resigned because of an attempt on his life. He had health problems but that wasn't why he stepped down. You'll need security. You'll need to be careful, keep your guard up. Can you handle the pressure?"

"Yes," Katherine said after a moment of pause. "I have my father's spirit to support me."

"I also selected you because you have steel in your backbone— I understand you argued your first Supreme Court case after leaving your father's deathbed."

She nodded. "We were on the way to the Supreme Court that day. My dad was to deliver the oral argument in *Hilton Head Corporation v. State of Georgia*, a property rights case. I was in the back seat, reviewing related cases while my mother was in the front seat drilling my dad with questions to make sure he was ready. I was checking the case references to his responses. His recall was faultless. Then, for no apparent reason, he pulled the car over a few blocks from the Court. Through the rearview mirror I saw him squeeze his eyes shut. He put the car in park. He was panting. Obviously in distress."

"What did you do?"

"I drove him to Howard University Hospital as fast as I could. He was having a heart attack, but was still full of fight. In the emergency room, he handed me his marked-up brief and told me to go deliver his oral argument at ten. I had just been admitted to the Supreme Court Bar and I was supposed to sit next to my dad. Instead, I gave the oral argument in his honor with great emotion—but no tears. Tears would have disappointed him. We won the case. Overnight, I became a national expert in appellate corporate law. His last words to me were: 'Kathy, this is your opportunity. Don't cry. You can do this—for us.' So I want to do this for *us*—Dad, me and We the People—I want to be a great Supreme Court justice."

The process began with flashing cameras as she entered the East Room in the White House where the President introduced her to the nation on live television.

Chapter Two

Washington, D.C.
Sunday, September 16

The day before her Senate confirmation hearing, Associate Supreme Court Justice Nominee Katherine Helena Ross moved through a field of friendly faces in front of Allen Temple A.M.E. Church as the path before her cleared. The press and her supporters snapped her picture. She climbed the steps with confidence, security officers at her side.

She looked straight ahead.

Two men ascended the steps behind them. They wore crisp combat fatigues.

Katherine's shoulder-length hair was hidden under a blue velvet hat that she held in place with her right hand. The hat had been the first item she selected that day, then a navy blue St. John couture suit with gold buttons, simple gold earrings with matching necklace, and low-heeled navy Ferragamo shoes with matching purse. Simple. Elegant. Polished.

At the entrance to the sanctuary, she scanned the vestibule to a spot beyond where the ushers were passing out programs. In the last pew, a well-dressed man with dreadlocks stood, not taking his seat. Troubled eyes. He wore a black conservative suit accented by a red, green and yellow African scarf with matching cap.

Katherine caught his glare and averted her eyes, feeling a bit uneasy.

She'd seen him before. Was he stalking her?

Once Katherine was seated, the pastor signaled the organist to begin. The choir marched in as the man with troubled eyes approached the podium from the left.

He clicked the microphone on.

He shouldn't be up there, she thought.

The announcements clerk rushed up from the rear, but not before the man began to speak.

"Don't be a heartless John Galt," he shouted from the hijacked podium, glaring at Katherine with fire in his eyes. "The Black Activists Mobilization Network—BAMN—wants to know are you gonna be for the oppressors or for us? Don't betray us. We're fightin' back."

She locked her eyes on him.

The pastor rose. The minister seated next to him tugged on his sleeve. In that pause, the man retreated as quickly as he'd come.

The shaken announcements clerk retook the podium, welcoming the visitors. The two men in combat fatigues stood up when their names were called.

They sat in the middle of Katherine's pew, just two empty seats away. *Who were they?*

Feeling like swarmed prey, she shifted her gaze toward the stained glass windows. Morning sunlight streamed through, exploding into a prism of colors. In the middle pane, a white dove swooped toward a target. Katherine knew the Bible verse that it represented:

I saw the Spirit come down from heaven as a dove.
—John 1:32

She felt God's spirit in the church.

Before her, an energized young-adult choir swirled like rhythmic waves to the uplifting tones of piano and organ, tambourines, saxophone, and drums. Several people rose to their feet and swayed, adding their energy to the flow of worship.

The choir's jazzy rendition of the hymn *Looking for You* pulled Katherine from her seat. She felt a gentle touch on her shoulder. An older woman blew her a kiss with a wide grin. Katherine returned the smile as she clapped and rocked to the music.

It wasn't long before the congregation became one body, swaying in unity. Then the man with the dreadlocks bolted from his seat again and jumped into the air in the center aisle. He held up his right hand balled into a tight fist, and pumped it in time with the music. Then he shouted the words to the song, "That's for the struggle. That's for the pain. That's for those dark nights…"

His attention-grabbing moves broke the unity.

Two deacons at the front of the church bowed their heads in a prayerful pose. Katherine sat down. One of her security guards moved toward the man and directed him back to his seat, sitting next to him on the outer edge of his pew.

Katherine's other protector moved to the aisle seat next to her. The two deacons in the front of the sanctuary resumed "at attention" postures, monitoring the frenzy of moving bodies.

Pastor Charles G. Adams, a guest minister from Detroit, wore a scarlet ministerial robe. Gold Latin crosses were embroidered on two black velvet panels down the front. Adams was not tall, yet his presence announced a man with stature. He rose from his knees after prayer at his seat, then moved with purpose to the pulpit.

"Revelations, chapter seven," Pastor Adams said. "Verses sixteen and seventeen. They shall hunger no more. Neither shall they thirst anymore. For God shall wipe away every tear…"

On cue, the musicians broke into *Revolution,* another upbeat spiritual song.

In a unified tribute of praise, the choir released the full power of their voices.

When the song came to an end, Adams opened his leather-bound Bible and said, "Turn to John, twelfth chapter, verses forty-five and forty-six."

The entire congregation read out loud:

"And he who sees Me, sees Him who sent Me.

"I have come as a light into the world that whoever

"Believes in Me should not abide in darkness."

"We're all blessed to be in this church today," Adams said. "Here, in a church founded by freed Blacks ten years before the first shots rang out in the Civil War. Here, in a church sitting on the Hill of Good Hope in the nation's capital. Here, in a church that supported former slaves who came to make their first homes as free people. Here, in a church burned to the ground once and rebuilt from the sweat and tears, pennies and dollars of those who didn't have a lot of money but had a lot of faith. Here, in a church where the stained glass windows bring a rainbow of colors and a rainbow of blessings. I'm honored to be here today."

Katherine pulled a pen and small notepad from her purse and began to take notes, because her mother had told her this man knew how to feed hungry souls.

She could not write quickly enough, because everything he said gave her something more to prepare for the challenges she would face in the morning. He had the spirit of God in his eyes, and the word of God on his lips. She wrote:

Learning and thinking are required of faith.

Follow your reason where it leads and have the faith to follow God's inspired path.

Understand there is a spiritual obligation to be intelligent.

Don't separate the mind from your religion.

Love must rule over all things. Remember this.

Don't fight against anything. Fight for reconciliation. Fight for God's grace.

"Katherine Helena Ross," Pastor Adams said to her.

She was about to underline *fight for reconciliation*—but couldn't. She glanced up.

"Soon to be the Honorable Supreme Court Justice Katherine Helena Ross," Adams continued. "God wants me to give you a

13

message. You have a spiritual obligation to display your God-given intelligence when you sit on the bench.

"Don't become a worthless token like our brother sittin' on high. When you get the chance to make things right—make things right."

Katherine sat up straight in her seat, a little uncomfortable knowing all eyes were on her.

"I didn't get to this place by myself." He pointed at her with sharpened eyes. "And you didn't get to your high place in life without some help. Black people working with caring white people opened the doors for us. We needed help. And that is the truth."

Several people in the congregation stood, applauded and shouted, "Amen."

"You've always been with us," Adams said. "Your father and grandfather were deacons here before they passed on, and your mother praises the Lord at the first service every Sunday. We pray for your confirmation. Fear no evil. You are blessed."

Coming to a close with a crescendo of spiritual instructions for all challenged in the struggles of life, the minister said, "as you fight to accomplish your God-inspired mission, remember this: When God is for you—nobody can stop you!"

Intensity of purpose radiated through Julianne LaSalle's eyes as she sped past the emptying pews and cut through an empty row to reach Katherine at the back of the sanctuary. Red glasses framed her eyes. She had brown skin and dimples, her ponytail held with a black clip. She wore a simple black dress with flowered scarf and red shoes. A childhood friend of Katherine's, she was a reporter with Urban Times Media.

She caught up to Katherine and said, "Walter Rodney was acting kind of strange. You better keep an eye on him. I'm a little concerned."

"What do you know?"

"He joined the church last week. He's trying to recruit youth in the church for a BAMN-like organization. I think he picked the name, Black Activists Mobilization Network, as a play on the acronym BAMN. Do you know about BAMN?"

"*By Any Means Necessary?*" Katherine asked, descending into a crowd of people in front of the church, Julianne fixed at her side. She waved to those she knew.

Julianne vied for her attention. "Do you know what their agenda is?"

"Off the record," Katherine replied, "I've been told they have an international socialist agenda. Coming from Asia. Were the men in combat fatigues with BAMN?"

"Don't know. But don't worry. I've alerted church security. The deacons on duty today are retired police officers. Armed. We've got your back."

Chapter Three

As Katherine approached the Cadillac sedan in front of the church, her driver hurried to open the rear passenger door. He monitored the churchgoers' movements and excited chatter as they passed her vehicle. A small boy pointed to the shiny black sedan as his mother dragged him along, forcing him to trot.

Katherine waved at the little boy. He waved back, keeping pace with his mother.

Before she reached the open car door, Walter Rodney, with two young men at his side, pushed through the crowd, blocking her path.

"So where do you stand?" Rodney hollered. "We don't need another worthless one."

The crowd closed in. Katherine's security grabbed her arm, pushing their way through.

"I stand on God's word," she responded, continuing her stride.

"Let her by," a voice shouted from the crowd.

Her security and the crowd nudged Rodney out of the way.

"You're gonna have to answer to the people if you get in," he shouted.

"I'll answer in the morning." Katherine settled into the rear seat and glanced at her watch. "I'll go directly to my mother's," she told her driver.

"Do you know that guy?" he asked, pulling away from the curb.

"Not really, but I know he could be trouble."

As they rolled down Good Hope Road, she gazed through tinted windows at several boarded-up buildings that had distinctive lettering in bold colors. She'd noticed the same lettering in many oppressed areas in the world. The writing seemed to be painted from the same energy—by one invisible hand working through the hands of many dispirited souls. Most would call it graffiti, but she thought of it as creative art.

After a few turns, they entered I-295 heading downtown. The freeway traffic glided along as they crossed the calm Anacostia River. Today, the water appeared as a glistening blanket from shore to shore, the sun's rays landing softly on its surface.

Katherine pulled a paper with the latest senate vote count from her purse and scanned it. She felt a quiver of excitement.

Now a seasoned veteran, she had argued before the Supreme Court on several occasions. Ironically, her father's death had set up the opportunity for her to gain the experience needed to become the head of the appellate litigation section of the leading law firm in the capital, mainly defending corporate rights. She often was consulted on important cases scheduled for oral argument at the Court, and was well known in elite legal circles.

Now on her cell phone, she called in favors. Her well-connected friends had told her not to worry. Six conservative votes were in the bag. Two more would join, if needed. Politics.

Her eyes closed again.

Her mind roamed to thoughts of *him*. She knew why: Her driver was wearing Old Spice cologne. She took in its scent with every breath. Distracting. *He* wore Old Spice.

She wondered if his scent was still in the sweater she had stored away long ago after he never returned for it. She needed to throw it away.

Katherine wished he didn't come to mind so much, but she had thought of him constantly since accepting the nomination. Even though she had avoided him for years, she knew he would support her. They had dated a short time while enrolled at the University of

Michigan Law School. She wished that that hadn't happened. But it had. He knew what he needed to know about her, so she decided not to visit the senator from Michigan.

Her last words to him had been, *I won't call you again.*

So, she hadn't.

And he never called her again, either.

Sixty-three votes were more than enough.

Katherine slid the vote count back into her purse. She needed to stop worrying about this.

She was good to go.

When they arrived at the Watergate complex, the driver took a moment to scan the calm street. He studied the vehicles parked nearby before opening the car door for her. As she approached the building, the concierge opened the door and escorted her to the elevator, and then notified her mother that she was on the way up. By the time Katherine reached her mother's apartment on the ninth floor, the door had been unlocked for her.

Her mother, Helena Ross, still taught adult Sunday school at the age of seventy-eight. She attended the early morning service then taught her class. Mrs. Ross was normally in her car by eleven, on the way home to cook. As a rule, Katherine showed up on time for Sunday dinner by three, after attending the eleven o'clock service.

Katherine entered her mother's waterfront condo which was expertly decorated with fine art, custom window treatments, and Baker furniture. Fresh flowers in decorative vases were placed in strategic positions in the living room—all a temporary distraction from the impressive view of the Potomac River.

The kitchen was painted a bright yellow that seemed to pull happy feelings from a person's soul. Two yellow Le Creuset cast iron pans and a black frying pan sat on the black glass modern cooktop. A stainless steel timer ticked away near the oven.

With her silver hair upswept into a French roll, Mrs. Ross executed in the kitchen with the precision of a well-rehearsed dancer.

She grabbed flour, butter and seasonings for the gravy. Put them in position. Checked the time. Pulled the roasting hen from the lower double oven. Checked the meat thermometer. Done. Turned lower oven off. Right front burner under the cast iron skillet turned on. Butter dropped into the skillet to sizzle.

Katherine savored this moment, knowing that her mother would always be the same no matter what was going on in the world. Efficient. Audacious. Resilient. She drew strength from her.

The aroma of homemade yeast rolls took Katherine back to her childhood. When the timer went off, she knew they had been in the oven for seventeen minutes. Exactly. Not too light. Not too dark. A perfect golden brown.

Katherine grabbed a towel. Heat escaped when she opened the oven; the warmth caressed her face. She placed the pan of perfectly-shaped cloverleaf rolls on the countertop. Seated on a stool at the counter, she brushed the roll tops with butter. Unable to wait, she grabbed one, broke off a cloverleaf section, and bit into it. As she savored the taste, she said, "Mom, nothing is better than the taste of your rolls."

"You say that all the time."

Her mother reached for the hen cooling on the counter. As she lifted the lid off the old black-and-white-speckled roaster pan, the aroma of rosemary escaped with the steam.

Soon they were seated at the table with a bouquet of flowers in the center. After blessing the meal of chicken, wild rice, fresh green beans with onions, and cranberry sauce, her mother reached for the bowl of beans. "I talked to Julianne LaSalle this morning. She said it's important she speak to you."

"She did. At church." Katherine cut the chicken for both of them. "What'd she tell you?"

Her mother pursed her lips. "She's working on a story about some socialist group. Pastor stopped them from meeting in the church. She's concerned they might get violent."

"I've asked my security to talk to her."

"If she's given you some type of warning you should take it seriously. You know her."

"Yes, I know she has a good nose for sniffing out trouble."

"Are you going out this evening?"

"No, I need to be well rested for my hearing. I'm going to bed early and read."

"Good. What are you reading?"

"Supreme Court briefs. What else do I have time for?"

"You shouldn't work on Sunday. You'll be ready."

Katherine gazed at her mother. She didn't know much about her side of the family.

"Mom," she said, leaning forward in her chair, "you've never told me much about your life before you met Dad. Is there anything I should know?"

Her mother stopped eating and let several moments pass.

With a soft voice she said, "There are some things I've never talked about that I know I should share. I've just been waiting for the right time. Yes, we have family secrets."

"What?"

Her mother closed her eyes and lowered her head. "I—I can't."

"Mom," Katherine said with alarm, "what is it?"

No response.

She stood, wondering if her mother might need help. "Are you okay?"

"Yes, I've been struggling with how to tell you." She gazed away, then turned to face her daughter. "Maybe it's time."

"Time for *what*? Am I adopted?"

"Of course not. You're my baby."

"Then what should I know?" She decided to wait out her mother's silence.

"Your father wrote something for you years before his death. A lot happened in my life before I met him. I'll have to go get it. It's in my safe deposit box."

"But I have a hearing in the morning. I need to know everything *now*. Just tell me."

Katherine could almost see her mother's mind at work by the expression on her face.

"I don't want to remember every dirty detail. Can't deal with it now. Understand?"

Katherine responded with cutting eyes. "No. I don't."

"You're better off not knowing yet," her mother said with twisting lips. "That way you can answer their questions honestly. If you knew, it could hurt you."

Chapter Four

Hart Senate Office Building
Monday, September 17

"Who the heck *is* Katherine Helena Ross?" Texas Senator Maxwell demanded. "You have no judicial opinions that we can review. We know you've been well paid to work on the Supreme Court filings of others, but that doesn't tell us what you independently think. How do we know you won't just flip out on us?"

"Flip out, Senator? How?"

"You know what I mean. Presenting yourself here for the Supreme Court with no judicial record. That takes some nerve. Most smart people wouldn't do it. They know you need to be a judge to have the experience to be a Supreme Court justice. We don't know what you might do. There's nothing to judge you on."

Katherine sat alone at a black-draped table before the eighteen members of the Senate Judiciary Committee, her back to the audience. Blazing floodlights shone above her head. The impressive hearing room boasted two-story-high ceilings, wood-paneled walls, bright lighting, and state-of-the-art communication equipment behind second-floor glass windows. The seal of the United States Senate was carved into the wall, centered above the semi-circular rostrum fitted with eighteen microphones.

Katherine jotted notes during Maxwell's attack. Her supporters were seated in the first rows behind her. The press was on the floor in front of her, their lenses trained to record her slightest reaction, so she kept her expression stoic and frozen although she reeled inside at Maxwell's comments. So far, she had made no serious mistakes in her testimony. She had thought he wouldn't be a problem, counting him as a yes vote.

Her mistake.

She asked, "Do you have any questions for me?"

Maxwell hit her with questions in rapid fire.

"Are you a liberal or a conservative?"

"Neither."

"That's not a good answer for me."

"That's the truth."

"What about state rights?"

"I believe in the U.S. Constitution and state rights."

"Do you think immigrants should have the same rights as American born citizens?"

"I respect the right of Congress to create immigration laws under our Constitution."

"Do you believe in same-sex marriages?"

"I believe people can fall in love with anybody, but the issue of marriage is a matter of positive law that has to be worked out in the political arena for the law to be stable and enforceable through time. When the timing is right, I think Congress will deal with the issue."

"Huh? Never mind. What do you think about capital punishment?"

"I am pro-life for all."

"That's a problem. Ya' see. You might flip out on us. Capital punishment is a state right."

"Life is an inalienable right. The Supreme Court must balance conflicting rights."

Finally he said, "I have no more questions. Maybe we shouldn't rush this thing. She'll probably twist things up. Who knows what she might do."

For seven hours that first day, Katherine had declined to answer questions in the abstract, deferring to the Court's established legal precedents as a defense to potentially lethal questioning. Yet she had explained her position on myriad topics with patience. Now she endured assaults to her professional image.

Maxwell had painted her as unqualified due to lack of judicial experience.

How did one answer the question: "Who are you?"

It was the kind of question that had kept her awake at night ever since the nomination.

Without moving her head, she caught a glimpse of Senator Skip Graham with his head down. He had sat through most of her hearing that way—reading and writing.

They had avoided direct eye contact all day.

"Very well," the judiciary committee chairman said. "If you have no further questions, I'll turn the questioning over to Senator Clay from the great state of Florida.

"Madam," Senator Clay began, "I, too, am concerned that we have no evidence on what type of judge you would be, and that bothers me—more than a little bit." He paused. "After listening to your testimony this morning, we know you believe that the full range of a justice's life experience influences how they look at the facts in a case. And therefore, I believe your life experience would impact your decision in a case. Is that a correct inference?"

"Yes."

"I know you won't answer a question in the abstract. Therefore, I feel compelled to ask a personal question that is not based on any hypotheticals: Have you ever had an abortion?"

Katherine could hear gasps from those surprised by the very personal question that had been considered out of bounds until now.

She glared at her interrogator. "Women have a right to privacy in such matters."

"Your medical records could become public," Senator Clay prodded. "They're digging."

"Then our legal system should punish those who would deny me my privacy rights."

"That response may not go over well with my supporters."

"Your supporters should know I am sickened by the thought of abortion and pray for the soul of every woman who has felt compelled to risk her life by having one."

"You need to answer my direct question, Ms. Ross. You know how this goes. I'm an undecided vote. I need to know what you stand for."

"I stand for what's right."

"Don't blow it at this point," he warned.

Katherine stared Senator Clay in the eye and said nothing, drawing strength from Pastor Adams' words. *When God is for you— nobody can stop you.*

"If you've never had an abortion, just say so," he said. "Why are you making this so difficult? If you've had one, you need to explain your decision to us so we can evaluate it."

"I have privacy rights. Nothing in the U.S. Constitution requires me to give up my personal rights to sit on the Supreme Court. If someone wants to break the law to look at my medical records, then let them. I'm not going to fear that."

"Very well then, I have no further questions."

Graham, *the* senator from Michigan, leaned forward and adjusted the microphone. "Let the record reflect the fact that about one-third of Supreme Court justices have had no judicial experience in their background before their nomination to the Court. So the fact that Ms. Ross has no judicial experience can't be a disqualifier from service for the first African-American female nominated to the Court. In fact, I think it would be an unconscionable discriminatory act if we used lack of judicial experience as a reason to reject this highly qualified nominee."

Katherine was relieved he had come to her defense, but she didn't want to owe him anything.

The chairman continued, "With that comment duly noted in the record, this hearing will resume at nine in the morning. We'll begin with questions from Senator Graham."

Katherine knew she wouldn't be able to sleep that night.

Chapter Five

The Watergate Complex

Helena Ross was far away in a happy place when she heard a faint ringing that grew louder as she was pulled back from sleep into her bedroom. She focused on the offending machine. Who could be calling her at eleven at night? Her caller ID said Julianne LaSalle. What could she want this late?

Mrs. Ross picked up the receiver and said, "What's wrong?"

"I hate to call you so late," Julianne said. "But I just got a call from the Associated Press asking me to help them confirm the accusation that Frederick Ross is not Kathy's father. Do you have a comment?"

"No. I don't have a comment on something so ridiculous. Frederick G. Ross is Katherine's father. Go check her birth record. Goodnight."

At seven in the morning, Helena Ross answered another call from a reporter whom she didn't know. When he identified himself, she quickly said, "No comment."

Next, the doorman called. The press had inquired if she lived at the Watergate. Of course, that information had not been confirmed but they had camped in front of the building anyway, waiting for her to emerge.

Mrs. Ross decided she wouldn't go to the hearing that morning in order to avoid the press, but she still had to venture out at some point to go to the bank and retrieve her husband's letter. She turned the television to CNN. *Maybe she could just walk to the bank. They wouldn't expect her to be out walking like a tourist today. Yes, she could walk over to Katherine's condo from the bank and finish watching the hearing there. They could talk after Katherine read the letter.*

Seated in her living room with a black cup of coffee, Helena heard the bacon sizzling in the skillet—but she didn't move before it burned. She was glued to the flat screen. When she finally got up at a commercial break, the bacon strips had disintegrated. She threw the blackened flakes in the trash and turned on the air vent over the stove to clear out the smoke, but that didn't change the smell. Turning water on the hot skillet in the sink, she was engulfed in steam. When she felt the heat, she decided not to deal with the mess until the skillet cooled.

It was important for Katherine to understand her family history, so she had been working on her memoir. She didn't know if it should be written as a work of fiction, because it contained information that some might view as criminal. She would let Katherine decide about the ultimate publication. She just needed to get the story out of her system, but it was hard to write. She would give it to Katherine at the right time.

But this definitely was not the right time.

Helena worked on her memoir in no particular order. When she had the energy to write about something in her past, she wrote it. Then sometimes she let the manuscript sit for months or years with no work effort. Her husband had encouraged her to write as a way to heal emotional wounds. He coaxed her by writing a chapter himself about how he had met her.

Over the years, they had worked on his love story many times, cutting things out, adding new details from their memories, and then cutting them out again because this was to be a story that would reveal the truth about the circumstances of Katherine's birth in a loving way. Mrs. Ross had tried to rework it as her story, but she couldn't.

Her version of the story was short. She had been traumatized.

Some memories had been erased.

She never wanted Katherine to feel unloved or unwanted. That was why she had never told her about the past. *Why couldn't they just let it stay buried?* She felt bad thinking about it and wanted to go back to bed. She wanted to sleep. But the phone kept ringing.

She knew it would make a difference, if everybody knew. Her private life story could derail Katherine's greatest opportunity in life. She had no doubt about that. Helena Ross didn't want to tell her daughter that she was born of an illicit relationship, nor reveal what had driven her to leave her family and cut off contact.

The way she figured it, there was only one way for Katherine to survive the vetting process: lack of knowledge was really her safest path.

How would that go over on national television?

Katherine was going to be mad, but it couldn't be helped.

She penned a note to her daughter that read:

September 17

Dear Katherine:

I did not intend to share the following information with you until after my death, but it seems giving it to you now is the wisest thing to do, given the rumors that have surfaced.

Your father and I debated about when to tell you certain things many times before his death. Your father did not agree with my decision to delay, but he honored my wish. So don't blame him for whatever you might feel after reading this. I am the one responsible. Forgive me. I've done what I thought was best for you over the years. I love you, Baby.

I decided the best way to tell you was by sharing the story about our love affair in your father's own words. Well, this is mostly his version of the story. You will be able to recognize the places where I added my two cents to his narrative. But this is not the whole story.

This is what I think you need to know as your hearing continues in the morning. I plan to be there to support you. But I will not answer any questions.

Make sure you are alone when you read your father's story. Have a glass of wine and know that we both love you with all of our hearts. Having you as a daughter was our greatest joy.

Love,

Mom

Chapter Six

May 6, 1987

Kathy,

I am sharing my story about how I met your mother so you will know what happens when a man falls in love. I hope your mom does not make too many more edits to my story, if I predecease her. But, we both know that she might.

I should have told you sooner, but your mother was never ready to discuss this matter with you. Talking about some things has always been difficult for her. Maybe she will never be able to share some details of her life with you. Don't push her. Think of her as an oyster with a pearl inside. Use too much force and the pearl could be damaged. I can only pray one day she will share her secrets with you. Don't expect them all to flow in one sitting. Her story will take time to unfold.

With regard to your own life, wait for the man who unconditionally loves you and is not afraid to express and show it. True love is patient and kind. You deserve the same kind of love that I've given your mother. I trust you will not settle for less. When it happens, it just happens.

I hope you will not be reading this after the death of both of us. If so, I'm sorry. Know that you have had my unconditional love from the day you were born.

Your Dad,

Frederick G. Ross

Chapter Seven

Harvard Law School Library
Winter 1959

The first time I saw your mother, I was a third-year student at Harvard Law School trying to study in the library. She was a new library assistant. I was instantly attracted to her. I picked a seat where I could watch her as she went from the circulation desk to the stacks. Her movement distracted me for hours on that first cold day. I was mesmerized for weeks. My studies suffered.

But who could blame me?

Her hair was silky smooth with bouncing curls just past her shoulders. Her complexion was flawless. Her almond eyes were hiding something. Pain. Your mother never smiled, but her eyes shouted the presence of a sweet soul, anyway. Her inviting lips were highlighted with bright red lipstick. With a natural golden skin color, her beautiful face was only missing a warm smile. I wondered why she didn't smile.

She was obviously a mulatto, like me. But unlike me, she didn't look like she had any Native American Indian blood. I wondered, but never knew for sure, if she had French blood, too. Whatever blood she had made an awesome genetic combination. Reserved beauty. Cautious. Regal.

I've often imagined the angel Cupid, with his little bow and arrow, taking aim at me on the first day I saw her. His arrow pierced my heart, penetrating the depths of my soul.

Day after day I watched her. Every evening I took the same seat to study and consider how to approach her. Somehow your mother seemed experienced—perhaps more experienced than I in matters of love. The other women in my life no longer interested me. All of my available time was spent in the library. Observing your mother. Wanting her.

I finally got my nerve up and asked her, over the circulation counter, "Will you go out with me?"

"No," she said with no softening comment to explain the rejection.

I walked away, trying to hide my disappointment. I felt sick; her refusal had a physical effect on my body. I actually felt pain from her rejection. I thought this was ridiculous. I didn't even know her. I wondered how she could affect me in this manner. I tried to control my feelings. I couldn't.

I was drawn to your mother as if she was a magnet and I was a metal paper clip. I was sure that we were meant to be because I could not stop thinking about her.

The next day, I went back to the same spot in the library. I was not strong enough to fight the attraction to your mother, even in the face of rejection. I took my same seat at a reading table along her path to the second-floor stacks.

As she walked by me, I could smell her perfume. The scent of vanilla reminded me of a warm summer night.

I wondered if God had a sense of humor. There shouldn't be distractions like your mother in the law library. It was bad. I had a crush. And it was strong, like the one my grandpa told me about. My French blood was flowing. I muttered to myself while trying to focus on the words in front of me.

What was she doing to me with no effort?

The next day she wore a white smock with a black skirt and flat black shoes. Her hair was pinned up. Attractive. Graceful. She approached my cubicle again with a pile of books in her arms without looking at me.

"Are you married?" I whispered as she came around the stacks again.

"No," she responded and sauntered away, out of my sight for the remainder of the day.

After the library closed, I waited outside of the rear exit door for her to leave the building so I could talk to her again. The night air was like the inside of a freezer. She attempted to hustle past me without acknowledging my presence.

"Do you have a boyfriend?" I asked.

"No," she answered without slowing.

I followed to catch up with her. "I want to take you out."

I thought your mother was trying to play hard to get since I'd always had my pick of girls. No girl that I invited had ever said no before.

Without looking at me, your mother said "no" again.

"Why not?"

"It's none of your business," she snapped. Then she hurried her pace. I sped up too, unwilling to just let her drop me without consideration.

"Why won't you at least look at me? I'm not that bad looking. Am I?"

Mom's Narrative: *Your dad was very attractive to me. Six feet tall with an athletic build, he had olive skin with dark brown wavy hair that he kept greased. For the record, I did notice him as he tried to study that day. But I could not allow myself thoughts of the possibility of having a man like that in my life at that point. I thought he was eye candy. Nothing more. So I resolved not to even look at him. I didn't need any more trouble.*

As you know, your father had mixed blood: French, American Indian, and Negro. I wasn't sure he was Black. I didn't know what race he was. All I knew was that he was a good-looking man studying to be a lawyer at Harvard Law School. A prized catch.

So I replied, "I am sure you can have any girl on this campus that you want."

"That may be true," your father responded in his arrogant tone. "But the rest of the ladies are not keeping me from sleeping at night. Can we go to the Wursthaus or the Oxford Grill, maybe, for a drink?" Now that I was looking at him, his voice took on a more confident tone.

"No," I said again and turned to walk away.

Not letting up, your father said, "I want to know why you won't go out with me." Then he grabbed my arm, turned me around, and drilled into my eyes. I couldn't speak. Tears threatened. Embarrassed, I breathed deeply, trying to stop the impending flood. But, I couldn't. [Edited by HR]

Dad's Narrative: With a flood of tears, your mother's hard shell crumbled, exposing her pain to me. I was shocked. Her tears pulled at my heart.

"Where do you live?" I whispered, showing my concern.

Your mother did not respond.

I touched her shoulder. "I'm here for you."

"In Arlington."

As she wiped her eyes with a tissue, she mumbled, "I'm so sorry."

Your mother tried to get away from me again. She headed for the bus stop. I kept up with her. My stride is longer than hers. (*Kathy, you are supposed to smile at this comment.*)

"What are you sorry for?" I softly asked.

"My life."

She slowed her pace and we walked the remaining distance in silence. As we stood at the bus stop, I waited for your mother to speak. She didn't. The bus arrived.

"Goodbye." She turned to get on the bus.

I reached for her arm and looked into her eyes again, and somehow felt the piercing wails of primal pain from the depths of her soul. Kathy, I knew I couldn't let her go then or I would lose her forever.

So I boarded the bus to Arlington with her.

We took seats near the rear, on opposite sides because there weren't two seats together. I think your mother was thankful for that. I watched her, struggling to hold back her tears in a frozen position.

For the entire ride, she didn't look at me. She kept her head turned to the window and the darkness of the night.

Soon she stood and reached for the pull cord. She made her way to the front. I followed her. We both got off of the bus.

"So, what are you going to do now?" she asked in a stronger voice.

"I'm going to walk you home," I said with a flare of chivalry. "I am not going to leave a lady with a wounded heart at the bus stop. How far?"

"Four blocks."

Mom's Narrative: *I wished that I'd met your father in another life. I felt that I did not deserve to be with a man like him. That my fate had been sealed. I felt hopeless. I was trembling inside.*

Again, I waited for your mother to speak. She didn't. She tightened the scarf around her neck and put on her gloves. I put my right hand in my pocket, my tax regulations casebook in my left. I didn't have any gloves. I kept switching hands to keep my fingers from freezing.

In silence, we walked the four blocks to your mother's little one-room studio. As we got closer to her place, I wondered what I doing out there with such a cold fish. I knew nothing was going to happen with her that night. She was too upset. With each step I told myself I was acting like a fool. I knew your mother might be trouble. But I didn't care. I still wanted her. I told myself she was going to have to say "no" at least one more time before I left her that night. I prepared emotionally for your mother's final rejection.

Persistence. That's how I've gotten everything in life. (*Kathy, remember this: If you really want something, don't give up hope.*) I wanted your mother. My confidence returned.

We arrived at her building and walked up the stairs. To my surprise, your mother lived alone. She opened the door and let me into her apartment. The first thing I noticed was her bed. It had an inviting yellow, orange and gold bedspread on it. Obviously luxury linens. I did not expect that. Her bed was neatly made with several accent pillows.

I remember her small dining table with just two chairs.

One for me, I thought.

A small beige and red couch with a coffee table faced the windows. A wooden dresser had a crate of books on each side of it. Yellow canopied curtains draped the windows, allowing light from the streetlamp to seep through.

I eased over to the couch and noticed several suitcases lined up next to the closet door. Her closet was open and full of very nice clothes. On a side table set a Singer sewing machine and a basket full of patterns. The pattern for the white smock your mother wore was on top of the pile, revealing her skill as a seamstress.

I watched your mother take off her coat, then turn and hold out her hand for mine without saying anything. I gave her my coat and placed my textbook on her coffee table. I stood watching her. She placed our coats on a hook behind the entry door.

Although small, her apartment had a nice, inviting feel to it. It smelled of her perfume. Everything was neat and clean, well-organized.

She faced me and her beauty warmed the space between us as her eyes made a plea.

"Can I have a cup of coffee before you throw me out into the cold?" I asked.

"Okay," she said to my surprise. "Do you want some tomato soup and crackers?"

"That would be nice."

As I looked out of her window, I saw icicles on the telephone poles. They looked like daggers that could kill a man. The wind howled against the windows. Everything made her place all the more alluring.

I settled back on your mother's sofa. Finally I could read my assigned homework cases and watch her, knowing I couldn't lose her. I had no desire to leave her that night.

I made up my mind: I was going to spend the night with her.

As she reached for the can of soup from a top shelf, I noticed her waistline.

She poured the can's contents into a saucepan, then added water. She placed the saucepan on the burner and turned on the flame. The coffee began to percolate. The smell of Maxwell House and tomato soup added to the hominess. Your mother placed china cups and saucers on a small tray with spoons, sugar and PET milk, then she positioned the tray on the coffee table in front of us.

She sat next to me on the couch in a guarded posture.

"So, where does your life story begin?" I asked cautiously.

"My life story is sad," she said in a barely audible tone.

Your mother told me everything that I needed to know. We stayed up talking all night long, ate soup and crackers, drank coffee, talked some more, and we touched. She cried. I comforted her with my love. I told her I would be with her as long as I had breath in me. If I am deceased when you read this, you'll know I kept my word to her.

We fell asleep, still intertwined.

Upon awakening the next morning, I held your mother in my arms and said, "This is right. Will you marry me?"

She accepted my proposal of marriage. We were married the following week.

Five months later, your mother gave birth to you.

By law, I am your father.

Chapter Eight

Tuesday, September 18

On the second day of hearings, Hart Senate Room 216 was packed to capacity when Katherine entered just before nine. Among the interested parties, Walter Rodney sat near the back of the room, which meant that he had been in line before dawn for seats issued on a first-come-first-served basis. She pushed alarm out of her mind, and moved on to the front of the room.

Senator Stephen "Skip" Graham entered the hearing room at nine exactly. A former NFL player, Graham was muscular and ruggedly handsome. Still fit, with the body of a gladiator, he had perfect white teeth that gleamed against a smooth mocha complexion. He sported a close haircut, trimmed mustache, and neat goatee. She noticed the yellow "M" on the lapel of his tailored navy blue suit—a former Michigan Wolverine.

She shifted her gaze to the reporters before her, not wanting to remember his touch.

A few minutes after the hour, the chairman called the hearing to order and ceded the floor to Graham. Katherine braced her emotions as Graham tapped the microphone.

"I'd like to take the questioning in a different direction this morning," Graham announced. "What is your position on reparations to address historical wrongs?"

"I'm aware of the fact that a reparations bill has been introduced in the House every year since 1989 to address the fact that former slaves were never compensated for their labor, which represents a denial of their basic property rights that affects the economic rights of their descendants to this day. That injustice has stood for over one hundred years with no political solution. Political action is needed. Bold action is long overdue."

"So you would grant reparations from the bench?"

"You know the Court precedents," Katherine said. "There would have to be a case based on existing law. The problem is, we don't have a reparations law and that's a political problem."

"What are you saying, lady?" Walter Rodney shouted from the back. "The Supreme Court should give us reparations now! What about our property rights? They got their property rights. We want ours for our children."

Without turning, Katherine recognized the voice.

The Chairman banged his gravel. "Remove that person!"

As the Capitol Police surrounded Rodney, he jerked away, and a small scuffle ensued. Rodney was finally escorted from the room in handcuffs. Katherine knew they couldn't hold him long on a misdemeanor charge of public disturbance. After paying a five-hundred-dollar fine, he would be back on the streets in twenty-four hours—but she couldn't worry about him.

Having restored order, the chairman said, "You may continue."

Katherine picked up as if nothing had happened. "Senator Graham, with all due respect to your position as chairman of the Constitution, Civil Rights and Civil Liberties Senate Subcommittee, I believe it's your responsibility to take action that will result in the passage of a law that addresses the breach in our society caused by the denial of basic property rights to over four million slaves at the founding of this country. The Congress should act."

"What do you think of the architecture of the Supreme Court building?" Graham asked.

"What kind of question is that?" Senator Maxwell blurted out.

"Let her answer the question," the chairman said.

"The symbolism in the Supreme Court reinforces the notion that justice is timeless across space and time. I think the Supreme Court building represents a temple of justice for all."

"What are the values you feel most passionate about?"

"I care deeply about human rights, freedom of speech, and freedom of religion."

"What do you think the primary consideration should be when a justice rules in a case?"

"To protect the rule of law embedded in the U.S. Constitution. We need laws to promote a nonviolent society."

"I know you to be a woman of passion," Graham said.

Katherine froze in her seat and gazed into the sea of cameras before her, annoyed.

"Your father cared passionately about civil rights. We know that's in your bloodline."

Senator Maxwell chuckled. "Well, it's rumored Frederick Ross isn't her natural father."

Katherine recoiled from the feelings of public humiliation overtaking her.

The chairman pounded his gavel. "You no longer have the floor, Senator Maxwell."

"Forgive me, Mr. Chairman. I didn't realize my microphone was still live. But I still have some time remaining. I'll have one more question for Ms. Ross."

"So noted," the chairman responded. "Senator Graham, you may proceed."

"Ms. Ross, your record shows you've given your professional time and resources to protect the interests of abused children. What else might influence your decisions on the bench?"

"As I said before, enforcing the rule of law is key to maintaining our rights and maintaining faith in our judicial system. I will respect the law, even when I disagree with it."

"Does that imply you don't believe in natural law?"

"I don't believe that term has been defined in a federal statute, so I think it means different things to different people. I think the simplest definition is: It is the law that one knows is right in their heart. But we can't have a predictable system of government based on natural law because we can't know what's in another person's heart. So I would tend to follow positive law. That is, statutes that have been enacted by the elective bodies and officials of this country."

"In *Hilton Head Corporation v. The State of Georgia,* you represented a Gullah family from South Carolina and convinced them to incorporate in Georgia to protect their property rights on Hilton Head Island. That allowed you to take advantage of rulings establishing the rights of corporations to win their land case in the Supreme Court. Is that correct?"

"Yes."

"Do you think corporations are part of 'We the People'?" Graham asked.

"States have defined corporations to be persons," she said. "The Supreme Court granted corporations constitutional rights in 1819."

"You haven't answered the question,"

"That's the positive law today. I believe who a person is under the U.S. Constitution is an area of the law that is ripe for another debate by the Supreme Court."

"Do you believe in state rights?" the chairman asked, challenging her with his tone.

"Yes, so long as they don't conflict with rights guaranteed under the U.S. Constitution."

And so it went for another six hours with only one break on that bruising day.

And throughout, above all else, she needed to know who her father was.

Chapter Nine

The Ritz-Carlton Residences
Georgetown (Washington, D.C.)

Katherine steamed, having just returned from dinner with the White House chief of staff who informed her that rumors were swirling and a massive effort was underway to discover her natural father's identity. Powerful interests were at work trying to derail her nomination. He advised her to confront the matter head on, regardless of the level of embarrassment she might face. If she were caught in a lie, her nomination would die.

Their conversation ran repeatedly through her head:

Is Frederick G. Ross your biological father?

Yes. I think so.

Well, your adversaries don't think so and you need to know before you say yes again.

The chief of staff warned her that her nomination was unlikely to survive the process if it were proven that she distorted critical information on her FBI background form. They would do what they could to handle the situation, but...

Katherine called her mother from dinner to tell her she would be stopping by.

No answer to her calls. So Katherine had gone home to simmer.

She got up from the recliner in her bedroom and grabbed the phone off her nightstand to call her mother for the seventh time that evening. The phone rang endlessly. She couldn't imagine where her mother could be after nine in the evening. It wasn't her bridge night. There was no meeting of the sorority. She wasn't at her godmother's house. Her cell phone went directly into voice mail. *Where could she be?*

Her mother had not been at her hearing, although she had expected her to be there.

Slowly her anger turned to concern.

Katherine snatched a running suit off her closet shelf and changed.

Ready in less than five minutes.

Rifling through her nightstand drawer, she found the keys to her mother's condo, located her red gym bag, and stuck the keys in the side zip pocket. With the gym bag over her shoulder, she sprinted the length of the empty hallway and took the elevator down to the garage to her black Jeep Grand Cherokee.

She zipped out of her building, barely braking at the stop sign.

Slow down, the voice in her head warned.

She called her mother again. Still no answer.

She called the Watergate complex. "Hi, this is Katherine Ross, Helena Ross's daughter. I've been trying to reach my mother in Unit 912 and she's not answering her phone. I'm concerned and on the way over. Will you let me in the underground garage when I arrive?"

"Let me check," the night doorman said.

"No," she said. "I don't want you to disturb her if she's asleep. I have keys. I just want you to open the garage door for me."

"I'm checking the permission-to-enter log," he said. "Yes, I do see that you have permission. Stop at the front desk when you arrive so I can check your ID, then I can let you park in the garage. The press just left."

"Okay, I'll be there in a few minutes."

As Katherine burst through the door, she found her mother in the living room seated in a comfortable chair facing the windows with a leather-bound Bible in her lap, a strong-minded look on her aged face, and a glass of merlot in her hand. She glanced up at her daughter.

"I expected to see you sooner," she said. "Would you like a glass of wine?"

"No." Katherine sank into her usual seat facing her mother. "Have you been out?"

"At your place," her mother replied. "I walked over. Tried to wait on you but didn't know how late you'd be, so I left to get back before dark. Did you get your Dad's letter? I left it for you on your kitchen counter."

"No, I didn't go into the kitchen."

"It's in a manila envelope. You should read it tonight. I have something else for you."

She handed Katherine the worn family Bible. "This was my mama's. The bookmark is a recipe that's been handed down through the years in my family."

"So you just let your phone ring when I called?" Katherine asked.

"Yes." She placed her wine glass on a coaster. "I didn't want to talk on the phone."

Katherine flipped to the Birth Records page of the Bible. Nothing was recorded.

"Who is my father?" Katherine asked.

"It's on your birth certificate. Frederick G. Ross is your legal father."

"I have a right to know who my biological father is," Katherine said in a raised voice.

"All you need to know is that your father is dead."

Katherine fought back tears of mixed emotions. Frustration. "You can't expect me to go back into the hearing tomorrow without knowing who my father is. You can't do that to me."

"I don't think a law exists that can compel me to tell you what I can't or don't remember."

"What do you mean you don't remember?"

"There are some things I've just pushed out of my mind."

"You know who my natural father is," said Katherine, "because you said he's dead."

"I've never told you that your father wasn't your biological father. I think it's best to leave some things buried. Your father is dead. That's a true statement."

"Is my biological father dead?" Katherine asked, enunciating each word carefully.

"Yes," her mother replied.

"Who was he? You don't have the right to keep a secret like this from me."

"Maybe one day we can talk about it, but not now."

"I demand to know now."

Her mother picked up her glass, took a sip of wine and said nothing.

A vein pulsed on Katherine's right temple. "The press is running search engines. No one will believe I don't know who my natural father is. Is that why you didn't show up today?"

"I didn't come today because I knew they were on the hunt, and I had to go to my safety deposit box to get your dad's package. I didn't want to draw any more attention."

"Well that didn't work," Katherine snapped. "I need you to face the truth with me."

"The fact that you're going for a high-level appointment does not change my privacy rights," her mother said calmly.

"I was expected to give truthful statements on the background materials I filled out."

"I assume you did make truthful statements. You were born in a legal marriage. Frederick G. Ross is your legal father. He is dead. The FBI has verified that fact. A valid public record of his death exists. Your biological father is dead. Enough said."

"Why do you always have to keep so many secrets?" Katherine stood to leave.

"To make it easier to get along in the world," her mother replied, placing her wine glass back on the coaster. Holding back.

"If they find out who my father is and why you've hidden it from me all of these years, my whole world might just blow up on the front page of the newspapers tomorrow."

"Trust me," her mother said, clasping her hands. "Now is not the time for you to know. Better to leave it alone. I think everybody's dead who can tell the whole story—except for me. They're just fishing. Don't worry."

Katherine knew her mother was manipulating her. But what could she do? Tears of frustration finally broke free. She yelled, "Who is my father?" Then, whispered, "You have to tell me, please. That's the only way I'll make it through."

Katherine waited for the dam to burst.

But it didn't. There was no crack in her mother's protective shield.

"I hate it when you half-tell me something, then clam up. You're not being fair."

"Read the letter from your dad. It might help you feel better."

Katherine slammed the door as she left. It banged harder than she intended. Marching down the hallway, she realized her explosion of anger hadn't mattered.

The dam would hold.

"Wait," she heard her mother call. "Please come back."

Katherine glanced down the hallway at her mother, standing in the opened door. She went back with hope. Her mother closed the door behind her.

"I just can't remember everything that happened to me. I don't want to remember every dirty detail—I can't deal with it now. Understand?"

Then her mother broke down in tears.

Katherine reached out, cuddling her like a baby.

Instinctively she knew that was all she could do.

Chapter Ten

Hart Senate Office Building
Wednesday, September 19

"You've been through a lot with us over the past few days, and I commend the way you've handled yourself under fierce questioning before this committee," the chairman said in his opening remarks on the third and final day of Katherine's Senate Judiciary Committee hearing. "I've saved my questions for the end."

Katherine felt like an animal chased through the woods by gaining predators. She readied for the final assault, considering everything that floated into her awareness. She remembered again: *When God is for you, nobody can stop you.*

She was ready for the final challenge.

But how could she survive?

"I'd like to take this in a different direction," the chairman said. "When do you believe justices should enforce rights, such as the right to marry whomever you please—rights that are not explicitly stated in the Constitution?"

Katherine paused to consider the unexpected question. She noticed Graham raise his head, glaring at the chairman. He seemed alarmed. She calculated the risks. "I view the right to marry whomever you want as a compelling claim for liberty. Compelling claims for liberty, like the rights of women to vote, must be upheld even when no specific language in the Constitution can be found for them. Our Constitution reflects abstract principles that great justices must struggle with over time, sometimes making politically controversial judgments—"

"Thought you said you would always follow the written rules of law?"

"I would anchor my decisions on the U.S. Constitution, deferring to legislative bodies in the case of a blurred constitutional line. But I would call a strike in the case of a clear miss. Supreme Court cases often result because reasonable people have different interpretations of the abstract concepts in our Constitution. The strike zone is not always clearly defined."

"You were nominated by a Democrat—are your political views liberal?"

"I'm a moderate with friends in both parties. I think of myself as an independent. I don't have extremist political viewpoints either way. I like to consider both sides of an argument."

"What twentieth-century justice's jurisprudence do you admire and why?"

"I have to say Rehnquist because he engaged in the facts of each case, following the relevant legal precedents, but he was willing to break rank with ideological commitments when the circumstances merited a different direction. Like Sandra O'Conner, he considered everything. They were often in the majority—both pragmatists who could end up in any camp."

"So you're not taking sides?"

"No."

"You're saying you would be an unpredictable swing vote. That might not work for everybody here. We all know there's been a pack of hungry wolves roaming the streets of Washington trying to find something in your background that would disqualify you as a Supreme Court justice. But to my knowledge, they've returned from the hunt without making a kill in spite of their best efforts to derail your nomination. I'm kind of surprised you haven't taken refuge in either political camp. People like to know what they're getting. But

I'm satisfied. I've spoken to people who have worked beside you and I'm convinced you're a moderate—and that's what we need for the good of the people—someone with a moderate judicial philosophy."

Was it over? Katherine had rehearsed her responses to questions about her father over and over again in her head. This was not what she had imagined in her nightmares.

She was ready to answer questions about her father.

"In closing these hearings I have one final question: Do you have any regrets today?"

She regretted never having children—but didn't need to say that. "I regret my father is not sitting behind me today, yet I feel his presence in this room. I have answered your questions over the past few days in his honor, as I think of the man who witnessed my birth and held my hand along the path of life for so many years. I feel blessed to have been raised in a family of love by my mother, who is sitting behind me today, and a father who was never afraid to publicly show his love and respect for my mother. I regret my father didn't live to see this day."

"Mr. Chairman," Senator Maxwell said. "I have time remaining and one more question for Ms. Ross before we adjourn these hearings. Perhaps you forgot."

"Yes, I did. You may direct your question to Ms. Ross."

Katherine tensed for the question she feared.

"Ms. Ross," Senator Maxwell said with a drawl. "I note that you were born five months after your parents' marriage. I've heard whispers in the Capitol corridors about that fact. We all have. Was Frederick Ross your natural father? It's rumored he's not."

The room fell into silence.

"I don't know who my natural father is."

The cameras trained on her mother.

Then back to Katherine.

"I deeply regret that I can't answer your question. I've asked who my natural father is. I didn't get an answer and my mother is refusing or possibly unable to answer that question for reasons I can't explain. My mother has informed me she is exercising her right to privacy in this matter. But I, too, no longer believe Frederick Ross is my biological father."

Her emotions welled up. Her eyes grew moist. She couldn't understand how her mother could shut down on her at this most important time in her life, leaving her high and dry in the public eye. What could be so bad? Would the press find out anyway and derail her nomination?

"Are you saying you don't know anything about your natural father?"

"I only know my natural father is dead," Katherine responded with sad eyes.

"That's enough," the chairman said. "Her parentage has no bearing on whether or not she can serve this country well. You don't get a seat on the Supreme Court by birthright. The fact that she does not know her natural father should not be a relevant consideration for this committee. This hearing should be about her, and we should vote her up or down based on her actions. The way she has handled these hearings speaks volumes about her character. I would hope that her qualifications and character are what matters most when we cast our votes."

He pounded the gravel. "These hearings are adjourned."

Chapter Eleven

Washington, D.C.
Monday, October 1

Walter Rodney walked away from the Supreme Court with a well-worn briefcase in hand. There had been no justice for him in the courts. Yale University had fired him as an assistant professor of African American studies years ago. His international reputation among his peers hadn't mattered. Academic freedom was a myth. Departmental politics prevailed. They had painted him as a political liability for the university. His views were too radical to be promoted.

The Supreme Court had declined to hear his case.

Now Howard University had fired him too. That ticked him off. He was within his rights, but on the wrong side of economic beliefs. He wanted justice for *his* people—the oppressed. The truth needed to be published. The young people needed his guidance. No. He wasn't finished. They couldn't stop him.

He would reach the young people another way.

From a distance Walter heard the familiar bleat of a police siren that stirred the stew brewing in his soul. Bubbles of anger surfaced from a churning sea of repressed emotions. He didn't want to entertain anger because he knew it meant losing control over his mind. He wouldn't give in to the rage. They would not be allowed to beat him down.

As his bus approached, he dashed across the street with a raised hand. The door opened. He paid his fare without a glance from the driver. As he headed for the back of the bus, he noticed that all of the passengers wore the same dazed look. Halfway down the aisle, he stopped amid the frozen stares and felt their wounded spirits.

Walter Rodney wanted a revolution in the spirit of the underclass.

"Whatever is wrong, you don't have to take it," Walter declared. "Don't let the capitalist power structure wear you down. We must unite. That's what we must do."

He pulled flyers out of his briefcase and passed them around. They announced a recruitment meeting for BAMN that evening.

"Sit down," the bus driver instructed. "No soliciting on the bus."

"I'll take my seat. But, you should consider resisting your oppressors instead of just saying what they tell you to say to keep us all under control."

A woman wearing a nurse's uniform raised an eyebrow and turned away as Walter passed. Others avoided eye contact as he walked to the rear.

He sank into a seat next to a young Black man with a fresh haircut who wore an ROTC uniform. They rode in silence for a few blocks, shoulder to shoulder. Both gazed out of the window at the passing decay of brick buildings and the occasional new construction project, fenced all around with padlocks. Secure, as contractors built over broken dreams. Shattered brown glass lay on the ground.

"What do you see when you look out of the window?" Walter asked.

The young man shrugged.

"I'll tell you what you see. They're making way for the power elite to reclaim Washington from its oppressed citizens. Gentrification. Transformation. Exploitation. The underclass makes way for the wealthy elite, the people with money. *Big* money."

The young man said nothing.

Walter pressed on. "They're going to crush the small property owners in this area, drive out the homeless, take the land from the poor for back taxes, or buy land from them on the cheap. That's what they always do. Know what I mean?"

"Yeah," mumbled an older man in rumpled clothing. "Dat's what they do."

This energized Walter. He was drawing an audience, but he kept his eyes on the young man and drilled on. "Know what happens next?"

The young man opened a box of Good & Plenty candy.

"They put up million-dollar condos, driving the poor out of the heart of D.C. Capitalism just makes the rich richer on the backs of poor people who don't make enough to pay the taxes. That's like it's always been, making us work for scraps."

"Some of us are gettin' over big time," the young man said.

"Yeah, the sell-outs do," Walter replied in an annoyed tone. "The drug dealers do, too. But most of us don't get over big time. But we can resist what's happening to us. Join us."

"I'm down with helpin', but I can't do nothin' now," the young man answered.

"There's no progress without struggle." Walter borrowed a line from abolitionist Frederick Douglass. "If we had continued to pretend to be stupid and just followed orders, we would still be slaves. Do you know your history young man?"

"What difference does it make?" The young man frowned. "I don't see no chains now."

"Never mind history, then. Our lives are turning to shit today. Know what I mean?"

"Naw, my life ain't shit." The young man popped a handful of white-and-pink-coated licorice in his mouth.

"If you think we haven't been exploited by the capitalist system then you've got chains on your brain."

"I'm not in chains."

"Use your brain, young man. Time's up. We must fight our oppressors."

"Man, I'm not oppressed."

"Ya' can't beat da system," the older man muttered, his shoulders slumped.

"Join them if you can't beat them?" Walter retorted with his eyebrows rising.

The older man turned away.

"I can work for the good of the people by makin' good grades and savin' myself from crime," the young man said.

"Be selfish and just look out for yourself?" Walter inquired.

"I'm a Christian. I care about others. I just don't believe the whole world is against me." He shoved another handful of sweet candy in his mouth.

"Not the whole world. Just the oppressors who've chained the brains of the weak. Come to the meeting. We can help you understand some things." Walter watched him chew the hard candy with little nutritional value, betting he didn't even know what he was chewing on.

"Can't," the young man said, swallowing. "I have to go to ROTC practice, then work."

"If you're going to be a freedom fighter, you need an education about the history of Black people before you give your life to the system. History is a legal weapon. You need to learn how to use it."

In retort, the young man returned his gaze to the street and his Good & Plenty.

"I'll be at the community center at 7:30 tonight," Walter announced. "First floor. If you want to join the brothers' fight for justice, show up."

Walter rose and pulled the overhead cord.

He strode down the aisle of the bus, energy beaming from his eyes, then turned and made his final pronouncement. "The people united, will never be defeated!"

Chapter Twelve

U.S. Supreme Court Building
Tuesday, October 2

"It's too dangerous," the white lawgiver said to the Black powerbroker. In the privacy of his ornate chambers, Chief Justice Harlan Gaines scoured the proposed constitutional amendment that would provide an involuntary retirement process for Supreme Court justices over the age of sixty-five. He read the words through progressive plastic-and-titanium glasses.

His small group of handlers had considered the risks. It was time. Senator Graham, seated across from Gaines, knew he needed to draw the Chief in. Privately, the Chief could shepherd Graham's proposed twenty-eighth amendment to the U.S. Constitution through the Congress or could kill it, just by making his preference known. Graham needed to make sure that the Chief had no serious objection. He noted that Gaines looked perturbed. Graham shifted his gaze toward the Chief's oversized windows and the view of the dominating Capitol Dome.

Only the ticking of an antique desk clock could be heard as the senator waited.

When finished, Gaines placed the draft on his conference table—face down.

"Let me begin by saying..." Chief Justice Gaines folded his arms. "I will not endorse this amendment because of the separation of powers doctrine."

"I understand," Graham said. "I did not expect an endorsement. I just wanted you to review the amendment before I went public with it."

"That's wise. I do think it's in the best interest of the Court for me to be responsive to your request for an informal review of this proposed language."

"What do you think?"

"You shouldn't set the Court's term in statute," Gaines said. "We have a tradition of ending the term in June—although we work all of the time."

"I'll change the language so it's clear that all five letters have to be submitted to the Judiciary Committee before the start of a new term; you'll still have the flexibility to control the length of a term. You can set a June date or extend it. Same power you have now."

"Since the triggering event is controlled by the Supreme Court, I will have no public objection to it, with that change."

"Will you privately support it? You know you've got a problem."

"No. The separation of powers doctrine should be respected. I think current provisions of the Constitution are adequate. If there's a problem, the House should impeach."

"I appreciate that position. I really do. But I think impeachment is too harsh in the case of a justice who falls ill. I don't believe most of my colleagues would view getting old as a high crime or misdemeanor."

"Our system has worked well up to this point." The Chief looked smug.

"That's a matter of opinion. We can look at the events leading up to the retirement of Justice William O. Douglas as a case in point. After his stroke no one thought Douglas was competent. And then, I understand, there was the odor issue—"

58

"Okay, I know about his incontinence, but…"

"All of the Supreme Court issues were not fully debated and resolved when the Constitution was adopted. This is a better process to deal with long-term health problems of justices who have served us well. Not everyone can or will admit they're incapacitated. This amendment is overdue."

"I think any retirement process for sitting Supreme Court justices should be handled within the Supreme Court," Justice Gaines said.

"From my view, Senate ratification is a necessary check on the actions of the Supreme Court. This proposal keeps the Court from playing politics by booting someone off who isn't incapacitated but just a pain to deal with for five or more justices. I think my proposal respects the checks and balances. The President appoints Supreme Court justices, the Senate concurs. The Supreme Court recommends the involuntary retirement, the Senate concurs. Like the best amendments, simple, elegant."

"We'll see. Tell me again what this language boils down to."

"If the proposed amendment is ratified, the involuntary retirement process could only be triggered after the chair of the Senate Judiciary Committee receives five individual letters from sitting Supreme Court justices certifying that a particular justice is incapacitated and unable to carry out the duties of office. All five letters must be received within a given term of the Court. If the chairman does not receive five letters by the end of the Court's term in October, the removal attempt fails."

"That's good."

"After the receipt of five letters in a term, nothing happens for the first thirty days to allow for a graceful voluntarily retirement. On the thirty-first day after receipt of the fifth letter, the chairman will hold a private hearing and the process will begin. The committee will be required to make a recommendation to the full Senate to remove or retain, culminating with a vote. There will be no public Senate hearing because it involves medical privacy rights."

The Chief picked up the proposed amendment to check the language again.

Graham waited until the Chief returned his gaze then said, "I hope you appreciate the fact that the Senate would have no power under the proposed amendment unless five sitting justices think we should confirm their actions to retire a colleague."

"Yes, I understand that part."

"Could you live with this type of process if it were adopted by the people?"

"Of course, if ratified," Justice Gaines said. "But good luck with that. Out of ten thousand attempts—only twenty-seven amendments have been ratified to date and the last one took over two hundred years for ratification. You know the odds."

"Yes. But it's time to deal with this issue."

"Maybe. Maybe not. It could be misused."

Graham simpered as he rose to leave. "I believe in the rule of five."

"When is the committee going to vote on Ross's nomination?"

"Don't know if we can pull her through. You know, presidential politics."

"If that's the case, I'd say the odds are against her making it. She'll die in committee."

"You should know she only needs one more committee vote. I'm still working on it."

Chapter Thirteen

Thursday, October 4

It was about ten in the morning when one of Senator Graham's junior staffers told him that BAMN was targeting the Supreme Court for protest efforts, and had signaled out Supreme Court Justice John T. Galt and nominee Katherine Ross for special attention. Ross was an attractive target because she had media attention and did not yet have full federal protection. But some BAMN members were vocally supportive of Katherine because she was known in the community—making Justice Galt BAMN's agitation target. Galt was the Black man whom the African American community wanted to hang for desertion. A puppet for the white man. A traitor.

BAMN just wanted to keep the pressure on Ross to make sure she did the right thing.

Graham feared things could get out of hand.

He debated calling Katherine to warn her, but didn't have her private number. Graham considered her circumstances—and their history—before making a call from his office desk phone.

"I need a favor," he said into a speakerphone. "It concerns one of our acquaintances."

"I need a story," Julianne LaSalle replied from her Urban Times Media office.

"Then we have a deal. What do you want to know?"

"When is the Judiciary Committee going to act on Kathy's confirmation?" Julianne swirled around in her seat. "People are getting nervous."

"In the morning."

"Is her confirmation in trouble?"

"Nope. We'll be recommending her to the full Senate."

"Then why the delay?" Julianne eyed the remainder of her lunch: a red apple.

"Presidential politics. You know how it goes."

"What's up?"

"I'm introducing a constitutional amendment that creates a process for the involuntary retirement of a Supreme Court justice over the age of sixty-five."

"What makes you think you can get it through?"

"Its time has come," Graham responded. "It's as simple as that. The Founding Fathers intended for us to make the U.S. Constitution a more perfect document through the amendment process, as issues ripened for resolution. With several Supreme Court justices well beyond traditional retirement age, it's clear this issue is ripe to ensure the integrity of our highest Court."

"How many of the justices are over sixty-five?" Julianne asked, munching on the apple.

"Five."

"How many are over seventy?"

"Four and three are over seventy-five."

"Are the ones over seventy-five functioning well?" Julianne threw the core in the trash.

"We don't know. It's a well-known fact their law clerks cover for them during illness."

"Yes, I've heard that too. Why hasn't there been an investigation of the matter by your committee?"

"Separation of powers. And by the way, have you followed up on the rumors about how Galt's chambers are running?"

"I'm working on it."

"You can't verify the story, right?"

"Right. I've tried talking to a couple of law clerks, but I couldn't get anything out of them. They told me they could get fired for talking to the press."

"Their law clerks are pledged to secrecy."

"Can't you subpoena them?"

"Separation of powers again."

"What do you think would happen if a justice were incapacitated and wouldn't resign?"

"I don't think the House would act to impeach them."

"Then what would happen?"

"I think the law clerks would manage the situation," Graham replied. "Even the Senate Judiciary Committee doesn't know how much power the law clerks wield when a justice is ill. The only real solution is a constitutional amendment. We'll face a crisis one day if we don't—"

"But wouldn't a constitutional amendment weaken the Court?"

"I think we can strengthen the Court with the right amendment. Something needs to be done, but there are no easy answers given the foundation laid by the Founding Fathers that shields the Supreme Court from undue political influence."

"Well we know the Founding Fathers didn't get it all right. Slaves counted as three-fifths of a person. I was shocked to read that in the original Constitution."

"Well, that's a long story of no consequence today. It was just a political deal. The best they could do at the time. Now you've got the scoop on Katherine's delay and you owe me. Off-the-record, I'm concerned that Walter Rodney's fixated on Katherine. Let her know he might be serious trouble, but don't tell her the warning came from me. Deal?"

"Okay, I'll make sure she understands the situation. But can I ask why?"

"No."

Chapter Fourteen

It was past two in the morning, but Senator Graham could not sleep. He lay in the darkness alone, the doctor's words playing freely in his mind: *"I'm sorry, your wife is gone."*

Graham still wasn't over Candice's death.

He could not restrain the memories of the accident on black ice that claimed her life in 1982. The memories still played in his head. They had been enrolled at the University of Michigan and commuted from Detroit. Feeling sick, she had wanted to sleep in that morning. But he wouldn't let her stay in bed because he did not want her to drive to Ann Arbor alone. A fearsome snowstorm was on the way, so he had insisted that she get up and ride with him. How he still regretted that decision. He should have let her sleep. He should have stopped at the airport. He should have found them a motel room before he lost control of the car.

But he hadn't done any of those things—and now she was dead.

It was his fault.

Every detail remained as fresh in his mind as if the accident had happened yesterday. The blinding snow had overtaken them as he passed the final exit to safety.

But it had already been too late when he saw the sign.

He couldn't have gotten over to the exit in time.

He wallowed once again in the painful memories until sleep finally came.

Dreaming, Skip saw Candice smiling at him through an invisible pane of glass. Without knowing how, he understood that he could not touch her. He also knew he was not really asleep. She was there, in his bedroom. He felt her enduring love.

"Don't worry about me," she said. *"It's cool over here. I'm happy. Find love again. It's all about you now. What are you going to do with the rest of your life?"*

Graham woke from the dream and looked at his bedside clock. 3:30 a.m. Recapturing the last moment with her was not a possibility. Yet a feeling of peace still surrounded him. He was sure Candice's spirit had spoken to him that night. He felt her presence. Now he knew for sure her spirit was still alive and that she wanted him to find love again.

For the next two hours, he lay in bed thinking of her. There were no tears, just warm memories of the love they shared. No regrets. No guilt. He felt good when he thought about how peaceful she had looked in his dream.

Candice was happy.

This night signaled the end of his grieving process. He felt different. A new lightness filled his soul. For the first time since his wife's death, he felt free to love again.

Chapter Fifteen

Friday, October 5

"Let's logroll," Michael Spade said to Senator Graham over lunch at The Capital Grille. Spade, a lobbyist at the law firm of Spade, Spark and Lightfoot, was an elite dealmaker on Capitol Hill with powerful clients who enjoyed their anonymity behind corporate veils. He carried the business interests' flag with potent financial firepower and strategic precision. Better to be on his side. His network of contacts went from A to Z, polished to corrosive.

Spade's connections reached all levels of government and included a complement of public relations firms and paid political activists. His firm also contracted an army of lawyers in other firms that had specialized skills and influential relationships.

Spade, Spark and Lightfoot was the firm to make things happen in Washington, D.C.

Spade continued his proposal. "You roll my log on the transportation bill and I'll roll your log on your proposed Supreme Court amendment."

"Ross doesn't have the votes to get out of committee," Graham said. "Can you get her through as part of the deal?"

"Can't do that."

"Then I can't help you."

"I said I'd get your constitutional amendment through—isn't that enough?"

"We both know I probably won't get a touchdown when it comes to state ratification, so you really aren't offering me anything. I need something more from you to play on the transportation bill. There's billions in it for your clients. You'll probably get a success fee worth millions. I know that. Help me with Ross and I'll help you."

Spade drew back in his seat. "Don't know what I can do with presidential politics."

"I need adequate consideration."

Spade's forehead rose as he processed Graham's request. "Senator Maxwell wants the transportation bill passed with the projects for his supporters. I think I can get him to vote for Ross now—but we'll have to put her full Senate vote on hold until after the election."

"And the amendment? I have to have that, too."

Spade nodded with a sly leer. "Okay. Do we have a deal?"

"One more thing. You promise to support her after the presidential election, regardless of the outcome."

"Now you're asking for too much." Spade stood slowly.

Graham knew he was calculating.

"But we have a deal," Spade said, reaching for his briefcase.

Graham was sure he could make Katherine understand why he delayed her confirmation when they got a chance to talk. He knew there was real risk that she would become a victim of presidential politics if her nomination were put up for a vote now.

He needed to control the situation in order to save her.

Seated at his desk on the afternoon before the committee meeting, Graham counted Katherine's votes again, noting those that might flip. Picking up the phone, he made a few calls to make sure he still had support from the key Republicans with whom he had trusted relationships. His colleagues were clear: they could not vote for her confirmation before the election but would honor their deals after the November elections were over.

He recounted her votes with the new information. *Too close.* But she had more than enough votes for her confirmation, regardless of the outcome of the presidential election, if voted on in the lame duck session. He concluded that was her only path to the Court.

Maxwell's staff confirmed he would vote her out of committee, but would motion to delay sending her nomination forward for the full Senate vote until after the election.

Graham would support his motion.

She had to wait.

Chapter Sixteen

Alexander Morris felt the power of the eagle rise within him. He watched as an American bald eagle soared over his head toward a vulnerable target on Lake Joseph in the Catskill Mountains of upstate New York. The determined eyes of the predator focused on unsuspecting prey. With its wings pulled in close to achieve drag, the eagle transitioned to a shallow glide and attempted to pluck a trout from the lake with clenching claws.

The weight of the large fish pulled the eagle underwater.

The eagle could no longer fly, but still fought.

Morris monitored the ripples in the lake as they moved to the shore.

He's hungry and won't let go, even if he can't lift it and drowns.

The captured fish never had a chance.

The eagle would not let go.

Death was the price for his life.

The famished eagle made it to shore with the large fish.

He dragged it onto land and took his first bite.

Red blood splattered his bright yellow beak.

Above, another eagle lurked, resting on a branch.

Without warning the rested predator attacked, snatching the remains of the fish from the hunter. There was no fight.

A weak eagle cannot survive.

Morris turned toward the Inn at Lake Joseph where he had rented a room. The scent of burning wood dominated the cool morning air as he made his way back. The sound of a crackling fire greeted him as he entered the lobby, enabling him to shake the chill. Morris headed for the library where he expected his wife Paula, a former Senate staffer and descendant of a powerful privateer, to be waiting.

Paula rose from her seat and kissed him. "This place is amazing."

"How was your drive?" Morris glanced back at the lake through a window.

"Quicker than I thought. I was a little delayed getting out of the city, but it only took two hours after I cleared the tunnel."

"Want to fish?" Morris asked.

"Yes. But you'll have to bait my hook."

"The Inn has several boats we can borrow. Let's go."

On the lake, Morris steered the boat to a special spot the desk clerk had told him about. He baited Paula's hook and handed her the pole. She nervously cast her line into the water. With flair, he cast his own line.

They waited for a nibble.

"I heard some new information about that BAMN group," Paula said. "That Black guy who got arrested at Ross's hearing has been busy."

"What was his name?"

"Walter Rodney. Now he's putting in a full-time effort trying to organize a militant group of Blacks. I asked Spade's firm to hire Stratagem to check the guy out. Rodney seems to be targeting the Supreme Court. We've got to protect our assets. We need to know what he's up to."

"You might be right," Morris said. "Nobody's better at infuriatin' grassroots groups than Stratagem. But we over-educated that one. He knows what he's worth on the black market."

"How are we going to deal with Katherine Ross? We can't have three unpredictable Supreme Court justices. Can't read the Chief anymore. We've got to instill confidence that we can deliver. We never should've made that deal with Graham."

"Spade said he was tough to deal with," Morris replied. "We needed his vote for the transportation bill. Ross was the only chit that would move him."

"What about the votes for his constitutional amendment? He got that, too."

"That was just cover. He knows the states aren't going to ratify it. He's no fool."

"Do you know Ross's views on the Hawaiian property rights case yet?"

"No, Ross has been too busy to arrange a meeting with Al. He's still trying…"

"I thought they were close."

"Al will find a way to see her." Morris pulled back on his line. "I think I got a big one."

"Don't let her get away," Paula whispered.

"Who else is close to Ross?" Morris gave the hooked fish a little more line.

"Nobody I know that we can use."

"I'll give Al another call and give his firm a bigger retainer. They'll deliver for the right price. He's still with that K-Street lobbying firm, right?"

"Right."

Morris grew quiet and focused his attention on the fight at hand, listening for each click of the reel. They fought for a while.

When the big fish tired and gave up his fight, Morris reeled him in with little resistance.

"Al's our hook," Morris said, "but we can't let a big fish pull us under. We'll give Ross some rope but if she's got too much fight in her, we'll have to cut the line."

Chapter Seventeen

Washington, D.C
Tuesday, October 9

"What happened?"

With her cell phone pressed against her ear, Katherine felt a dagger in her back.

"It's not as bad as it sounds." The White House chief of staff gave an assessment. "You were unanimously voted out of the Senate Judiciary Committee, but a deal's been struck to hold your confirmation vote up until after the presidential election, in exchange for passage of Graham's proposed constitutional amendment. You're still alive."

"So Graham rolled over me?"

"He's in your corner. You must appreciate the fact that you were voted out of the Committee with a unanimous recommendation for approval. It's not about you. It's politics. Not only Graham's proposed amendment for the Court, but there's the transportation bill headed for the Senate that's one vote short for passage, too. Graham made a deal to vote for the transportation bill in the Senate if they provided the three votes he needs in the House to pass his amendment."

"So," Katherine said, barely able to control her temper, "Graham is taking my scalp for three votes on an amendment crapshoot with less than a one percent chance for ratification. Is that what you're telling me?"

"It's a little bit more complicated than that. Your confirmation is 'On Hold' for now."

"I think 'On Hold' means 'No Go'."

"I think it means, 'No Go Now'. Your Republican friends will vote for you after they're out of the line of fire with their contributors."

"I'm not so sure what I can expect from my so-called friends."

"Cheer up," he said. "We plan on winning this election."

"If they win, they're still going to vote for me?"

"That's what I've been told. If I were you, I'd talk to Graham. He's cutting the deal. If we lose, the President-elect will be calling the shots. In that case you'll need six Republican votes in the lame duck session to get through."

Great. She wondered how many times Graham got to mess up her life.

Chapter Eighteen

Katherine hung up the phone and then placed a call to Al Carlton, who had been her behind-the-scenes mentor for over thirty years. Al had been a close friend of her late father, despite the fact that he was a conservative Republican. After her father's death, Al had always been available whenever she needed a door opened or a bit of counseling.

They agreed to meet at The Capital Grille for a drink at six.

Katherine was already seated in a secluded booth at the far end of the room when he arrived. He smiled as he approached her table.

"I was expecting a call from you," Al said, giving her a kiss on the cheek.

Immediately, a waiter appeared beside him. Al turned and asked, "Do you have a bottle of Camus Special Selection Cabernet Sauvignon 2007?"

"Of course, sir."

"Then that's what we'll have tonight. We're celebrating."

"An excellent choice, sir. It's the best red we have in the house."

"We're celebrating my being put on hold?" Katherine asked once the waiter had gone.

"No, celebrating your ability to weather the storm. You just have to walk the halls of the Senate and work the politics to get a quick confirmation vote after the election."

"I don't like politics."

"Play the game now and win, and you won't have to play it ever again. I was worried you wouldn't survive when your father died and left you with his law practice. I don't know how you turned that practice around so fast and then had it successfully acquired by a major firm, making a nice profit for you and your mother. You know how to take care of business. The Supreme Court will be the icing on the cake of life for you."

"Failure was not an option for me. Not with my mother."

"I gather she can be tough to deal with."

"Tough? More like impossible. If my nomination depends on her revealing the name of my natural father, I'll have to withdraw."

"I don't think it's going to matter," he said. "I think you handled it well. Do you want me to help with your Republican politics?"

"Al, I'd appreciate all the help I can get."

The waiter poured a small tasting of the wine into Al's glass, twisting his wrist as he stopped the pour, then wiped the bottle's rim with a white cotton napkin to avoid any spill.

Al inhaled its bouquet and leaned back. Before taking the first sip, he swirled his glass on the table then sniffed again. He nodded his approval after he tasted. "Your Honor, what do you want me to tell them about you?"

Katherine watched the waiter pour her a full serving of red wine before she spoke. "Tell them that I, like Chief Justice Harlan Gaines, have no overarching judicial philosophy." She sniffed her wine before adding, "Tell them I have conservative legal views as they relate to business and that I have conservative friends, like you, whom I listen to and respect."

She tasted her wine. "This may be the best wine I've ever had."

"Glad you like it. But, Kathy, I need to ask you some personal questions."

Katherine cradled her wine glass in both hands, looking him straight in the eye.

"If the Republicans win the White House, it could get ugly. Other than the issue about your father, is there anything else in your background they could dig up?"

"No, I don't think so."

"I hate to ask this, but somebody might ask me. Any abortions?"

Katherine went silent, gazing at the white halo that ringed the surface of her wine.

"If a Republican puts his or her neck on the line supporting your nomination, they're going to rely on somebody they trust to tell them what you stand for. I need to know."

"Al, are you really a single-issue friend? You know me. If I had personal circumstances that forced me to make the gut-wrenching decision to end a pregnancy, should that decision negate all of my professional accomplishments?"

She swirled her wine with one hand, giving it lots of air. "Ask them, would I be less of a lawyer if I got pregnant as a dependent child and my parents wouldn't allow me to have a baby? Am I qualified for a seat on the U.S. Supreme Court if I bow to political pressure now?"

"If you don't answer the question, you might not be qualified as a political matter."

"They're going to have to vote me up or down based on my professional record."

"Are you saying you had an abortion?" he asked.

"I'm saying I am going to demonstrate my intellectual brilliance, just like Harlan Gaines did, by not answering questions people don't have a right to ask."

He shook his head.

"I'm going to defend women's rights by defending my own rights. Whether or not I exercised my legal right to have an abortion is irrelevant. The question is out of bounds."

"Well, what am I supposed to tell them when they ask about your position on abortion?"

"Tell them you don't know. Tell them that you asked and I wouldn't answer. Tell them I'm standing on my professional record and nothing more."

"Why can't you just say what you need to say, then do what you need to do?"

"I *will* do what I need to do. I'll answer truthfully or I won't answer."

"I don't want anything to blow up in my face."

Katherine asked, "Are you going to help me?"

"Not until you give me a better story to tell."

"I know you can help me."

"Well, I have this advice for you. If you find yourself in a senator's office and you're asked if you've had an abortion, don't—and I repeat don't—start invoking your rights. Just tell the truth. You may be embarrassed, but sometimes you have to give up rights to gain privileges."

She reached for her glass again, stalling. "I hate this process."

"But you love winning. If you can't give the right answers, consider withdrawing your nomination if the Republicans win the White House because you won't get through."

Katherine leaned back in her seat without comment, focusing on the halo in her glass.

"I understand," she said with resignation, finishing the last drop of wine.

"Well, it's time for me to be going." He gathered his belongings. "Look, when they ask you about abortion tell them you're pro-life all the way. You know I'll help you if I can."

Al then placed a package on the table. "You should read this—I have an interest."

In the days that followed, Katherine told the Republicans she was pro-life in response to their questions about her abortion position.

Like her mother, she did not lie.

She protected her privacy.

77

Chapter Nineteen

Tuesday, October 30

With her arms folded, Katherine waited for her hairdresser. Again. "This can't keep on happening. I'm gonna have to fire you if you keep on making me late," she said.

"You know you love me too much to do that," Ken said, efficiently flat-ironing a section of neatly partitioned hair on the crown of Cheryl's head.

"He can't help it," Cheryl said.

Cheryl and Katherine were best friends. They'd been coming to Ken's Salon on U Street near Fourteenth since the days when the area was considered the ghetto. Now it was a trendy destination for the up-and-coming. Katherine was part of his core of loyal clients.

They were all friends.

"Just come at six in the morning," Ken said. "By eight, you'll be ready for the cameras."

"I was here three hours last week," Katherine said, her wet hair dripping on a white towel around her shoulders. "We're supposed to meet Jo and Merle in fifteen minutes."

"Calm down, ladies," he said. "The bid-whist game will hold. You'll be out in no time."

"You know he can't help it," Cheryl said in an accepting tone.

"He's gonna have to help it," Katherine said. "I don't know why you're the only man I haven't been able to fire and make it stick."

"Because the others aren't as lovable as me," Ken said, twirling the brush through Cheryl's hair. "Has the player called you lately?"

"I should fire you because you have too much history," Katherine said.

"I wanna know, too," Cheryl said. "Have you heard from Skip?"

"No, I haven't heard from him," Katherine said with unconcealed irritation. "Why would he call me? He derailed me for a constitutional amendment that's going nowhere."

"I think he'll call," Ken said. "He knows he messed up."

"*She* messed up," Cheryl said. "I told you to call him. He would have called back."

Ken twisted a curl; white smoke escaped.

"Stop it," Katherine said, shaking her head. "You don't know what happened."

"She's getting mad," Ken whispered into Cheryl's ear. "We'd better quit."

Cheryl shifted in her seat. "Hey, is our summer shopping trip to London still on if you get confirmed?"

"No reason we can't keep our tradition. The Court's term ends in June. That shouldn't be a problem."

"What're your plans over the next few days?" Cheryl asked.

"I might go over to Philadelphia. I'm brushing up on our history. My mother said we might have family roots there and to check out the rare bookstores. They have some good ones."

"What day you going?" Cheryl asked. "That might be fun."

"Thursday."

"I'll go with you," Cheryl said. "Hey, I just read Thomas Jefferson had a Black family."

"You didn't know that?" Katherine asked. "I thought everybody knew about Sally Hemings. They nailed it with DNA a few years ago. I found out Jefferson served sweet potato biscuits at the First Continental Congress. My mother said her grandmother kept *her* grandmother's original sweet potato biscuit recipe in the family Bible and passed it on to her."

Ken reacted. "Your great-great-great grandmother could read and write?"

"Yes, but she wasn't a slave, and her children were well taken care of."

Cheryl leaned forward. "Like Jefferson took care of Sally?"

"Something like that," Katherine said. "But I don't know the whole story. My mother's family is full of secrets that people took to their graves. The sweet potato biscuit recipe is all I've been able to pry out of her. She gave me a laminated copy in a blue leather-bound Bible a few weeks ago. She told me to research Margaret Thomas—then she clammed up on me."

"Well, I know you're researching Margaret," Cheryl said. "Whatcha know so far?"

"In early 1776, George Washington hired Margaret Thomas as his seamstress. She was a freed mulatto woman—sometimes she was called the washerwoman. Margaret married Billie Lee, Washington's most revered slave. I'm thinking she could have been in his spy ring."

"George Washington had a spy ring?" Cheryl asked.

Ken placed the pressing comb into an electric stove, preparing to straighten-out the kinks.

"Yes, it was called the Culper Ring."

Cheryl raised an eyebrow. "You think you might be related to Margaret Thomas?"

"Maybe, but probably impossible to prove."

At last it was Katherine's turn. She settled into Ken's chair for transformation while her thoughts ran on, leaving the narrow path of conversation. What could derail her?

Katherine checked her internal compass, her thoughts shifted to her conversation with President Greene and all that was at stake. Inalienable rights for the people, not corporations, had to be protected. No one knew better than she the games that could be played with corporate entities. Corporations had super-rights as citizens. That was dangerous.

It had to be addressed.

Did she have the courage to take on the tough property rights cases? She thought so. If she were effective, she'd make enemies. She might lose some friends. That was okay.

If she did the right thing, there might be a price to pay.

What would she do in the face of a death threat?

Two days later, Katherine and Cheryl arrived at Philadelphia's 30th Street train station with Katherine wearing a baseball cap and sunglasses. She had slipped away from her security detail. They thought she would be home all day, but she had escaped.

She wanted a day of freedom, so Cheryl had picked her up in her basement garage.

As they waited in the long line for a taxi, it moved quickly.

"We're going to Bauman's Rare Books on Walnut," Katherine said to the taxi driver. "Do you need the address?"

"Naw, I got it," he responded.

"We have a one o'clock appointment."

"You need an appointment to get in there?" Cheryl asked.

"Yes, if you're to be taken seriously and get your hands on something that's really rare."

"What did you tell them you wanted?"

"I asked to see any papers, books or letters related to intelligence gathering during the Revolutionary War. I have a hunch about Margaret Thomas."

"What do you think you might find?"

"A hint into the past. I don't know. I'm just looking for something illuminating."

They rode up the elevator in the historic Sun Oil Building to the nineteenth floor, home office of Burnam Rare Books. As they entered the elegant space with its dark, wood-paneled walls, they were met by the gallery manager. He directed them to the conference table on a colorful oriental rug where he had been cataloging a shipment of current acquisitions.

"I'm sorry," he said, "but we don't currently have any George Washington original letters or anything on a Margaret Thomas. But we do have a rare official document signed by both George Washington and Thomas Jefferson related to the issuance of a Letter of Marque to a sloop of war. It's very rare, framed, and has a price of $50,000, if that would interest you."

"No, that's not what I'm looking for."

"When we get George Washington letters, our established collectors normally snap them up immediately. It's unlikely you'll be able to locate what you're looking for unless you find it in a private library or museum. Sorry we couldn't help you. Try the African American Museum."

Then she noticed the book that the gallery manager had been working with when they entered the gallery on the table, staring at the book jacket.

"There was an author named John Galt?" Katherine asked.

"Yes, a very famous Scottish author working at the end of the enlightenment period."

"What's the title of that book?"

"*The Radical: An Autobiography*. Published 1832."

"May I see it?"

Katherine sat down at the conference table and quietly perused its pages.

"How much for Galt's book?" she asked.

"I'm still researching it to set the price, but I could sell it for $1,000 at a profit."

"I'll take it."

Over at the African American Museum, the curator shared documents and stories related to the thousands of freed African Americans who had made Philadelphia their home in the aftermath of the American Revolution—a period during which enslaved Blacks were still considered property. The museum's next major exhibit would be called *Audacious Freedom.*

To Katherine's great disappointment, they had nothing on Margaret Thomas. So she left Philadelphia with a hint into the past, but not the historical link to her family history that she had hoped to find.

Chapter Twenty

Tuesday, December 11
8:30 p.m.

A little more than a month after the presidential election, Katherine received the call she had thought would never come. She listened intently, in disbelief.

The President's chief of staff said, "The Senate will be voting on your confirmation in the morning before they recess for the holiday break. It appears your nomination will be approved. I've just confirmed the last Republican vote. Your Senate vote has been scheduled for 10:00 a.m. You should be present in case there are any last minute questions. I'll be escorting you and will pick you up about nine. Goodnight, Your Honor."

At home, Katherine leaned back in her desk chair, her heart palpitating. Several books were spread around her related to the Founding Fathers, the Federalist Papers, and the Constitutional Convention. Over the past few weeks she had waded through a dozen books and spent countless hours on the Internet confirming and testing her understanding of matters related to the legal foundations of the Supreme Court. Was she ready?

There was no more time to prepare for another hearing.

But she had to do something, so she reached for a book about the Constitutional Convention, turning to a random page for insight.

She read the words of George Washington written shortly after the Convention adjourned in September 1787:

Your own judgment will at once discover the good and the exceptional parts of it, and your experience of the difficulties which have ever arisen when attempts have been made to reconcile such variety of interests and local prejudices as pervade the several states will render explanation unnecessary. I sincerely believe it is the best that could be obtained at this time; and, a constitutional door is open to amendment hereafter ... If it be good, I suppose it will work its way good.

The Court had been left with a big job to work out over time, she thought.

Everything wasn't settled.

Scanning webpages, she discovered that one of the first Justices of the Supreme Court, James Wilson, proposed the three-fifths slave compromise as a member of the Committee on Detail that produced the August 6 draft of the Constitution. Politics. Dred Scott.

Slavery was a property rights issue at its core—the ultimate oppression of property rights.

Next, Katherine printed out the minutes of the 1787 Constitutional Convention from the Library of Congress website and placed them in a three ring binder. She placed the binder on her bookshelf for later reference, realizing that upholding the Constitution of the United States meant upholding the political decisions that shaped it. Positive law. Repose.

When should natural law trump positive law for justice?

That was the line she must discover for herself.

Her job would be resolving conflicts inherent in the Constitution and laws of the land.

Should corporations have the same property rights as human beings?

Katherine thought of the Hawaiian property rights case, *State of Hawaii v. Office of Hawaiian Affairs*. Those papers sat atop a pile of Supreme Court cases she wanted to tackle. Then there was the white paper on Hawaiian property rights prepared by the National Association of Bankers that Al had asked her to review.

She wanted to crystallize her position on property rights.

The Hawaiian case was a good place to start. She glanced at the clock again. It was late. She would just peek at it. In less than thirty minutes, she had processed the unanimous Supreme Court opinion in that case. Politics. Repose? She would have to get back to this case later. At this point, she had to put her faith in God to carry her through.

There was nothing more she could do.

At ten in the morning, Katherine sat in a room alone in the north wing of the Capitol, near the Senate chamber. Ready. She watched the Vice President of the United States call the U.S. Senate to order on television. The chair of the Senate Judiciary Committee rose and called for a confirmation vote on the nomination of Katherine Helena Ross to the U.S. Supreme Court.

Senator Graham called for the question to be voted on without debate.

Sixty "Yes" votes to call the question. Passed.

The Vice President called for a roll vote.

Sixty "Yes" votes confirming. Enough. She cried out in joy, staring in disbelief at the screen. She sent up a prayer to God for courage. Her life had just changed forever.

Graham eyed Katherine in the hallway, leaving the Capitol with her protectors.

She diverted her gaze.

He did not pursue her. He would wait until the timing was right.

That evening, Katherine reviewed the list of family members and close friends who would be invited to attend her Judicial Oath ceremony.

Senator Graham did not make the list.

She attached the completed list to an email to Chief Justice Gaines informing him that she wanted her mother to hold Lincoln's Bible during the ceremony. She hit the *SEND* button with a triumphant flare of her finger. She had made it to the Supreme Court.

With the holidays upon them, her formal investiture ceremony at the Supreme Court could not be scheduled until January 4. Katherine was glad to have a few days of unscheduled time before her official duties began. Starting the term ten weeks late meant she wouldn't have time for leisure or background reading after taking her oath pledging to uphold the Constitution of the United States of America.

She grabbed the book on the 1787 Constitutional Convention again, searching for insight and inspiration. She would read until she fell asleep. As she drifted, images of George Washington floated through her mind. Sleep overtook her with the book opened to a page with Benjamin Franklin's comments made to the Constitutional Convention just before their historic vote when the fate of the Constitution appeared doomed.

Franklin said:

I agree to this Constitution with all its faults, if they are such; because I think a general government necessary for us. I doubt, too, whether any other convention we can obtain may be able to make a better Constitution; for, when you assemble a number of men, to have the advantage of their joint wisdom, you inevitably assemble with those men all their prejudices, their passions, their errors of opinion, their local interests, and their selfish views...

She dreamed that Franklin whispered into her ear, "*E Pluribus Unum.*"

Out of many, one.

Chapter Twenty-One

Wednesday, January 23

The smell of Maxwell House coffee filled the chambers of Associate Supreme Court Justice Katherine Helena Ross. She lifted her father's Supreme Court mug and sipped, always remembering him when she drank from his cup. It was still unbelievable that she was a United States Supreme Court justice and that these personal chambers belonged to her for the rest of her life.

Her new life still felt like a dream. Some nights, the dream turned into a nightmare when she considered the consequences of her actions and those who depended on her to right the wrongs. Life wasn't fair to all. Yet every morning she arrived at her chambers excited and thankful for the opportunity to serve her country in such a critical role.

Having more Supreme Court work experience than she had, Katherine's new law clerks and secretaries were selected by the sitting justices at her request, and assigned to Chief Justice Gaines for supervision, pending her confirmation by the Senate. As a result, Katherine had not met her staff nor did she know their identity until a few weeks before, trusting the advice of a retired Supreme Court justice as to their competence.

In the weeks since her swearing-in ceremony, her life had been completely rearranged. New office. New schedule. More power. More attention. Less freedom. A lot less sleep.

Opinions were already rolling out from the Marble Palace.

At 7:30 a.m. Katherine's first law clerk arrived. Ron Payne walked through the door, said good morning, and placed a pile of equal protection cases on her desk. "I've done summaries for your review. They're on the top."

At twenty-nine, Ron sported a well-developed upper body. Rounded biceps bulged in his long-sleeved golf shirt. He had an angular jaw with a straight chin, a face full of promise. Ron could pass as a well-tanned white person, but most Blacks recognized him as one of them.

"What do you think?" Ross asked. "Any worth taking?"

"I was up until after midnight summarizing these cases. The only one I think you should consider is the one from Texas."

"Sit down. Tell me the facts. Quick."

Ron sat and leaned forward.

"Meyers vs. State of Texas. Black male. Twenty-one. No physical evidence. No history of violence. High-publicity case. The defendant has an alibi with three family witnesses. He's not from a violent community—only two murders in his county all year, both were domestic violence. I saw a quote in the local Texas newspaper from the president of the NAACP saying that the sheriff arrested all of the young Black males in the county aged sixteen to twenty-one. Thirty in all. Put eight of them in a line-up. Eyewitness identification by the victim. Now there is new evidence. A key witness signed a note on her deathbed saying she regrets her testimony and does not believe the defendant is guilty. Fifteen years after his conviction, she wants to save his life. She died eight weeks ago. But this case has a new twist—he argues the equal protection clause. If the state can't take the life of a corporation for criminal acts, it shouldn't have the right to take the life of human beings for criminal acts. That's it. The rest are not compelling cases."

"What's that judgment based on?" she asked.

"No new evidence, some missed the deadlines for filing, most are just boilerplate, exhausting appeal rights with no real hope of delaying their inevitable dates with God. The question we have to consider is: Was there a constitutional misstep in the application of the law? As a matter of practice, we don't second-guess the lower courts on assessing the facts of a case. I didn't see any new evidence in the other capital cases. I think you should vote to hear the Texas case, but I think even that case is going to come up one vote short."

Within seconds, Katherine announced her first decision of the day at 7:50 a.m.

"I'll vote to hear the Texas case," she said. "I'll take it home, read it tonight and then try to convince someone to join me. The equal protection angle is compelling. An individual has a constitutional right to life, just like corporations. Humans can't have lesser rights than corporations. If you can't kill corporate persons for wrongful acts, the states shouldn't be allowed to kill the class of persons who are human beings."

"That's what I thought."

"The Texas case is good because half of all U.S. executions occur in Texas," she added. "Tell me who hasn't voted to hear it."

"I'll have to find out, but I'll bet Galt won't vote to hear it."

"How do you think the Chief will vote?"

"Hard to say."

"I'll take the whole pile of cases home with me tonight. This is death. I'll make my decisions on the other appeals in the morning. I may try to lobby Galt on the Texas case."

"His heart is hardened," Ron said. "Don't waste your time."

But she wasn't convinced Galt couldn't be reached.

Ron continued, "If you want to hear the Texas case, you'd better work on somebody else. The Chief is a better shot, but he's still a long shot. But he likes to exercise his brain cells—I'd try him."

"How?"

"Send him a handwritten note. Just ask if he will join you in hearing this case and send our summary. See what he says, then decide what to do."

"Just a note?"

"That's all. I don't see any other death penalty appeals in that pile we can get five votes for consideration. That's the political reality you're facing here. My advice to you is don't stay up all night reading if you can't make a difference."

"If my heart tells me a man is innocent, I'm going to fight to hear his final appeal."

Ever so slightly Ron pulled his head back with raised eyebrows. Katherine didn't miss the message in his subtle body language.

He questioned her judgment. To do his job, he needed to know what she believed. "If the states fail in protecting the inalienable rights of our human citizens—we have a job to do. Juries are made up of humans. Humans make errors. States can err. People's lives are at stake." She picked a pen up from her desk to make a point. "Giving the government the right to take a human life is dangerous and must be monitored by this Court. We must always be on guard to protect a person's right to life."

She flung the red pen that she was holding.

He jumped. "So you're gonna try to tinker with the death machinery?"

"Without a doubt. I don't think the states have the power to kill innocent people by a simple majority vote under our Constitution."

"Does that mean you're taking on the abortion issue too?"

"I'll listen to my heart on issues like that," Justice Ross said, continuing her train of thought. "Pay attention to the handwritten appeals. Look for the egregious cases of trampled human rights. Allow yourself to feel which ones pull at your heart."

"Okay. Is there anything else I need to know?"

"Yes. I'm willing to listen to natural law arguments, even though I believe following statutory law is best. Thanks for the heads up on the internal politics. I needed that."

"My pleasure."

"Ron," she said in a softer tone, "you should be comfortable expressing your viewpoints to me, even when we disagree. I value your viewpoint. Now, time is of the essence."

Justice Ross turned in her black leather executive chair and faced her computer, signaling their conversation was over. She entered her pass code and pressed enter.

It was 8:00 a.m. Justice Katherine Helena Ross was ready for a full day of work at the U.S. Supreme Court. She'd keep her powder dry on Galt for now.

Chapter Twenty-Two

Allen Chapel A.M.E. Church
Sunday, March 10

With a bounce in her step and her hair styled in a no-nonsense French twist, Katherine put on dark sunglasses as she exited the white brick church and made her way toward her waiting sedan. Her tailored black suit accented with a form-fitting, lace-trimmed purple camisole trim revealed the natural curves of her body. Yet the look was still conservative, with low-heeled black Chanel pumps and a matching purse.

Reaching her Cadillac sedan with the open door, she sank into the rear seat.

Her black car crossed the I-295 bridge over the Anacostia River. Eventually they merged onto I-395S on their planned route. Traffic moved easily. No accidents. Katherine closed her eyes for a short rest. The periodic thump of the sedan's wheels registered as they crossed connected sections of highway pavement. A few moments later, she felt the vehicle slow. Then they came to a complete stop.

She opened her eyes.

A sea of red taillights lay ahead of them on the two-lane exit ramp. In the distance she spotted the green sign for the Twelfth Street exit near L'Enfant Plaza, maybe a thousand feet away.

"What's happening?" Katherine asked Hal Barnes, her security officer.

"I don't know. Nothing's moving. Look behind you."

Katherine turned. A parking lot of bumper-to-bumper cars came into view.

"Sorry, I should have stayed on 395. We're blocked in. Not a good situation for us."

Impatiently, Katherine's thoughts wandered from the words she had heard at church to the draft opinions on her desk that awaited her full attention. She glanced at her watch. 2:45 p.m. They had already sat for twenty minutes.

A metallic blue BMW in back of Katherine's vehicle moved into the emergency lane and passed them. A few cars ahead, the BMW merged back into a legal position.

Katherine saw why: A DC police car was backing up the emergency lane, past her vehicle to the split at the beginning of the Twelfth Street exit. The police car stopped, made a three-point turn at a right angle—then the sound of its siren pierced the air.

The idling cars in the two exit lanes parted, making way for the screaming beast with flashing eyes. Its wheels screeched, as if it were in pain.

Katherine watched in disbelief. That was too dangerous—even for an emergency.

She frowned as the police car sped away, sirens off.

Next, she noticed the BMW move backwards into the emergency lane again, passing Katherine's vehicle. When it reached the split, it repositioned and sped onto the freeway.

Following the examples of the police and BMW, car after car backed up to the beginning of the split, and made the life-daring charge to merge into the free flowing traffic.

Several car lengths ahead, the driver of a cream-colored Ford F-150 truck decided to completely turn around and go in the opposite direction of on-coming traffic on the exit ramp.

"Do you want me to back up?" Hal asked.

"No, that's no example to follow. Move to the right a little when you get a chance."

Following her instructions, Hal positioned the security sedan in the middle of the double lane exit, blocking the cars behind them.

"Don't move," Katherine said as three car lengths suddenly appeared before them. "No one can pass us. If this persists, someone might get killed."

With the F-150 continuing in the wrong direction, all of the stalled traffic ahead of them disappeared. Katherine knew the F-150 couldn't turn around again nor could it make a mad dash for the fast lanes with traffic moving at maximum speed limits. She wouldn't make it. She'd die.

"Blow at her!" Katherine said, waving her hand to attract the driver's attention.

The driver of the F-150, a woman with a red bandana tied around her head, glanced at Katherine and gave her the finger. The cars behind them started to honk their horns. In response, Katherine got out of her car and stood in the emergency lane behind the F-150, waving for the woman to backup. From three cars behind her vehicle, a man exited his car and cursed at Katherine. Then she noticed him. Walter Rodney laid on his horn and glared at her.

Walter was following her.

Hal turned off their vehicle and joined Katherine. The former football player with his athletic build towered beside her, standing in a ready-for-action posture, focused on Walter.

The F-150 stopped at the split.

Then they heard police sirens. "Let's go," she said. "I don't want to make a scene."

"You already have. Just be glad I sent out a distress signal for backup before you decided to get out of the car. That guy from the church might be unstable. Did you see him? Next time, please stay in the car so we're both out of harm's way."

"I'll try. But someone might have been killed if we had done nothing."

"I'm going to say this again," Hal said, annoyed. "Don't get out of this secure vehicle no matter what is going on around us without the door being opened for you. Even if I get hurt, don't get out of this car. If you can drive, drive us to a safe location. Otherwise just wait in the vehicle until help arrives. That's your security protocol. Your life may depend on it."

"Sorry for being late," Katherine said as she entered her mother's condo and kicked off her shoes in the hallway. "I feel like I'm losing control over my life."

"What's wrong, baby?" her mother asked. "Why are you late?"

"Traffic. I'm just feeling overwhelmed with everything. Running my chambers is like setting up a small law firm—then I have to deal with oral arguments, conferences, a never-ending flow of cert petitions and the spilt decisions. Don't know when I'll catch up."

Katherine took her seat at the dinner table. The food was waiting and she was ready for it.

"Take your time with the split decisions," her mother said, cutting a standing rib roast. "You'll be making the decision for the Court and signaling what your jurisprudence will be. Make your father proud. I wish he were alive to see you now."

They blessed the food after her mother was seated.

"I wish he were here, too, to debate some of these cases with me over dinner like we used to do. Most people could never imagine our Sunday dinner conversations. He was always sharp."

"In more ways than one," her mother said, reminiscing. "In his pinstriped trousers, vest and jacket, he looked like he was ready for them. He had thought of every possible question and had an answer that would lead them right back to his main point."

"Just like he was the day he died. You were ready for them, too. You were a great team."

"I learned so much from him about the law and being prepared."

96

"I hope you've learned not to let the legal profession work you into an early grave. Sixty-five was too young for your father to die. You look tired."

Katherine poured hot gravy over her white rice. "I am. I feel like I'm being challenged to find my deepest reserve of energy." She sighed.

"But you're up to it."

"You know, all of the opinions are due by mid-June and they are the toughest constitutional issues facing the Court—split decisions at the appeals court level and now split at the Supreme Court. I think I'm the only true moderate. I wish I had someone I could lean on."

"So how much sleep are you getting?" her mother asked with concern.

"Four to five hours when I take time to exercise. I have a trainer meet me at least three days a week at the Court gym at six. So I'm up at five most days."

"You'll be okay." After a pause her mother asked, "Have you met with JT yet?"

Katherine's mother had given Justice John T. Galt the nickname "JT" during his confirmation hearings. Katherine had no idea why. She hadn't heard anyone else call him that.

"I haven't been able to set an appointment with him yet. He's guarded with me."

"You have to meet with him," her mother urged. "There's too much at stake."

"But what can I do? I'm not going to just walk into his chambers."

"We've got to reach him for the good of the country. I suspect he has a good heart. He's just protecting himself. You can reach him. I know you can."

"Nobody else has. He's polite to me, but he just keeps putting me off."

"Ask him to meet you for breakfast in a public place. Julianne said he's a target."

"A target?"

"Walter Rodney's antics at the church have been stopped, but he's over at the Douglass Community Center now, agitating against the super human rights of corporations that are crushing the little people. Hal advised me to find a safer place to take yoga."

"Really? I didn't know that. What else did Julianne say about him?"

"She said he's got a speech that he keeps repeating about Galt and the co-optation of Black people in leadership positions. He's calling for opposing the system by any means necessary. Fighting in the streets, if that's what it takes."

"Fighting in the streets won't work."

"We know that," her mother said. "But a lot of the young people feel the government has failed them. You need to be careful. People use violence when they feel the system doesn't work for them. Baby, you represent the system now. To some people you look like a puppet."

"I'm not a puppet."

"I know that. Getting back to JT, he represents what's wrong with the system to a lot of people. But you still have to reach out to him. It's the right thing to do."

"Okay, I'll send him a note and ask to meet for breakfast. Does that make you happy?"

"For the moment."

"Will you make me happy by telling me who my father is?"

Her mother slumped back in her chair. "Not now."

"Mom. Why can't you tell me?"

"It's hard. I've written a few chapters of my memoir. But it's not ready yet. I'll give it to you when it's ready." Her mother reached for a pile of envelopes and handed one to Katherine. "Here's an invitation to a fundraiser I want you to attend with me."

"I don't want to go to a fundraiser now." She dropped the invitation on the table and felt her emotions erupt, but spoke calmly. "I want to know who my father is."

"Please, come to the fundraiser with me. I'm working on it— you can have it soon."

Chapter Twenty-Three

Arlington, Virginia
A Few Days Later

Justice Ross entered the dining room of the Ritz Carlton Hotel at Pentagon City and a few heads turned as she sailed by. On the wall, she admired an oil painting of a fleet of warships in an ornate gold frame. Scanning the dining room she didn't recognize any of the attorneys scheduled to argue before the Court that week.

The waiter took her to a reserved booth near the end of the room.

A few moments later, Justice John Galt appeared—her black-skinned counterpart on the Court. His hair was trimmed with sharp lines. Dressed in a black suit with a Yale-blue tie, he looked down at her through large-framed lenses and extended his hand for hers.

"Let's eat at the buffet to save time," he said before sitting down, then turned away.

She got up and followed him to the inviting spread of foods, then back to their table with full plates.

"Have you been reading our security briefings?" Katherine asked, spreading her napkin.

"I don't worry about threats. After you've been here for a while, you'll learn."

Galt poured maple syrup on his waffle.

She took in his dismissive attitude.

"I think you should pay attention," she said. "I think Walter Rodney is dangerous."

Galt forked into his roasted potatoes.

Katherine continued, "Our community is losing hope that America is the land of opportunity. And that just makes it easier for groups pushing socialism to recruit our youth to protest. Racial tensions are rising again. Things could get violent."

"Those efforts will fail," he said, reaching for his juice.

"How can you be so sure?"

"They always fail. They're weak people. All they'll do is protest. You have to do something productive to make a difference. Look at us. We're successful in this society."

"Yes," Katherine said. "But we had help."

"Affirmative Action didn't help me. I helped myself."

"We need not debate about our different views of reality."

"There is only one truth."

"Let's get back to Walter Rodney," Katherine said, recognizing a dead end. "BAMN—"

"They're fizzling."

"You're wrong. They're still trying to organize our youth."

"The health of our economy is what matters now," Galt said. "We must protect the business interests. In the long run that's what's fair to all. Money is the great equalizer."

"When people feel they're economically oppressed and lose hope, they revolt, and that's why we need to pay attention to what's happening on the streets. That's why you need to read your security briefings and understand what's going on with Walter Rodney."

Galt cut the soft golden brown waffle and took a bite. Katherine bit on dry toast and watched him enjoy the delicate syrup-drenched waffle as he chewed.

He wiped crumbs from his mouth with a black napkin.

She knew he expected her to keep talking.

She decided to wait him out.

"So who is this Walter Rodney?" Galt asked finally after his waffle was gone.

"An angry Black man who lost his job and can't find another one. He's organizing a group called the Black Activists Mobilization Network. It's called BAMN, too. Understand?"

"Yes. It's the acronym for 'By Any Means Necessary.' What does he want?"

"He's calling for reparations."

"Same chant. It hasn't worked yet. Maybe he should find a new one."

She leaned in. "You should know, there was a meeting on Good Hope Road last night where Rodney had the whole room chanting, 'Galt Must Go!' He's targeted you."

"I'm not going anywhere. How do you know that?"

"Julianne LaSalle called me last night to warn me. She thinks they're plotting a violent protest directed against the Court. I notified security."

"Julianne has your home phone number?"

"She called my mother. She's in my mother's Sunday school class."

"Anything else I should know about Walter Rodney?"

"He's making progress with the reparations message."

"The weak trying to demand loot from the productive is not new."

"Reparations is a valid legal issue for the descendants of slavery. The Jews got reparations. The Japanese got reparations. The issue is still ripe for justice."

"We can't solve the country's problems by focusing on minority group issues."

"If the rights of an identifiable minority group are trampled…"

Galt looked her straight in the eyes and leaned forward. "We can't create legislation from the bench just because we want the Constitution to say something that it simply does not say. Our Constitution protects the inalienable rights of the individual."

There was a prolonged silence.

Determined glares of gladiators locked.

"What about corporations?" Katherine asked.

"State rights. That's in the Constitution."

Katherine glanced at her watch. "It's time to go. Oral arguments at ten."

She rose, knowing there was no time left for a meaningful debate on state versus individual rights. She didn't like how he made her feel. Discounted? Ticked? Powerless? Smiling at him for the benefit of any interested spectator in the room she said, "I bought you a gift." She handed him a book, giftwrapped in gold paper with a red, white and blue bow.

"Katherine," he said before she could walk away, "you should do some homework on the Commerce Clause. The Civil Rights Act rests on the Commerce Clause and that is the only legal foundation that it has. The Civil Rights Act is not going to stand forever because it does not have the Fourteenth Amendment as its base. You should know the end could be near."

She looked down at Galt. "I know the business interests you support co-opted the Fourteenth Amendment, and that the rights intended to protect the former slaves are primarily used to further the interests of corporations today."

"You must understand…"

"I understand corporations are not human beings—but they have superior rights in the law. That's why my father put his clients in corporations whenever he could to defend their economic rights. I believe the Commerce Clause *is* going to stand."

Katherine slung her black bag over her shoulder and exited the room, leaving Galt to settle the bill. After retrieving her coat, she hurried to her waiting car and settled into the back seat for the short ride to the Supreme Court building.

She gazed out at the frigid Potomac River deep in thought about the conversation she had just had with Justice John T. Galt. His warning was disturbing.

As the armored sedan crossed the Fourteenth Street Bridge, Katherine wondered if Galt—a Black man who had experienced racial discrimination—would really vote to strike down the Civil Rights Act if the right case came before the Court.

Katherine could only hope he wasn't a fool.

Chapter Twenty-Four

U.S. Supreme Court
Friday, March 22

The next morning, Katherine shook hands with Chief Justice Harlan Gaines who stood at the top of the white marble spiral staircase on the north side of the building, peering down five stories to the bottom. As she took in the magnificent view from the top, she could hardly believe this was now her everyday reality. In awe of the symbolism and beauty that surrounded her, she silently gave gratitude to God for bringing her this far in life.

Chief Justice Gaines, dapper in his traditional red bow tie and black suit, explained that the circular staircase was self-supporting. Each step attached to the marble wall, and the only additional support of the entire spiral structure was due to the proper placement of each step a few inches overlapping the one beneath it.

Gaines pulled back a red velvet rope, motioning with his hands and a slight bow of his head for her to proceed onto the landing.

Katherine placed her right hand at the beginning of the bronze railing. It felt smooth and cool to her touch. Her hand moved back and forth on the rail.

Her next step would be an act of faith.

Little shivers tingled down the length of her leg as she placed her black low-heeled pump on the first descending step and allowed her weight to shift to her right foot.

Below, several stories down, one of the Supreme Court docents stood in front of the spiral staircase with a tour group. The docent's voice echoed up.

"We have visitors," Gaines said, looking down the staircase. "Probably VIPs since this area is not accessible to the general public. Let's go introduce ourselves."

Katherine felt a little fear as she glanced down knowing that only a few inches of marble strategically placed at each step supported the massive staircase. It reminded her that the Supreme Court, as an institution, was self-supporting with few anchors.

She paused on an extended landing area facing Gaines, about one floor level from the top. "Do you know the quote by Francis Bacon, 'We rise to great heights by a winding staircase?'"

"'All rising to a great place is by a winding stair,'" Gaines responded. "Of course."

She took her next step, tightening her grip on the bronze railing. "I think I'll walk up all five floors of this staircase, reciting that verse as a mantra, whenever I have a tough decision to make. If I can't make it—I'll seriously consider resigning."

"I don't think you'll be the first," he said. "Sometimes I think of man's cyclical journey in life, moving from one state of being to another. Often we return to the same vertical axis with a little higher elevation and a slightly different perspective on what justice means."

"But sometimes we fall short in delivering justice," she said. "We make compromises."

"That's why we keep circling around and around an issue until it's clear to a majority of us what's right. That's why some issues keep coming back."

"How long do you think we're going to uphold the socially constructed reality that corporations should have the same rights as a living person? We can't uphold…"

"Forever. All the states agree: The corporation is a person. So there's no controversy in how the lower courts view that issue. As it stands, there's no basis for review."

"Well, I think it's a pillar that may be crumbling at its base," Katherine said. "It's kind of like pretending slaves were three-fifths of a person. It's a constructed reality that can't stand…"

"It's the best vehicle in the world to promote the free market. It's standing."

"With the expansion of corporate rights over the years, we've created a vehicle for foreign interests to play in our politics. A speeding vehicle that will cause major casualties…"

"I just don't think it's wise for us to deal with the definition of who is a person now," the Chief said. "Most legal eagles think that's a nonissue. It just isn't ripe for our consideration."

Katherine felt dismissed. She knew that was the majority view. Was she powerless to make a difference? How long were the power players going to be able to make that rule of law stick? She answered her own thought: *Until the people wake up.*

They continued down the last few stairs without comment until they reached the docent and escorted guests.

The docent introduced them.

Gaines asked, "Who are our guests?"

"Law students from the University of Virginia," the docent replied. "They're meeting with Justice Galt in the East Conference Room at two for a lecture."

"Does anyone have a question for me?" Gaines asked.

After an awkward moment of silence, a girl in a white blouse and black slacks asked, "Do you read all nine thousand certs petitions filed with the Court every year?"

"I must tell you the truth," Gaines said. "Most of us don't read all nine thousand certs. Our law clerks screen them for us. We give our clerks clear guidelines on which certs are to be brought to our attention. I read those. It takes four votes for the Court to hear a case. We also pool our clerks to reduce our workloads, but participation in the pool is voluntary. We have a talented staff that helps us get through the tremendous volume of cases filed here every year. We only accept about a hundred cases each year for review."

"What's the most interesting part of your job?" the same woman asked.

"Oral argument, when I get the chance to ask tough questions," the Chief answered. "I like to see an attorney rise to the occasion."

"Some justices are on record saying they personally read all nine thousand certs," a male student said. "Justice Ross, are you going to try to read all of them yourself?"

"I haven't decided yet if I'm going to use the cert pool. My clerks were participating in it before I was sworn in. At this point I'm reading all certs with three votes for a hearing."

"Thank you," the docent said. "We should be moving along."

Gaines overruled. "As the Chief, I get to decide when this session is over. We have a few more minutes to shape these developing legal minds."

A Hispanic male raised his hand. The Chief acknowledged him with a nod.

"Justice Ross, will you be asking questions during oral argument?"

"Yes. If I think there's a relevant legal issue that has not been brought to light by either party, I may want to probe it."

A young Black man who somehow seemed familiar to Katherine asked, "Is it constitutional for a state government to give collectives of anonymous economic interests or groups of foreigners the same rights as natural born citizens under the U.S. Constitution? You know what's happening. BAMN wants to know if this Court has the courage to deal with the moneyed interests who seek to control us through corporations and malevolent foundations."

Katherine was alarmed. She felt vulnerable. Violated.

How did he get into the restricted area?

Gaines responded before she could. "Without a specific context or decided case, we can't say more. It's been good to meet all of you."

They turned toward the highly secured area that led to their private chambers.

The Supreme Court police covered their backs.

Chapter Twenty-Five

"I want to put one of the interns on Walter Rodney full-time," Julianne said, charging into the office of her editor, Sam Knight.

Sam glanced up from the papers on his worn desk with an occupied expression.

Julianne took the seat in front of him, intending to engage him for a while.

"I thought you had an intern investigate him months ago," Sam said.

"I did, but the semester ended and the student went on to other things. He was a little timid. Didn't want to join BAMN. Thought it might get dangerous. Graham told me Rodney was recruiting people to stalk Ross and asked me to warn her, off-the-record."

"That seems strange. Why wouldn't he use a more formal channel?"

"Don't know. They don't appear to be very chummy."

"I don't know about using the interns if you think it's going be dangerous," Sam said.

"This is going to be a big story. I went to Rodney's meeting last night and they were shouting, 'Galt must go!' He had a big crowd riled up. I'd love to keep going to his meetings myself, but they may not be as open with a reporter in the room."

"I think everybody knows how you feel about Galt. You'd fit right in."

"I'm objective. Frankly, I just don't want to be viewed as being part of BAMN."

Julianne was Galt's most lethal critic in the media. She was an opinion leader in the Black community—regularly featured on cable network news and political talk shows.

"Why do you think he's dangerous?" Sam asked.

"Rodney is an intellectual guerilla. He's a leader who can influence people to revolt."

"Do you think he could be a terrorist?"

"No. He's a freedom fighter who isn't afraid of violence. But what really concerns me are his socialist views. He's calling for a revolution and I don't want to get labeled with that."

Chapter Twenty-Six

J.W. Marriott on Fourteenth Street
The Next Saturday Night

Katherine spotted Senator Graham from across the main ballroom. Her heart jumped. Again. He wore a navy blue business suit with his signature maize and blue tie. Sharp, like her dad.

Intelligent. Poised. Desirable.

The images came at her. The night she gave herself to him, believing he had room in his heart to love her, *too*. Her surrender. His strong yet tender touch. Her inexperience. His caressing embrace. Her love. The sting of his rejection was still as fresh as if it had happened yesterday, as was the pain that followed. She still mourned the life they could have had together and could not recover.

No. She wasn't going to let her emotions run wild again.

Katherine caught his gaze and turned away.

She glanced at the list of host committee names for the fundraising event for the new president of the National Association of Historically Black Colleges and Universities. Graham was a member. She should have looked more closely at the invitation. In general, she did not accept invitations where she knew he would be present.

But now she was here, and people had noticed.

That night, Katherine Ross didn't look like an Associate Justice of the U.S. Supreme Court. She looked more like a mature high fashion model ready for a strut down the catwalk in her designer suit, yet her position as a Supreme Court justice demanded reserve. She sipped on a glass of merlot at a high-top cocktail table with an entourage of defenders positioned around her.

Her persona resonated power.

Now in the spotlight, she wondered if he would approach her. She'd made up her mind—he would have to make the first move or they would never speak. That was her final decision and had been for the last thirty years. Final judgment. No appeals from her heart.

Case closed.

Katherine watched her mother from across the room as she mingled with old friends and made new ones. Mrs. Ross sat at a table chatting with the wife of Howard University's president. A constant flow of people stopped by their table to speak to them.

She continued surveying the room—full of well-dressed Black achievers who could afford the two hundred fifty dollar admission price or had the right connections. Loud voices echoed through the crowded room as old friends traded tales about their triumphs and challenges. Guests celebrated recent professional advancements while lamenting the changing climate and closing doors of opportunity.

The band played a mixture of old school and new music to the delight of the crowd. Katherine recognized *Wishing on a Star*, a popular old tune.

Not that song, she thought. *Not now.*

Music had a way of taking her back. With him in the room along with that song, her emotions stirred.

She considered leaving.

"Katherine?" Senator Graham caught her placing her empty glass on a tray.

She turned to face him.

"Are you avoiding me?"

"I'm here," she said, noticing her mother talking to Julianne LaSalle. "So I haven't avoided you."

"But you didn't even stop by to ask for my vote."

"I did ask for your vote. Didn't you get my letter?"

"The form letter you sent to the entire U.S. Senate?"

"Yes."

"I expected more from you than a form letter, given our past."

"I didn't think more was necessary, given our past."

"Okay, I can accept that," he said. "Can I take you out to dinner when this is over?"

"No, I can't."

"Some other time then?" he asked, handing her his business card.

"Maybe," Katherine replied, taking the card. The scent of his Old Spice cologne drifted her way. *No. Not again.* "I don't want to make any commitments now—I'll call you later."

"Should I hold my breath?" He gazed into her eyes. "I was holding my breath."

"I wouldn't do that if I were you." She turned away.

"My cell phone number is on the back. Call me."

She did not reply as she made her way through the spirited crowd, her security detail trailing her. When she reached her mother's table, she glanced back once more.

Senator Graham already had another smiling female at attention.

She knew he had multiple interests.

Weeks later, Katherine stared at the phone as the speckled rays of morning sunshine hit the desk in her chambers. She had thought of him every night since the Howard reception. The memories disturbed her sleep. Seeing him again had opened up a dam of emotions within her that had been contained until then. She couldn't call him.

She was an Associate Justice of the United States Supreme Court.

Call him, her heart said.

No, replied her ego.

Why couldn't she stop thinking about him?

She felt the old ache. Again. Katherine sighed as she blocked all thoughts of him.

She wasn't a schoolgirl with a crush anymore.

Justice Ross processed and initialed the pile of cert disposition memorandums before her and cleared her desk of all clutter. But the memories of Skip Graham could not be dismissed.

Chapter Twenty-Seven

Russell Senate Office Building
Monday, March 25

Cold. Bleak. The wind picked up as a rare snowstorm gathered energy and moved toward Washington, D.C. Sleet formed icicles that gave the trees along Constitution Avenue a translucent glow. Papers on the ground skipped forward, pushed by gusting winds. The sun, covered by clouds, barely lit Capitol Hill, which heralded the blizzard approaching from the west.

Cars moved in slow motion. Travel was already dangerous. But Graham's office worked late in spite of the imminent storm, united in their efforts to find a way to knock Galt off the playing field of justice because he was a major impediment in their fight for equal opportunities. They hoped to improve their chances of removing him with a constitutional amendment.

They were too close to the goal to let up now.

Just before the presidential election, the National Conference of State Legislators had endorsed Graham's proposed constitutional amendment. Since Senator Graham was on the Executive Committee of the National Conference, getting the endorsement hadn't been very hard for him.

Twenty states ratified Graham's proposed amendment in the first six weeks after the election. The President announced his support in late January, followed by an endorsement from the

National Governor's Association in short order. Another fifteen states ratified over the next six weeks, bringing the total number of states ratifying to thirty-five.

That same evening the California legislature would vote on the proposed amendment. Ratification by three-fourths or thirty-eight states was needed to amend the U.S. Constitution.

The vote would be close.

Senator Graham also couldn't leave his office early because he was expecting a visit from Justice John T. Galt. The week before, Graham and his staff had huddled and strategized about how to handle recent reports about the management of Galt's chambers. Those discussions had led to the planned meeting today.

Galt walked into the senator's office with white-framed prescription glasses perched on the bridge of his nose as if to make a statement by their mere presence—the glasses being in sharp contrast to his dark skin tone.

"Let's get right down to business," Graham said, taking a seat. "I understand you and your wife are making public comments against my proposed amendment."

"We have separation of powers and my wife speaks for herself," Galt said. "You have no power over me other than my salary, which you can't lower—and I have a lifetime appointment."

"Section One Article Three of the Constitution makes it clear that a Supreme Court Justice has a term of service based on their behavior."

"Gosh," Galt said with wide eyes. "I should have said I have a lifetime appointment unless I exhibit bad behavior. Am I being accused of bad behavior?"

"Not yet," Graham answered. "But incompetence is a form of bad behavior."

"We already have an impeachment process in place to handle that situation."

"Nobody outside of the Supreme Court knows enough to impeach a justice when they're in decline due to advancing age."

"If we have an incapacitated justice on the bench, you should do your job and impeach."

"You know impeachment is in the hands of the House," Graham said. "If the House doesn't act, the Senate and the President are powerless regardless of what we know."

"You think the Senate can better judge the competence of a Supreme Court justice?"

"I think five Supreme Court justices can judge the incompetence of one of their own."

"We must respect or at least tolerate each other now," Galt said. "We act like a family. That might change under your proposal. That's my concern."

"Can we talk about equal opportunity for a minute?"

"Shoot," Galt said.

"Why do you think you're successful?"

Galt paused, considering the unexpected question. "Education, intellectual capacity, hard work, politics, faith and my grandfather's influence. But by and large, I've made my own way."

"Most successful people had help," Graham said. "When one gets on the road of opportunity and performs, better opportunities seem to keep appearing in one's life."

"Equal opportunity programs just take opportunities away from the qualified," Galt asserted. "Opportunities should be given to the best qualified."

"How do we decide who is best qualified for an opportunity when a large pool of qualified people exists for limited slots? Opportunities like going to Yale or Harvard. At elite institutions, legacy is often used as a tie-breaking factor. Why is that fair?"

Galt let the chance to speak pass.

"Those with the highest grades are sometimes rejected because other factors are considered. Should physical attributes determine who gets early opportunities in life?"

"Of course not. Race should not matter."

"What about size?" Graham asked.

"Size?" Galt repeated with an incredulous look.

"Yeah. You know, like the opportunity I had to play football because I was big for my age. Like the opportunity I had to go to the University of Michigan. One opportunity built on another." He leaned forward. "I'm here because some white people got to know me and opened doors for me. That's how it works. Now tell me about the opportunities that allowed you to become a Supreme Court justice."

"My grandfather took me in," Galt said. "He gave me discipline, put me in a Catholic school. He gave me the opportunity to learn. But I did the rest."

"Did you play sports?"

"Yes, basketball."

"Born before June?"

"Born in May. What difference does it make?"

"People born before June tend to get more opportunities because they tend to be a little bigger and a little smarter than those born later in the year. Who helped you with homework?"

"I had a college-educated cousin who lived around the corner," Galt said. "She bought books for us and helped me learn to read."

"So you had the opportunity of being tutored by a college-educated relative, attended a private school, and played sports. You also learned how to disarm white people."

"Disarm?" Galt asked.

"Yeah, I understand you're great at telling jokes about yourself."

"I deliver more than just good jokes."

"We can manifest the things we want in life because of education. Some people never figure it out because of poor education. We're not better than them. We were just lucky."

"People can change their life circumstances if they have the will to do so and use their intellect."

"That's not always true." Graham reached for the file before him. "Everybody isn't dealt a winning hand in life. Let's talk about your jurisprudence. Help me understand that."

Galt took off his glasses and stared at Graham. "I am an intellectual defender of the Constitution of the United States. I stand for rational decision-making in my judicial decisions."

Graham opened the file and read a portion of a Supreme Court dissenting opinion in the University of Michigan Law School affirmative action case:

The Law School seeks a façade—it is sufficient that the class look right, even if it does not perform right ... The law school tantalizes unprepared students with the promises of a University of Michigan law degree and all of the opportunities that it offers. These overmatched students take the bait only to find they cannot succeed in the cauldron of the competition ... This cruel force of racial discrimination must continue until the beneficiaries are no longer tolerated. While these students may graduate with law degrees, there is no evidence that they have received a better legal education than if they had gone to a less "elite" law school for which they were better prepared.

"Do you agree with this type of legal opinion?" Graham asked.

"No collective group has the right to anything that robs another person of a right."

"We've had collective rights in this country from the beginning. The collective rights of our Founding Fathers trumped the individual rights of the slaves and women. We both know the collective rights of corporations are trumping individual rights today."

Galt shrugged.

"I understand you believe the Constitution should be interpreted based on the intent of the Founders when originally drafted. Is that a fair statement?"

"Yes." Galt paused. "I also rely on the timeless principle of natural law."

"Natural law," Graham stated. "What does that mean to you?"

"It means, all men are created equal by God. No one has divine rights over another—and that leads to my core belief that individual rights should be supreme under the law. The right to own property, the right to bear arms, the right to personal freedom, the right to due process of law, and the right to religious freedom are all individual rights that drive the decisions within my chambers. People can only be governed by giving their consent."

"I don't think the former slaves gave their consent to be governed."

"Man gives consent by his failure to resist. We have a natural right to fight oppression. Liberty, that's what the Revolutionary War was about."

"How do you apply natural law to interpreting the U.S. Constitution?"

"I apply self-evident truths," Galt replied. "Individual rights must reign superior to any collective right because history has shown that collective rights are always co-opted for the benefit of a few. People should have equal rights. That's natural law, simply stated."

"You do know some people believe racial inequality is natural," Graham said slowly.

"Race is a myth. A social construction used by some folks to further their political agendas. As long as we accept the illusion that race is real, we'll be held back."

"Do you view corporations as persons? Is that natural? I think not."

"I respect state rights. Fighting for special rights is a trap for us. People should have equal rights. We cannot sacrifice our individual rights for collective rights based on race from which only a few benefit—because history has shown collective rights are always co-opted for the benefit of an elite few."

"An elite few?" Graham asked.

"You know what I mean. Most Black folks haven't benefitted from affirmative action. The masses were left behind. You know the races are mixing. Most people have mixed blood—even if they don't know it. Why focus on something that will naturally die?"

"Because racism is still alive in this country. Justice for the oppressed requires equal opportunity programs because most of us won't get opportunities without the force of law."

Galt stood. "You should know, I do not believe in kneeling from a position of power."

"Hope you aren't blinded by the snow," Graham said. "Black ice can be deadly."

After Galt left, Graham turned on his computer screen to monitor the progress in California. He smiled. California had passed by a one-vote margin. Thirty-six states had ratified. Two more states to go. If the amendment passed, another deal could be made.

Galt was not untouchable.

Chapter Twenty-Eight

The Ritz-Carlton Residences

Katherine arrived home late that evening after a long day debating with her clerks and finalizing her first majority opinion in a five-four decision. They had worked late because it had to be perfect. Everyone in her chambers had found something to change during the course of the day, and she had found the last typo at eight.

At last, there was nothing more for her to do or say about her first opinion.

In her kitchen, she spotted an envelope on the black counter where her dad's letter had been placed a few months ago. Her mother had been there. She eyed the thick manila package with a sense of foreboding. She knew what it was, and realized instinctively that the knowledge it contained could make a big difference. That knowledge was part of understanding who she was and why she had been raised as she had.

Guarded. Restrained. Protected.

Katherine longed to know why her mother was so secretive, and how she had buried a secret so deep that the search engines of the national press couldn't find it.

Why did her mother cry as a defense against telling the truth?

Katherine took the precious package into her bedroom. She placed the two-inch thick envelope on her nightstand and prepared for bed. She wanted to be comfortable when she settled in for a deep read. She climbed into her bed and reached for the package. She read the words scribbled across the seal were in her mother's handwriting.

Don't read this now if you have important things to focus on. This can wait.

Not anymore. Katherine broke the seal. She had waited long enough.

She eased back against her periwinkle pillow sham and pulled a loose-leaf manuscript from the envelope. Clipped to it was a short note from her mother.

Be alone when you read this. It records my darkest hour. I found voice to write it, but I still can't talk about it. I've written it as Hattie's Story to protect you. In case somebody else picks it up. My name was Hattie Mae Cobb. Now you have it. I don't want to talk about it again. Please understand. I love you.

Placing the note on the nightstand, Katherine stared at the title page for a moment. In bold block letters the title jumped out at her, ***HATTIE'S STORY.***

She took a deep breath and turned the page…

HATTIE'S STORY
Chapter One

April 1946
Dublin, Georgia

I accept my fate.

It happened in the late afternoon on a comfortable spring day when I was eleven.

It was my fault. Mrs. Polk caught me cheating on a test. My father told me to never cheat in school. He told me that I was smart and I could grow up to be a schoolteacher. As soon as I got home every day I did my math homework first. I loved the challenge of solving those problems. I was good at it. It was rare for me to get a problem wrong.

I got straight As in math.

I was going to be a math teacher when I grew up.

I had a crush on a boy named Jimmy Wilson. He was chocolate brown with the brightest white teeth. I would have done anything to get Jimmy Wilson's attention. He worked so hard and didn't pay much attention to me. But that didn't matter. I loved Jimmy Wilson. I thought about him all the time.

Before Jimmy came to school, he had to milk the cows and get his little brothers and sisters ready for school. Jimmy's father had left his mother with six children when he was nine. So Jimmy got a job after school to help his mother buy food, and became the man of the house. He accepted his responsibility to make sure his family had food to eat. I liked him for that.

Often Jimmy fell asleep during school because he worked so hard and never got enough sleep. Some days, he didn't have his homework done and I let him copy mine. I helped Jimmy a lot. He was a good boy with a good heart. That's why I loved him.

I helped Jimmy whenever I could to be close to him. I sat next to him in class. Every few minutes I lifted my paper when the teacher wasn't looking so he could see my answers.

I didn't want Jimmy to fail.

One day, I let Jimmy copy my answers on a multiple choice math test. I got mixed up and skipped a problem. As a result, most of my answers were wrong. Without noticing my error, I put the answer down for the last problem twice. I showed him my paper. He quickly wrote down my answers.

He winked at me at the end of the test. I blushed. In my mind's eye, I can still see Jimmy. My heart leaped with joy. We turned in our papers.

The wheels of fate were set in motion.

The next day, as Mrs. Polk passed out our graded exams, she paused at my desk and dropped mine in front of me. I was shocked to see a big red "45%—SEE ME AFTER CLASS!" written on the top of my exam sheet.

I knew I was in trouble.

"You cheated," Mrs. Polk said as she looked first at me and then at Jimmy. "You two got exactly the same answers right and wrong on the test."

Trying to defend me, Jimmy said, "Hattie didn't know I was copyin' her paper."

"She knows how to cover her paper," Mrs. Polk said. "Don't think I didn't see you two this morning before class on the side of the building—cheatin' again. You cheated on today's homework, too," she growled. "Cheaters, both of you."

"I'm sorry," I said as I looked down at my new brown leather shoes.

"Sorry is not good enough," Mrs. Polk said. "After school today you two have to clean this room up, empty the trash, wash the blackboard, sweep the floor, and mop it. I want this room to be spotless before you leave here today."

After school, Jimmy and I worked as fast as we could to clean up our classroom. He emptied the trash. I swept the floor. He mopped. I washed the blackboard—twice, before Mrs. Polk was satisfied.

I think Mrs. Polk thought that Jimmy and I would walk home together. But she didn't ask. She probably saw our friends waiting for us in the distance. She knew we would all be late but didn't care. We needed to be punished.

So, that's what happened.

When Jimmy finished mopping the floor to her satisfaction, Mrs. Polk hopped into her car. As she drove off she said, "I guess you two have learned your lesson."

She was wrong.

My friends tried to wait for me. I saw them through the window as we worked, but they couldn't miss choir practice because we got caught cheating. The youth choir sang every second Sunday at church. My friends waited for me as long as they could.

I watched them leave.

I knew it wasn't their fault.

Jimmy saw them leave, too, and knew what that meant.

"I have to go to work," he said in a distressed tone as he put the mop and bucket in the closet and turned to face me.

Jimmy worked at the Do-Drop-In Restaurant. He would have to walk almost two miles in twenty-five minutes to be on time. He could not be late again. The owner had warned Jimmy that he would find another boy who could get to work on time if he couldn't.

"I'll be okay," I said. "Go ahead. Don't be late. I'll see you later."

I watched as he sprinted away toward the west side of town.

I started toward the church alone.

I walked along the main road at a quick pace. Almost jogging, I reached the footpath that led to the shortcut through the woods.

I gazed at the setting sun. Orange and yellow bursts of color streaked across the warm blue sky with white balls of cotton candy floating in the distance. It was beautiful.

I peered down the shortcut path. I didn't see the other kids ahead. I didn't hear their voices, only the sound of the wind as it rustled dry leaves.

Everyone was long gone.

I wondered if I should take the shortcut.

When in a group and running late, my friends and I always argued before we took the footpath through the woods. Somebody was always scared. Our parents repeated over and over a warning to scare us so we would not go into the woods alone: "Raw Head and Bloody Bones gonna get you if they catch you in da woods alone. They eat little chillums for dinner when they can catch them alone."

"N-e-v-e-r go down dat path alone," my father warned. "Ya never know, who ya gonna meet on dat path."

I thought, *I'm not a little child. I need ta get ta church 'fore my part. I gotta hurry. Nothin' ever happen in dem woods around here. Walkin' down da main road alone dainjus too. Day jus' tryin' ta scare da little chillums so day don't git lost.*

I took the shortcut.

I can still hear my Uncle Wash telling the story of what happened that day.

His truck broke down, forcing him to walk into Dublin to pick up some motor oil and a fan belt to make repairs. He rushed through the newly plowed fields set with spring plantings, hoping to get to town before Tim's Garage closed at 6:30 p.m. It was a little over a five-mile walk into town.

It had been after 5:00 when he realized his truck wouldn't start.

Uncle Wash had no time to spare if he was going to make it to Tim's before closing, so he took the shortcut through the woods, too.

He needed to hurry.

Deep in the woods I scrambled down the dirt road. I heard pecking. I gazed up: it was a redheaded woodpecker, hammering. Then I was startled by loud, short screeches from something close above my head. All I could hear was *caaw-caaw-caaw.* I moved past it. Then stopped. I was afraid to turn around. But I had to know. I knew it was some type of a warning when I saw a single black crow with iridescent black feathers barking at me eagerly. I started to run away. I wanted to get out of the woods before something caught me.

But I ran into trouble.

Two white men appeared on my path carrying fishing poles, a cooler, and a rusty bucket. They wore dirty overalls with no shirts. Sunburned skin. Badly worn-out shoes.

"Looky here at what we done caught," one of them said.

I moved to the side of the road to let them pass, like we had always done when we met white people on a narrow path.

"Told you it was too soon to give up," the other one said. "Come here, sweet meat."

I couldn't process what was happening. But I knew it was bad. Fear gripped me. I turned and bolted. Knowing I couldn't look back. I ran as fast as I could, but they caught me.

I cried out in fear while the two savage beasts taunted me.

They touched me with their filthy paws.

I pleaded, kicked and screamed in an attempt to delay the inevitable.

I put up a valiant fight to protect my prize.

But I was no match against adult male strength.

They enjoyed my childish struggle and made a game out of it. Kind of like playing with a cat using a string. They showed me a path of escape as a possibility, then blocked my way and dragged me along the ground, removing a piece of my clothing each time I attempted an escape.

Finally, I had nothing on. There would be no escape for me.

The game was over.

They took me.

I was repulsed at their smoky beer breaths, rotten teeth and foul-smelling bodies. But they could have my budding body because I was just a Black girl and they were white men.

One of the animals grabbed me and pulled me to the ground on a bed of broken branches and dead leaves.

The other one said in a mocking tone, "Don't be so mean. She can use me as a mattress." He lay on his back, pulled me over on top of him and held me while the other man leaned over me. I closed my eyes.

At the forced entry, I screamed at the top of my lungs.

A howling scream of despair.

Terror raced through my veins as pain ripped through my body in waves. I felt like my tender parts were being ripped from my body by wild animals hungry for their victuals. The assault on my body was the ultimate act of violence against a child. Nothing could ever hurt me more. Not even childbirth. I was defenseless. Petrified. Screaming. Bleeding.

More than ready to give up my ghost to end the agony that ripped through me.

Pain shocked every cell of my body as the force of their body parts bruised my delicate skin repeatedly, without regard for the damage to my deflowered body and soul.

They enjoyed hurting me.

I'll never forget their glazed eyes.

I was dying.

Some distance off the footpath, Uncle Washington heard my screams. He hesitantly advanced toward my cries as they reduced to moans of agony.

He told me a voice in his head said, *"It's a rape."*

He knew he couldn't just walk away because he knew they might kill me.

He looked around for help.

There was no one in sight.

Uncle Wash moved closer toward my moans. He stopped a safe distance away, out of sight, and saw two rednecks and my light-skinned black legs.

Uncle Wash recognized one of the men. He had seen him in town at the Farmer's Market off Route 319 a few weeks before, but he couldn't get a good look at the other one.

He could not see my face. He could only hear my wails of torment. He said my cries sent fire alarms throughout his body.

I shrieked, "Ohhhhh, my God help me!"

Uncle Washington said then he recognized my voice. I was his brother's child. I was his favorite niece. Uncle Wash was enraged.

He wondered what he could do? Outnumbered. Unarmed.

But he knew he had to save me.

Uncle Wash remembered passing a house under construction down the road and ran back to look for a weapon. He scanned the building site for anything to use while sweat popped from his brow. He said he felt blood pulsing through his temples. He had to find something quickly that could kill.

But all of the building tools had been removed.

Then he spotted a pile of bricks and wood. The bricks were made from red Georgia clay and cement. Heavy red bricks with sharp, rough edges. Uncle Wash knew they would work. Red bricks had been known to kill when thrown with enough force.

He knew the bricks could become lethal weapons in his hands.

Uncle Wash was strong.

He had a body like Hercules. I can see his tightened jaws. I can imagine the lines of tension frozen into his face as he prepared to act, wide nostrils fully flared like an alligator, taking deep breaths as his body readied for a death fight.

He said he was ready to die if he had to.

He prayed for help and mercy.

He knew somebody was about to die.

He picked up three red bricks and put a two-by-four under his arm before returning to the scene of my misery. He said he moved like a snake, looking for an opportunity to strike. He peered through the bushes, ready to do whatever he needed to do to stop my attackers.

I was pinned to the ground like a paper doll.

When one finished with me, he simply watched while the other one took his turn with me. I felt like a wounded animal, surrendering to death.

Weeds, dried leaves and blackness were my only comfort as my torturers changed my position for their pleasure. The dead branches didn't hurt anymore.

I was silent.

I'd gone within myself for comfort.

Seeing me apparently near death, Washington took one brick and the two-by-four, one in each hand. With slow deliberate steps, he moved closer.

Both men had their backs to him.

Washington put the two-by-four on the ground; then he hoisted the brick over his head with both hands. With all of his might, he threw the red brick.

I heard a loud grunt, followed by a thud. I felt wetness on my face and a shower of rocks as a massive weight crushed me.

The red brick had split the scoundrel's skull, killing him instantly.

His body landed on me.

I did not move.

Blood covered my face.

His blood ran into my eyes.

I could barely see when I tried to open my eyes. I heard deep breaths.

It seemed like time froze.

Then I heard my father's voice in my head—*Fight back!* I pushed the lifeless body off of me and reached for a tree branch that had fallen by my hand.

The other attacker lunged toward me.

I scooted away, escaping his claws.

Uncle Wash whirled back around with the two-by-four raised, ready to strike.

My attacker turned toward him.

I grabbed the tree branch and swung at my attacker. The long dead branch broke into a thousand pieces. Dust flew. Dust in my hand.

I recoiled into a fetal position.

My attacker lunged toward me again.

Uncle Wash advanced, swinging the two-by-four like a mighty sword. After the two-by-four split into two pieces, Uncle Wash finished him off with his bare fists. I heard each blow as Uncle Wash beat the man who had taken my body as his plaything.

He beat my attacker to death with his fists, sending him to his rightful place in hell.

Dripping with blood and sweat, Uncle Wash turned toward me.

"You gonna be okay," he said in a breathy voice. "But we have ta git outta here—fast. Put ya' clothes on."

He turned around, not wanting to see my nakedness.

I wiped my face with my arms as I gathered my torn clothes.

"All torn," was all I could say in a cracking whisper.

Uncle Wash unbuttoned his bloodstained shirt and gave it to me.

"Here," he said with his back to me.

I put his shirt on while he searched the dead men's pockets. He found car keys and slid them into his back pocket.

"We gotta go." He turned to face me.

We walked toward the main road in silence. I looked down at my bare feet as we walked. I could only find one bloody shoe and left it behind.

Uncle Wash looked for the attackers' parked vehicle as we neared the road. He spotted a burgundy pick-up truck parked by a tall oak tree in the distance.

He took my hand and pulled me until I trotted with throbbing steps.

Just as we reached the truck, a car went by with a white lady driving who stared at us with a knowing eye. It was Mrs. Jackson, the town gossip who ran the Inn on Main Street. Her eyes bugged as she slowly drove past.

It wasn't a look of sympathy.

Then she sped away.

Uncle Wash mumbled, "We can't go home now."

He got in the truck. Taking a deep breath, he turned the key. The dusty pickup started with a jerk.

"Get in!" he shouted.

I was dazed. I remember brushing a whiskey bottle off the seat as I got in and slammed the car door. I remember staring at my bloody feet.

"We got no choice," he said. "Black people killin' white people means hangin' 'round here. Mrs. Jackson goin' to da Sheriff. He'll find da bodies. Should've gotten rid of dem. But no time. Can't put da bodies in da truck now. Can't run in dis truck either. We're goin' get caught if we stay in dis truck. Gotta leave town. White mob hang me for what I did. No choice. We gotta run."

I closed my eyes.

There was nothing I could say.

Uncle Wash was talkin' out loud to himself. "Where can we go? Uncle Eddie in Atlanta? Naw, not 'nough gas. Need money. Can't go to the relatives. They'll kill them. St. Cecilia's... Yeah, St. Cecilia's."

We headed for St. Cecilia's Catholic Church on the edge of town.

Uncle Wash worked the grounds at St. Cecilia's in Dublin on Saturdays. I remember the cut and trimmed grass having the appearance of lush carpet. I gazed at the magnificent flower gardens as we entered the property.

Uncle Wash mumbled, "Will dis be da last time I see dis place?"

We proceeded to the residential quarters on the south side of the church and found Father Frank Ryan in his study with an open Bible.

Father Ryan offered us water. "Did anybody follow you here?" He poured two glasses.

"I don't think so," Uncle Wash said.

"Was it rape?"

"Yes."

Alarmed at my physical condition, Father Frank immediately went for a nun to attend to my needs. None were available. All of the nuns were away on a trip for a Summer Bible School Teacher's Retreat. Father Ryan went through some of the drawers in the nuns' living quarters.

He found a dress and a blouse for me that he thought would fit. All of the nuns' shoes were too big. He gave me a couple of towels. I went to the kitchen outside of his study, washed myself, changed clothes, and returned to the study in my bare feet.

Father Ryan handed me a hairbrush. I tried to brush out the dirt, bugs and branches from my hair as best I could. Uncle Wash told our story as I picked at my tangled hair.

Uncle Wash confessed he had killed two human beings. He asked for forgiveness.

"Do you know them?" I heard Father Ryan ask, referring to the rapists.

"No, but I've seen them before at the Farmer's Market."

"Hattie, do you know them?" Father Ryan asked me.

"I've seen them passin' on the road before."

"Are you sure they're both dead?"

"I know da man dat I beat to death was dead," Uncle Wash said.

I spoke staring into space. "The other one dead, too. He died with his eyes wide open."

"What about the lady in the car?" Father Ryan asked. "Do you think she knows you?"

"She drives past our place all da time," Uncle Wash said with sad eyes.

The priest sighed. "Then they'll know who you are, where you live."

"Yeah," I uttered. "We live jus' down da road from Uncle Wash. She seen me, too."

"I'll go talk to your people," Father Ryan told us. "I think all of you have to leave here. Your whole family. They'll be lookin' for somebody to hang for this."

It was clear: we had to leave town before death had the opportunity to make another visit. My Uncle Wash and Father Ryan agreed—there was no time to spare.

With dread on his face, Father Ryan realized that at least two dangerous trips would be needed for all the Cobbs to escape Dublin. His Pontiac station wagon had three rows of seats that could comfortably carry eight people. Fifteen of us were in danger.

There was no one else he could call to help.

Most peace lovers were not willing to put themselves in harm's way to oppose unlawful evildoers, so the practice of lynching prevailed when the mob felt offended by a Black person. That day, Uncle Wash had offended the KKK by killing two of their own.

Father Ryan said he was sure we would be killed if we did not run for our lives.

I knew my daddy wouldn't run. But I said nothing.

My family had purchased eighty acres of land in 1867. We worked the land as sharecroppers for thirty years before it was finally paid off. It was often a struggle, but we had managed to keep the eighty acres in the family for close to a century. When my grandparents died, my father and each of his three brothers inherited twenty acres apiece.

My family lived peacefully on their land. They earned a decent living, owned cars and trucks, built sturdy homes. We were never hungry. Always had what we needed. The extended Cobb family all lived and worked on our own land. We built our own church and had our own cemetery. We had, could make or buy everything we needed for a good living. Even though we worked from sunup to sundown, we were content with the life we had on our own land. Our family was happy, staying out of white people's way.

Father Ryan decided to visit my parent's house first. I watched him leave the church grounds in his new 1946 Pontiac Streamliner station wagon with wood paneling. He made a right turn on Highway 319, traveling north. I stared out of the window, following him on the route to my home in my mind's eye.

This is what I learned happened that afternoon.

My father invited Father Ryan into our home. It was a wood framed house with a long front porch. We were so proud of it. Father Ryan sat on our dark blue sofa near the window. My father sat in his big armchair across from him.

My mother was out of sight in the kitchen.

Father Ryan told my father the frightening chain of events. At first, he said nothing.

My mother silently wept.

Father Ryan told my father we had to run to avoid a lynch mob.

My father responded with righteous anger. He said, "I'll be damned if I let them run me off of my land. I'd rather die than run like a coward."

Father Ryan told my father they would come lookin' for blood when they found the bodies and the trail led to our home. He told him about the lady in the car who passed us.

"I'm not runnin'," my father told him. "Washington can leave if he wants to. Go talk to his family. My family's not leaving dis land. We're fightin'."

Father Ryan asked about me. He asked what was going to happen to me. What was going to happen to Washington, if they all stayed and fought?

My father replied, "I told dat girl not to go off alone in those woods. Let Washington take her with him. She'll be better off with him… Hard-headed girl."

My father used profanity. My mother wailed.

Father Ryan told my father I needed clothes.

My mother, with tears in her eyes, scurried to the back of the house. She came back with a pink pillowcase full of my clothes. Father Ryan said she had dried her eyes. There was no time to cry.

Father Ryan asked about my shoes.

My mother told him she didn't have any shoes that fit me. My old shoes and Sunday shoes were in the shop. I was a size six-and-a-half. The rest of the women in the house were size eights. My mother told him to ask Washington's wife for shoes, since she was a seven.

Father Ryan pleaded again with my father to leave.

My father refused. He told Father Ryan, "I'm dying right here. My father ran away from the lynch mob and left us. I'm not gonna run from them. I'm gonna face them like a man. You better leave now. Made up my mind, I'm not runnin'. I'd rather face a violent death than die a coward."

Down the road, Father Ryan found Uncle Washington's wife making a pound cake. Beef stew simmered in a large pot on the wood-burning stove. Cornbread batter was already in a pan, ready to be placed in the oven.

"Where are your sons?"

"In the field, plowing."

"Call them in. Now."

"Is something wrong?"

"Yes, get them now."

Without hesitation she ran out of the back door toward the field and shouted, "Fire!"

Her boys came running.

With a bucket of water in his hands, Ademus, her oldest son, said, "Ain't no fire."

As the younger two brothers rushed into the house, their mother said, "I feel fire."

"Washington killed two white men," Father Ryan said.

"What happened?" Ademus asked.

Father Ryan spoke with urgency. "Hattie was raped. Washington caught them and killed them to save her. I got Hattie's things but no shoes. You have to leave town now if you want to be with your husband. Get Hattie some shoes. She can't go home."

Washington's wife said as she rose from the table, "I'll get our things."

"Fast," Father Ryan said. "If the boys stay behind, they might just lynch all of you in your father's place. You're not safe here. I think all of you should come with me."

Her sons gazed at each other, understanding the truth in the words just spoken.

They all sensed the imminent danger.

Without another word, they got up from the table and moved with furious energy, grabbing their guns and ammunition. Fishing poles. Knives. A big pot. Clanking cooking utensils. Some grease. Sweet potatoes. A smoked ham. Candles. Matches.

They only grabbed a few personal things, stuffing them into pillowcases.

Washington's wife stuffed an extra pair of her shoes for me into her pillowcase, leaving her favorite housedress. No room.

They didn't bother with the food cooking on the wood-burning stove. They left.

Later that evening, the Sheriff arrived at our house. The sheriff parked his car across the road from the house. Alone in his car he puffed on a cigar. He let his left arm hang out of the front window as he flicked ashes onto the ground. Waiting. Guarding against an escape. Just watching our house from a safe distance.

My father, mother, three sisters and four brothers were all in the house, having been rounded up to face a certain challenge from an angry white mob. They peeped out of the windows, wanting peace but prepared for a fight to the death. There were no other vehicles in sight. But they knew that would change soon.

My father considered his move. He had a losing hand. He walked slowly to the sheriff's parked car, unarmed, hands showing at his sides.

"Can I help you?" my father asked the sheriff.

"Yaw know anything 'bout two white men killed in the woods?"

"Yes, sir, I do."

"What cha know," the sheriff asked as an eyebrow rose and his eyes narrowed.

"They raped my daughter and they died for it," my father said. "I know da lynch mob be here in a while and they'll kill my family if I don't give myself up. Life ain't worth living if a man can't protect his family. So I'm turning myself in."

"Then you're under arrest." The sheriff got out of his car. "Confessin' makes my job a whole lot easier. Turn around."

The sheriff reached for his handcuffs and began to put them around my father's hands when my brothers burst through the front door. Guns aimed. Ready for death.

"Don't shoot!" my father shouted out. "I told you. I'm giving myself up. You'll be safe if I do. Take care of your mother. I'm goin' with the sheriff. It's the only way."

"No!" my mother screamed from the porch.

My brothers lowered their guns.

My sisters pulled my mother back into the house as the sheriff loaded my father into the back of the car. It took all three of my sisters to restrain my mother, who was kicking and screaming. Within minutes, our living room looked like a tornado hit it. Broken glass and overturned furniture lay everywhere from my mother's struggle to be with her man.

She loved him so. She worshipped him.

"No!" she cried as she swung my sisters around the living room. "You can't take him from me. He didn't do anything! No.

Please, don't take him from me." At the top of her voice she yelled, "He didn't do anything! He didn't do anything!"

My sisters blocked the front door with their bodies.

My mother fell to the floor on her knees with her hands clasped together prayerfully. "Where is God? Please God, don't let them kill him."

My mother sobbed on the floor until she was totally exhausted.

"I can't live without him." She cried all night long. She knew.

She would never see her husband again.

Father Ryan got back to the church with Uncle Washington's immediate family. We headed for Savannah, about ninety miles southeast of Dublin.

Soon it would be dark.

We spent the night parked in the woods off one of the back roads on the way to Savannah. We rested like cats, sitting straight up in our seats, ready to jump into action if any white glint broke the blackness of the night. We listened for sounds of alarm.

Nobody slept.

I began to shiver uncontrollably. I was sitting in the front row between Father Ryan at the steering wheel and Uncle Washington, who cradled me in his arms. I wept silently against the backdrop of shrills from crickets, cicadas and katydids.

We kept the car windows down, enduring the bites of gnats and mosquitoes. It was stifling hot. There was little water. We needed fresh air and needed to listen for the sounds of danger. Washington took the bug bites without moving. He shielded me with his body as best he could. I didn't move when I was bitten, either.

My bug bites were minor in relation to the gaping wound in my spirit.

We endured the physical discomfort of that night rather than face certain death at the hands of an angry mob in the name of justice. Father Ryan told us, if we were caught, he would not be spared. In

1946, white people who didn't follow Jim Crow were lynched, too, along with any offending Blacks. That's just the way it was.

With a loaded gun on the dashboard, Washington kept his eye out for any sign of trouble. There was a sudden rustling sound from the ground about 100 feet away. Washington reached for his gun and pushed me over to Father Ryan.

Ready to fire.

"Rattlesnake," Washington said, breaking the silence after several minutes.

I wept until I could no longer produce tears. My life had changed forever. I could never go back to Dublin. Nor could Washington Cobb and his immediate family, go home.

I worried about the fate of my family.

Would they kill my father? He'd fight. He taught me to fight back. He'll die fighting. *He's dead. I know he's dead. It's my fault. I'll never scream for help again. I'll die before I scream. No white man will ever make me scream again! I won't fight, if I can't beat them. I won't scream again. I'll die first.*

I closed down my emotions and tried to forget the details of what happened by simply repeating my ABCs in my mind, blocking out all other thoughts of what had happened for the rest of the night.

As the sun peeped above the treetops, I silently prayed to God:
Please, forgive me for cheating and disobeying my Daddy.
It's my fault. I want my Mamma.
Strengthen me so I will only cry to you.
Help me to be strong. Forgive me. Please. Let us live.
Have mercy on my father's soul. He did the best that he could.
Amen.

The next morning, my brothers found the smoldering remains of my father hung from a tree with a burned cross at his bare feet. They cut him down and took him to the family cemetery. The men in the family dug a grave. My mother was not present.

141

My father confessed to the sheriff for the crime of killing two white men. There was no stronger evidence that could be marshaled. The fact that they were raping his daughter was irrelevant. No question of his guilt. A Black man confessed. No need for investigation.

Nor a trial or a jury.

When the angry mob appeared at the jailhouse seeking instant justice, the sheriff threw them the keys to my father's cell and walked away.

The case was closed.

*****

When Katherine finished reading the first three chapters of her mother's story, she was near tears. She couldn't read anymore.

The clock on her nightstand read 10:15 p.m.

She slid the manuscript back in the manila folder and carefully placed it in her bottom nightstand drawer under some important opinions she wanted to review.

She must remember: *A confession may not be unquestionable proof of guilt.*

In bed, Katherine reached for her Bible to search for a few words of comfort. She closed her eyes and blindly opened the Bible to Ezekiel 34, and read the verse about the shepherds and sheep. As she read, she thought of the African American community as sheep.

In particular, she thought of her grandfather as a slaughtered lamb. Forced to sacrifice himself for the lives of his loved ones. Then she thought of her mother. She had paid the ultimate price for disobeying her father: Separation from him for the rest of her life.

No father. No mother. No wonder her mother never talked much about her parents.

She felt crushing pain in her heart.

Her soul was troubled as she considered the oppressive history of her race. Race was still a problem in America. Katherine got out of bed and onto her knees.

God, I'll be a shepherd for the oppressed. I won't hide in fear for my life, if you call me into battle. Use me. Some things are worth dying for. Give me the strength to live up to my calling. Help me understand what I am called to do in this life, in your name. Amen.

Then Katherine got under the covers. Her head rested against a soft six hundred thread-count pillowcase as she tried to surrender to sleep. The soothing scent of lavender rose from her bed sheets. Yet she could not find a comfortable position in her king size bed.

She wrapped the navy blue comforter around her shoulders. The sheets felt cold against her feet as she moved them under the covers. Turning, she folded into a childlike position, pulling the comforter over her head to further darken her space.

Then she wept on her pillow as she felt the numbing pain that her mother had tried to bury so many years ago, as it burst from her heart. She allowed herself to feel all the injustice that was bottled up inside her. Her thoughts drifted to the innocent man on death row, then back to her defenseless mother as an innocent child under attack.

She felt crippling pain.

Katherine said her ABCs until the pain stopped.

Was her father a rapist? Now *that* was her big question. And she could understand why her mother wouldn't want the world to know that.

Chapter Twenty-Nine

Upon awakening the next morning, Katherine found her Bible in bed with her under the sheets, still open to Ezekiel 34. The digital clock read, "*6:51 AM OFF*." She had forgotten to set the alarm. Her driver would be downstairs waiting for her at seven thirty. Nevertheless, she reached for her Bible, propped herself up with pillows and read the verse again. She closed her eyes for a moment of silent prayer for her mother and lost family. Then she reached for her lap desk, a pen and a sheet of her personalized stationery. Using her Bible for reference, she wrote:

Justice Galt:

Would you be willing to meet me for breakfast again? Last night, I read the following passage in the Bible before retiring:

"Therefore, you shepherds, hear the word of the LORD: As surely as I live, declares the Sovereign LORD, because my flock lacks a shepherd and so has been plundered and has become food for all the wild animals, and because my shepherds did not search for my flock but cared for themselves rather than for my flock, therefore, O shepherds hear the word of the LORD: This is what the Sovereign LORD says: I am against the shepherds and will hold them accountable for my flock." (Ezekiel 34:7-10).

Might we be shepherds for lost black sheep?

Katherine

A week later, seated at her majestic desk processing a pile of correspondence, she opened a small envelope that contained a handwritten note from Justice Galt on ivory-colored card stock with his initials "JTG" embossed on its folded face.

As she unfolded the note, Katherine gently placed her engraved silver letter opener, a gift from her mother, on the desk and straightened up in her seat as she read.

Justice Ross,

I would be pleased to meet you for breakfast in the Court cafeteria next Wednesday at 7:30 a.m. In regard to your question about the shepherds and sheep, I do not think we are shepherds for the African American community. But, if we are, this is what the Sovereign LORD said to me last night: "I will shepherd the flock with justice." (Ezekiel 34:16f). And, I believe the Sovereign LORD wants justice for all members of the human race. That's my view. New topic this time?

JTG

What could she say?

Chapter Thirty

Monday, April 8

"We must always struggle for our liberty." Jennie Galt held up a glass of Moët champagne and offered a toast at her retirement bash. At fifty-five she still retained her youthful figure and sported a size-six haute couture red, white and blue evening gown. Golden locks draped around her shoulders like a cape. Always the cheerleader, she ended her remarks with a pledge. "You can always count on me to be in service on the battlefield for liberty."

The small group applauded. Jennie concluded her scripted remarks and descended the stage in the dark paneled library. High-top tables around the perimeter of the room were lit with candlelight, as were five round tables for six in the middle of the space. The guest list for this event had been carefully screened so everyone could relax and enjoy candid conversations at their tables. A pianist in the corner resumed his play, camouflaging the condescending chatter in the room sparked by her remarks.

Jennie headed for the table in the middle of the room and took a seat next to her husband, Justice John Galt, who sported conservative black glasses that evening.

Also seated at Jennie's table was Paula Morris, wife of Alexander Morris, the invisible crown prince of the legal elite. Paula was Jennie's best friend. They had been classmates at Harvard Law

School. They counseled and supported each other, and they often traveled together.

Paula's husband, Alexander Morris, was seated next to Chief Justice Harlan Gaines at another table, with Al Carlton seated at his table, as well. Everybody who was important to the conservative legal cause was present at Alexander and Paula Morris's Virginia estate to celebrate Jennie Galt's retirement as a lobbyist for the National Gold Chamber of Commerce.

After twenty-five years, Jennie was leaving one of the most powerful lobbying positions in the nation to become head of the Liberty Train Foundation, a nonprofit with the goal of protecting and restoring the nation's constitutional values and freedoms, and dedicated to protecting the free market. Liberty Train was a foundation funded by her moneyed K Street clients through corporations that protected their personal identities from the public.

Jennie had become an icon on K Street. She represented a brand of tough knuckle politics with a maniacal commitment to purpose that was respected as a force for change in the nation's capital.

Her corporate clients paid well, and she normally got whatever she went after.

Everybody in the room knew that about her.

Her values defined her character.

Everybody respected her relationship with her husband.

Although Jennie's retirement was the reason stated for the gathering, most knew the real reason: so that the conservative elite could size up their short list of potential nominees to the U.S. Supreme Court.

It didn't matter that there were no current vacancies on the Court. The polished group of about thirty wanted to be prepared, since their presidential candidate had won the election. It was only a matter of time before President-elect Abraham Canty would have a slot to fill. And they wanted to be ready when the time arrived. Therefore, they needed a short list of nominees to begin their vetting process, candidates who would further their conservative legal agenda: welcome religion into the public educational domain, reduce union influence in the public sector, expand presidential executive powers, reverse Roe vs. Wade, strip the Commerce Clause of power, kill affirmative action, protect state rights and speed executions to save public dollars.

Legal agents committed to demolishing the major pillars of the New Deal.

"I think at least three seats will open up this term on the Court," Morris said to Judge Godfrey Hocks, the former Chief of the Third Federal Circuit Court of Appeals.

"I only see two likely retirements," Hocks replied. "But three retirements would ensure our majority. I guess we need three, when you look at how Ross is shaping up."

"You should make the short list of three we're working up for our new President." Morris glanced across the table at Gaines. "If I were you, I'd have a private chat with the Chief before he leaves. That might help. He'll be having dinner with our candidate soon."

"How many people are being seriously considered?" Hocks asked.

"Five were invited tonight," Morris answered. "But one didn't show up. He was above the need to socialize over dinner with us, so I think our list is now down to four."

"So it's down to you, Bates, Clemons and Melville," Al Carlton said. "I don't think you'll have any problem making the cut."

"I wouldn't be so sure about that," Morris said.

"I think Melville will prove incendiary with time," Al said. "He's just written too much that he can be tagged with. Being on the bench for decades gives our opponents too much ammunition to use in the hearings. Melville would be great, but I just don't see him making it through the process."

"Ross should have been incendiary, but we had to hold our fire with Graham's deal. Now we don't know what we have and she's probably got years on the bench, if she's healthy."

"Graham's deal could work to our advantage," Al said.

"I don't see how," Morris said. "I think we never should have let that amendment out of Congress for ratification. But nobody ever thought Graham would be able to get it so far. Now we could have a big problem, if it gets through. Have you had tea with Ross yet?"

"Not yet. She's been buried."

"Well, we don't like the way her first opinions are leaning on business issues," Morris said to Al directly. "I thought you said she was pro-business."

"She is."

"Well, Jennie doesn't believe she's going to follow the script."

"She'll be okay. I know her. I'll talk to her."

"You'd better do it soon. I just heard from Jennie that an important corporate case is split and sitting on her desk. If she goes the wrong way, lots of important people are going to be upset with you."

"She'll rule the right way," Al said.

"I think she's unpredictable. If you'd told us she was a free thinker we wouldn't have let her through. Jennie said she's trying to sway Galt to rejoin the tribe."

"Well, we both know *that* won't work," Al replied.

"I'm still concerned she might get in front of our train."

"Don't worry about her. I'll blow the horn and get her attention."

"She needs to know there's a line she can't cross without consequences."

"Not a problem."

"Let me be clear." Morris looked Al in the eye. "We're not going to tolerate a problem at her level from someone who went in with a blessing from us."

Later that evening Alexander Morris called Stratagem, his private security operative, to confirm the arrangements for dealing with the problem.

"What are your plans?" Morris asked.

"I've infiltrated BAMN," Stratagem reported. "They're a group of frustrated Blacks organizing over on Good Hope Road. We need to take over. I need the right cover to execute, and an extra million to put together a covert team with the appropriate skills and resources. Have you heard of Shawn DaPeoples from Seal Team Six?"

"Yes, as a matter of fact, I have."

"He's my right hand man on the streets. A perfect fit for our team. We're on it."

"Okay. Do what you need to do to protect our assets. But Ross is expendable."

"Understood."

Chapter Thirty-One

A Few Nights Later

"Jennie's concerned about Galt," Paula Morris said to her husband when they were alone in their elegant master bedroom suite ready to retire for the night.

"What's the problem?" Alexander Morris asked, unzipping her dress. "I thought Galt was under her love spell, like you have me."

She moved into her Roman Walnut-paneled walk-in closet. He followed, placing his cuff links on her marbled center island and throwing his tie on her white bench. Her dress followed.

"Jennie said he's been withdrawn lately, spending a lot of time in his library reading."

"He's back to reading again?"

"Yes." She moved away to grab her robe.

"What's caught his interest this time?"

Opening a jewelry drawer with deep blue velvet lining, she dropped her pearl earrings, diamond bracelet and wedding ring into their proper compartments before answering. "A rare book by the Scottish author John Galt."

"Hah. He's discovered him. Where'd he get that?" Morris sat on the bench, moving their discarded clothes out of the way.

"Don't know. But Jennie said he's enthralled by it."

"I thought he was enthralled by her." He watched her unpin her dark hair and shake it.

"The book seems to be competing with her entertainment."

"Well that's no good." He unbuttoned his shirt; then dropped it on the floor.

"Nathan told Jennie he's doing a bit more than just signing these days."

"Who's Nathan?"

"Nathan Butt—one of the law clerks we selected for him," Paula said.

"That could be a problem." He stood and his pants hit the floor.

"So far it's been nothing major, but he's starting to edit Nathan's drafts before signing."

"If you and Jennie selected him, I'm sure Galt's no intellectual match," Alexander said pointedly, moving toward his wife. "Have Jennie tell Nathan to push back if he sees the need."

"Galt's starting to act like he thinks he's in control." Paula hung up her dress.

"Well, if Jennie doesn't think she can control him, we can use BAMN as a cover to get rid of him. If he's not of value to us, he's not one of our protected assets."

"When Jennie asked him what he was thinking about, Galt told her, 'ego eases out God.'"

"Is he getting religious on us?" He kicked her shoes out of his way.

"No. Worse. She's worried he might no longer share our moral values. He keeps saying they don't need any more money, and maybe he should retire. Galt seems to be getting confused about a lot of things. But Jennie will let me know if there's a problem with him."

Morris dimmed the lights and led Paula to their bed. "Stop worrying, baby. Galt knows he can't retire until it's time for his lights to go out. Jennie understands what needs to be done. Glad we never told him she's in the family."

Paula and Jennie were more than just best friends—they were distant cousins—committed to protecting the family's interests in America.

Chapter Thirty-Two

U.S. Supreme Court
Monday, April 15

Justice Galt wondered if they were going to try to kill him. That was a possibility. He moaned and moved slowly through the silence of his chambers in the Marble Palace. From where he stood, Galt couldn't see the rising sun. He reached for the light on his massive oak desk and plopped into his black leather chair.

Conflicted.

He closed his eyes, attempting to release the toxic thoughts that had robbed him of critically-needed sleep the night before. He felt a sharp pain in his gut, a pain that had been more frequent and severe in the past few weeks. On some level, he knew what was wrong.

There had been other signs.

A knock came at his inner chamber door.

Roy Smith entered. He was an older Black man from Georgia with humble eyes, a retired Metro police officer. He now worked as Galt's personal security officer.

"What brings you here so early this morning?" Roy asked.

"Breakfast with Justice Ross. It's almost time to meet her."

Galt felt another pain and began to scribble a note to his secretary to schedule his annual physical exam around the first of July. He had no time for the doctor before the term ended.

Bad news could wait.

"What can I do for you?" Roy asked.

"Nathan Butt may be a problem," Galt said slowly. "Keep an eye on him. I overheard him talking on the phone the other day. I was shocked. I intend to show him who issues the opinions in this chamber. He's confused and thinks he's a Supreme Court justice."

"Is it that serious?"

"Could be."

"Why don't you fire him? He's just a law clerk."

"Might not be the wise thing to do," Galt said. "Gotta keep the trains rolling on full speed to get to the end of the term on time. He just needs to be managed."

"We will keep an eye on him."

At 7:30 a.m., the line in the Supreme Court cafeteria started to form. Galt waited for Justice Ross just outside the entrance. He checked his watch.

In a moment, she rounded the corner to greet him.

They got in line behind two of the Chief's law clerks. After the clerks placed their orders, the short-order cook in a white uniform turned his attention to Galt. He ordered two scrambled eggs, hotcakes, and bacon.

Then Katherine said, "Oatmeal and two boiled eggs."

The sound of sizzling bacon, rattling pans and cracking eggs mixed with the buzz of serious conversations as the cook prepared multiple orders with flare and a broad smile, delivering plate after plate to the glass countertop.

"In your mind, does statutory law always trump natural law?" Katherine asked.

Suddenly, Galt seemed to cringe as if in pain.

"Are you okay?"

"Yes," Galt continued with a quick recovery. "We, as the Supreme Court, can carry out the self-evident truths of the Constitution."

"I take that to mean you see natural law in our Constitution."

"Right." He turned to face her. "It's the foundation. I can't do this job without God."

"To be honest, I thought you were an atheist."

"I once lost my faith in God. Now I see his presence everywhere. I believe in God and there it rests. My faith honors reason and the power of the mind to discern the wisdom of God. Truth must stand up to rational reason."

"What my God expects of us might not always be rational," Katherine replied. "Rational self-preservation fails in the face of love. I know that to be true."

"How so?"

"My father and my grandfather made irrational decisions in the name of love."

"I think people who make irrational decisions for the benefit of others are not likely to find happiness in this life."

"It might not be all about this life."

"We can agree on that point," Galt said.

The cook placed their orders on the counter. When they proceeded to the cashier, Katherine grabbed the bill. "I'll pay this time."

They took seats in a quiet corner.

Galt spread butter on his pancakes. He sneaked a peek at her out of the corner of his eye as he busied himself, preparing his food to his liking.

Katherine broke the silence. "Did you read the capital punishment cert from Texas?"

"I've turned in my disposition memorandum on that appeal already. I voted no."

"It takes courage to go against the norm."

"I know that. I'm the one who feels like a stray dog around here."

In a low tone she said, "I wish we could find some common ground. Did you read the book?"

"Yes, I was shocked to see my name on such an old book. Where did you get it?"

"A rare books store in Philadelphia."

"I've been thinking about things," Galt said. "Let me tell you the parts that have been playing in my head since I read it. There was once a little boy who exasperated his mother. He saw himself as entitled to everything everybody else had, and when he couldn't get something he wanted, he felt a great injustice had occurred. He bucked against his parents' authority when he thought they wronged him, and saw parental discipline as extreme cruelty against an innocent child's nature. He believed in God, but not church authority.

"Many of the church rules made no sense to him. He was kicked out of his parish school because he couldn't figure out why the teacher kept trying to tell him that if A=B and B=C, then A=C. He thought on a higher level and could only rationalize in his mind that A=A. In his world, A was A, B was B, and C was C. It made no sense to pretend otherwise.

"Now, one day, the little boy was hungry. On his way to school, he walked past a fenced-in apple orchard. The trees were full of luscious bright red apples. He looked around. No one was in sight. The boy thought the apples might spoil, but, more than that, he wondered why it was wrong for him to pluck an apple and eat it if he was hungry. After all, hadn't God put apple trees on earth to feed man?

"The little boy had a lot of questions for his parents and teachers that they could not answer. Why does a person get the whole apple tree for himself and his children for all time? Why is a person who has erected a fence around an entire apple orchard with forced labor entitled to all of the fruit from all of the trees in the orchard? Shouldn't the hungry man rebel and take what God intended them to have by right of birth? Should the property rights of bullies persist for all time?"

Katherine broke in. "I have a more fundamental question: Why are the original land property owners entitled to own property in the first place? If the original land right granted by the British king is counterfeit because the king had no divine power from God to divvy up this earth—why isn't the bestowed property right counterfeit?"

Galt continued his story. "The little boy wondered, 'should individual men be allowed to own God's land for all time, or should we just have a right to use it during our lifetimes?'"

Katherine started to answer but Galt continued. "I used to think I knew the answer to these questions. Now, I'm not so sure."

"If we keep ignoring gross injustice because of politics, we might not have clean hands in the eyes of the people," Katherine said. "When did you read the book?"

"Last week. I could see myself with those thoughts, asking those questions in another place and time. I was a radical in my early life—but this profession changed me."

"Has the book really challenged your thinking about property rights?"

"Yes." Galt finished his last strip of bacon. "But there's a lot going on. We could end up seeing things the same way when you consider all of the risks and forces at work here."

"What makes you so sure I'll see things your way?"

"You want justice." Galt rose to leave. "But the price might be violence. I hear there's another corporate land rights case from Hawaii on the way to our chambers. Repose. That's the issue. Maybe the time has come for us to hear that case. I might vote to hear it."

"You might?"

"Yes," Galt said. "But don't tell anybody I told you that."

Chapter Thirty-Three

Monday, April 15
5:30 p.m.

In his two-bedroom apartment near Fourteenth and M Streets, Walter Rodney sat in his small living room watching CNN's *Worldwide News Reports* on a flat screen. The sounds of gunfire in a late-breaking story about a sniper attack in Israel overwhelmed the street noise that normally ricocheted around his apartment. Vibrant images of death filled the screen. He watched death take its victims in high definition; breathtaking colors beamed from the digital screen without any obvious emotion registering on his face.

He was relaxed, with an ice-cold Coke Zero in his hand.

Synchronized beeps from his cell phone announced a text. He spotted his phone on the table, peeking out from under the *Ebony* magazine, and grabbed it, noting that the text was from one of his more outspoken recruits, Larry Stratagem, now the most energetic comrade in his BAMN group.

What could he want?

As Walter read the message, his eyes widened and a calculating smile appeared on his face.

> *Galt at Morton's having dinner. Working tonight as cook. Get carryout. You can eat while you wait. Then follow him home. We need to know where he lives. Come now. Stratagem*

Walter pecked his response: *OK. Will see if Shawn can get Temple van.*

I'll put in a steak order for you. He's eating alone. No visible security, Stratagem wrote.

OK, Walter tapped back.

Thirty-five minutes later, Shawn and Walter pulled up in the Temple of Mali van and parked about six hundred feet from the restaurant. Walter strolled into Morton's and approached the hostess station.

"Do you have a carryout order for Walter Rodney?"

As she fumbled through a couple of bags on the counter behind her, he glanced into the main dining area. Galt was nowhere in sight, but he couldn't see in the booths.

"I called it in," Walter said before she could speak. "A man took my order."

"Let me go check."

"Okay, where is your restroom?"

"Over there," she said pointing. "Near the back."

Walter proceeded through the main dining area and spotted Galt in a booth having some massive chocolate concoction for dessert. He noticed a female with her eyes locked on him. He'd seen her before. Who was she? His security? She looked away, reaching for her purse.

Walter spotted the men's room sign.

On his return, the hostess pulled the cash register receipt from a white carry out bag and handed it to Walter. Sixty-two dollars for a steak. That was robbery.

He handed her his MasterCard. She ran the charge through the machine and handed him the receipt. He looked at the pretty hostess and wrote in an eight-dollar tip, totaled the bill and signed with a carefree scribble.

The steak better be worth it.

On the street, an eerie feeling crept over him. He looked around. Several people moved like busy ants in all directions.

Galt must have security somewhere.

The wind blew paper and leaves along the street. He heard a construction drill and the sound of a bus passing by. He could not account for it, but felt something just wasn't right.

Looking around as he approached the van, he could see the passenger-side door was unlocked. Where was Shawn?

Walter stepped up onto the side rail on the passenger side and settled himself in his seat. The smell of grilled steak, garlic mashed potatoes and onions filled the parked van. Walter's stomach growled.

He glanced in the side view mirror and noticed a man wearing jeans, a sweater and a dark knit skullcap approaching the van from the rear, close to the curb. He popped the door locks on, thinking some crackhead might be trying to rob him.

That would have been bad.

Walter pulled out his cell phone, glancing from door to door before punching out a message with speedy fingers.

Where are you? Galt's ready to leave.

Walter did not notice the man in the black skullcap brush closer and position a small magnetic device across the van's passenger door.

Walter pressed the send button as his eyes shot back to the activity on the street.

The incoming text to Walter was almost immediate. *Had to go to bathroom. Go without me if you have to. Keys in box under your seat.*

Walter felt under the seat for the box and found it.

He placed the box on his lap and waited.

Finally Galt exited the restaurant and proceeded in the direction of the parked van.

Walter noticed a man he believed to be a U.S. marshal emerge from the shadows and head with urgency toward the justice. The man in the skullcap was about a hundred feet from Galt. Walter thought that he must be a U.S. marshal protecting Galt from the crackhead. He'd known Galt had security somewhere. Suddenly both men grabbed the justice, turning him with force, and distancing him from the van. Yes. His security was working.

Gotta go now. Can't wait on Shawn.

He opened the box on his lap.

Walter trembled in disbelief at its contents: a ticking bomb.

In the next instant, the van exploded.

Metal, plastic, glass, flesh, hair, fragments of clothing, and bright red yods of blood flew through the air then settled like raindrops. The force of the blast blew a hole in the right side and roof of the van. Walter's body was split in half. The sounds of breaking glass, transforming metal, and fire alarms vibrated for over a mile.

Then, stillness.

When the red thunderstorm was over, Justice John Galt's back was sprayed with the blood of Walter Rodney, mixed with his own. The bodies of his protectors lay, lifeless, at right and left angles to Galt's shoulders.

Chapter Thirty-Four

U.S. Supreme Court
Monday, May 6

Katherine felt violated by the attack on Galt, as it was really a blow struck against the entire Supreme Court. She felt as if her life had been picked up by a cyclone—dislocating her personal relationships, her Sunday routine with her mother, and other simple pleasures that private citizens took for granted. Now, a walk along the Potomac alone in the evening was forbidden. Security was her constant companion.

Gloom filled the high ceilings of the Court under lock down.

Galt was still in a coma.

At nine in the morning she sat at her desk, staring at the four walls of her oak-paneled chambers adorned with priceless oil paintings, her coffee untouched. Divergent facts and rumors swirled about the assassination attempt on Galt. She didn't know how to assess what was happening. She read the troubling petition again.

The cert petition concerning the native Hawaiian property rights had landed on her desk. The case had arrived at the Supreme Court the week before. She knew a political resolution was called for—but what should happen if the politicians never dealt with making things right?

Shouldn't the Supreme Court be the check and balance for the people?

She stared at the recommendation from the cert pool. Deny. In spite of what Galt had said, she thought the odds of overcoming that recommendation were slim. The corporate rights in the case were clearly established throughout the land. She knew the Chief's position.

She couldn't imagine four votes for the case without Galt's.

Surrounded by carts of legal briefs, she picked up the draft disposition memorandum from her staff; it also recommended denial of the native Hawaiians' request to be heard. It noted that the case employed a novel angle—one that was not likely to win.

The beachfront land in question was owned by a Delaware corporate entity which the state of Delaware defined as a person. That legal precedent had been in place for over one hundred years. By law, corporations could exercise human rights. That made the Fourteenth Amendment of the U. S. Constitution apply to corporations. That was today's legal reality. The case challenged the right of the corporation to exercise human rights, arguing that the Founding Fathers had not foreseen the current situation.

The shareholders of the Delaware corporation were foreign interests—not U.S. citizens. Should foreigners be able to buy U.S. Constitutional rights by simply buying a U.S. corporation? Certainly the Founding Fathers had not contemplated foreign interests— possibly our enemies—being able to play in national politics behind corporate masks. How had things gone so far?

Did this case create an opportunity to look at the foundation of corporate law differently? Was Galt evolving? Critically thinking for himself? Could this case be why he became a target?

Maybe Galt really was going to vote for the Hawaiian case to be heard. She thought of the story of the little boy that he had shared with her. She wondered if he would really vote to challenge one of the pillars of corporate law given the facts in the right case. And was this it?

Katherine had been up late the night before reading the 2009 Hawaiian Supreme Court ruling. The heavy reading weighed on her conscience. When she arrived at the Court that morning, she had called up all of the filings and records associated with the Hawaiian case.

The pile now sat before her.

She picked up a folder labeled "Joint Resolution." Inside she found a United States joint resolution signed by former President William Clinton. She read the 1993 Congressional Apology in disbelief at what had occurred.

> *...On January 14, 1893, the United States Minister John L. Stevens conspired with a small group of non-Hawaiian residents of the Kingdom of Hawaii, including citizens of the United States of America, to overthrow the indigenous and lawful government of Hawaii ... Armed naval forces of the United States invaded the sovereign Hawaiian nation on January 16, 1893, and positioned themselves near Hawaiian government buildings and the Iolani Palace to intimidate Queen Liliuokalani and her government...*

Reading on, she discovered that on the afternoon of January 17, 1893, a Committee of Safety representing American and European sugar planters, descendants of missionaries, and financiers deposed the Hawaiian monarchy and proclaimed the establishment of a provisional government. Then John Stevens extended diplomatic recognition to the provisional government without the consent of the native Hawaiian people, in violation of treaties between the two nations and of international law.

Stevens had no presidential or congressional authority to overthrow the queen.

When informed of the risk of bloodshed with resistance, Queen Liliuokalani had yielded her authority to the United States government. She yielded to the superior force of representatives of the U.S. Navy under the armed threat of certain loss of life—expecting the United States government to undo the actions of John L. Stevens.

Clearly, the queen had expected justice from our government when she surrendered. This was a case with enormous political implications. Could things be made right now? Katherine was appalled at the behavior of the United States of America. How could the native Hawaiian's property right claims be denied in the face of such injustice?

Katherine's emotions churned. She did a little more research. Before Stevens's land grab for the provisional government, the native Hawaiian warlords fought and took land from each other. How did the queen's property right arise? Queen Liliuokalani was only in power because her ancestors engaged in war and took land from other indigenous groups.

If she were on the Court in 2009, what would she have done?

In a unanimous decision, the U.S. Supreme Court kicked the issue of the United States of America illegally taking land from the native Hawaiians in 1893 back to Hawaii to let the political process "work its way right." That was wrong. There had been no justice.

Al told her that he had been retained by the Hawaiian Banking Association to lobby an issue that might turn into a Supreme Court case when he gave her a white paper entitled, *The Impact of Native Hawaiian Land Use Rights on Real Estate Lending in Hawaii.*

Now they had a cert petition. She felt certain it was the same case that Galt told her he would vote for. The week before, Al asked her to read the white paper before their scheduled meeting.

So she had. Now Katherine decided to cancel their meeting.

She wasn't in the mood to be lobbied.

Chapter Thirty-Five

That afternoon the stack of cert disposition memorandums occupying the corner of Katherine's large desk still blocked the view of her cluttered conference table. The pile of certs had not yet been reduced to vacant space because of her research on the Hawaiian land case.

Her thoughts turned to Galt.

Katherine recalled Galt's voice as she replayed the image of him chugging along to his chambers and moving his arms in a circular motion like the pushrods of a train. He had been telling jokes to his clerks in the private hall just outside of her chambers on the day of the blast.

"Gotta keep the trains rollin'. Ten weeks to term's end. The pressure is on."

Now Galt lay in a coma. He could lose his right arm. It had been almost completely severed at the shoulder. The doctors could not predict if the reattached arm would ever be of any use nor could they give any assurance that he would regain consciousness.

They would only say they expected him to survive.

Katherine rose from her desk and walked over to one of the oversized windows that was framed by flowing navy brocade draperies with jeweled trim, opening them to let in some sunlight.

Gazing out, she realized the role of the U.S. Supreme Court was more crucial than the Founding Fathers foresaw. Chief Justice John Marshall had created a Court with awesome power and a crushing workload that only a few had the mental capacity to handle. With the fallout from the blast still hanging in the background of her mind, the quiet and seriousness of her chambers began to feel like a prison. From then on, would she have to confine herself to those walls to feel safe? She trained her eyes on the barricades blocking the white marbled steps to the main entrance of the Court.

The crowds of tourists that used to mill in front of the U.S. Supreme Court were gone.

In their place, a detail of armed security guards stood on alert.

On a side table next to the windowsill, Katherine noticed a copy of the *Journal of Supreme Court History* with an article about the Dred Scott case that had set the stage for the civil war. The worst decision ever made by the Court. In 1857, the Supreme Court ruled that slaves were not citizens of the United States.

That decision had been wrong.

Just like the Court's decision to give corporations constitutional rights.

She scanned the article and thumbed through the *Journal*. Following the Dred Scott article there was a piece on golf as a pastime for Supreme Court justices. She skimmed the golf article and thought of the serene settings—then made a decision to dismiss the gloom that clouded her mind. The sun was shining brightly. So she would to go play golf with her clerks. There were substantial precedents for it.

She thought they would be safe at the club.

Chapter Thirty-Six

Katherine reached the entrance to the Congressional Country Club in Bethesda, Maryland. In the driveway, under a large pear tree with pink blossoms, she stepped out of her armored Chevrolet Suburban. Other vehicles crowded the parking lot.

A full assortment of firepower was present. For her?

Upon entering the clubhouse, Katherine reached to turn off her cell phone, honoring the club's policy. As she pressed the "off" button, her phone chirped.

"No cell coverage in this area," the receptionist said. "The signal blockers on the roof have been activated again."

She was not surprised.

Her advance security detail was already stationed on the course ahead of them as Katherine and her clerks gathered at the first tee, ready for play. Carl, a Stanford Law graduate, sat in a golf cart at the beginning of the Blue Course. Katherine pulled up in a cart alongside him. Hal and another security officer kept a safe distance behind them.

The manicured grounds were just beginning to come to life.

Pam, a fiery redhead from the University of Chicago, bounced toward Carl's cart and jumped in. She gazed down the fairway. "This is beautiful. Lots of sand to the right."

"I'm not going there," Carl said. "Galt still out?"

"Yes," Katherine said. "He still isn't responding."

"Lots of buzz about Senator Graham's amendment in the press this morning," Carl said.

"Nothing can stop an idea whose time has come," Ron said, walking to the first tee with a driver in his hand. Ron was a Harvard Law School graduate. "Only two more states needed for ratification. The media attention on Galt might just push it through."

"It's time," Pam declared. "New Hampshire is debating the amendment in its Senate tonight. I think it's moving along just fine. If Galt wakes up, do you think he'll resign?"

"I think he has to," Ron said. "He can't write."

"So what?" Carl said. "He might be able to dictate. I can hear him arguing he doesn't have to read or write to keep his job, as long as he's alive and decides. He's not a quitter."

"I read he won't be able to come back until the fall at the earliest," Pam said.

"What's going to happen to the cases he was drafting for the majority?" Ron asked.

"They'll have to wait until he returns or is replaced," Katherine said.

"William O. Douglas returned disabled after a stroke," Carl said. "Physically and mentally disabled but he held onto his seat way too long. If Galt wakes up, he'll just hold on."

"I wish Galt would wake up and resign to save us the trouble of removing him," Pam said. "On second thought, we might be better off if he doesn't wake up."

"Shhhh," Katherine said with puckered lips. "Ron's about to hit."

Ron positioned his driver behind the ball. After eyeing the target, he executed a near perfect swing. His ball landed in the middle of the fairway.

"My turn," Carl said, settling into position at the more advanced white tees. He whiffed, then swung again. The ball veered to the right, barely fifty feet from the tee. "Dang it."

Katherine stepped up to the white tees. Checked her distance to the flag: 339 yards. *Whack!*

"It would have been a great shot if it had gone straight," Carl said.

"Yeah." Katherine slid her driver back in her bag. "Rushed my shot. Let's go."

"I still have to play my shot," Pam said.

Holding up a stack of papers, Ron said, "You need to decide on these certs today."

"I know," Katherine replied. "I'll play the first six holes with Carl, switch to Pam on number seven, and we'll start processing the certs on thirteen. We're playing ready golf."

"I'll just pick up and hit from the reds with Pam," Carl said in a sheepish tone.

Pam swung. The ball bounced forward and rolled to a stop, about a hundred feet away.

"Not great," she said. "But not bad for me. At least I made the fairway."

Carl hit, sending his ball in pursuit of Katherine's errant ball.

"Well, boss," Carl said. "What can we do to improve?"

"Be of one mind with the ball when you execute a shot," Katherine said. "A great shot happens when you trust your preparation, control your emotions, and execute a fundamentally perfect swing in your mind's eye first. Only focus on the ball at your feet. That's it."

"Is talking about work going to be a problem all day?"

"We can talk about work, but we need to clear our minds when ready to hit." Katherine drove toward the sand traps. "Did you review the 2009 Hawaiian property rights case?"

"Yes." Carl's brow furrowed with a clear expression of displeasure on his face.

"What are you thinking?"

"I think the native Hawaiians got screwed. They're too weak to deal with the state. They are now less than twenty-five percent of the population of Hawaii. The state of Hawaii is never going to fully restore their land rights because they're going to protect the property rights of the corporations. We know that."

She stopped the cart and Carl continued. "The Court has a precedent of respecting state rights, but we reversed their Supreme Court decision in the matter. Not good."

Katherine walked to her ball and took aim. It landed in the fourth sand trap. "I don't believe it." She approached it with two golf carts following her. In the trap, she dug her heels into the sand, addressed the ball and swung. The ball landed just shy of the green.

Pleased with her shot, she returned the club to her bag. "Carl, if there was a fenced-in apple tree over there with luscious apples on its limbs and you were starving, would you have an inalienable right to pluck a piece of fruit from God's apple tree to satisfy your hunger?"

"We have to have property rights," Carl said. "No way around it."

"I agree," she said. "But what constitutes a legitimate property right? Who gave the British king the right to give God's land away? Should property rights that were obtained by violence or force be upheld in our judicial system for all time?"

"You're getting deep," Carl said. "If you go there, you're going to need a lifeline."

"I'm going deeper," Katherine said. "Should the descendants of bullies be allowed to benefit from the illegal acts of their ancestors in perpetuity?"

"Working out property rights is political," Carl said. "After weighing everything, I believe we have to let the Hawaiian land rights case work itself out in the political process."

"But we interfered last time," Ross said. "I think the decision of the Hawaiian Supreme Court to issue an injunction should have been allowed to stand while the residents of Hawaii worked out their politics."

"Corporate property rights were in danger," Carl said. "The case was too hot."

171

They made a beeline to Katherine's ball. She skillfully chipped it onto the green.

"You know Galt's clerks are still working on the draft opinions assigned to him."

"I know," she said. "We're concerned because we know he isn't driving the bus."

Katherine and her team were up and down all day. The only constant was the furious exchange of critical information, silenced for that one moment of total focus in their quest for the perfect shot. They had moved from topic to topic in two-way and four-way conversations on all of the major issues to be decided in her chambers, efficient exchanges of information as they attacked the course with anger, glee and careful consideration.

At the eighteenth tee, Katherine prepared to swing after gazing at the treetops to her left in the distance—then she stopped. She heard vehicles approaching from behind on the cart path. Her eyes darted to the alarming sounds. The guards tailing her pulled their carts off the paved path, jumped out, and were rushing toward her.

What was happening?

She scanned quickly and made a quick step toward Hal, but tripped over the tee box and fell. Black SUVs screeched to a halt on the pavement near her. Before she could rise, she felt the weight of bodies on top of her. Keeping her down. Was there a shot? Was Hal hit? Out of the corner of her eye, she saw the SWAT team with high-powered rifles drawn move into shooting positions around them.

She almost couldn't breathe. A few minutes seemed like an eternity. Stillness. Quiet.

"Stand down," one of the SWAT team members said.

The weight on her lifted.

Hal helped her up. "Are you okay? I thought you were hit."

"I think so," Katherine said, twirling her right ankle. "I thought you were hurt."

"We got a take-cover signal. There must have been some type of serious security breach. I'll find out what happened. Give me a few minutes. Are you going to finish?"

How could she focus on the ball now? What had gone wrong? To her surprise, she felt her cell phone buzz in her pocket. Glancing at its screen, she recognized Gaines's identifier.

"Yes?" she said, placing the phone to her ear.

"Sorry for the misunderstanding," Chief Justice Gaines said. "I didn't realize turning off the signal blockers at Congressional would trigger a red-alert security protocol. Guess I pulled the wrong string. Secret Service orders still rule there. Not the club president. But I thought you should know as soon as possible that Justice Galt just regained consciousness. He's talking."

As Justice Ross's black Suburban exited the gates of the country club, Stratagem watched from the shadows of the trees down the road. Two black SUVs trailed her Suburban.

New vehicles. She would probably be riding in the equivalent of a bulletproof tank soon.

They needed a new plan.

Chapter Thirty-Seven

Saturday, May 11
The Ritz-Carlton Residences

Katherine felt incarcerated.

SWAT team in the basement. Police on foot patrols. Plain clothes officers. Could they really keep her safe? They said she was safe at home. How long was she to stay at home?

Alone in her bed, she feared her home had become nothing more than an upscale prison. Since the assassination attempt on Galt, she had gone to work every day, but had not resumed her social life. Her personal life had effectively been put on hold. She couldn't let anybody new enter her life now.

She spent most of her days reading and writing—during the week and on the weekends. Her body was getting stiff from the sedentary lifestyle that had been thrust upon her.

The day at the golf course had helped. She needed to get out.

Cheryl was the only person she could talk to freely. Her mother was hard to talk to.

Maybe she should give Cheryl a call.

She wanted to talk about how her social life had died. Her security didn't want her to go to church. They didn't want her to go to London. They didn't want her to have dinner at her mother's every Sunday, even though her building was considered safe. She even had to alter her regular hair appointments. She hadn't seen any of her friends in weeks.

Katherine didn't like what she was being forced to do for safety.

She thought about Washington Cobb and her grandfather.

They had not cowered in the face of threats. But she was afraid to go out. Could they protect her? Yes, they could. But at what cost?

Security could not keep her on lockdown forever. She had to stand up now.

Katherine decided to go see *Motown the Musical* in New York—that evening. The need to go was urgent. Fear had to be dismissed. She picked up her cell phone and called Cheryl.

"What!" Cheryl said. "Are you crazy? Galt almost got killed last week. Now you wanna go see a play in New York? Tonight?"

"I'm not crazy, but I just can't live my life in fear. If I don't deal with the dread of going out now, I'll never go anywhere."

Katherine's voice cracked. "You know, I read the first part of a book my mom's writing about how she grew up in the south. It was tough back then, with the KKK and everything else. As a young girl, my mom learned to live with fear and abuse. The men in my family had to run or face being lynched. They didn't cower in the face of threats—they faced them. I have to learn how to live my life in the face of threats or this job will crush me."

"I get that," Cheryl said.

"So if you don't want to go with me, I—"

"I'm going. I just needed to know where you are, psychologically. If that's what you need to do to be okay, I'm with you. How we going?"

"U.S. Airways. Meet you at the ticket counter at three. We'll catch the four. Check into the Grand Hyatt. We can walk over to the Lunt-Fontanne Theatre on 48th. Show's at eight."

"Hal is going to have a fit," Cheryl said. "Wear that short gray wig to change your look. Sneak out of the Ritz and catch the Metro. I'll get the tickets."

Cheryl and Katherine swayed to the music that transformed America and eased the racial tensions of the generation. The music was soothing to Katherine's soul. It was a part of the history of her life, and transported her back in time with its stories of love and the pain of being in love, when love was not returned. Rejected love. Joyful love. Hurting love.

One song in particular took her back to that enchanting evening with Skip. *Baby, I Need Your Lovin'.* He was part of her history, too, just like the music.

She danced in her front row seat, letting her feelings flow. She joined the masses doing the *Cool Jerk* dance to the Funk Brothers' Motown beats, with striking upper-body moves.

She sang, forcing her fear to take a backseat.

She felt back in control, enjoying the gift of the present moment.

Chapter Thirty-Eight

George Washington University Hospital
Tuesday, May 14

As Julianne LaSalle strode down the long hallway that led to Justice John Galt's hospital room, she noticed two armed guards stationed near the end of the hall. She thought they were U.S. marshals. One was seated in back of a small portable desk next to an unmarked door, while the other guard stood near the nurses' station with a view of the entire length of the hallway and multiple screens of patient monitors.

The steady beeps of medical devices danced through the air as patients' lives were managed and held in balance with life-giving fluids.

A mixed scent of fresh flowers and disinfectant filled the air.

She stopped at the guard's desk just short of the entrance to Galt's room.

"I'm Julianne LaSalle with Urban Times Media," she said in her most professional tone. "I believe Justice Galt is expecting me."

The guard opened a notebook to a blue tab labeled, "Visitors." He found her name, checked it, then noted the date and time in the space next to her name.

"May I look in your bag?" He put on a pair of turquoise rubber gloves.

Julianne handed him her well-worn black leather Coach bag. He opened it, moved a couple of items around with his gloved fingers and handed it back.

"Please open the briefcase."

The guard removed two books and an assorted pile of flyers, papers, and notepads. He fanned through a collage of documents, then rose to scan her body with a metal detector.

"You can go in, but your briefcase, keys and hairpins need to stay with me."

Julianne saw a sea of flowers in Galt's room. She loved the smell of roses. A slight glint of sunlight came through the bottom of the lowered window shade and hit the floor.

The dim lighting echoed the Justice's physical state.

An array of monitors flanked Galt's bed. An IV was attached to his left arm, while a clear plastic tube was wrapped around his head, forcing oxygen into his nose. His face, bruised with swollen eyelids, made him look like a prizefighter in his last round. As she crept toward the bed, Julianne could not tell if his eyes were swollen shut. His right arm was heavily bandaged.

As Galt took in each breath, Julianne watched his yellow blanket lift up and fall down.

She did not know if she should speak or remain silent.

She lowered herself into one of the chairs beside the bed. The sounds of the life support machines around the crown of Galt's bed were temporarily drowned out by the siren of a passing police car. The piercing sound did not move the justice into consciousness.

She thought he was a weak excuse for a man—just a puppet for the white people.

Why had she been placed in the middle of this drama with him?

Twenty minutes passed with no sound other than the periodic beep of the machines.

Her thoughts ran wild. *No, she wouldn't give him CPR, if he needed it—she would die first. She wished he would do the country a*

178

favor and just resign or die. Either way worked for her. He knew she was not one of his fans. He surely could not be one of hers.

Julianne looked at her watch. *Thirty-three minutes. Gone. Maybe she should leave.*

Julianne sighed and twisted in her hard seat.

Finally, he opened his eyes.

Julianne stood and moved to his bedside. Leaning, she said, "I'm Julianne LaSalle."

"I know who you are," he said in a weakened voice. "You wouldn't be here if I didn't."

"Why am I here?"

"To interview me."

"Are you going to resign?"

"I'm doing fine."

"Are you going to answer my question?"

"My job is not complete. I will not quit my office."

"But you've been permanently disabled. You can't write."

"I'm not disabled," Galt said in a stronger voice. "So go tell the world I'm not going to die now, and I'm not retiring anytime soon. Go print that. You may leave now. I need my rest."

Justice John T. Galt closed his eyes.

Julianne had been dismissed.

Chapter Thirty-Nine

Real Times Media Office
Later that Same Day

"He might make it." Julianne strolled into Sam Knight's office and plopped into the single chair in front of his battle-worn desk. "And Galt's not going to resign."

Her editor's desk was piled high with paper, like bunkers created from any late-breaking story not important enough to stop the printing presses. In reality most late-breaking stories lost their value, like empty seats on a departed plane, once the digital presses of the Urban Times Media started to roll. Yet Sam found it hard to throw away stories that might be transformed into a front-page article with the right set of current events.

Julianne spotted her latest effort on the top of one of the bunkers.

"You didn't like it?" Julianne angled her head trying to see the markings on her draft.

"I'm not gonna run it now," Sam said.

"What do you mean? You gotta run it."

"No, I don't. It's not ready yet."

"So what're you gonna run?"

"A story about Walter Rodney. He was an expert on the slave trade and its impact on the development of capitalism in the world.

The community needs to understand his message." Sam flung a red file folder over the bunkers to Julianne.

The caption on the article was: *Walter Rodney: A Revolutionist.*

"I think Walter Rodney was a nonviolent militant who quite possibly stirred others to violence with his motivating oratory—both his supporters and his oppressors—without personally engaging in any act of violence himself."

"From what I've heard that's going to be a hard line to sell."

"Walter Rodney was a guy working on children's books when he died—children's books he hoped would break down racial tensions. He'd completed African and Indian books in a series to promote racial harmony." Sam leaned back in his chair. "Our readers need to be aware of Rodney's full message so our youth are not led down the wrong path toward violence."

"I can see the spin Fox News will put on this story. The conservatives are going to use the attempted assassination of Galt to spread fear of a communist takeover."

"Where did you get that?" he asked.

"Everything in this town is political, and they're going to spin this article as overeducated Black men pushing the world toward socialism. Can't you see it?"

Julianne peered through her red frames at her editor. "The assassination attempt on Galt was meant to create fear of the Black man. Galt's the symbol of the hanged man in Black America. We don't know who killed Walter Rodney. It could have been the Feds, international operatives of BAMN, a power play, or just somebody trying to get rid of a useless token on the bench. Whatever happened, it's clear to me that Rodney didn't kill himself by accident."

Sam looked at his watch. "What did you find out from your visit with Galt?"

"Nothing. Galt told me he wasn't resigning or dying and he needed his rest."

"You didn't talk about Walter Rodney?"

"No. He said what he wanted then dismissed me. What was I supposed to do?"

"Well, I guess there wasn't much you could have done under the circumstances. Go write a little something that leaves the door open for him to invite you back for another interview when he's feeling better. Don't burn the bridge with him."

"As far as I am concerned, the bridge was burned a long time ago."

"Just tell our readers what he told you to tell them," Sam said. He then wrote the following caption on a blank piece of paper:

Galt Expected To Survive: No Plans to Retire

"See what you can do with this by five. You've got 250 words."

It was three o'clock.

Two hours until her deadline.

Chapter Forty

U. S. Supreme Court
Thursday, June 13

As the first to enter the Justice's Conference Room, Katherine paused to admire the crystal chandelier that hung over the conference table, beaming with a radiant force that lit the hollowed space. Its oversized beads, in the shapes of diamond drop earrings, hung like icicles. Reflective waves of light bounced off the sharp edges of its dangling crystal nuggets, creating a sparkling cloud below the recessed ceiling. At its center hung a crystal ball that was almost the size of a soccer ball.

A feast for tired eyes.

Not even the President of the United States was allowed a seat at the conference table in this magnificent space where the deliberations of the Supreme Court justices were held.

Katherine stood on an oversized oriental rug that softened her steps and realized the gravity of the decision on their agenda today.

Tension hung in the air from working around Justice Galt's clerks plus his wife's authoritarian notes and instructions. Katherine went to her seat to the left of the chandelier as Chief Justice Harlan Gaines entered the room from his adjoining chambers.

"I went to see John this morning," Justice Gaines said. "He was heavily drugged. In a lot of pain. Obviously out of it. Then I returned here and found five draft opinions with a note from his wife saying John wanted to know if we would join him in issuing them."

"Did Galt say anything to you about them?" Katherine asked.

"No," Gaines said. "As you will recall, I assigned the Rumpsy and Beam Opinions to Galt for drafting the day before the bombing. Drafts for both were issued from his office today. Perfect work products. But no initials from Galt. I assume because he can't use his writing hand. Given his condition, I'm sure he didn't read or review them."

"So is his chamber running on auto-pilot?"

"Sure is starting to look that way. This situation can hurt our credibility."

Justice Martin entered the room and joined the conversation.

"Did you ask him about resigning again?" Katherine asked.

"He closed his eyes," Gaines said. "I took that as a 'No'. We have to do something about this situation. I don't think we can issue any opinions drafted by his clerks while he's in the hospital and under the influence of drugs. He can't be the fifth vote on any majority decision."

Justice Martin, the most conservative justice in the room, folded his arms, then said, "Isn't that like nullifying the vote of a sick justice? What's your constitutional authority for that?"

Chief Justice Gaines flinched.

"I'm in the majority in those four cases," Gaines said. "I've reconsidered my position and I'm withdrawing my vote on all four."

Two more justices with sour lines on their faces walked in holding copies of the four draft Galt opinions. They shook hands.

"Are we going to allow this?" Justice Marge Sadler asked, holding out the four draft opinions. "He is obviously not in the engineer's seat in his chambers—but his clerks are still working like he's at the throttle with his train going full speed ahead. This is a crisis."

"It's been done in the past," Justice Martin said. "Let's maintain the status quo."

"Do you think Jennie's calling the shots?" Katherine asked.

"I wouldn't put it past her to do that," Sadler said. "She'll argue they're one."

The other four justices entered the conference within seconds of one another as the clock struck two. After shaking hands, they were all seated. Galt's seat remained vacant.

The Chief spoke first. "After reading the four draft opinions from Justice Galt's chambers, I have decided to withdraw my vote for an affirmative ruling in all four cases for reasons that should be obvious to all of you."

"That's not right," said Justice Martin, who was in the majority. "Those opinions were brilliant. We should issue them now and, as Galt would say, 'Keep the trains running.'"

"But Galt didn't contribute to their development," Justice Wilson said.

"I'm sure we've all gotten at least one opinion drafted by our clerks where we didn't want to change one word because of its brilliance—and put our names on it for publication."

"I've never done that." Justice Helen Goodwell, seated to Katherine's right, flung her head back and frowned. "We can't let Galt's train run at high speed without him."

Justice Marge Sadler said, "I see the invisible hand of Galt's conductor materializing before our eyes. Did you see Jennie Galt's note float by your desk this morning?"

"Yes," Justice Martin said. "I thought it was fine."

Justice Goodwell roared back. "I thought it was a crime."

"Let's go around the table and take a vote to see where we are," the Chief said. "Should Galt's wife be allowed to give his vote on the four cases we've discussed? I vote no."

"Yes," Justice Martin said. "He has constitutional power we can't take away."

"No," Justice Kramer said. "It's obvious he's incapacitated and nobody nominated or confirmed Jennie Galt to the Court."

The justices went on responding in the order of seniority around the table.

"Yes," Justice Smith said. "We don't know how long it will be before his condition improves. We need to be practical. We should not stop the process if we know what his vote is. We all heard what he said and he hasn't said anything different about these four cases. We're not authorized to take his vote in this manner."

"Yes," Justice Kane said. "If I get sick I don't want you to take my vote. Treat others as you wish to be treated. That's the golden rule."

"I vote no," Justice Goodwell said. "We should not weaken the Court by allowing law clerks to harness the power of Galt's chambers through his wife's oversight."

Folding his arms on the table, Justice Frank said, "We should not weaken the Constitution by taking the vote of a living justice away. I'm with Galt on this. I'm voting yes."

"We have lifetime appointments as long as we exhibit good behavior," Katherine said. "Closing our eyes and allowing Galt's wife and clerks to wield the power of his office would be bad behavior on our part so I vote no. We are deadlocked four to four."

"If we count Galt's vote as a 'yes' we are five to four."

"I am reporting a four to four vote to the Clerk," Katherine said, "with a note stating Justice Galt is in the hospital and thus is unable to cast his vote at this time."

"Since we have a tie," Chief Gaines stated, "these four cases will be held over to next term and rescheduled for a second oral argument if a new justice joins us. I withdraw my prior votes on these four cases. They will not be decided until we have five votes excluding any vote cast by Galt. As it stands these cases only have three votes. This is how I will manage the situation in Galt's absence since we don't have the authority to do more."

Chapter Forty-One

Monday, June 17
The D.C. Community Cultural Center

Julianne LaSalle knew Stratagem was not a fanatical street-corner preacher who could only deliver a message to the already converted. No, he was much more than that and Julianne needed to know more about him.

She was sure the situation was a story in the making.

Larry Stratagem had been voted in as BAMN's new president at the last membership meeting. After Walter Rodney's death, Stratagem had no competition for the group's leadership. BAMN's membership had exploded in the days since Rodney's death.

The name *Black Activists Mobilization Network* was catchy. And Stratagem knew how to promote. Daily email blasts called for the rejected to become members of BAMN. A motivational message arrived every day for each person on the recruitment list with an email address. Anyone committed to the cause of opposing economic oppression was welcomed to join, at a membership meeting or online.

Julianne had not heard of Larry Stratagem until his email blasts caught her attention.

Now she wondered if she could be witnessing the birth of a powerful community leader.

She watched him stride like a military leader through the crowded room of mostly brothers toward the front of the meeting hall.

A large black drape with stripes of red, green and yellow provided the backdrop for the raised platform on which he would stand.

The scent of ganja smoke and incense laced the room.

Stratagem felt the energy of angry emotions in the air. Pent-up energy. Ready for explosion. *Good. They were ready.* Tonight, he would set the stage for action.

He gazed at his audience, sipping water from a glass on the table. Observing. Collecting his thoughts. The excited chatter in the room diminished as he adjusted the microphone. He listened to the private conversation of the small group in front of him who had yet to focus their attention on him. Organizing his papers with his head down, Stratagem directed his attention to them and their words drifted through his mental processor. He waited for the right cue to trigger his response.

"Hey man, you know what we gotta do now," a man in the front row said. "They done killed Walter. It was a setup. We all knows it was a setup."

"How you know dat?" a fat man wearing a bright red oversized t-shirt asked.

"Everybody on the street know dat," said an angry man with a Caribbean accent. "Strong Black men talkin' too loud just get taken out. They always cut 'm down."

"Black man don't have no chance if we don't dance to the tune of the master."

Stratagem commanded the talkers' attention with his gaze. They fell into silence, lured in by the leader's powerful dark eyes. He focused on each man before he spoke.

"We have no master other than God," Stratagem said with force. "We are free."

He allowed the words to hang in the air.

"Are my brothers free who're behind bars?" shouted a teenager in dreadlocks who had leapt to his feet. "What good is freedom with no money and no way to make money?"

"We can't find a job no more even if we do dance to the man's tune," said a man with a clean haircut. "Over-educated. Under-employed. Now they're bulldozing the public school system and making our teaching degrees worthless. Throwing us in the streets with the unemployed. Calling us lazy. All Professor Rodney wanted to do was teach us, but they forced him out onto the streets with the rest of us. Making us desperate animals fighting in the jungle for survival. At the end of the day, even Professor Rodney with a Ph.D. couldn't find a job."

"Stop looking for a job," Stratagem said. "Rodney created his own job to service the community. The man ain't gonna treat you right. The people gotta make things right. Listen up. A man must become free in his mind first. We gotta have a revolution, just like they did."

"A revolution? Are you crazy? They'll annihilate us."

"A true revolution begins in the mind," Stratagem said. "We gotta stop thinking we're powerless. We have boundless power. If we unite, they can't control us."

"They'll kill us," the fat man in the red t-shirt said.

"Listen," Stratagem said, raising his voice. "The price of freedom is death. We'll never be free unless we're willing to join Malcolm X and Martin Luther King. A man who is afraid to die will never be equal to a man without fear. They will always be slaves to the system."

He paused for impact.

"There can be no peace in this country until the Black man is given his due.

"Tell me: Why should the descendants of our ancestors' oppressors be allowed to pass on their ill-gotten gains from generation to generation in perpetuity?"

Stratagem let the question float for effect. "This is a political question we must force an answer to with violence, if necessary. The courts will not hear us if the people don't make our right to economic justice from past acts of aggression a compelling national issue."

His eyes moved across the room.

He raised his head to the heavens with open arms.

Then he shouted at the top of his lungs, "We are still due reparations."

The crowd roared in agreement.

Flinging his arms wide, his hands balled into tight fists, he said, "The wounds of slavery are too deep for a few decades of failed government programs to heal us."

Then he lowered his voice. "But something is changing. Oh, yes. Something is changing. When an educated Black man loses a job, he often finds he's over-educated for the low-level jobs available for the underclass, and under-educated for the available high tech and skilled jobs. Today, the market only values highly skilled Black men."

"Yeah." A laid-off schoolteacher, who had stopped Stratagem on the way in to warn him that undercover police were present, stood with a smoldering glare. "But some things haven't changed. Very little has changed for the educated Black man who doesn't know how to keep his mouth shut. We're being cut down on all fronts and that includes the sell-outs."

"Co-optation," Stratagem said with narrowed eyes. "That's what they do with highly educated Black folks. Let them in the upper-class country clubs. Tell them they're better than the lot they came from. Tell them they're equal and then put them on display in some high position. But it's still a mess backstage when the curtains go down—the exploitation goes on.

"But let's not hate on those who are getting over," Stratagem continued. "We need them to join us. Divided, we fall. Didn't they say 'give me liberty or give me death?'"

"Respect me or put me to death," the youth with dreadlocks shouted. "That's what Malcolm X said, the same damn thing the Founding Fathers said back in 1776. Makes you wonder why we weren't freed back then, don't it?"

"We weren't freed then because we didn't fight for our freedom like they did. The slaves accepted a life in chains out of fear for their lives. You can't be free if you're afraid."

Stratagem checked the audience for their full attention before saying in a powerful voice, "We must unite to resist oppression and claim what is ours by birthright."

Applause erupted throughout the room.

"How we gonna do dat?" the man in the red t-shirt said.

"Start a revolution in the minds of the people," Stratagem said. "A revolution starts in the minds of individual people who are willing to die for their loved ones and freedom. That's what Walter Rodney wanted—a revolution! And that's why they killed him."

Chapter Forty-Two

Senator Graham sensed the portal of opportunity would not stay open long.

The *New York Times* article that he held in his hands explained his proposed constitutional amendment and described the state ratification process currently underway. It elucidated in detail why over ten thousand attempts to amend the U.S. Constitution had failed. Yet, in spite of those odds, Graham's proposed amendment was unbelievably close to passage.

The article commented on the circumstances that had led to the retirement of Justice William O. Douglas. Stroke. Obvious incapacity. Incontinence. The Douglas situation was a glaring example of the need for the involuntary retirement amendment. An editorial urged the New York State legislature to ratify.

But would it be enough?

The caption on the *New York Times* article read: *Two States Short: Will it Die?*

Graham pulled an analysis of progress on state ratification efforts from his side file drawer. Thirty-six states had approved. Ten states had voted not to ratify. Only four states were still undecided.

Graham feared the ratification process in these states would die if no action were taken now. Technically, the states had six years to ratify an amendment, but rarely did they approve it past the first year of a request. Time was of the essence. Only two weeks remained.

The final states' legislatures were scheduled to recess by the Fourth of July.

Graham picked up the phone and called the chair of the New York Assembly's Ways & Means Committee. "This is Senator Graham from Michigan. I sit on the Senate Judiciary Committee in Washington. We have a big problem we're trying to manage over at the Supreme Court. Did you see the *New York Times* article on Justice Galt?"

"Yes, I glanced at it this morning. Didn't know about the Douglas issue."

"Quiet as it's been kept, dementia is a serious matter threatening the integrity of the Court," Graham continued. "We need New York. Do you think you can shepherd it through by the end of your term? We need your leadership to make it happen."

"Don't know if I can get it through now. We've got to balance the state budget by June thirtieth. We've got some tough issues. Our politics are messy. I'll try in the fall."

"I think this is the best time for a ratification vote," Graham pushed gently. "This is important for the country. Huge. We can't let the legal elite manage Galt's seat."

"I'll see what I can do, but I'm not making any promises. Things are crazy around here."

"It's crazy everywhere at the end of the term. I'm counting on you."

Graham turned and called out to his chief of staff, "Call every legislative office in New York and explain the amendment situation to them. Call my contributors with a New York address. We need New York."

"Yes, sir, I'm on New York."

Then Graham called the chair of the Senate Appropriations Committee in Colorado and gave him the same line. He barked to his legislative aide, "You've got Colorado. Get on it."

Next, Graham called the Capital Budget chair in New Hampshire, who agreed to champion the matter. New Hampshire was assigned to his executive assistant.

Finally, Graham made the distress call to the Senate Majority Leader in Utah.

Graham briefed him, then recruited him to motion for a vote on the amendment. The Utah senator told him there was little hope for ratification in his state. But he would push it.

Graham gave the Utah assignment to his press secretary.

"Launch a public relations campaign for passage in each state," Graham said.

All day long, his staff fielded calls from legislative staffs in the last four undecided states: New York, New Hampshire, Utah, and Colorado. Graham personally made appeals. He canceled his lunch appointment. With calls coming in and going out at a furious pace, there was no time for a leisurely lunch with K Street lobbyist Michael Spade. Spade would have to wait.

In two weeks, New Hampshire and Colorado ratified.

There was a celebration in Graham's office.

When John Galt learned of the amendment's passage, his mental defenses fortified. Calculating his options, he had one dominating thought: *he would not be forced out*. He knew that was why Graham had worked so hard to get the amendment passed—to get rid of him.

Galt needed to figure out how he was going to do battle with the devil.

Chapter Forty-Three

Urban Times Media Office
Friday, June 15

Sam Knight plopped the telephone receiver on its cradle as Julianne LaSalle barged into his office gripping her latest submission. She smelled cigar smoke and located the offending odor rising from a pile of ashes on his desk. A cancer threat she couldn't ignore.

She frowned at his ashtray, then at him, pursing her lips while leaning to the left.

Without regard for her obviously sour disposition, Sam was in a cheerful mood.

"The little piece you wrote on your hospital visit with Galt hit the mark."

"What do you mean? Did he resign?"

"Nope."

"Well if he's still on the bench, I missed the mark."

"I just got off of the phone with Senator Graham and he's gonna call for Galt's retirement on Thursday due to physical incapacity to serve."

"Why waste the effort? Galt's not going to resign."

"It's not going to be wasted effort. New Hampshire and Colorado ratified last night. Graham got the magic number of thirty-eight ratifying states to amend the Constitution. It's done. An involuntary retirement process for the Supremes is now in place."

"Are you telling me the truth?" she asked with wide eyes.

"The stars lined up. The integrity of the Court had to be protected."

"You really think my article helped make it happen?"

"With a little help from Galt's law clerks who tried to do too much, plus the reports of Jennie Galt taking control of his chambers, and the piece on the retirement of former Justice William O. Douglas that appeared in last week's *New York Times*."

"Wow," she said. "But still, nothing's really changed. We only have four justices—"

"Senator Graham obviously knows something we don't, or he wouldn't be calling for the retirement. Graham is setting the stage."

"What's the process for involuntary retirement again?"

"Five of the justices send letters to the Chair of the Senate Judiciary Committee which culminates in a Senate vote to ratify the action of the Court. That's it. A simple majority of the U.S. Senate concurring and it's done."

"Giving the Court the power to force involuntary retirements might make more of the justices retire at a reasonable age—instead of holding on until the eve of death."

"Tell me what you're going to tell our readers about the separation of powers argument. Somebody's going to argue this is a violation."

"Let me think," Julianne said. "The Supreme Court keeps all of its power, so long as they don't try to boot anybody out of the Marble Palace. If they do, they are checked first by the Senate Judiciary Committee, then the full Senate. The Senate only gets to ratify or reject their decision if the Court puts the ball in play. It's like the Supreme Court has the ball, but the Senate doesn't get to swing at a curve ball unless the Court decides to pitch it."

"You've got it. That's a good analogy. Use it in one of your stories."

"But given the current players on the Court, I have to call Galt safe."

Sam shot back, "I'm calling Galt out. Senator Graham was just appointed Chair of the Senate Judiciary Committee. I think my man has a game plan."

"I hope so. But meanwhile, what's wrong with this?" Julianne held out her draft of an article for publication. On the top of the draft, *SEE ME IMMEDIATELY* was written in red.

"Nothing. I just wanted to see you as soon as you came in. I've already got it set for the front page. Great work. I enjoyed reading it."

"You upset me for nothing?"

"I had my reasons."

"What?"

"The chambers of Justice Katherine Ross just called. She's granting your request for an interview. Her secretary said to call the marshals' office at the Supreme Court to be patched through to her chambers for a time. I just wanted to make sure you got the message."

Chapter Forty-Four

Monday, June 18
U.S. Supreme Court Building

In the Justices' Conference Room, Katherine spoke on the sixth case discussed that day. It was the Texas capital punishment case. The oral argument had been made forty-eight hours before. Galt had missed it. He was still at home recuperating from the blast and the amputation of his right arm; his left hand was of limited use as he was right-handed. As a result, Galt's wife now signed his name on memos and notes giving orders to his staff.

His chambers controlled his signature stamp—used without Galt's active oversight.

In reality that meant Nathan Butt, a law clerk, was in control of Galt's chambers.

What she said now wouldn't make a difference to Galt since he wasn't there to hear her.

Adding to her frustration, she knew it didn't matter to him what she thought because he had already cast his vote without listening to the oral arguments or the viewpoints of his colleagues. Had he even read the case? The process wasn't supposed to work like this.

Katherine was nervous, placing her glass of water on a coaster and gazing toward the Chief Justice. She was the last to speak on the case. Her moment had arrived. Inside she felt a repressed, angry energy stiffen her back as she realized she was powerless to make a difference in this case. Five votes against the defendant had already been cast to uphold the state's decision to execute the petitioner, if Galt had already voted as expected.

She willed the anger of injustice away as she surrendered to the Supreme Court process of decision that was unfolding before her, and she respected the dissenting viewpoints of her colleagues at the table—trying to understand their viewpoints. But she didn't understand. This was wrong.

With a clear voice she stated her dissenting position with vigor.

"We are the Supreme Court—and I believe the Framers had a clear vision that we should be deciding issues of federal law—constitutional and statutory—that are binding on all state and federal courts. We cannot protect the right to freedom of all Americans without ensuring no life can be taken in retaliation or error by the government under any circumstances. That is a core value of liberty. The innocent man on death row should have hope that the highest court in the land will take action to reverse a clear error in the judicial system. I do not respect a state's right to execute innocent people when there is compelling evidence that an error had been made."

She continued, her voice electrifying the space with energy. "Our Founding Fathers, of diverse religious beliefs, formally established life, liberty and the pursuit of happiness as inalienable rights. The Fourteenth Amendment extended those rights to all persons. The state of Texas does not have the legal right to take a human life in error. I vote to save the life of the petitioner. Based upon the new evidence, I believe he is innocent."

There was a moment of silent respect for her position.

Katherine eased back into her cushioned seat with deliberate silence and an unrelenting power gaze at Chief Justice Gaines.

"As previously stated," Justice Gaines said, "Galt's staff has notified my chambers that Galt cast his vote against the petitioner. He supports *stare decisis* in this case. The vote stands at five to four against the petitioner. I assign the writing of the majority opinion to myself."

"I would respect this decision-making process more," Katherine said, raising her chin, "if we looked at the new evidence in this case. I see an innocent man on death row expecting justice from this Court. I see judicial errors and suppressed evidence in this case that have been properly brought to our attention. I will be writing a dissent in this case."

"That's your privilege," Justice Gaines said, pulling his head back at an angle. "You asked me to support the cert in this case. I did. After considering the issue and the increased workload that would result from a change in precedent, my opinion about how the Court should handle death penalty appeal cases did not change. I would be happy to discuss the history of the Court's position on this matter with you privately—"

"Yes," Katherine said. "I would welcome that. But I'm still hopeful we can reach a decision to spare the life of an innocent man on death row."

"Justice Ross," Gaines said in a firm tone, "let's arrange a time to discuss this later. Moving on to another matter, we should discuss Galt's continued absence from our conferences. That, I believe, is the weakness in our decision-making process we should address. Galt should retire. Since he has refused my repeated requests for his resignation, I've decided to issue my letter to Senator Graham."

"Me, too," said Justice Wilson, who was seated across from Katherine.

"I won't hold Galt to a standard that I would not want to be held to, myself," said Justice Martin.

"We should be patient with him," said Justice Kane. "He'll resign in due time."

Sadler fumed. "John Galt isn't going to resign as long as he has breath in his body,"

"I think he needs to go now," said Justice Goodwell.

"I agree," Justice Sadler said. "I'm issuing my letter."

"Under the Constitution, we have a lifetime term," Justice Kane said.

"We have an unlimited term as long as we exhibit good behavior," Chief Gaines said.

"Nobody can prove what he's doing from home," Justice Martin argued. "We all work from home at times. I say we give him a pass. I'd want the benefit of doubt."

But you won't let the man on death row off the hook—that's hypocrisy at its finest.

Katherine slowly placed her Mont Blanc fountain pen on the table, gazing across the expanse of the large conference table at two senior justices and one empty seat. Ever so slightly, she shook her head from side to side.

She felt the tension in the air as all eyes focused on her.

"I am not prepared for this discussion or vote," Katherine said, picking up her notepad. "The vote stands at four to three. I am sure it would be four to four if Galt were present. It takes five letters to begin the involuntary removal process. So I will have the final say."

"Justice Ross," Chief Justice Gaines said, "I believe the integrity of this Court is being tarnished. The press knows Galt is not actively engaged with his law clerks at the Court, yet his individual dissents and opinions keep on rolling out of his chambers."

"That's a problem," Justice Kramer said.

"I wasn't finished," Chief Justice Gaines said, his eyes trained on Katherine. "Politics aside—we need to act now to prevent the possibility of irreversible damage to the Court—before we recess and you leave for London."

Creating breathing space, Katherine slowly put her notepad on the table.

The Chief had no more power than she did. She would not be bullied into a quick decision. Katherine sat up straight in her chair, then said, "I appreciate all of your viewpoints, but I am not yet convinced Justice Galt should be removed."

Several eyes around the table grew wide in surprise.

She continued, "I think Galt should resign, but I'm not sure going through an involuntary removal process is in the Court's long-term best interest. So I'm still deliberating."

Chapter Forty-Five

The U.S Supreme Court
Thursday, June 20

Julianne LaSalle downloaded information from the BAMN meeting that she had attended a few days before and slid it across a conference table to Justice Ross. "I think Stratagem is going to be much more effective in organizing the community than Walter Rodney was. He's got charisma. Great oratory skills. They've definitely got—"

Katherine cut Julianne off in mid-sentence and slid the papers back to her. "Ask to see Hal—my security officer—and give this to him. How many were in attendance?"

"Close to five hundred. He's really stirring them up. You need to be careful. Have you issued your letter to Graham?"

"No." Katherine was surprised at the question. "Why do you ask?"

"Senator Graham said he had him."

"Has who?" Katherine's tone conveyed annoyance.

"Galt. This morning at the Press Club, Graham said, 'I've got the Chief's letter for Galt's retirement. That makes four. I expect to have the fifth letter by the end of the day.'"

"Did he really say that? Well, I'm not issuing a letter to Graham today, and I don't know how he gets to five without me. The senator shouldn't be so confident. Don't print what I said."

"Why not? You have to—"

"No, I don't."

"If you don't, you could become a target," Julianne warned. "They're serious."

"I won't be intimidated."

"But everybody expects you to take him out. If you don't issue your letter, everybody will be wondering what's wrong with you. They'll think you're a sellout."

"There's a lot to consider. I just haven't decided yet. Print that. I'm worried it could hurt the Court. Things could get too political over in the Senate."

"But Gaines has issued his letter to Graham," Julianne said. "His was the letter nobody thought would be issued."

"That doesn't make it right."

"If you don't issue the letter this week—"

"Nothing will happen."

"You'll be holding us back and helping racism rise again."

"The problems that hold us back are greater than just race," Katherine said, pursing her lips. "Class matters. Fear paralyses. Greed prevails. Rational self-interest rules everywhere."

"That's why the radicals have taken to the streets pushing for socialism."

Shaking her head, Katherine said, "Socialism is not the panacea for our economic ills."

"Has the Supreme Court been co-opted by the business community and wealthy elite?"

"I can't answer that. Appointments to the Supreme Court are political. I'll be the first to admit that. That's why we have the confirmation hearings—to allow the people to have a say in who gets on the Supreme Court through the political process. Unfortunately the confirmation process is broken and has been turned into an embarrassing spectacle that needs to be fixed."

Katherine paused as Julianne wrote at the speed of a racecar.

"Money and votes—that's what drives the political process. No one group of people is in total control of this country. With nine justices randomly appointed over time, the chances of the Supreme Court being controlled by any one party or group, like the business community, is reduced. But if our Court has been co-opted, it's because the masses let that happen by not understanding that their power at the ballot box drives the political process."

"Are you saying the business community is not driving the decisions of the Court?"

"All I can say for sure, Julianne, is they're not driving my decisions."

Julianne completed her note and leaned forward in her chair. "Okay. Let's get back to the news of the day. Why won't you issue a letter to take out Galt now?"

"It might not be a wise thing to do."

"Please explain to me why leaving him in place is a wise thing to do."

Katherine said nothing, annoyed with the persistent line of questioning.

"Don't just leave me to speculate on why you won't take him out," Julianne said.

"I need to speak to him before I decide—and I don't know when that will be."

Julianne felt the silent vibration of her cell phone. She pulled it out of her pocket and viewed an incoming text. Her eyes widened. The message was from Senator Graham.

The text read: *Four letters on my desk. Waiting on Kathy. Can you help with her?*

"Excuse me," Julianne said, tapping a reply.

Her message was short: *No!*

"Four letters for Galt's involuntary retirement are now sitting on Graham's desk," Julianne said. "The pressure for you to issue the fifth letter is on. Do you have a stronger comment for the community on when you might issue the fifth letter?"

Katherine stood up. "If Galt is incapacitated, he should resign before I take action."

She folded her arms. If Julianne misquoted her, she wouldn't be back.

Julianne put her notepad away. "Okay. It's on you, Kathy."

Chapter Forty-Six

Friday, June 21

Give me a call. We have personal matters to discuss.

All night long, Katherine tossed in her bed with the sound of Graham's voice repeating like waves crashing against a seawall. She felt possessed by an unwanted feeling of attraction. She had seen him again at a White House dinner a few weeks before.

She realized he was near when she smelled his Old Spice cologne.

He said in a low tone near her ear, "We need to talk about us."

The alarm beside her bed went off at 5:45 a.m. But her thoughts of him continued their dance.

At 5:50 a.m. she willed herself to a seated position. Where had the five minutes gone? She got up, showered and dressed.

Her driver would be waiting for her at 6:30 a.m.

At 6:35 a.m., Katherine slid into her fortified Suburban holding a metallic coffee mug in one hand and her black leather briefcase in the other.

"Good morning," Hal said, cranking the ignition. "How are you today?"

"I'm dragging." She closed her eyes for a moment—then added, "I didn't sleep well."

"The work getting to you?"

"No, the wrong guy."

"A guy?" Hal grinned. "That's good news. You've never mentioned a guy before."

"No," Katherine replied without smiling. "Not good news. He's no good for me."

"You've got a crush," Hal said, teasing. "Do I know him?"

"Everybody knows him."

"Must be a great catch."

"Why would you say that?"

"If everybody knows him and he's keeping you up at night thinking about him, he has to be a great catch."

"If he were, somebody would have caught him by now."

"Maybe he's just waiting for a woman of your stature. Has he called you?"

"No. He's waiting for me to call him."

"Did he give you a private number?"

"Yes, he gave me his cell number."

"Your Honor, I think you should call him."

Katherine did not respond.

The driver continued, "You don't expect him to file a pleading, do you? Don't be so uptight. There are only a few men who would be right for you. Listen to your heart."

"You don't know who he is," Katherine said, closing her eyes. "Let me rest for a few moments."

Katherine's vehicle moved down Independence Avenue on the way to the secure garage beneath the Supreme Court Building, with another black SUV on its tail.

Stratagem got a text from Shawn: *They'll be crossing your path in fifteen minutes.*

Perched on top of a building with a high-powered lens, Stratagem snapped a picture of Hal and the license plate of Justice Ross's vehicle as it approached First Street.

Katherine remained out of view behind black glass with her eyes closed.

Stratagem texted Shawn back: *The timing must be exact. It took ten minutes. We'll check it again next Friday.*

At 6:55 a.m., Katherine walked into her inner office, closing the door behind her. She was the first to arrive. Bright sunlight hit the flowers on her desk making their rainbow colors vibrant.

She surrendered to impulse, picking up the phone on her desk and dialing the cell phone number written on the back of Skip's business card.

He answered on the third ring.

"This is Kathy."

"How are you?" the senator asked. "I've been waiting to hear from you."

"Yes," she said with hesitation in her voice. "It would have been longer if I hadn't called you."

"But you said you would call me," he said. "So I've been waiting on you."

"You don't expect me to believe that, do you?"

"Of course I do, because it's true."

"If you wanted to talk, why didn't you call me?"

"I was afraid you might hang up on me after so much time had passed."

"Thirty years is a long time to wait for a guy to follow up." Anger forced its way up her throat and took over. "You're right. If I were smart, I would never have called you. I should hang up now. I do know what my risks are with you."

"I hope you don't, because I've waited thirty years for you to break down and call me."

"Why did I need to break down to call you?"

"Because that's the only way that it could work. Especially now with all that's going on with Court politics."

"Yes. You've been plenty busy with us."

"Somebody has to be." The senator paused. "When are you submitting your letter on Galt?"

"I don't know. I'm not sure it's the right thing to do."

"Not sure? How can you not be sure? You do know Justice Gaines submitted his letter? You can take Galt out with the stroke of your pen."

"What I do to him, I do to myself."

"The people need you to protect us from him. He needs to go. You know that."

Katherine spoke in her professional voice. "Well, I'm still deliberating on the matter. Nobody knows why the Chief rushed and submitted his letter to you, and I'm not going to speculate on his motives. I have an independent job to do to protect this country. You'll get it when I know it's right."

"You're the fifth letter," Skip said. "There are four letters on my desk right now certifying he's not able to carry out the responsibilities of his office from your fellow justices. A letter from you, a private committee hearing, and it's over for Galt. It can be over in ninety days."

"I told you, I'm deliberating."

"I'm counting on you, just like you counted on me without having to say a word."

"No, I didn't count on you. In fact, after thirty years, I had no reason to count on you for anything. Not even a phone call. So I didn't count on your vote. And you shouldn't count me as a sure thing."

"I'm sorry," Skip said in a lower tone. "I shouldn't have brought it up."

"No, you shouldn't have."

"I told you about my wife. You knew I wasn't ready for a serious relationship back then. I always knew you were strong and I—"

"Skip," she said, cutting him off before her emotions reached the boiling point. "I shouldn't have called you. Things between us can't work now. I have to reach my own judgment on Galt. I can't let you influence that. I'm not there yet. So let's just leave it alone. Goodbye."

She quickly replaced the phone in its cradle without waiting to hear his reply. Her attention immediately turned to the pile of legal briefs and memos on her desk.

She worked with quiet resignation as random thoughts of him continued to play in her mind. Each time, she reminded herself, she was not going to give him another chance to hurt her. She had work to do. She had had enough of him.

Within minutes, she had closed the emotional shield to her heart as she blocked out all thoughts of him. Assuming the mentality of an executioner, Katherine focused her mental capacities on the tasks at hand.

All memories of the senator were erased and placed on a shelf in her subconscious mind.

Waiting for a summons.

*****

Skip looked at his phone in disbelief, realizing that she had actually hung up on him. That had not happened to him in years. Normally he could handle the ladies without a blowup. But dealing with her had always been different. Although they hadn't spoken intimately in thirty years, there was still chemistry between them.

He could feel it.

In fact, that was the reason he had pushed her away before. He simply hadn't been ready to feel love again. Love hurt too much. He knew he had hurt her by pushing her away.

He had been wrong.

Skip scrolled to his phone log and saved her unattainable private number. He keyed in the name Kathy with one bull-headed thought: *It's not over yet.*

Then he summoned the courage to call her back and pressed the send button over her highlighted name. To his surprise, the number being dialed showed all zeros on his phone's display.

The automated operator stated, "The number that you have reached cannot be completed as dialed. Please check the number and try again."

He scrolled back to her number. It was a four-digit number. 1959.

The year of her birth.

Now that he was ready to pursue her, there was no way he could privately call her back. Calling her public office number was out of the question.

Skip knew her. She wouldn't take his call under the present circumstances.

He considered her security protocols as a sitting justice on the United States Supreme Court with the Court on high security alert. He considered his position. Separation of powers.

She didn't have to speak to anyone she didn't want to speak to.

He was blocked.

Chapter Forty-Seven

Sunday, June 23
The Ritz-Carlton Residences

At 11:00 a.m., Katherine sat in her workout clothes at her kitchen counter, a glass of iced tea cooling her hands. Hal, her security officer, had finally convinced her to alter her Sunday routine, including dinners with her mother. There was no place safer than her own kitchen. Sometimes Katherine cooked. Other times, they just ordered in from a nearby restaurant in the Georgetown section of the city. That day, they had a take-out meal of veal piccata from Café Bonaparte, one of Katherine's favorite restaurants.

"Did you report what Julianne said to the marshal's office?" her mother asked, throwing away the empty containers.

"Yes. They seemed concerned and asked me a lot of questions."

"What did they ask?"

"How long was Walter Rodney a member at the church. The nature of my relationship with Julianne. Whether or not she can be trusted."

"What did you tell them?"

"That I don't know how long he's been at the church. That I don't know him at all. Julianne's concerned BAMN might turn violent. She sees a rebel mentality growing."

"They should have known you didn't know him," her mother said with a slight tone of indignation. "What did you tell them about Julianne?"

"She's a childhood friend. Hates Galt and has always been vocal about it. But she's nonviolent and will pass on information to me if she feels I'm in danger. She expects me to issue the fifth letter and thinks I have a moral obligation to the Black community to issue it. I feel conflicted. Will Galt be able to perform in a few months? Nobody knows. The community expects me to issue the execution order. Even Skip asked me about it on Friday."

"You talked to him?" her mother asked, edging closer in her seat. "I saw the way he looked at you at the reception at the Marriott a few weeks ago. What's going on?"

"What do you mean?" Katherine was unwilling to open to her mother's attempt to pry into her past relationship with the senator. Again.

"You know what I mean."

"Please."

"Well, don't lose yourself trying to help a boy."

"That's what you always say." For the first time, she understood why her mother had always issued that warning—but then decided not to reveal that she had started to read her memoir. "I'm not going to take out a Supreme Court justice just because Skip wants me to."

"Don't let him put you in a vulnerable position."

"Mom, how many times have you said that to me?"

"Not enough, yet."

Katherine thought the time might be right. "Are you ready to tell me who my father is?"

"Not now. It's a long story."

"We have time. I'll have a glass of wine with you."

"It's a painful story for me," her mother said, getting up and moving toward the bottle of merlot on the far end of the counter. "It's hard for me to talk about it."

"I still need to know." Katherine watched her reach for a wine glass.

"You might not like what you find out."

"Mom, I believe in facing the truth, no matter how painful it might be."

Her mother poured herself a generous glassful. "Have you finished reading Part I?"

"No."

"If you couldn't handle that, you're not ready for Part II. I know you started it."

"Why can't you just tell me who my father is?"

"I can't," her mother said, taking more than a small sip. "You just have to accept that. You need to understand everything to understand me. You had a privileged upbringing. I don't want to be judged out of context. When you finish Part I, I'll give you Part II."

"Can I read it now?"

"No," her mother snapped.

Katherine waited, hoping her mother would break the silence. She didn't.

"Okay. I know I can't force it out of you. When I finish Part I, we'll talk."

Changing the subject her mother asked, "Did you promise the senator anything?"

"No. He understands my position. And I'm sure he doesn't like it."

"I know how much pressure you must be under. Be strong."

"I think all of us on the Court will be more vulnerable if we take him out."

"If that's true, why did Gaines issue his letter? Is it some type of power play?"

"I don't know. The Chief hasn't said much."

"What did he say?"

"'I hereby give notice to the Senate Judiciary Committee that Associate Justice John T. Galt is unable to carry out the duties of his office.' That's all he's publicly said on the matter, and I can't say what he said in private conference."

"There's no scuttlebutt about why Gaines issued his letter?"

"Nope. The main scuttlebutt is about me. Everyone expects me to issue the fifth letter."

Her mother broke in, "You can't. Not before you try to save him."

"Why not? I cried when I read his cert memo on the Texas capital punishment case," Katherine said with sadness. "His rejection was heartbreaking. Cold. Mean spirited. He didn't have to say everything he said to kill the man's spirit. Galt might be beyond salvation."

"Don't judge him yet. Assume he has a good heart under his battle-worn exterior."

"His actions indicate he has a hardened heart, if he has one at all. Last I talked to him, he was willing to let the innocent die on death row. But he told me he might reconsider his position on some things. He told me a secret—I don't know if I should believe him or not. I need to talk to him before I decide."

"Maybe he didn't have a chance to change his position."

"That's the point. If he's competent and in control, he should have changed his vote before we discussed the case. I just don't know how he could issue some of the opinions he's issuing." Katherine's emotions spewed. "I feel sick reading some of them."

"Maybe his clerks got some things by him to make him look bad."

"Maybe I should hold him accountable if he hasn't read everything that's been issued in his name."

"Kathy, don't be so quick to issue your letter," her mother said. "There could be more going on with him than meets the eye."

"I'm not—but maybe I should. I don't believe Galt's thinking for himself, but it bothers me that the Chief issued his letter so fast. So I'm not going to be quick making a move until I understand the end game."

"Well, maybe he'll see things different now that the Chief has turned on him."

"Maybe."

"Where is he on religion?" her mother asked.

"He says he's spiritual but not religious. I still believe he's an atheist."

"My childhood minister use to say 'an atheist may be closer to God than a religious person who has made no real attempt to know God.' So don't be so quick to judge."

"The current opinions rolling out of his chambers certainly don't reflect a change of spirit. I really think he's an egoist. That would explain his decisions."

"An egoist?"

"Yes, he's surrounded by them. They believe rational self-interest is a virtue. I think John Galt is a character who worships his own human spirit above all else."

Her mother said nothing for a moment, clearly in thought. "Didn't he go to seminary to be a priest? If Galt seriously sought God as a young man, he might not give up his quest as an old man. His views could change."

"It's more likely his views haven't changed. That's what the evidence suggests."

"Katherine, he went to a seminary. Think about it. He might be spiritual just like he says he is."

"I just don't think he's a sage who believes in selflessness and concern for others."

"He's just had a near death experience. You'll know if JT's changed when you see him."

"If I get the chance."

"So what are you thinking?"

"I'm thinking there are only two possibilities: Galt's an atheist with great acting skills or a highly developed spiritual person. If he told that story about the apple tree to anyone else—he could have a problem keeping his supporters."

"Baby, don't issue your letter if things aren't adding up. What's your gut saying?"

Katherine closed her eyes.

"Right now my gut is saying, 'hold.'"

Chapter Forty-Eight

Justices' Conference Room
Thursday, June 27

Tension filled the air.

"Chief, I believe you have an obligation to decide on the thirty cases that you've been holding up," Justice Kane said. "There is no constitutional authority to strip Galt of power. He's still exercising his constitutional power. I urge you to fulfill your responsibilities to the Court."

"All we know for sure is that Nathan Butt is exercising Galt's signature stamp," Justice Goodwell said. "If Galt isn't incapacitated, where is he? This is the end of June and he was injured on April fifteenth—his chambers have been running for over two months without Galt."

Chief Justice Gaines turned toward Katherine. "Justice Ross, we need your decision before Monday. By then Galt's office will have issued twenty-five more opinions and five dissents in his name. We know Jennie Galt is issuing written orders to his staff in his name, maintaining that's her right as his wife. The people have empowered us. We need to act."

"I still need to talk to Galt," Katherine said in a calm tone. "It's my understanding I have until Sunday, October 6 at midnight to issue the fifth letter. Am I correct?"

"We've set the end of this term as June 28," the Chief said. "That's when it's ending."

"The Court's term begins on the first Monday in October," Katherine said. "So I believe we can just take a recess and extend this term until October 6 for the purposes of considering Galt's incapacity to serve. We have that power. The cases that need Galt's vote can still be held over to the next term."

"She's right," said Justice Sadler. "If five of us agree, and I can count to five."

"For Christ's sake, we need to get on with it," Justice Martin said. "The press will kill us if we carry forty opinions over to the next term."

"Why would we hold them over?" Justice Kane asked. "We should issue our opinions with Galt's vote until he's dead or removed. That's what the Constitution calls for."

"Justice Ross, we need to act now to prevent the possibility of irreversible damage to the Court," Gaines said. "We need your decision now."

"Why are we having this discussion?" Justice Kramer asked, elbows on the table, both palms up. "The Constitution didn't ask us to vote as a group. It requires us to issue individual letters, if we believe the circumstances warrant it. We don't have to act in unison."

"I'm not just thinking about Galt," Katherine said. "It's about all of us. I just haven't decided yet. I won't be pushed."

Then Sadler scribbled a note and slid it over: *Don't jump off the bridge for Galt.*

Chief Gaines glanced at Katherine with an expression of irritation. "We can't cripple the Court while Justice Ross decides. As long as five letters have not been issued, we should not strip Galt of his constitutional power. I reinstate my previous votes in the cases where my vote would make five. Galt's opinions will be issued as submitted. We either deal with him or we don't deal with him. Katherine, it takes five of us to deal with him. The ball is in your court."

"I'll issue the fifth letter when I'm sure it's the right thing to do," Katherine said. "I'm recording five votes to extend this term to October 6 with our traditional summer recess beginning on June 28. Are there any corrections to my count of five votes in favor? If not, we are adjourned."

Feeling her power among equals for the first time, Katherine rose to her feet.

Four sets of eyes glared at her.

Chapter Forty-Nine

Monday, July 1
London, England

The caller-ID on his cell phone had read *Unknown Caller*, but Stratagem recognized the voice immediately and listened with interest.

"Surprised you're in town. We're long overdue for a face-to-face. Got big plans. Can we meet on the campus for lunch at one?"

"I'm setting something else up right now," Stratagem said. "Two would be better."

"Okay then—our table at two."

Larry Stratagem wore crisp combat fatigues for the meeting with his old friend on the busy campus of the University of London's School of Oriental and African Studies (SOAS), a futile breeding ground for those with socialist views. They had first met years ago in an economics seminar on international reform and development.

Thus they shared the same worldviews on political economy.

Forged after hours of intense debate.

Stratagem knew that his old friend was a representative of *The Cabal* in China—an influential group of entrepreneurs, now ruling from the top in Shanghai. All of the members of *The Cabal* were billionaires many times over. *The Cabal's* growing economic power in China could not be ignored, but their controlling influence over China's government was always denied.

Stratagem's old friend had told him about the existence of *The Cabal* years ago but had never revealed his real name. Stratagem had simply known him as Joe since the days when they were graduate students at SOAS. In spite of not knowing his real name, they had become lifelong friends and stayed in communication over the years. From time to time, Joe would call and give Stratagem lucrative assignments to further the cause.

With a capitalist education, they agreed, the money was all that really mattered to them.

Money was the power needed to rule the world.

At three, they huddled over tuna fish sandwiches in the student cafeteria at a table they had shared many times before. Joe wore olive green cargo pants with a matching jacket. Over Joe's head hung a sign announcing the next BAMN student meetings.

They both had been student members.

"So it's a disruption strategy," Stratagem said. "How can I help?"

"Can you wake up the Black community?" Joe asked. "They're ripe for agitation."

"What do you want to happen?"

"Destabilize the national government. Riots in the streets, starting with D.C. Then move a wave of fear across the country. Shake their faith in the system. Startle them."

"That will cost a lot of greenbacks," Stratagem said, tilting of his head. "A royal sum."

"Name your price," Joe said. "We're ready..."

Chapter Fifty

London, England
Friday, July 5

Katherine and five of her college classmates—Jolene, Cheryl, Merle, Ronnie and Debbie—stepped out of the Dorchester Hotel. Across the street from the hotel, about one hundred and fifty feet away, the paparazzi stood like a roped-off herd.

Stratagem fit right in with his camera focused, drawing no attention from Katherine's security.

As the women stood in front of the hotel, several photographers snapped pictures of the posse of Black women in jeans, sporty blouses, jeweled baseball caps, sunglasses, and designer jackets. Rare shots of what could be the ladies' last day on planet earth. Money-making pictures.

Hitting Justice Ross in London would make international headlines.

And that would be good for business in more than one way.

With Debbie in the lead, the girls turned right onto Knightsbridge and headed for Sloane Street, an avenue lined with designer stores. Classic black and brightly painted British taxis buzzed by them, moving like schools of fish up and down the crowded street. A red double-decker bus passed. The girls promenaded down the boulevard at a fast clip, chatting along the way.

"Ladies, shall we have tea this afternoon?" Debbie asked in her best snooty voice.

"I don't want tea," Katherine replied. "I want to go over to Pasta Brown. They've got the best food I've had in London at any price. It's little, but nice and reasonable."

"Okay," Ronnie said. "We'll go to Pasta Brown for dinner before the play."

"We'll have to use cars for this evening," Katherine said. "But that will take the pressure off finding taxicabs after the play. It's been arranged."

"Speaking of the pressure," Ronnie said, "when are you going to issue the fifth letter?"

"You know how I feel," Katherine replied. "But I can't right now."

"What do you need?" Debbie asked. "A laxative? You need to just shit him away."

"I can't talk about Galt," Katherine said, while the others jabbed and laughed. "I have a lot to consider. So let's talk about something else, like who can save the most money on a percentage basis on what they buy—the losers have to give the winner a hundred pounds."

"I'm game for that," Ronnie said. "It's *sale time* and we shouldn't be payin' full price."

The girls continued their march to Sloane Street on their hunt for the best summer bargains in London. Entering Harrods, they headed for the bags on the first floor.

Debbie held up their first find. "Look at this a travel bag."

"Now that's bad," Jolene said, gazing at the glitzy silver bag.

Debbie looked at the tag. "Fifty percent off—I'm buying it."

"Over here." Katherine motioned with her hand. "Lavender crocodile."

"That's your color," Jolene said.

"Ohhh, no," Katherine exclaimed. "It's three thousand pounds and it's not on sale."

"That man over there keeps looking at me," Jolene said. "See him? He's following us."

Katherine looked over her shoulder and spotted Hal, her security officer. "Don't worry," she said. "I didn't want to tell you, but I have a security detail. That's probably who Jo saw following us. They'll let me know if we're in danger. You know how things are."

Katherine returned the lavender croc to its display holder.

The girls shopped for hours, and had lunch at the pizza counter in Harrods' Food Hall. The morning passed in a blur of designer offerings, thick sweaters, and the exotic scents of the perfume counter. Everybody found something to buy, but not everyone found great deals.

The shopping party returned to the Dorchester with bags galore. Dropping off their purchases, they made a quick change before hopping into cars with drivers for dinner at Pasta Brown.

Shawn DaPeoples snapped their pictures. Again.

Larry Stratagem shadowed them in a black Range Rover, keeping a safe distance back.

Chapter Fifty-One

On the way to Pasta Brown near busy Leicester Square, Katherine spotted the rare books store she had visited with her mother and father years before. It brought back fond memories of her first European trip. Her father had purchased an original 1881 copy of *Uncle Remus: His Songs and Sayings* by Joel Chandler Harris at her mother's urging.

Because of *Uncle Remus,* she had recognized the Gullah dialect in *Hattie's Story.*

A brightly lit OPEN sign hung in the bookstore window.

She hoped it would be open later.

The girls were hit with the aroma of simmering tomatoes and Italian seasonings at the door of Pasta Brown in Covent Gardens. The tiny restaurant had modern decor with dark paneling, a mirrored wall, and chrome finishes. A waiter pushed three small tables together, making a table of six for them. Each table was set with a single yellow rose and two wine glasses. Simple. The history of the Italian family who owned the restaurant was written on the mirrored wall behind their tables, with the dessert menu posted above Katherine's head.

The old friends had red wine and chatted gaily about the bargains they'd found. They began their meal with bruschetta, mussels marinated in white wine, and king prawns sautéed in garlic butter. Next, their waiter served platters of bright green broccolini and spinach, pizza, spaghetti and lasagna. They all shared, family style. Plates and glasses clanked.

"I can't help it," Merle said to Katherine. "I gotta ask—What's up with Galt?"

"I haven't figured him out yet."

"You don't have to figure him out," Jolene said. "You gotta take him out."

"I've got to do what's right," Katherine said, looking Jolene in the eye.

Merle pushed. "Then you gotta take him out. He'd take you out, if they told him to."

"Look," Katherine said with a look of steel, "can we drop it?"

"No," Jolene replied. "We can't drop it."

"What could be worse than leaving him on the bench?" Debbie asked. "I wanna know…"

"Putting a Roger B. Taney on the bench," Katherine replied.

"Who's he?" Ronnie asked.

"The Chief Justice who wrote the 1857 Dred Scott decision that said slaves aren't protected by the U.S. Constitution and can never be U.S. citizens. It took the Fourteenth Amendment to undo its damage. Hey, I'm on vacation." Shaking her head and waving her hands she added, "So conversation about Galt *is* over for the rest of this trip."

"Well I guess she's ruled." Debbie pouted with mocked attitude.

"Have you heard from Skip?" Jolene asked with a knowing glance.

"No," Katherine replied in a quiet voice. "Not really."

"Not really?" Ronnie parroted. "Come on, girl. You're holding back on us."

Katherine's chin went up. "I hung up on him and I don't want to talk about it either."

"You hung up on the chair of the Judiciary Committee?" Merle asked.

"No, I hung up on Skip when he stepped out of bounds and I called it. Game over."

"Not before a touchdown," Cheryl jabbed. "Seeing anybody else?"

"I haven't had time to see anyone else," Katherine said. "I'm a hard match."

"Well, if you think that, why are you giving Skip such a hard time?" Jolene asked. "I never understood why you two couldn't figure it out. We know you have a thing for him."

"He's no good for me," Katherine said, feeling flushed. "Besides, our positions won't allow it. Can we change the topic?"

"Well, I think it's your position that makes it work," Ronnie said.

"Yeah," Merle said. "A senator and a Supreme Court justice—that works."

"Not if he's chair of the Senate Judiciary Committee," Katherine said, holding back sharp words. "Sort of a conflict of interest, I think. We're finished. And I really want to go around the corner to a rare books store I saw. We've got a little time. Want to go with me?"

"I'd rather go to a big bookstore," Jolene said.

"Me, too," said Cheryl. "I saw one down the street. I want to buy a paperback book."

"I'm going with Cheryl and Jolene," Debbie said. "Meet you at the theatre."

"Count me in," Ronnie said to Debbie. "I want to find a great meditation book."

Katherine felt like her friends were deserting her. Even Cheryl had groaned at her.

"I don't really want any books," Merle said. "I'll go with Kathy. Keep her company."

After paying the bill, Merle and Katherine made their way back to the rare books shop. When Katherine attempted to open the door, she was surprised to find it locked. She located a buzzer and pressed it. A young man with blond hair peered through the door.

"May I help you?"

"I'm interested in making an investment," Katherine said.

He unlatched and opened the door to the dimly-lit store.

As Katherine entered the cramped space, she could smell the old books.

"What's your best buy at this time?" Katherine asked.

"A first edition printing of *War and Peace*," he said with an English accent. "It's a thousand pounds. Is that within your budget?"

"That would be in Russian. I need English."

"Then it would be Adam Smith. Volume One and Volume Two of *An Inquiry: Nature And Causes of The Wealth Of Nations*. A very rare find."

"How much is *The Wealth of Nations*?"

"Seventy-five thousand pounds," the bookstore clerk said with an English air.

"That's over a *hundred thousand dollars!*" Merle exclaimed.

"What's the most a copy of *The Wealth of Nations* has sold for?" Katherine inquired.

"A bound copy of the first edition with additions and corrections for the first and second editions sold for ninety-five thousand pounds at auction a few years back."

"You really thinkin' about it?" Merle asked.

"Maybe. When was it published?"

"March 9, 1776," the bookstore clerk replied. "The year the American Revolutionary War started. George Washington had a first edition copy. The one we have for sale was owned by the famous American financier Robert Morris."

"Can I see it?" Katherine asked.

"I'm sorry," the storekeeper said with an air of superiority. "That book is very rare and only potential buyers are allowed to handle it."

"And what makes you think I'm not a potential buyer?"

"You would need a black American Express Card to handle those books," the storekeeper said, raising his nose. "Unless you have another bank relationship we can verify."

Katherine reached into her purse and held up her black card as she said, in a mocking English accent, "Will this do, sir?"

The storekeeper gazed at the black titanium card in shock. "Of course."

He scurried to his cluttered desk past a wooden ladder that looked a hundred years old. There he put on white gloves before rushing back to retrieve the rare books from a vault.

He placed Volume One of *The Wealth of Nations* on a foam cushion and handed Katherine a new pair of white linen gloves in a clear package.

She examined the volumes with satisfaction sparkling in her eyes. "Can I get them for less than seventy-five thousand pounds? The bindings are worn."

"No. I'll get my price."

She bargained. "I would buy them for fifty thousand pounds now."

"Sorry, no deals on Adam Smith. The price is the price."

Katherine turned and headed for the door, hoping he would stop her. She put her hand on the doorknob. Would he let her walk out? She waited before turning around.

"Okay." Katherine reached into her purse again for her wallet. "I'll buy it."

"I can't believe you'd pay that much for old books," Merle said.

Katherine explained, "There's more than one way to hold wealth. These books are an investment. Our economy is based on the principles espoused in these books. They're part of the knowledge associated with the founding of our country. This is a significant investment for me."

Bouncing down the street with excitement, Katherine thought of Robert Morris. She would have one of her clerks do some research on him. How had these books passed hands for over two hundred years, ending up in London for her purchase that day? Coincidence? Fate?

Katherine glanced over her shoulder, again feeling she was being watched. But she knew her bodyguards were behind her. Watching her every step. She sped up.

Merle complained. "Why are you walking so fast?"

Katherine didn't answer. It was dusk. Then she noticed the shadow of a man as he paced in front of her. He wore all black. She was spooked.

She told herself there was no need to be paranoid; her car was waiting around the corner.

As they dashed to make the opening of *A Chorus Line*, Stratagem's shadow lengthened in the alley while he tracked the movement of her vehicle with his mobile device.

Chapter Fifty-Two

"That was a great show," Katherine said, exiting the Palladium Theater on Argyll Street with her friends and stepping into the night. She surveyed the bustling atmosphere and noticed a broken streetlight on their path. The earth's light had been swallowed. Darkness surrounded them. Her gut quivered. She felt danger. Unexplained, but real. Feeling the cool breeze, she buttoned her tweed jacket. They trudged through the crowds. Everything appeared normal: the bright lights, hip-hop dancers, and busy bistros—but she knew something was off. Her steps quickened. In the distance, Katherine spotted their waiting vehicles near the corner, two black Mercedes with dark tinted windows.

Instinctively, she slowed her pace as they approached the vehicles. *Should she stop?*

"What's wrong?" Cheryl asked.

"The doors should be opening," Katherine said.

At that moment, Jolene's driver got out of the second Mercedes and bowed his head in a greeting to them. From the alley entrance in front of them on the right, two men dressed in black emerged and moved toward them.

From behind them, Katherine heard the code word, "wind."

She stopped in her tracks.

"Let's go," she said, turning on her heels in the opposite direction and speeding back toward the theater. Within moments two male security officers flanked Katherine in front of the tight pack as they pressed through the crowded street.

"The vehicles have been compromised," Hal said. "Glad you picked up the breach. You almost got too far ahead of us."

"Where are we going?" Katherine asked.

"Oxford Circle. The Tube. Underground."

"How far?"

"A couple blocks. Let's move it."

Two more security officers, one male and one female, joined the rear.

As they reached the top of the stairs leading down to the Oxford Circle Underground Platform, they heard a loud explosion.

"Go," Hal ordered. They ran down the stairs along with the stampeding mob. Katherine, surrounded by her protectors, waited on the platform, pinned in the center, uncertain of what would happen next. It was hot. Sweating bodies were everywhere. Pressed together. When the doors of an arriving train opened, they were propelled forward and crushed by a sea of bodies. The door closed and the train took off.

"Was that a bomb?" Ronnie asked.

"Don't know," Katherine replied. "Let's talk later." She turned away and stared at the graffiti on the dirty tiled underground walls that flashed before her, periodically displaying the name of a station stop. Finally, the signs with bright red circles and the word *UNDERGROUND* across the horizontal axis read *Knightsbridge Station.*

"We're getting off here," Hal said as the train came to a stop.

Amazingly, all eleven of them had stayed together. Along with a few other passengers, they proceeded to the escalators. Two vans waited on Knightsbridge.

As they approached, the doors to the vans opened. Katherine slid into the first van between Hal and another security officer. Her friends were directed to the second van.

"We recommend you cut this trip short," Hal said. Their van made a turn in the opposite direction of the Dorchester Hotel. "Explosives were attached to your vehicle. We don't know what happened to your driver. There's an active chapter of By Any Means Necessary at the School of African and Oriental Studies. We don't know if they're involved, but we did get a reliable tip from an informant on campus. You now appear to be a target in London. I'm sorry—you can't behave like a regular tourist traveling with your friends anymore. We're moving you to the U.S. Embassy until we can arrange travel back to the States."

"What about my friends?"

"You and your security detail can be accommodated at the Embassy. We'll move your friends to another hotel. More than likely they can fly back to the States with you, if they want. A government plane will come for you, unless we make other arrangements."

Katherine backed deeper into her seat as the realization of what had almost happened sank in.

She felt hunted, vulnerable, and anxious.

What had she gotten herself into?

That night Katherine settled into a Chippendale armchair with a red seat cushion in the U.S. Embassy and opened the manila folder containing her mother's manuscript. She had brought it along since she had not had any time for recreational reading. Plus, she had not wanted to deal with the painful emotions that made her mother cry. Katherine had felt that she needed a vacation to dig into her past. Time to deal with her mother.

She needed a diversion.

At a side table, tea service with small cakes on a silver platter was her only company for the remainder of the evening. She took a sip of tea. It was bitter in spite of two teaspoons of sugar.

It had steeped for too long.

She turned to the first page of Chapter Two.

HATTIE'S STORY
Chapter Two

Savannah, Georgia
The Morning After It Happened

We reached the city limits of Savannah about eight-thirty in the morning. The city was just waking up, with cars and trucks moving along the busy streets. The sun's rays were already beating on the tops of the tall oak trees that lined Abercorn Street. We parked under flickering shade created by a canopy of branches that protected us from the scorching rays of the sun.

We felt a little safer.

In gratitude, we gave thanks in prayer because we had survived the night.

When I opened my eyes, I saw a lady walking her dog. She wore a beige shirt, white sleeveless ruffled blouse and a beige hat. The sun's rays intermittently bounced off her bobbing blonde curls.

Father Ryan caught her attention. "Where do the coloreds live around here?"

"Everywhere," she said with a southern accent. "Some live with the families they work for, some own houses in town, some live in Needle Pointe."

"Needle Pointe?"

"Yes, about ten miles south of here."

"I've got a good, hardworking colored family with me looking for work," Father Ryan said. "I can't afford them anymore. Could they get jobs in Needle Pointe?"

"I don't know," she said. "Them coloreds kind of keep to themselves, livin' off the land and sellin' crabs to the factory. Don't know a lot 'bout Needle Pointe."

"I was thinking about an old rice plantation where most of the colored help might have gone north—except for the old timers. Do you know a place that needs the help of a whole family?"

"You might try the Jackson Plantation near Moon River," she said. "I heard all of their coloreds left and moved north a few weeks ago. Go see Jackson. He might jump at the offer."

After thanking the lady, Father Ryan started the station wagon and turned us around heading south. With the windows down letting in a cool breeze, we drove out of Savannah.

"Let's eat the pound cake now," Uncle Wash said. Ademus, Uncle Wash's oldest son, reached into the pillowcase and pulled out the cake wrapped in waxed paper. He cut it into seven pieces and passed them around. As we got closer to the Jackson Plantation, the scenery became greener and more vibrant. With a sweet taste in our mouths, we gained a sense of hope. We felt relief from the stress of our late-night drive through the back roads from Dublin.

The fresh morning breeze eased our fears.

Chapter Fifty-Three

Katherine put the pages down. She still felt fear in the confined space around her, although her windows were shut tight and locked. The cookies were tasteless. She peered into the darkness outside of her window. She was behind concrete barricades.

Imprisoned for the night.

Unable to sleep, she turned another page.

HATTIE'S STORY
Chapter Three

Needle Pointe, Georgia
Spring 1946

The Jackson Plantation lay in a serene setting not far from the Isle of Hope off the Atlantic Ocean. It had been a rice plantation during slavery days, with several acres on marshlands adjacent to tranquil waterways. The entrance to the five-hundred-acre estate had a white wooden archway with the name "Jackson Plantation" inscribed in large black letters. A winding dirt road led to the main house with a balcony supported by four columns. Huge oak trees with hanging Spanish moss lined each side of the road, creating a canopied alley. A white picket fence ran around the perimeter of the big house, enclosing a picnic area by a pond off to the right.

A side path led to the horse stables and a smokehouse, while another side path further along the main road shot off to what had been the former slave quarters, now abandoned and fenced-in with decaying wood.

When we arrived at the still magnificent main house, appropriate for an aristocrat of the antebellum south, Father Ryan left us in the crowded station wagon. He crept up the stairs and inspected the expanse of the porch with its peaceful view of a pond. He knocked on the front door. Clayton Jackson answered it.

"Hello, I'm Father Ryan," I heard him say. "I'm doing the Lord's work trying to help deserving Negro families find better working conditions."

"Where you from?" Clayton asked.

"South of Atlanta," Father Ryan said. "These poor people have been working like they're still in slavery and wasn't gettin' hardly nothing for their labors. They been treated real bad. The young girl— well you'll see her—she's had a hard time. I'm helpin' them move on."

"Why you come here?" Clayton asked.

"A kind lady in Savannah told me about you. I understand you need help runnin' this place. If you'll pay them ten dollars a week and give them room and board, the family would be willing to work for you. That's five workers for ten dollars a week."

Mr. Jackson jumped at the offer. "Yes, I think I can help them."

The truth was Mr. Jackson needed us. Even though he was a big time lawyer, he struggled to maintain the lifestyle his ancestors had enjoyed, without the free labor of slaves.

We moved into the former slave quarters, taking the largest cabin. It had a cooking area separate from the main living part with a large table that could seat ten people. We all smiled when we saw it. We were used to eating together as a family. The outhouse had two seats and a door. That was an upgrade. We worked hard and created a new home.

In some ways, it was better than the home we had been forced to desert.

In the backyard, we found apple, orange, fig and pear trees. In front of the cabin were tall oak trees, palm trees, and azalea bushes. A river flowed in and out with the tides about one hundred and fifty feet from our front porch. When the tide came in, we could catch fish from our front yard. We had our own garden, a chicken coop, and a watermelon patch.

Everything we needed to survive.

Often we ate watermelon on hot summer nights. One of life's simple pleasures that we could share as a family. We put a little white picket fence around our cabin. In the spring, when the azaleas bloomed, the setting of our new home looked like heaven.

Uncle Wash and his sons worked as field hands. His sons grew up angry because of the strict discipline he imposed on them. He kept them in line and respectful of the white man. If the boys got out of line, he beat them savagely. Uncle Wash often said, "Better for me to beat dem than da white man. They'll do as dey told, if they're gonna live with me."

My Aunt Annie worked as the Jackson family cook in the big house while I worked as her helper and their maid. Before long, I was given a room in the big house on the first floor, since I often worked after dark.

Charlotte Jackson, Mr. Jackson's daughter, always had something for me to do.

We kept the Jacksons' house and grounds in picture perfect condition.

I did what I was asked to do and kept to myself.

I never complained.

*****

Katherine now realized why her mother had beaten her for minor acts of disobedience as a small child. That's how the children in her family had been raised. Beat the children to make them behave, so the whites wouldn't kill them.

Understanding this for the first time, she turned another page.

HATTIE'S STORY
Chapter Four

Needle Pointe, Georgia
March 1947

It was a starless night with a full moon. Curled up in my bed, I heard the men talking downstairs. Somebody was going to die. There was nothing I could do. So I was silent.

Curtis Adams was a Black man who had restored the sawmill on the Needle Pointe plantation. The sawmill had been abandoned since Sherman's March to the Sea in 1864. Nobody owned it. Adams repaired the sawmill, and made quality wooden planks for construction. His business grew rapidly. At first, he only provided planks to the Blacks in Needle Pointe to build their shacks. But he couldn't make much money just selling to Blacks because they didn't have a lot of money.

There was no way for him to make a lot of money.

One day a white man showed up and bought some lumber from Adams. Adams's wooden planks were better than the ones sold in Savannah that cost three times more. It wasn't long before more whites started to buy their wooden planks from Adams. Most sent their Black workers into Needle Pointe to make their purchases. For many years this arrangement worked well.

Adams's business boomed as he participated in the free market. He charged the whites a little more. After a few years, he was able to buy a used 1933 Ford truck. That meant he could haul lumber into Savannah to sell, providing jobs to Black men in Needle Pointe.

Adams competed with the white sawmills for business. His price was always lower. One day his competitors found out he wasn't working for a white man—he was working for himself—and that was unacceptable under Jim Crow. It was okay for Curtis Adams to sell low-priced lumber to the Blacks, but it wasn't okay for him to sell cheap lumber to whites. It was an affront to white contractors for him to deliver lumber to building sites in Savannah in broad daylight. The whites were outraged at the arrogance of an uppity Negro from Needle Pointe.

Negroes had no right to compete in the free market with white folks.

Never mind the Fourteenth Amendment. This was the South where Jim Crow was the law. Every now and then, Negroes had to be put back in their place. Fear was their weapon.

I heard the white men say Curtis Adams had to be dealt with. They left to get torches, rope, and their white robes. I had seen Mr. Jackson's white hood and robe in a hidden closet.

I heard him go to that forbidden closet.

I was so frightened.

I told no one that Mr. Jackson was in the Ku Klux Klan.

I just pretended not to know.

Later that night, I saw the flames from a safe distance through my second floor bedroom window in the big house. I cried in silence in my bed, alone. Afraid to move. Balled into a tight fetal position. The strong smell of burning wood forced me to think of my daddy's breath being taken away by the smoke and flames at his feet.

With the bed covers over my head, darkness was my only companion.

I felt the presence of evil. I closed my eyes, saying my ABCs.

This is what I learned happened that night.

That night, fifty Klansmen appeared outside of Mr. Adams's small cabin in Needle Pointe. They pulled him off his cot and onto the wooden floor. He was dragged outside and down the narrow dirt road to the sawmill. Burning crosses ringed the sawmill. He was sure they were going to kill him. Yet, he remained calm.

A teenage boy who lived in back of the sawmill ran toward Needle Pointe Hall. A shot rang out. He fell. He cried out, "Help!"

They shot him again. His lifeblood was running out. But no one dared to help him.

Cabin by cabin, candles and oil lamps were extinguished after the residents of Needle Pointe peeked out their windows at a ring of fire around the sawmill.

Several of the hooded men poured gasoline inside and all around the sawmill as they hooted racial insults and hollered with delight at the coming destruction.

Curtis Adams watched without a sound, without movement, without emotion. The sawmill was not his property. He always knew that. He was just using it.

The bullies could burn it to the ground, if they wanted.

He had no attachment to it.

He simply stared at them—with a look revealing that he was not afraid to die.

Adams did not beg for his life because he had already given it to God. The Grand Wizard put a torch in Adamss' face. Adams looked directly in the Wizard's eyes. They communicated without words. Adams kept his eye contact and composure.

"Take it, boy, and torch it for me," the Grand Wizard shouted at Adams.

He took the torch and slowly walked to the sawmill.

Adams threw the torch inside the sawmill.

He watched the wooden sawmill ignite; then he sauntered away. Defenseless. Away from the flickering flames and toward the white-robed mob armed with guns and torches—his head up.

He faced the Grand Wizard.

Out of the corner of his eyes, Adams noticed one of the hooded men holding a rope with a readymade noose.

The hooded man shouted, "I'll give ya' a chance to run, boy."

Keeping a locked gaze with the Grand Wizard, Adams strode toward the lynch mob, stopping a respectful distance of six feet away. He saw a glimpse of recognition in the eyes staring back at him from behind the white hood.

He stated softly, "I am a widow's son. Is there no mercy for a servant of God Almighty in this incarnation?"

He stood erect, his shoulders squared, eyes locked. Curtis Adams was ready to die like a man with no attachments to this earth.

He won the stare down with the Grand Wizard.

With the sawmill engulfed in flames behind him, the Grand Wizard suddenly said, "It's over. Let's go. He knows his place now. We won't have no more trouble outta him."

The Grand Wizard turned and strode away. The mob followed. They all drove off.

Curtis Adams had held his ground like a man.

Adams stood tall until the last car left Needle Pointe.

With the threat in retreat, he rushed to the bleeding boy on the ground. He knelt beside him and felt the boy's chest, getting blood all over his hands.

"Do somethin' ta help my baby," the boy's mother screamed, running toward them.

"He's gone," Curtis yelled. "I felt 'um—Can't do nothin'—Go back!"

"Oh Lawd, not my baby." The grieving mother fell to her knees on the dirt road. Her wails could be heard over the crackling of fierce fire. Flames danced on the rooftop of the sawmill with various shades of orange embers floating into the night air. Adams noticed that the wind was blowing in a southeast direction toward the coastline.

God's breath had spared Needle Pointe by directing the deadly embers to the sea.

Adams rose and gave thanks to the Lord for his deliverance.

He stood alone in complete stillness for six long hours, watching the sawmill burn to the ground, until the first hint of the sun's light appeared on the distant horizon.

No one attempted to extinguish the flames.

They were all afraid to leave their wooden cabins before the dawn.

With the arrival of a new day, Adams got in his truck and drove to his family's farm in Liberty County about thirty miles away.

Many times I heard Curtis Adams tell his story. He would end by saying, "I will fear no evil as long as I can live off of my own land and have God as the master of my life. If they don't kill me, I won't give up. If they knock you down, get up. They can only win if you give up."

Curtis Adams rebuilt the sawmill for the exclusive benefit of the Needle Pointe community—respecting the Jim Crow laws. It was bigger and better than the old sawmill.

He did not give up.

He made it.

*****

Katherine found herself lost in the story.

How could her mother have known all of this? Was Curtis Adams her father?

The only way to find out was to keep turning the pages.

HATTIE'S STORY
Chapter Five

After years of hiding, we became less afraid. One day, my cousin Ademus wandered past the Jackson property line. Ademus had made friends and learned the history of Needle Pointe. Its former residents were among the few former slaves to get the forty acres promised under the Freeman's Act of 1862. The brutal overseers who had run the Williams Plantation before the Civil War had fled when Sherman's March to the Sea reached Savannah. As a result, the Williams Plantation had been subdivided and deeded to several former slave families, creating an all-Negro community in the late 1800s.

The new landowners named their community Needle Pointe.

For generations, they were happy just living off the land.

Most of the former slave descendants never moved beyond Needle Pointe's boundaries. Their wealth was the inherited land and Moon River. For generations, the Wiggs family provided spiritual leadership for the tight-knit community. I can still see Reverend Abraham Wiggs preaching and swinging his arms while the congregation screamed and hollered, praising the Lord.

Reverend Wiggs had extraordinary oratorical skills for a man with limited formal education. The Lord just seemed to speak through him every time he got up to preach.

On Sundays, we put on our best clothes and went to church at eleven. If somebody had a Sunday hat, they wore it. But most of us didn't have a Sunday hat. I never had one.

During the service, we listened to some of the best voices in Georgia. We prayed. We sang. We cried. I cried a lot for my daddy. I thought I would never get over his death. I just sat and cried for many years about everything I could not control. For a long time, I found it hard to give thanks to the Lord for delivering us through the trials of life as Negroes in the South because I was still living in my own personal hell. Locked up in my mind.

I was forced to attend church every Sunday and sit in that chair until two or three, crying until the tears stopped. Most people just left me alone.

Everybody knew I had had a hard time. They knew what had happened to me.

I didn't make any friends because I was afraid to leave the Jackson Plantation without my Uncle Wash. The boys were invited to parties at Needle Pointe Hall. I didn't go with them.

I stayed to myself.

Needle Pointe Hall was a small one-room wooden structure on the main dirt road through the community. It was always jumping on Friday night with the radio blasting and corn liquor flowing. Those few residents with radios would bring them to the community hall so everyone could listen if something big was being broadcast, like a Joe Louis fight.

Everybody shared whatever they had. It wasn't much. They fished and caught crabs, selling their catch to the oyster and crab factory down the main road for money. They didn't need much to be happy in such a beautiful setting with fruit trees everywhere.

No one ever went hungry.

They were free. Content with their simple lives.

But I was never happy.

I couldn't forgive myself.

Ademus was good at telling stories. He tried to cheer me up. I can still hear him—going on and on. Sometimes he could make me laugh. I talked to him more than anybody else in the family. He understood me. He was my closest cousin. Ademus would tell me what happened when he went over to the parties in Needle Pointe.

What follows is the story of how Ademus met and married Leila Freeman.

My life story is impacted by Ademus to this day.

He's the family link that matters.

In late July 1947, Ademus was invited to a going-away party for a young man named Danny who had enlisted in the army. He met Leila Freeman at the party. She had on a simple blue dress, no makeup. She looked shy. He said he winked at her. She blushed.

"I've seen you around a few times," Ademus said. "What's your name?"

"Leila," she replied without looking at him.

"Say, can ya at least look at me?"

"Whut?" she said in a broken Gullah dialect.

"You're talkin' to me, but you're not lookin' at me."

"Whut we talk'um 'bout?" She glanced at him, then looked away.

"Why your eyes so sad? You're at a party."

"Me don't wanna see Danny go." She spoke with rapid words. "He like brother ta me. His family looks out for me."

"Looks out for you?" Ademus asked.

"Yeah, my mama die a few months ago. Me live next door to dem."

"Do you have older brothers or sisters?"

"Naw," she said.

"Younger?"

"Naw." Leila looked down again. "Jus' me."

"Who ya live with?"

"Live 'lone. My ma never married."

"How old are you?"

"Fifteen," she lied. Leila was just thirteen.

"I'm seventeen," Ademus said. "Can I get you a drink?"

"Yeah, git me somethin' strong."

"I don't know if I can git dat for you, but I'll see."

Ademus walked to the drink table, returning with two drinks.

"Orange juice?" Leila asked with a nervous stutter.

"It's orange juice and with a little corn liquor so you can relax," Ademus replied. "No one's at your cabin to run me away at night?"

"Danny, 'e look out for trouble at my place," she said with the first sign of a spark in her eyes. "People like you comin' round. 'E say I shouldn' be neckin' and carryin' on wit boys like you. 'E might run ya 'way, if 'e saw you at my place."

"What did you say?" Ademus asked, easing toward her.

"I ain't got no mama or daddy. I ken have company, if I wanna."

"If you want me to stop by ta see you, put a red ribbon in your window," he said.

"Okay. Will ya walk me home?"

"Yeah, but I won't come in 'til Danny's gone."

They talked for over an hour and he walked her to her door.

"Goodbye," he said, giving her a quick hug after looking around. "I gotta go."

"Wanna go crabbing with me tomorrow?" Leila asked as he turned away.

"Gosh, I git up early. Gotta do my chores. Can you take the noon heat?"

"Me a Georgia girl," Leila said in a spunky voice. "I'm used to crabbin' in da heat of da day. Got some chicken bones for bait."

"My Daddy's got a good net. You ever crab with a net?"

"Yeah," she said, "I can make nets and use'm for fishing. But most times, jus' use a stick. I'm real good at dat."

"I'll bring my Daddy's net. Ya can catch a whole lot more crabs with a good net. We can make some money. I'll show ya how ta use it, so bring a big basket."

"How big?"

"Real big. We just slaughtered a cow so we've got some cow lips. You know, they make da best bait for crabbin'."

"I know'um."

"See ya later," Ademus said.

Leila was happy for the first time in months. Finally she had something to look forward to. A boy. She laid awake all night long thinking of him.

The next day, Washington found Ademus in the barn. "What ya doin' with my net?"

"I'm goin' crabbin'.'"

"Thought ya said ya couldn't go with me."

"I'm goin' wit somebody else," Ademus replied. "Can I have da cow's lips."

"Who ya goin' wit?"

"A girl."

"We need ta talk before ya start seein' girls... Who's da girl?"

"Leila."

"Dat sounds like trouble," Washington said. "Don't dat girl live alone? You need to go crabbin' with me first, son, so we can have a man-ta-man talk 'bout girls. Need to leave dat girl alone. She's too young. Jus' trouble waitin' to happen. Ya hear?"

Finding a good spot on the coast, Washington and Ademus crabbed, drank Coca-Cola, and ate ham sandwiches. They talked for hours. Finally, Washington told his oldest son in foul language to stay away from Leila's door—to avoid temptation's path to hell.

Ademus stayed away for a while.

After many weeks of unending chores, Ademus got a chance to go to another party in Needle Pointe. Entering the community hall, he looked for Leila. She wasn't there.

He left the party and crept toward her cabin. As he approached, he saw the red ribbon in her window. He wondered if the ribbon had been on display for weeks.

At her door, he knocked. He didn't have to wait long.

Leila appeared at the door, dressed for the party. Excited to see him, she let him into her small, untidy space with a broad grin. Without words, she reached to kiss him. He didn't know what to do. She rubbed against him.

He responded.

"Nothing but neckin' and carryin' on," she whispered.

"Okay." He breathed hard.

There was no more conversation.

Her door opened to him.

Over the next few months, Ademus visited Leila when he could. But that wasn't often. He saw her no more than once a month. He had to sneak. Still under the control of his strong father, Ademus was not allowed to be out all night. He had a midnight curfew.

When Washington began to suspect Ademus was still seeing the girl, he stopped his son from going to parties in Needle Pointe. But his preventive measure was too late.

As Leila began to show, the "news" started to fly in the close-knit community where everybody knew everybody. There was much sympathy for Leila, as she was too young to be alone. Everybody knew Ademus was the father-to-be.

They also knew Leila had a father.

The rumors finally reached Reverend Wiggs.

He decided to pay Curtis Adams a visit.

"I hate to bring this up to you," Reverend Wiggs said, sitting at the dining room table in the neat Savannah home of Curtis Adams. "But have you heard Leila's pregnant?"

"No," Adams said, "I haven't heard that."

"Did you know that girl was living by herself?"

"I thought she was living with her aunt. That's what I was told—"

"So you did ask about the girl after her mother died?"

"Yes," Adams said in a meek tone. "I did."

"You know everybody thinks you're the girl's father. Dey think it's a shame ya done nothing ta help her. They asked me to do somethin'. So I'm here askin' you ta help da girl."

Adams tried to defend himself. "I never was sure…"

"Well, she's dark skinned like you, has them big ears and a chin just like ya folks—and we can't ignore her nose. Da nose and pinball eyes shout ya her daddy to me."

"I—"

"If I were a betting man, I'd bet she's ya daughter. Ya owe da girl somethin'."

"Her mother could have been with somebody else," Adams said. "I was never sure."

"Her mama was sure. She told me you're Leila's father 'fore she died."

"She never told me dat."

"You got married without even tellin' her. She had no reason to lie on her deathbed."

"She never told me!"

"I don't know anybody else who thinks dey might be dat girl's father—other than you. And that girl needs help. I hear dat Ademus Cobb from da Jackson Plantation is da father of her baby."

"How old is he?" Adams asked.

"Ademus? Sixteen. Maybe seventeen."

"Well, he's just a child, too."

"Well, they were grown enough to make a baby so they grown 'nough ta get married. Curtis, are ya gonna help dat poor girl?"

"I don't know," Adams said.

"For Heaven's sake—why don't ya do da right thing?"

"Okay, I'll go see Wash Cobb and demand Ademus marry da girl."

"That's da least dat you should do."

*****

Katherine was confused by her mother's story. Why was she having her read all of this? This was not a story about her mother's life. She wasn't even born in 1946. Her mother was from Dublin, Georgia—Ademus was her mom's cousin. So what?

Why did the story of Ademus and Leila matter? *Why?*

Finally, sleep captured Katherine.

She faded away, still befuddled.

The next morning Katherine boarded the first class cabin of a commercial flight from the tarmac through the food service entry. She settled into her seat without attracting the notice of any other passengers. Hal was already seated behind her. Her friends would fly home on a government plane with a female decoy later that evening.

They had decided to leave London with her, but Hal demanded she make an unexpected departure on a scheduled flight. Katherine thought she should have decided, but that's not what happened. It was his responsibility to keep her safe and he had only given Katherine an hour's notice that they were flying commercial back to the States.

She knew Hal was proud of his record.

He had never lost a person under his protection.

Three hours later, the jet cruised along at thirty-five thousand feet over the Atlantic Ocean on the way back to the nation's capital. After pondering her circumstances and the potential role of BAMN in the bombing attempt, her thoughts went back to her mother's story.

She knew who Leila's father was. So what? She still didn't know who her father was. And she didn't know why Curtis Adams was relevant. Pressing her lips together, she realized that thinking about her mother's story was taking her from fear to annoyance.

Maybe that was a good thing.

Katherine reasoned that irritation was a better emotion than fear—so she reached into her briefcase and pulled out the manila envelope to continue. Her mother's story had stopped her from thinking about her situation for a few hours on the previous night. Maybe it would work for her again.

She had to stop telling herself stories about what BAMN might do. She did not want to think about the attempt on her life. Like Curtis Adams, she would not let fear reduce her to nothing.

She pulled energy from the story. Adams had been fearless. She would try to be, too.

With questions still unanswered, she turned the page.

HATTIE'S STORY
Chapter Six

Savannah, Georgia
December 1947

Curtis Adams, a very dark-skinned man, had married a light-skinned schoolteacher from Savannah. His new wife, Emma, had flowing black hair usually worn pinned up in a bun. Her father was a doctor in town. Her mother was a teacher. She was from one of the elite Black families in Savannah. Her family did not think Adams was "good enough" to marry her.

But she had married him anyway.

After their wedding Curtis told Emma, "I might have a daughter in Needle Pointe that you might find out about, so I'm telling you. I've never seen her. She might or not be mine. I don't know. Her mother doesn't bother me and I don't bother them."

That's how Curtis Adams explained away his parental responsibilities to his new wife.

Adams worked hard to provide a good home for Emma. He wanted her family of doctors and educators to respect him. Adams only had a fifth grade education—but he was smart.

Adams became the wealthiest Black businessman in Savannah. He thought making more money than the doctors in her family would make Emma proud of him. Adams started several businesses: bricklaying; lumber; wood cabin building; and fuel, milk and ice delivery.

Yet in spite of this wealth, Adams had not provided any financial support to Leila's mother, and the woman refused to beg him for help. She faced her pregnancy and efforts to raise the girl without any financial support from Curtis Adams.

But Adams knew he had an obligation. When he spoke to his wife about Leila's pregnancy she had said, "You know that girl's your daughter. If she wasn't, you wouldn't have told me about her when we married. You need to do something about this. Go talk to the boy who got her pregnant and make him marry her."

"I don't wanna to talk to the boy," Adams said. "I'll talk to his father."

After the meeting with the reverend, Washington forced Ademus to marry Leila.

Ademus moved into Leila's dirt-floor cabin in Needle Pointe. Its furnishings were meager. A wood-burning stove for cooking. Pots and pans in a wooden crate. A rusty tin tub for bathing. Wooden table with two chairs. A couch and bed. Curtis Adams gave Ademus and Leila two hundred dollars as a wedding gift.

That was a lot of money to them.

Curtis also gave Ademus a job working for him on the weekends delivering ice, milk and kerosene fuel in Savannah for six dollars a day. It wasn't much, but it helped with the fifteen dollars a week he made working on the Jackson Plantation.

Ademus had just turned seventeen when Leila became his responsibility.

They used the money from Leila's father to fix up the cabin. They bought a new bed, a dresser, a sleeper sofa, a table and four chairs, a new round metal tub, kitchen utensils and a crib for the baby. They spent about a hundred dollars. Ademus hid the other hundred for an emergency.

They made a comfortable space for their new baby in the small wooden cabin.

Their baby, John Thomas, was born on May 2, 1948. His family nickname was "JT."

Leila became pregnant again and had a second son, Charles Lincoln or "CL" to the family. Annie Beatrice soon made an appearance—they just called her "B"—followed by a third son, Doyal Wilson, whom they simply called "DW".

Using initials for nicknames was a Cobb family tradition.

Had been for generations.

A few months after DW's birth, Leila was pregnant again with a fifth child. Their cabin was chaotic with Leila hollering at the boys from sunup to sundown. Ademus was almost never at home, day or night, so Leila leaned on JT for help around the garden and house.

Leila knew she had a husband who did not want to be married to her.

She tried to please him, but nothing worked.

Ademus, an attractive light-skinned man with a slight streak of red hair on the right side of his head, wanted to explore the big city life in Savannah. He found the nightlife there exciting. Now, he was a man. His father couldn't tell him what to do anymore. He was free.

Even though Ademus didn't own a car, getting to Savannah on a Friday night was no problem. Often he caught a ride into town from the Needle Pointe community hall. Somebody was always going into Savannah on Friday night after the dance. Or he'd ride with some of the folks who had moved from Needle Pointe into Savannah who came back on Friday nights for the dance. There were always rides going to "The Joint," an after-hours drinking place for Blacks.

"Will you take me to The Joint with you?" Leila pleaded on Friday nights as Ademus washed up and put on his best clothes. "I never get to go nowhere."

"Ya need to stay home and take care of da babies," Ademus replied. Always the same reply. At two or three in the morning, when Ademus had not returned to their bed, Leila would cry. She would stay awake all night in tears—praying for him to come home.

When she would hear him come through the door—in the wee hours of the morning—she would pretend to be asleep. She didn't know what to do or say to him, other than to pretend that nothing was wrong with his late-night habit.

Leila knew Ademus would return home for his kids. She watched him hold them, kiss them, and play with them for hours when he was at home. After he lost his job at the Jackson Planation, Ademus went to catch crabs every weekday, selling them to the local crab and oyster factory, just down the main road, for five cents a pound. JT and CL by his side. Happy.

It wasn't much, but it was the only job that Ademus could find after Clayton Jackson caught him gazing at his daughter Charlotte with wanting eyes—after she had made a suggestive motion to him. Clayton had told him to stay away from Charlotte in the clearest of terms. After Clayton fired Ademus, the young family struggled. Ademus never told Leila why he had been fired.

Leila busied herself taking care of her babies, tending their small garden, washing their clothes, taking care of working peoples' kids, and cooking. She worked hard but didn't earn much money, not charging the people she babysat for because they had helped her.

In Needle Pointe, people helped each other for free.

With four children to care for and another on the way, her work was never done.

Ademus complained to Leila, "Why can't ya clean up this place? My mother worked for the Jacksons' and kept our cabin clean. I can't live in this filth. Da house is always a mess."

When he said these things, Leila would cry and he would walk out the door.

Ademus was used to a clean, neat cabin on the Jackson Plantation. Leila tried to clean things up, but she had never lived in a neat cabin. She just didn't know how to keep it clean.

Ademus took naps whenever he felt like one. He was the man of the house and Leila didn't work. Or so he thought. If he had been out late, he simply didn't go catch crabs the next day. But on the weekends he did have to make deliveries for Mr. Adams. That six dollars a week was badly needed, since Ademus only made five cents a pound for his crab catches and could never be sure what his earnings would be in any given week.

Somehow Ademus always seemed to have enough money to take care of his family's needs. The kids didn't need much. Leila had a Sunday dress, a housedress, and work clothes for the garden. Ademus had his work clothes and a choice of going-out clothes.

That's just how things were.

Leila's main concern was keeping Ademus as her husband.

She knew Ademus did not love her. He was seeing other women, coming and going as he pleased.

She did not challenge him.

This went on until the end.

One night in the spring of 1949, Ademus approached his home in fear. He noticed his clean clothes still pinned to the clothesline in the backyard. He grabbed them. Quietly, he opened the cabin door. With bare feet, he inched across the dirt floor to the corner in the living room where his children slept. JT and CL slept on the couch and B slept on a cot while the baby boy, DW, was in his crib. Leila was in the bedroom with the door closed.

Ademus bent down and kissed the two older boys gently on the cheek so as not to wake them, and then turned to the baby's crib. As he looked at the sleeping baby, who had his mother's distinctive facial features and his own light skin, tears fell from his eyes.

The sounds of crickets pierced the silence of the night.

He picked up the baby and wandered onto the small wooden porch in front of the house.

With the baby in his arms, he knelt to pray.

Ademus looked over his shoulder at JT as he stirred on the couch, then back to the innocent face of the baby he held to his chest. Love overflowed for the young children he was about to abandon.

"Don't want y'all to end up like me," he whispered. "Seems like da men in dis family always gotta run ta stay alive. Sorry, I can't take ya with me. Ya better here. I pray to God y'all never have to run away, y'all never have to kill a man. Ya better off without me."

His shoulders heaved with silent sobs.

"When ya become a man, leave dis place and make somethin' uh yo' life. I pray to God, ya'll break the curse of bein' Black by usin' ya mind and makin' a way out of no way. Sorry. I gotta go." He wiped his tears with the baby's blanket.

Ademus kissed the sleeping baby and returned him to his small crib before grabbing a pillowcase and stuffing his boots and clean work clothes in it.

JT woke and saw the shadow of his father packing his clothes. He dared not move.

Ademus did not enter the bedroom where Leila pretended to be sleep.

She silently wept as she waited in bed for him with her back to the door.

But he left without saying a word to her.

When JT heard the car motor crank, he bolted out of bed and ran after Hattie's car, crying out for his father to stop. Ademus stopped by the community hall. His son ran into his arms.

"Daddy, don't leave us," JT wailed.

Ademus shook JT and told him to stop crying. He told his young son that he had killed a white man and had to run away or the lynch mob would kill him. That he could never come back to Needle Pointe. He told JT the white man would kill him and his grandpa, if he talked. JT had to stop crying or they all might die. Ademus told JT to take care of his mother and never tell anyone that he had seen him leave—not even his mother.

Traumatized, JT wouldn't talk to anyone for months.

Leila told people Ademus left her for another woman.

That's what she believed.

*****

JT? Katherine thought, putting the manuscript down. Could Galt be JT? But her mother wouldn't just make up a story like this. She recalled that he had changed his name to Galt. Galt was disassociated from his father's family. Her mother was right: she didn't like what she had found out—and she hadn't needed to know this before her hearing, if in fact Galt was JT.

Yes, that could have made a difference during her hearing.

She wondered what Galt knew.

No way to know for sure—but she still needed to know who her father was.

With another hour left in the flight, she picked the manuscript up and turned to Chapter Seven. Katherine's interest was primed when she saw the date, a year before her birth.

Finally, the answer was near.

HATTIE'S STORY
Chapter Seven

Savannah, Georgia
Sunday, August 24, 1958

Clayton Jackson, owner of the Jackson Plantation, was a widower. His wife died during the birth of his daughter, Charlotte, his only child. At the age of twenty-three, Hattie Cobb was the acknowledged mistress of Clayton Jackson. He saw her often.

One night, Clayton had stopped by Hattie's place on his way home. She had company so he didn't stay long. Hattie's friends from college had come to visit from Atlanta for the weekend. Hattie did not want her college friends to know about him. So Hattie and

Clayton visited in the small house in back of the main house, away from her friends.

Hattie never dated in college. Her private time was reserved for Clayton. The "affair" between them began when she was fifteen. Over the years it had matured into a consensual romantic relationship, even though it had been birthed from an abusive act against a young colored girl who just gave in with no defense.

What else could she do?

No crime had been committed when Hattie consented to have sex as a child. Jim Crow was the law. She was desirable with no rights of defense against white males—other than the rights granted by a white protector. Clayton was her protector.

She only had to worry about pleasing him.

He was an important white man in and around Savannah. A lawyer, descended from a family line of plantation owners, lawyers, and judges—his brother was the most powerful judge in Chatham County.

From past experience, Hattie knew to keep her mouth closed when Clayton made his first personal requests of her. She knew her fate couldn't be changed without putting others in danger. She would not scream and put Washington's life in danger again.

In return for her silence and compliance, she had been educated. Hattie attended Chatham County Public Schools in Savannah and rode the school bus with Clayton's daughter, Charlotte. Hattie was the only Black child from the Needle Pointe area attending a Black public school in Savannah. In a way, she was privileged.

On the ride into town, Hattie was not allowed to speak to the white children on the bus. She rode in the back of the bus. At first, her fast Gullah/Geechee dialect was a problem with the Blacks at school, so, with Clayton's tutoring, Hattie learned to speak proper English.

In time she became bilingual.

She read in silence on the long ride to and from school every day, becoming lost in books she borrowed from the library. In her senior year in high school, she read great books. Clayton told her which ones to read—in addition to those assigned for reading in her classes.

That's when Hattie's love of books was born.

Hattie helped Washington's sons learn how to read. Often she brought books for Ademus' children and read to them after Sunday dinner. She bought JT a copy of *Walt Disney's Uncle Remus Stories* for his seventh birthday. Hattie had read the original version. It was her favorite book. The Disney version became JT's favorite book. The *Uncle Remus* characters talked like them. They were funny. Resourceful. For a while, Hattie read *Uncle Remus* stories to JT every Sunday. He was a quick learner.

Hattie taught JT how to escape into another life through books.

When Hattie graduated from college, she moved to Savannah. Clayton had sent her to Spelman College in Atlanta, a historically Black college, where she graduated with her B.A. degree with honors in 1957.

Hattie started a real estate agency and became one of the first Negroes in the state of Georgia to pass the real estate broker license exam. Clayton helped her study for the state licensing exam, sharing law books from his library with her. She spent hours preparing for it with Clayton. He saw to it her exam was properly scored by the examiner simply by letting his interest in her application be known to the chair of the licensing board.

That's all it took for her to be treated fairly.

With Clayton's help, Hattie became a Negro businesswoman in a town that only had a few Negro businessmen. In fact, the Blacks were resentful of her financial success, as many of them had had their business efforts thwarted by competing whites. But Hattie didn't have that problem. Clayton protected her.

He was a lawyer at the town's largest law firm.

In Savannah, Hattie was protected so long as she didn't violate Jim Crow law. So her business was limited. Nevertheless, she was responsible for several homes in Savannah, previously owned by white people, being sold to Blacks, and she was proud of that fact.

But Hattie needed a steady income in Savannah to support herself. She wanted to be independent. So she appealed to her lover for financing for another business venture.

Clayton helped Hattie buy one of Savannah's grand old houses on Henry Street, in the city's decaying historical district. It was an Italian Renaissance mansion made of red brick with ornate ironwork railings on its balconies. Hattie fixed it up. She ran an after-hours joint from the mansion, selling booze and renting rooms at hourly rates. The mansion had large rooms with fifteen-foot ceilings on the upper floors. The lower level had a large bar with a fireplace and was big enough to accommodate a partying group of fifty plus live entertainment. Many of the local Black musicians played at Hattie's Place on the weekend.

There were also two large private rooms in the basement that were used for a variety of group activities. Hattie's Place, as known to the Savannah locals, provided a wide range of entertainment to its customers. More than just booze and good food could be had. Several of the local area prostitutes serviced their customers from Hattie's Place.

Coloreds entered through the front door of the mansion and used the upper level of the house for their entertainment activities, while the white patrons used the former slave entrance because it was more discreet. There was a separate smaller house on the backside of the mansion that had formerly served as the slaves' residence. It was just a few feet away from the discreet slave entrance leading into the lower level of the main house. Prominent white Savannah customers used the former slave house in back of the mansion for their private parties.

Savannah's elite Black social community shunned Hattie. Although she was college educated, she was not married to one of the doctors, lawyers or educators—and she didn't make her money the right way. The Black elite treated her like degraded trash.

In general, Black business people and entertainers were not welcomed into the elite Black social clubs of Savannah, regardless of how much money they made.

They simply were not "the right kind of people."

Hattie didn't care to belong to any of the social clubs in Savannah. She had her own social world in which Clayton treated her like a queen within the confines of her palatial home in the historic district of Savannah. Her friends were her customers, and the musicians and singers who patronized her place. That was enough social life for her. Music was her elixir.

Hattie made good money. She wore fine clothes. Clayton was a good man to her.

On some level, Clayton and Hattie loved each other. They needed each other. Their love blossomed without interference from others. Neither of them had other sexual partners nor wanted any. They were a committed couple who could never marry because of societal limitations, and limited to a secret love that would never be blessed.

When Hattie became pregnant, he said he loved her and that they would work it out.

When Hattie realized Clayton could no longer protect her, she decided to leave Savannah. There was no hope for her in the South. Not with him. Not alone.

She wanted a better life for her baby.

*****

Katherine's face tightened. She was irritated by what she was reading and thinking. Irritated on a lot of levels about a lot of things that she had read.

She closed her mother's memoir and, deep in thought, gazed out her window at the mounds of puffy white clouds that formed an endless blanket below the jetliner. She looked at her skin. Yes, she could have had a white father. Yes, it could be Clayton Jackson.

She didn't know how she felt about that possibility.

Was Jackson a true love or a rapist?

She couldn't believe her mother really loved him. Could he have fallen in love with her? Or had her mother romanticized the story to make her feel better about the circumstances of her birth? She noticed that the writing had changed to third person. Her mother would do something like that to make things look better. Yes, she would cover-up the abuse. It wasn't love.

At least Katherine now understood why her mother had pushed her father to buy the first edition copy of *Uncle Remus* when they found it in London years ago. *Uncle Remus* was the only happy tie back to her family—the only link to her family background that she had fully shared with any kind of joy, even though she hadn't said it was a link to *their* past.

Galt might be JT. No. Must be thousands of JTs in the world. Couldn't be.

Could be.

When she saw Galt, she would have to ask him about *Uncle Remus.*

No point in asking her mother about it.

The captain's announcement broke into her thoughts.

"We are approaching the Baltimore Washington International Airport. Please stow all materials used during flight, turn off all electronics such as computers, and return all seats to their original position. We will be landing shortly."

Complying with the request, Katherine slid the manuscript back into her briefcase and closed her eyes with pictures of the old South playing in her head.

As she heard the cracking of the jet's landing gear, then felt the jolt of the wheels bumping the tarmac, she wondered—*what else could have happened to her mother as a young Black woman in Georgia during Jim Crow to make her leave her family when she was in a state of pregnancy?*

Why couldn't Clayton Jackson protect her anymore?

Was he really her father?
It was only implied.

When the newspapers reported a terrorist bombing in London, she was thankful the articles did not mention that she had been the target. Her security team had swished her out of harm's way without alerting the press of her presence near the scene.
She didn't tell her mother about the close call.
Katherine could keep a secret, too.

Chapter Fifty-Four

U.S. Supreme Court Building
Friday, July 26

Katherine looked up at the enormous arrangement of flowers that her secretary carried into her chambers and placed on the conference table. The gigantic bouquet was an eruption of her favorite colors: lilac, pink, yellow, and red. Yellow roses dominated the arrangement. Her curiosity was piqued as she rose from her desk.

"There's a small package with a note," her secretary said.

"I'll take the note. I have to decide if I'm going to keep them."

"Really?"

Katherine did not respond.

She slowly opened the sealed envelope and pulled out the folded notecard with the United States Senate emblem. Her heart jumped as she recognized his handwriting. She sighed as she took in the words. The note read:

Kathy,

In the small package, you will find a single CD of Al Green's Tired of Being Alone. *This is how I feel about you. I hope you still have some love in your heart left for me. I'm sorry I hurt you. Please understand.*

You were the first after... You know. It was confusing for me. I didn't want to hurt you. I just didn't know what I was feeling, thirty years ago. Now I know my feelings for you are not fleeting, since they have not passed with time. I think of you often. Perhaps you, too, have discovered that what happened between us has not been erased by time. Enough said.

The next time you find yourself at home alone thinking of me, please play this CD. If you get the message that I'm trying to send you, give me a call. I've included the words to the song for you to consider now. We've missed the last thirty years without each other. We shouldn't miss another day.

Skip

Katherine unfolded the single sheet of lyrics. *Tired of Being Alone* was a song she had listened to many times over the years. She started to scan the sheet of lyrics, then slowed to a stop, rereading more than once the words on the very personal note as she took in the private meaning of the lyrics. His message was clear.

He wanted her back in his personal life.

But... why?

Repressed memories exploded into her consciousness—with long guarded images from their past. She could hear Al Green singing the words in her head. A full band of emotions emerged from her soul. This was not the right time.

She reached for her fountain pen, a sheet of her light blue stationery, and wrote the senator a reply.

Skip,

Thank you for your warm note. I already have an Al Green CD, so I am returning the flowers and the CD to avoid any appearance of impropriety. I'll listen to the song later and reply back to you again at a more appropriate time.

Katherine

She considered the message she was sending to the senator. The package accompanying the flowers was left unopened. The beautiful yellow bow with gold speckled ribbon remained untouched. After placing her response in a matching blue envelope, she put her reply where his note had been, then summoned her secretary by pressing a buzzer under her desk.

"Mary, will you send the flowers and package back to Senator Graham with this note. Have one of the Court's police officers hand-deliver them to his home address." After Mary left her chambers with the flowers, she slid his note and lyrics into her purse and placed it in her side desk drawer. She wouldn't let Skip influence her. She couldn't report the flowers. Had to keep her guard up.

Now, back to work.

While exercising that evening in her building's gym, Katherine listened to Al Green on her iPhone. Again. And again. The words of *Tired of Being Alone* were full of meaning to her. She considered the message he was sending her.

She told herself a lot of stories.

She remembered…

As Katherine fell asleep that night, Skip slipped into her dreams.

Chapter Fifty-Five

Russell Senate Office Building
Friday, September 6

Senator Graham had accomplished the impossible by getting a constitutional amendment passed for an involuntary retirement process for Supreme Court justices. Now Kathy was holding him up. The Judiciary Committee had reports that Galt had not been seen at the Court since the blast—four months before.

The time was ripe for Galt's removal.

But he knew why she was holding him up. She was playing hard to get. He knew her. Well. He saw in her eyes that she still had feelings for him. He still had feelings for her. But Galt was the issue now. They would work it out in time.

Graham stared at the four certifying letters that had been lying on his desk for weeks. There were only four weeks left in the term. He had reports that Kathy's failure to act decisively was putting her life in danger. He had to make her act before it was too late.

The Supreme Court's current term was scheduled to end on October 6.

He had a month to get Kathy's letter. The bull emerged.

He would have to make things happen.

Graham placed a call to Galt at his home that morning. "I wanted to give you notice that I'm expecting the fifth letter anytime," he said, leaning back in his chair with a smug look.

"I understand that," Galt said.

"Are you incapacitated?" Graham asked.

"No, I'm at home recuperating."

"It's been over four months. How long will you be away from the Court?"

"I've been to Court since the bombing."

"For how long?"

"Don't know—I'm not required to punch a clock. I was in before nine the other day."

"So you're not confined to home?"

"No."

"I know this is short notice, but I think we should have a conversation before the fifth letter appears on my desk. I also have something more personal that I want to share with you."

"What?"

"We should meet privately."

"When?"

"How about today at three? Maybe we can work things out."

"I'll come to your office. Might make a good photo op for the press. Three is fine."

"I can come to you," Graham offered and then added, "Less attention."

"No. I'll come to your office. I can show you I'm mobile."

At 3:00 p.m., Graham's secretary announced Justice John Galt.

Galt rolled in, alone, in a navy blue motorized wheelchair with an oxygen tank attached, transparent tubing wrapped around his neck. A brown artificial hand peeked from his right sleeve. He operated the wheelchair with his left hand, cruising into Graham's office at a turtle's pace.

Galt's distracting white-framed prescription glasses were perched on his nose in defiance of those who did not appreciate them, making a statement by their mere presence.

Galt stopped. There was no open space for his wheelchair to park.

"Justice Galt." Graham swirled around at his desk. "I'm sorry there's no space." The senator shouted out to his secretary, "Please make a space for Justice Galt next to the sofa, then place the four letters in front of the justice so he can reach them with the report. He might want to take a look at them while I finish up over here."

The wall behind the sofa was plastered with pictures and awards. There was a photo of the senator with the President, another with the governor of Michigan, and a third with the entire Congressional black caucus. Graham's University of Michigan Law School degree was displayed in the middle of the wall.

Graham worked at his computer screen with his back turned until his secretary had rearranged the meeting area. "Please close the door when you leave," Graham told her. "Hold all of my calls and don't disturb us."

He moved to the sofa and sat, then leaned toward the justice with a reserved stare. There was a moment of silence as the two men sized each other up.

Justice Galt's white-framed eyes went vacant. No emotion.

Graham picked up the report from the sofa and positioned it on the table within Galt's view. It was entitled, *The Influence of Jennie Galt on the Supreme Court.*

Graham spoke first. "Some of your wife's actions have been questionable for you, as a sitting Supreme Court justice. Haven't they?"

"My wife has protected rights under the U.S. Constitution. I don't try to limit her personal activities. I am a defender of her rights as an individual. Another question?"

"Then you won't defend her actions."

"Her actions don't need a defense."

"Even if she's wrong?"

"We share the same values," Galt said with a stony look. "Let's move on."

"When you have your private conference with the Senate Judiciary Committee regarding your competence, I want you to know that I'm not going to take any cheap shots. You will know in advance the moral and legal grounds that I will use to declare to the country that you are unfit to serve as an associate justice of the U.S. Supreme Court. But I'm always open to reconciliation."

"Reconcile to what end?" Galt asked in a firm tone. "We both know this is political. You want me out. I've decided to stay. There's nothing to reconcile."

"When are you going back to work full time?" Graham asked.

"I'm working full time. I did not miss making a decision on any case last term."

"That's my point. How were those decisions made when you were incapacitated?"

"I was never incapacitated. I could always think. I could always talk. I was always connected to my office while in the hospital and while at home."

"Your office was running on autopilot at the end of the last term."

"An efficient, well run chamber of an associate justice of the U.S. Supreme Court is not against the law."

"How many hours a week are you spending in your chambers?"

"Enough to get the job done. It varies."

"Have you read the four thousand certs received by the Court since you were injured?"

"Nobody reads all of them. We have a pool."

"When was the last time you went to an oral argument and asked a question?"

"I don't recall."

"When was the last time you went to oral argument and didn't fall asleep during it?"

"I don't recall."

"When was the last time you spent eight hours in your chambers?"

"I don't recall."

"Do you use your wife to help direct your law clerks?"

"Communications between a husband and wife are privileged."

"Can you sign your name?"

"No, my right hand is gone. I'm in rehab."

"In your state of incapacity, has your wife signed or initialed Supreme Court documents for you to direct your law clerks and staff?"

"I can manage my chambers any way I want to."

"Will you resign now? That would be best for the country."

"No," Galt said. "I won't bend for you, and you have nothing to trade with."

"A tree that does not bend in the wind can be uprooted in a strong storm."

"What did you expect from me? I don't care what you think."

"Nothing. But I do expect the fifth letter to appear on my desk one day soon."

Chapter Fifty-Six

The U.S. Supreme Court
Tuesday, September 10

Julianne hustled toward the second floor chambers of Justice Galt. As she reached for the polished brass doorknob she heard a clock chime 9:00 a.m. She entered a reception area where two administrative assistants were preoccupied, working with piles of documents all around.

One of the law clerks motioned her through the next doorway then he returned to his work. To her mild surprise, Julianne went through into an antechamber where four white law clerks worked with their heads down. Mountains of paper camped on every available space on their desks and the floor. Volumes of legal books stuffed the shelves. Colored coded briefs rested on wheeled carts. She noted intense facial expressions. Focused energy.

A male law clerk with blond hair motioned for her to proceed without taking his eyes off his computer screen. The other three law clerks did not even glance up as she passed through their space like an invisible spirit. Surprised at the four white law clerks, she guessed that he couldn't find a qualified Black. Clearly there was no equal opportunity program here.

As Julianne entered Galt's private chambers, she noticed a seven-foot grandfather's clock with golden hands in a far corner. Elegant touch. A priceless oil painting of the original Supreme Court justices hung in an ornate gold frame. Appropriate. Bookcases of law books hugged the oak-paneled walls. High windows with a Capitol view were showcased by elaborate draped brocade window treatments. A bit much, but this was the palace of egos.

Then she saw the beautiful oil painting of Frederick Douglas that hung above an antique writing table behind Galt's massive desk. The picture seemed out of place. Why was it there?

A yellow legal pad and pen lay on the right side of his desk.

But he couldn't write. Galt's chamber of power—and it was all a lie.

On a small table to the side of his desk she spotted two computers side by side. Why two computers? She'd have to remember to ask.

Julianne heard a cough and turned toward the sound.

Galt smiled at her from his seat at the conference table. "Close the door."

He held a marked-up brief in his left hand. A brief he could not have marked.

"I'm surprised you asked to see me again," she said, moving to close the door.

"I wanted to thank you," Galt said in a low baritone voice. "Have a seat over here." He pointed to a chair close to him. "And I wanted to know why you helped me."

Julianne remained standing, not wanting to sit that close to him. "I did it to help Justice Ross. He's been tracking her, too. I saw Walter casing you at Morton's that night. He was obvious. Eyeing your moves."

"I know you saved my life. That's why I'm giving you an opportunity. I can use you…"

"You can't use me, not after the way you've hurt our people."

"I've been pushing for the people," he said, shifting in his seat.

"Yes you have. You pushed us back a hundred years."

"How many articles have you written about me?" he asked.

"Not enough." She looked at him with contempt on her face that screamed without voice what she had written so many times about him. *Worthless token. Sell out. Traitor.*

They locked glares.

"Do you hate me?"

"I hate what you've done to our country in the name of conservative politics. I hate what you stand for. I…"

"Hating seems easy for you."

"Well I was taught by white America—and by you."

"You've got me all wrong."

"I don't think so," she snapped. "What did I get wrong? May I have a seat over here?"

She started to sit in one of the chairs across from him.

"No," he said, glancing up at her. "I'm out of time."

She looked at him with scorn. "I wish you were."

"You might get your wish," Galt said. "I'll see you on Monday at seven-thirty. I suspect the fifth letter will be sent to the Senate Judiciary Committee. So I've made a decision: For saving my life, I will grant you an exclusive right to cover me over the next ninety days. You'll be the only source of direct quotes from me in the press. You need to know me better."

She stood in shock.

Finally he said, "You will become my public voice."

Chapter Fifty-Seven

The Urban Sentinel Offices
Wednesday, September 11

Sam Knight had his back turned and was facing his computer as Julianne eased into his office unannounced. "You didn't accept it?"

Sam did not turn around, focused on his screen. "Wait. Deadline."

In the background, Julianne heard the staff in the production room discussing the front page setup and adjustments needed to accommodate the much smaller AP wire story on Galt.

After hitting a key with finality, Sam whirled and faced her with a stone face.

Julianne knew she was in trouble.

"Let's go over your notes from the interview with Galt," he said.

Julianne cringed. She didn't have any notes. She should have been listening. But she had debated him. Now she had nothing to show. Her shoulders dropped.

"I'm sorry. The exchange between us was so swift, I—I didn't take any notes."

"Did you record?"

"Security took my recorder when I entered the building."

"Then go make some notes now. Write a letter and ask Galt to review them."

"That's a good idea. He might give me something in writing we can use."

"Right. Look, I want you to produce a series about Justice Galt that is worthy of being an exclusive historical record of not only the events related to his involuntary retirement, but also an insight into the man. That's what I want from you."

"Insight into the man," Julianne said with a frown. "That's a tall order."

"So your interview with Galt was a fight? Did you win?"

"I'd say it was a draw. I didn't land any knockout punches."

"So you lost. Our readers expect something to jump off the page when they read an exclusive interview by Julianne LaSalle. I think you're capable of better work."

She avoided his eyes, her chest caving. "What do you want?"

"I want you to go to a new level as a reporter. I expect an ass-kicking piece from you about Galt, appropriate to be an AP piece because that's what it should become."

What could she say?

"We've never had an opportunity like this," he said. "A chance to give the nation a story they can't get anywhere else. This is a great opportunity and I'm not going to let you blow it."

"Blow it?"

"Yes, you didn't make any new points in this piece."

Sam pushed her draft back to her.

"You're right," she said, taking the draft. "I didn't like his energy. He made me angry."

"You've got to control your emotions. If he's willing to see you again, you'd better believe he has an agenda. So you better have an agenda, too."

Galt's sick energy had gotten to her and she had let it happen.

"Julianne, you've got an inside track on what could become the biggest story in the country. You've got to make this man transparent. Dissect him. You need to do some investigative reporting to get a new angle. Dig into his background. Look at everything and how it can bring something fresh."

"Since when do we get budget money for investigative reporting?"

"I've got $25,000 in discretionary spending," he said. "That's your budget. Why don't you use Robert Freeman to work with you? He's retired from *The Washington Post*. He might do it for $10,000."

"You don't think I can do it by myself?"

"I think investigative reporting is better done with two heads," the editor said. "This is big. Galt must have an agenda. For some reason, he wants to use you. You need to figure that out. Once we get going on this, every article, every week has got to shine. We need some help."

"Okay—but I just don't understand him."

"Write about the nature of his jurisprudence. Pick a legal issue and break it down so our readers get it. Make it simple. Get into his head whenever you get the chance. What shapes his thinking? Figure out what makes him tick. That will be news."

"You're challenging me to understand his psyche," she said. "I don't know if I *want* to understand the devil who rides him at night."

Chapter Fifty-Eight

The National Gold Chamber of Commerce was the most exclusive and powerful club of organized business interests in the country. In most political circles, it was just referred to as the NGCC.

They were everywhere in the political ether.

Nobody became a presidential appointee under Republican administrations without its approval, and that extended to appointments to the U.S. Supreme Court. With an annual budget of over $450 million, the NGCC had a large research budget to produce data supporting their public policy positions. They funneled data and position papers to their mentored appointees on a regular basis, and expected them to implement their policy positions or be removed.

Sometimes appointees resigned if they felt that they couldn't fulfill their political assignments rather than face certain removal. Contrary to general public knowledge, it was not the U.S. Chamber of Commerce calling the shots for business interests in Washington, D.C.

It was the NGCC.

Senator Graham wondered if the source of the note he held in his hands was the NGCC. That was a definite possibility. If so, what was their motive? Was Galt falling out of grace?

October 7

Senator Graham,

This is the scoop on the making of Justice John T. Galt.

At the time of Galt's nomination to the U.S. Supreme Court, the Republican administration was under attack in the media for not having any African American appointees in the Cabinet. The Republicans needed an African American symbol of legitimacy to maintain their socially constructed reality that racial discrimination was a thing of the past.

Finally, at a state dinner for the new Ambassador for Russia, the President of the United States was overheard saying to the president of the NGCC, "Find somebody you can live with, I'm tired of the heat. If we have to make somebody, make somebody."

The impossible assignment to find an African American who shared the conservative values of the NGCC and could be shaped, controlled, and monitored by one of its operatives went to Jennie Hale, an attorney and the Chief Lobbyist for the NGCC.

Attached is her story about their union as equals. I think it has implications for issues under debate about Galt's service on the bench.

I trust your judgment to use this information as you see fit.

Anonymous

Senator Graham leaned back on the couch, rereading the note from the unnamed source. Who wrote this document? Not Jennie Galt. He wasn't going to fall for that.

Chapter Fifty-Nine

The Union of Two Objectivists
By Jennie Galt

"A man falls in love with and sexually desires the person who reflects his own deepest values."
—Ayn Rand, *The Virtues of Selfishness*, p. 77

This is the story of how I met John T. Galt. This is first and foremost a story of love about the union of equals, two people who share the same core values in life. I'm writing this so those who question our love will understand the strength of the foundation that supports it.

A love like ours will survive the test of time.

Sitting at my desk, I was looking down at the busy traffic on J Street as I made up a list of five possible Black candidates for Solicitor General of the United States of America.

John was not my first choice.

A few days later, I learned John was to speak on affirmative action at an upcoming conservative think tank conference sponsored by the Heritage Foundation in New York. The conference was to be held on March 30. Perfect timing.

At that time, John was the Virginia State Attorney General, serving one of the most conservative governors in the nation. He had the required party credentials so I added him to the list of candidates under consideration. He was number five.

On the day we first met, I sat in the back of a conference room at the Grand Hyatt in New York. John told great jokes and kept the room laughing, poking fun at himself. He commanded the room with witty commentary that one would not soon forget.

I liked him.

I found him intellectually engaging.

He said all the right things.

Mentally, I moved him up on my list of possibilities to number one.

When his presentation was over, I left without introducing myself. There was just enough time for me to make my flight.

I went out the second floor exit of the hotel to the taxicab stand to look for my limo. It wasn't there. I was told it was tied up in the tunnel and would be late. I couldn't wait.

I dashed down to 42nd Street and stepped into a torrential downpour. The rain sounded like a marching band drummer practicing on a crab shell road, to the accompaniment of swishing cars and passing taxis. The line of waiting passengers was too long.

I scurried to Grand Central Station—but there were no taxicabs there either. I was going to miss my plane.

I could not miss a 9:30 p.m. meeting with my boss, president of the NGCC, to plot strategy on a tax bill to be voted the next morning.

I walked over to the ticket counter. "What time is the next train to Washington, D.C.?"

"Next train leaves Penn at 5:39," the ticket agent said. "You can make it."

"I can't. No taxis—it's raining."

"Take the gray line to the red line," he said.

"What?" I uttered. "I can't take the subway."

"Then walk."

I bought an umbrella at a stall along the way. I got soaked. My white blouse was sticking to my skin by the time I arrived at Penn Station.

I made it to Track 7 with only moments to spare.

The train jerked forward and we were on our way.

I pressed the door pad to open the business class door. Then I saw John.

I paused, checking the ticket for my assigned seat number. To my horror, it was the seat next to him. I continued to the restroom. But there wasn't much I could do. My mascara was smeared around my eyes, making me look like a masked bandit. I wiped my face clean then brushed my hair back straight.

On the way back to my seat, our eyes met. I felt the current. He nodded. I stopped.

"I've got the seat next to you," I said.

I was nervous. I avoided eye contact, settling into my seat.

"Weren't you just at my presentation at the Grand Hyatt?"

"Yes, I was. I'm Jennie Hale."

"Then you have me at a disadvantage. What can you tell me to even the score?"

"You don't really want full disclosure, do you? That could be too much information."

"Too much information? Does that mean you have something to hide?"

"Yes. It does."

"Okay," he said. "I'll assume you're a secret agent on my trail."

"That's a good assumption."

"I want full disclosure from you. In the dining car, perhaps?"

"That sounds good to me."

The waiter showed us to a table with white linen tableware and a small red plastic flower arrangement. He lit the tea candle and gave us menus. We ordered red wine.

The speed of our conversation matched that of our express train to Washington. I didn't really notice when our food arrived or what it tasted like. We ate between words while the city and industrial landscapes sped past our window.

At one point, he paused. He gazed into my eyes.

As I returned his gaze, I felt like I could see his soul.

So pure. Tender. Sweet.

We laughed at nothing. Maybe nervous energy.

I told him how I fell down carrying a bucket of manure on my grandfather's farm, spilling it on my only pair of school shoes, and how they stank for a day.

He told me a similar story of being unmercifully teased because of the way he smelled after doing his farm chores.

We traded stories without embarrassment.

"What's your favorite book?" I asked.

"*Atlas Shrugged,*" John replied, "without a doubt."

"Mine, too." I said with excitement.

We bantered about the objectivist theory embedded in the book. Our conversation flowed like water. We agreed that rational self-interest was the only way to pursue one's happiness. We related our life experiences to the book—they were remarkably similar.

I was an outcast at school.

He was an outcast at school.

We both saw Republican Party politics as a way to fit into the mainstream, and wanted to leave our painful childhood memories behind. Yet we could laugh at them with each other.

I had never opened up to a stranger like that before.

I told him about my upbringing in rural Iowa, my Christian beliefs, my education at a small religious college, and my activities as a conservative Republican Party activist.

He talked about his summers on a Georgia farm, his Gullah/Geechee background, his early education in a white Catholic school, and political activities as a Black conservative.

He talked about his concern for the survival of the historically Black colleges. He had a lot to say about his responsibilities as a

Black father and the resentment he felt from the abandonment by his father at an early age.

We talked about everything we could think of: our first day in kindergarten; our first loves; rejection by social clubs; economics; the problems with public education; the law; Republican Party politics; our mutual dislike of unions and collectives; the failings of affirmative action; race relations; and, of course, our religious views.

To our amazement, our values completely mapped. We bonded.

Then he pulled back in his seat and said like a little boy, "Gosh, I feel like I've always known you—am I falling off a dangerous ledge alone?"

I knew what was happening between us.

We were falling in love.

"No," I replied. "I feel like we're soul mates."

Then he really opened up to me about his early upbringing in coastal Georgia near Savannah during Jim Crow. Some of it was funny. Most of it was sad.

John shared his soul with me, remembering his grandfather, Curtis Adams. Over the years, John shared with me over and over again his grandfather's deathbed advice to him:

> *You can make it in this world if you use your mind, work hard and never give up your values. Keep your faith in God. Most who fight the white man end up dead. But don't fear death, either. You're gonna die one day. Accept that. Be ready. Remember what happened to me. You can only count on yourself in life, and if you're blessed, maybe a good wife.*

I became convinced that John was a perfect man who stood on sound moral values and could not be compromised by a mob mentality that attempted to take away from individuals to protect the tribe. I believe John would never give up a battle he believed in. He would be resilient. Strong. Someone I could depend on to do what he said he would do.

I glanced at my watch as the train began to slow.

It was 9:00 p.m.

Our marathon conversation from New York to Washington was coming to an end.

We agreed that true love only came to individuals who found mates who were their equal in intellect and moral values; and that sex was really just a celebration of finding someone who shared one's deeply-held values in life.

I heard the train whistle screech, breaking my trance.

I asked him, "Do you believe in spontaneous love?"

"I believe in the love I feel in my heart," he replied.

"I've held out for someone who shares my moral code. Color is not one of my issues."

"Nor for me. It may be for others, but I don't let others define my issues."

I felt the train slowing as it entered the station and made a quick decision.

I said, "I've decided to pay whatever price I have to pay to be with you."

"I can't believe what's happening between us. I've never seriously considered dating a white woman before." Then he asked with concern, "What about your family?"

"I can make it right with them," I said.

"My son. I can't abandon my son for you."

"I wouldn't want you to. If you were the kind of man who would abandon a son, I wouldn't have you. So, tell me about him."

"He's a great kid," John said with pride. "He's ten. His name is Joshua. He lives with me and we do a lot together. He attends a private school. So that's where all of my money goes. He's good at sports, but he's a free spirit with the wisdom of an old man."

"I think we could be a match."

As the last passengers in our car shuffled past us, I offered him a deal.

I said, "I could trade you up the food chain, if you're willing to put your own personal self-interest first and develop your rational brain to its fullest potential."

"Are you sure you want me?" he whispered. "Physically?"

"Yes," I said without hesitating.

"You must understand my boy is a package deal with me. Joshua dances to drummers only he can hear. You won't be able to mold him…"

"I only want to mold you," I said with my heart pounding.

"Will you be my Dagny Taggart?" John asked.

I blushed knowing what he meant.

Then I replied, "Yes. I could never say no to John Galt."

*****

After reading it several times, Senator Graham decided to pass *The Union of Two Objectivists* by Jennie Galt on to Julianne LaSalle for investigation. He needed more firepower. She needed more ammunition. Their interests were aligned. He'd heard that Julianne had access.

They both needed to know if this document could be turned into a loaded assault rifle.

Was Jennie Galt exercising the power of Galt's chambers?

That's what they had to prove.

Could this be proof?

Chapter Sixty

The ping of Julianne LaSalle's cell phone announced an incoming text message: *Instead of meeting in my chambers tomorrow morning, let's meet at the International House of Pancakes on Jefferson Davis Highway in Arlington. Jennie will be with me. J.T.G.*

The next morning, Julianne sipped coffee while waiting for the Galts. She jotted down notes with questions, thumbing through the strange document Senator Graham had given her. It was hard to believe Jennie Galt would have written such a document. She was sure Jennie would deny being its author. But would she confirm the basic facts? The document didn't have to be written by her hand to make a front-page story.

What would she say to the question: Did you really make a deal with John Galt to trade him up the food chain?

Julianne gazed up. Jennie Galt plodded toward her.

Where was John?

"So glad you're going to be working with us," Jennie said, sitting down. "John wasn't feeling well this morning, so I had to come alone. Let's get right down to business. You've got a lot to learn and we don't have much time. To be honest, I have my doubts about you."

"The feeling is mutual, but we're both here because your husband has an agenda—and it's my job to find out what it is. If you deal with me straight, I'll deal with you straight."

"That's all we need from you. Accurate reporting of our views."

"You'll have no control over what I write."

"Understood." Jennie signaled for the waitress. "I'll have a cup of coffee. Black."

"Then I have some tough questions for you," Julianne said, preparing to write. "Do you mind if I record. I don't want to misquote you."

"That would be fine. We both want you to get it right."

"Why did you marry John Galt?" Julianne asked.

"For love, of course."

"Did you write *The Union of Two Objectivists*?" Julianne showed Jennie the document. "The Senate Judiciary Committee has a copy."

Jennie pulled back slowly before she answered, "Yes."

"Why would you write something like this?"

"I wrote it for a workshop I taught several years ago on Ayn Rand's theory of ethical egoism. John is the best public figure to demonstrate the theory. The story of our meeting, marriage, and political accomplishments is a shining example of its power. I'm not ashamed of it."

"So to you, love is?"

"A powerful emotion that only happens and thrives when two people share the same moral values. For us, it was spontaneous love on the first date. A love that can't be shattered."

"Whose idea was it to change his last name to Galt?

"Mine. I started calling him 'my John Galt.' The name fit him. He is the perfect man to me. So I asked John to change his last name to Galt. His real last name didn't mean anything to him, but the name John Galt signaled his character, and made it easier for me to help him. That's why he changed his name to Galt."

"Before or after you married him?"

"Before. When we got married I changed my name too. I became very close to his son, Joshua, and adopted him as my own.

We decided to change his last name to Galt, too. We became the close knit family that John Cobb never had."

"Galt is estranged from his father's family?

"Yes. His father deserted the family. That forced John to grow up fast. His father was always drunk or out chasing other women. He was never home long. His father beat him."

"You said you helped John? What kind of help did you give him?"

"I had the power to open closed doors. We played politics. The conservatives could relate to a Black man who had changed his name to John Galt. I shepherded his appointment through the political process to become U.S. Solicitor General. Then I seized the political opportunity to capture a permanent seat for him on the D.C. Federal Appeals Court—good experience for a Supreme Court justice."

"Did you trade political chips with the power elites to get his Supreme Court seat?"

Jennie paused a second too long, after the waitress placed piping hot coffee before her.

"I'll take that as a yes," Julianne said, writing.

"Just say I didn't deny it," Jennie said with grit. "You can withdraw the question."

"You've been quoted as saying, 'The world should know that I am perfectly content helping John accomplish his objectives from the co-pilot's seat.' Is that a correct quote?"

"Yes." Jennie tried to take a sip, but her coffee was still too hot.

"When did you say it?"

"During his confirmation hearings. I let the world know I would and will carry out my wifely duties to him behind the scenes. He was confirmed with that statement on the record."

"Can you give an example of the type of wifely support you've given Justice Galt behind the scenes?"

"It's a well-known fact I made the political deals to save his nomination."

"Can you give me something more specific?"

"I helped write and type John's last speech to the Senate Judiciary Committee when it appeared certain that his nomination was going down in flames. I encouraged him. With only a few hours of disturbed sleep and me at his side, John marched into the Capitol to face the Senate Judiciary Committee. He took the high ground, defending his private life as just that—private."

"As Justice Galt's co-pilot, do you ever take over the controls of his chambers?"

"I don't think you want to go down this road with me."

"Are you involved in the hiring process for your husband's law clerks?"

"Not officially."

"Unofficially?"

"Of course. What do you want to make out of it?"

"When John brings home work from his chambers, do you help him?"

"I'm his helpmate in the full biblical sense of the word—his rock. We are one."

"He can't write," Julianne said. "Do you sign for him now?"

"He doesn't need to write to perform his job."

"He's rarely at the Court."

"He can work from home."

"Are you running his chambers and directing his law clerks?"

"This interview is over. You should stay on track if you don't want to get derailed. At some point you need to understand power, and realize you're not in control."

Chapter Sixty-One

Friday, September 13

Mrs. Ross wanted to talk to JT. She wanted him to talk to Katherine. She wanted to save him before it was too late. Katherine was under a lot of community pressure to issue the fifth letter.

The nation needed JT's careful consideration of the facts at play in each and every case. Moderation was the only way to avoid violence in the nation. This was about saving all of them. The nation needed him to use his heart. She knew he had one. It had been good. She had looked into his innocent eyes before he started hating his father.

She had to do something. But what?

The pain came again while she was sitting in her armchair overlooking the Potomac River. She rose from her seat and let out a sigh, waiting a few moments for the pain to subside before straightening her spine. Stiffness. She needed to move more. She hadn't been to yoga in months. Her body was complaining.

That led her thoughts to Joshua Galt's yoga class. Roy, Galt's personal security officer, had mentioned it to her in the basement of the Supreme Court building while she waited for Katherine a few weeks before. Why hadn't she gone yet?

That was a sure way to reach JT.

The Court's security officer wanted to drive Mrs. Ross to her class, but she insisted that they walk to the Capitol City Yoga Studio on K Street. Once there, she approached a petite young lady with short curly hair and bright eyes at the reception desk.

"Do you have anything for seniors?" Mrs. Ross asked.

"We have a great class called Healthy Backs. It's slow and a lot of people start there."

"I think that might be the class for me. It's been several months since I've been to a yoga class. Do you have an instructor by the name of Joshua?"

"Yes, as a matter of fact we do."

"Does he teach Healthy Backs?"

"On Monday, Wednesday and Friday mornings at eight-thirty."

The next morning, Mrs. Ross arrived at the studio at eight and signed in. Joshua stood at the front of the room, flipping through CDs.

He was medium height with a well-built upper body, fully developed shoulders, and bulging biceps that pushed against his smooth skin. Tight workout shorts revealed a toned behind. Attractive. He flashed a warm smile as he greeted his regular crowd of students who gathered at the front of the room.

Mrs. Ross picked a spot in the far back corner and spread out her mat.

Joshua approached her. "Is this your first yoga class?"

"No," she said. "But I haven't been for a while."

"Well, take it slow. Are you exercising?"

"Yes." Mrs. Ross wondered if he recognized her. "I have my own treadmill."

"Then you should be fine. If you can't do a pose, don't worry about it. Just do what you can and focus on your breath. If you do nothing but breathe properly for the entire hour, you will have made progress."

At 8:30 a.m., Joshua turned on soft music with the sound of flowing water in the background.

He instructed the class in a soothing voice. "Sit on the floor with your knees folded in front of you. Close your eyes. Breathe deeply. Focus only on the rhythm of your breath."

Mrs. Ross rested her hands on her knees, eyes closed. She felt his movement in the room as she followed his voice and moved into various positions with the others in class.

"Stretch," Joshua said, helping her into a strong warrior position. "Stretch as your oxygenated blood sends rich nutrients to every cell in your body. Just be in this moment, in this place, at this time. Be present with every breath you take—flushing toxins and negative emotions from your body with your every breath. Breathe in healing energy from the universe."

Mrs. Ross kept her eyes closed, struggling to maintain the downward dog position.

Joshua whispered in her ear, "Just go into child's pose and rest."

The class went on until they were all lying flat on their backs, fully stretched out, arms spread, with all eyes closed. Total silence.

Mrs. Ross became so relaxed she lost consciousness.

Joshua bent down and touched her on her shoulder. "Are you okay?"

"I fell asleep," Mrs. Ross said, embarrassed when she realized that class ended.

"You're not the first one." He pulled her up. "Have we met before?"

"In a way," Mrs. Ross said. "We saw each other in the basement of the Supreme Court a few months ago before your father got hurt. You were talking to Roy."

"Mrs. Ross."

"Yes. I mentioned to Roy that I needed to find a new yoga class because of the questionable activities over at the community center where I attended classes. He told me you were a yoga instructor here and that his daughter was in one of your classes."

"Yes," Joshua said. "His daughter comes to my Ashanti class and, yes, I think I can help you with your stiffness. But it looks to me like you already know how to just be."

"Yes," she said. "A long time ago, I learned how to leave my body, forget my past, and just stay in the present moment—as you say, 'to just be.'"

"That's why I got into yoga. It's not easy being his son."

"It's not easy being her mother," Mrs. Ross teased back. "Have you had breakfast? I was going to the café across the street. It's on me, if you've got the time."

"Sure," Joshua said. "But can we go down the street to the Street Side Café? That's where I normally go after this class. I'm a creature of habit. They're expecting me."

The Street Side Café was busy. There was a counter with eight seats, all taken. The sound of clanging dishes filled the room while the aroma of coffee served as a wake-up call. Glasses of orange juice added color. Two yellow plates with stacks of pecan pancakes and a little pitcher of warm maple syrup floated past them on the way to happy faces.

"Hi, Josh," the owner said. "Your booth is waiting for you and the young lady."

"Thanks." Joshua led the way to his favorite booth.

Mrs. Ross slipped in with her back facing the door. The owner placed two mugs before them and poured coffee while handing them the menus.

"Any specials today?" Joshua asked.

"Yes. We have a lump crabmeat scramble with tomatoes, chives, spinach, and mozzarella cheese. Served with an English muffin. It's very good. I'll be back for your order."

"This is my favorite place," Joshua said. "The specials are always good. I love the bacon-pecan pancakes, but normally I can't resist the mystery of the special."

"The special today certainly sounds good."

"And, what can I serve you?" the owner asked.

"We'll both have the special," Joshua replied. "With a large orange juice for me."

"I'll have a small orange juice," Mrs. Ross said. "And may I have one mixed berry pancake instead of the English muffin?"

"That will be two dollars extra," the waiter said.

"Okay," Mrs. Ross said. "No problem."

"I'll have two bacon-pecan pancakes instead of the English muffin," Joshua added.

"Another two dollars extra for you."

As the owner turned away, Joshua said, "I never knew I could have my pecan pancakes and the special, too."

"That's because you accepted an assumption that wasn't true."

"That sounds like something my father would say. Are your arms sore?"

"Yes. My arms are the weakest part of my body."

"You'll probably be sore in other places in the morning. So, take an Espom salt bath tonight. If you've got a big bathtub, use at least four pounds. That's a half-gallon carton."

"Four pounds! That's a lot of salt."

"Think about it," he said. "The instructions say two cups per gallon for soaking. How many gallons will your bathtub hold? Soak for twenty minutes and the soreness will be gone."

"What do you do other than yoga?" Mrs. Ross asked.

"I'm a writer. Normally I go home and write three to four hours, then come back to the studio for my evening classes."

"What are you writing about?"

"Injustice on Hilton Head Island. Property rights lost."

"That's surprising—does your father know what you're writing about?"

"Nope. Not really. He thinks I'm writing a novel about Frederick Douglas and Reconstruction. But it's turning into more. Much more. I've been able to piece together a lot about my grandmother's family and the properties they lost during Jim Crow. The Gullah/Geechee history and culture is fascinating."

"You know about Gullah/Geechee?"

"Yeah," Joshua replied. "My grandmother spoke Gullah. She talked fast. Real fast. I never could understand a word she said when she got mad. It's like another language. I asked my father about the Gullah background in our family when I learned about a ten million dollar federal grant to save the culture. He told me some pretty wild stories."

"Can I share a secret with you?" Mrs. Ross asked, gazing into his clear brown eyes.

"Sure." Joshua returned her gaze.

"Both of us have to be careful about who we talk to in Washington."

"I know I do. Please don't mention my writing project to your daughter. I don't want her to say anything to him about me. He's understandably paranoid."

"I know what you mean. I'm writing my memoir, and there are parts I haven't shared with my daughter. I've never fully answered her questions about my family."

"My father never fully answers my questions about his family, either," Joshua said. "He says he doesn't know much about his father's family history."

"He might be telling you the truth." Mrs. Ross toyed with her omelet. "I lost track of my family when I was young. I tragically lost my father when I was eleven."

"I'm sorry to hear that," Joshua said, placing his fork down.

"I've dealt with it by not talking about it."

"I didn't expect your secret to be so personal."

"I haven't really told you the secret yet."

Joshua leaned forward. "Are you going to share it?"

"I haven't told my daughter yet. Can I trust you?"

"We're each other's confidant now."

She was silent for a moment, then said like a speeding motor, "Da' buckruh' hogmeat flabuh me mout' 'tell uh done fuhgit uh hab sin fuhkill'um."

"What?" Joshua's eyes widened.

"I speak Gullah," Mrs. Ross said, perfectly enunciating her words with a smirk. "I said: 'That white man's pork flavored my mouth so that I forgot the sin I committed in killing the hog.' I was talking about the bacon and the ham we ate—somebody had to sin by killing the pig."

"Where're you from?"

"Georgia," Mrs. Ross said. "The Savannah area."

"Well, you know, my dad's from Needle Pointe. Not too far from Savannah."

"Yes, I knew that."

"You're bilingual," Joshua said with a little chuckle. "My dad speaks Gullah, too… Does your daughter?"

"No. Not really. I've always spoken perfect English around her."

"Well, this is what I think my dad says to himself when he's listening to confusing oral arguments and an attorney badly missing the mark. 'Don' gimme dat W'ich en' w'y dimmycrack talk.' If you can speak Gullah, can you tell me what he's thinking?"

"You're giving me a test?" Mrs. Ross asked, raising an eyebrow. She took a bite of her pancake before she said, "Don't give me that confusing Democratic talk."

Joshua smiled at the correct answer. "Now, don't ask me to say anything else in Gullah because that's all I know. Do you think in Gullah?"

"No. But I do think it sometimes, when I get angry. I remember my daddy talkin' Gullah real fast when he got mad. Movin' his head. That was one of his sayin', that is, sayings."

Joshua laughed at the facial expressions she made.

She laughed, too, and then went silent as her thoughts lingered in the past a bit too long.

Joshua picked up on her changing mood. "I'm sorry."

"It's okay," she said, bouncing back. "How much have you written?"

"I've just started. I only have a few chapters."

"I've got about thirty pages of my memoir ready for a review. I'm searching for the beginning of my story. Maybe we can form a writer's group. Just the two of us."

"That might work. A secret writing group that meets after my class."

"Do you think we can get away with it?"

"We should keep our professional relationship on a confidential basis." He chuckled. "Just as the justices keep their business confidential from us. Agreed?"

"Yes," she said. "We'll be partners in silence. Except you might let your father read a couple of my chapters, since he is familiar with the setting of my story."

"I'll see if he's up to reading anything that he doesn't have to read. He's still recovering."

"Sorry. Maybe I shouldn't have asked. I just thought he might find it interesting. I happen to have the first two chapters with me. Want to take them now?"

"Sure, I'll bring the first two chapters of my story to class next Wednesday. It's about forty pages, double-spaced. We can focus on your writing next week and my writing the following week... Breakfast here on the sixteenth?"

"Yes." She pulled a large manila envelope out of her oversized purse. "My pen name is Hattie Mae Cobb. Let's promise no copies are to be made. I think that's best."

Chapter Sixty-Two

Angry Justice: A Memoir
By Hattie Mae Cobb

Chapter One

On a sweltering night in the summer of 1958, Ademus was out drinking again at an after-hours joint frequented by Blacks in the historic district of Savannah.

He was loud. He was drunk. He was late.

Weeks earlier, Charlotte had learned her father would be out of town on a business trip to Atlanta this weekend and sent a note to Ademus through Hattie. Charlotte had invited Ademus to be alone with her in the big house on that steamy Georgia night.

She promised Ademus the comfort of her bed instead of crushed leaves on the ground.

Ademus got into his cousin Hattie's 1949 Ford and headed south for about ten miles toward the Atlantic coastline. But instead of keeping straight to go home, he turned left onto a winding dirt road that led to the old Jackson Plantation where he had once lived with his parents behind the big house that he could see, off in the distance. His heartbeat quickened. This was insane.

The Jackson house was a small mansion with eight bedrooms, formal and informal dining rooms, two sitting rooms and a library situated next to a pond. The large sitting room and library had red brick fireplaces and were decorated with imported French furniture, Turkish throw rugs, and Old Master paintings acquired by the Jackson family before the Civil War, when plantation life was in its glory. On the white painted porch, six rocking chairs were arranged in a line with little tables between them, three on each side.

Charlotte's bedroom was on the second floor. Her light was on.

Ademus pulled the car off the main road onto a side path that led to the modest but neat cabin where his parents and brothers still lived. Carefully, he parked the car behind some trees, hoping it would not be visible to his family or anyone else who should happen to travel the road that night.

Charlotte was waiting for him. He wanted to resist her, but couldn't. He could no longer combat the desire to see her again.

He didn't care what happened. He had to see her that night.

So infatuated, he would die for her.

Ademus threaded through the magnificent oak trees' with hanging Spanish moss toward the big house. Reaching the back gate, he used the key he had had for many years. It squeaked as he opened it. He paused and gazed across the blackened expanse of Moon River. The bright moon was hidden behind clouds.

Approaching the former slave entrance to the big house, Ademus hoped that his mother, who still worked as the Jackson's cook, was visiting their relatives as she told him she would be that weekend. He could not think of a good lie to tell her, should she happen to see him.

But he couldn't worry about that now.

Unrelenting desire, like water flowing downhill, drew him closer to Charlotte's door in spite of the risks.

He anticipated Charlotte's embrace and playful moves. She was always finding ways to tease him with little gestures, like unbuttoning her blouse to reveal her ample bust line as she fanned herself. Or, just a private lustful stare in the presence of others, revealed only to him.

Her brown eyes spoke to his heart on many levels. Sometimes they shouted for his touch. Whenever the two of them were alone, she asked him to hug her. He always complied. As children, the back of the barn had been their favorite meeting place late at night. Or, they met in the woods.

Hiding their love from the world.

Their love was mutual, but it was not a relationship of equals. Their love was illegal. He was married. She was engaged. He was Black. She was white.

Their love was a crime, punishable by death.

Charlotte Jackson was like the vanilla ice cream sundae with strawberry topping that Ademus could never have as a child. Her skin was creamy white and she had to be careful to protect it from the hot Georgia sun, often wearing flashy hats that matched her outfits. When her long reddish-blonde hair wasn't under a hat, she pulled it back into a ponytail with a matching ribbon or pinned it up in a neat French roll on her head. Charlotte was a fancy dresser, always concerned that her accessories matched perfectly.

That night, she wore a white night gown with lace around the low-cut neckline, her breasts pushed out beneath the soft white satin. The outline of her nipples showed under the thin material. Her hair flowed around her shoulders and down to the middle of her back.

She peered into her dressing mirror. Perfect.

Not wanting to break into a sweat yet, she moved in front of the fan. Still, she started to melt in the heat of the night. A bead of perspiration formed on her chest. She patted the moist hollow between her beasts with a handkerchief, growing impatient.

Where was he?

As she peered out the kitchen window again, she saw storm clouds forming in the distance. He might not come in a storm. A sense of loss engulfed her. The glow of anticipation faded from her face. She checked the clock on the wall. It wasn't too late yet. But Ademus should have arrived by then.

They should already have been together.

Why was he was making her wait? She wanted him. She felt cursed. Flopping onto a chair in the kitchen, she sighed.

With her eyes closed, she wished he would appear before her when she opened them. It had been weeks since she had seen him last.

She fought back tears. Considering her fate—a future life married to a man she did not love with no hope of an on-going affair with Ademus—her mood took on dark energy.

She felt the loss of childhood love.

Then she heard a sound outside.

Jumping up, she peeked out of the kitchen window once more. Her face lit up with a smile as she saw him approach the rear of the house.

"I been worryin' 'bout you," she whispered in her southern drawl. "I was gettin' afraid you weren't goin' come tonight. I didn't think I could endure another night without seeing you."

"I tried not to come," Ademus said, pulling back a step.

"Why?"

"You know why. You're engaged ta a rich white man now. You can't be messing around with me like dis. You know it. No tellin' what would happen if we git caught. I tried ta drink away the urge ta see you. You know dis is dangerous."

"Stop it!" Charlotte demanded. "Right now, I don't care what happens. I don't love him. It hurts like a vice around my heart when I can't see you. Just make me happy tonight. That's all that I ask. Make me happy now. Look at me."

He gazed into her lustful eyes, and then reached for her. She stepped back. Then reached for his hand, leading him up the stairs toward her bedroom.

With a beguiling smile she said, "I knew you would come. You belong to me."

She pulled off his silky shirt and let it drop on the stairs as they climbed.

In her room, she closed the door and turned on the radio to complete the candlelit atmosphere.

Eager for each other's touch, they kissed, caressed and fondled one another.

Lost in passionate foreplay, they did not hear the sound of the approaching car.

Clayton Jackson, Charlotte's father, parked and glanced up at Charlotte's open window. At first, he just heard the radio playing.

Clayton was surprised she was at home. She was supposed to be out of town. As he entered the foyer, he heard Charlotte's moan over the radio music.

Then he noticed the fancy shirt on the stairs.

He tapped his fingers on a side table in the entrance foyer, thinking what to do. Then he listened for a few more moments to be sure of what he was hearing. Charlotte was not in distress. She was enjoying her company, her moans getting louder. He decided not to confront the situation then, and left the house without making his presence known.

He would have a serious talk with each of them later.

Some things were best left alone, when grown folks were making love. It sounded like healthy lovemaking to him. After all, the girl was engaged and a big wedding was already being planned. The marriage needed to happen soon anyway. He would just tell Marcus, 'you're gonna marry her now' and that would be that.

Slamming his car door with force, he hoped they heard it.

He drove away with a devious smile on his face.

Young love, he thought. *Best not to disturb the lovebirds.* He would just go into Savannah for the night.

As Clayton drove down the road, he noticed the silhouette of a car parked behind a huge oak tree, off in the distance to the north. He knew that was one of the few good places to hide a car on his property, so he always paid attention to that spot when he drove by.

He thought it strange, though, that Charlotte's fiancé Marcus Turner would park there.

And there had been no car parked outside of his house.

Clayton became alarmed. If Charlotte was not with Marcus, who was she with?

In his gut, he knew the answer.

Clayton pulled his car off the road, parked it, and eased toward the parked car, keeping out of sight of his house. The car was blue. Marcus's car was red. As he drew closer, he realized that it was Hattie's blue car, and should have been parked at the Cobbs' cabin. Slowly, anger began to build within Clayton as he confirmed who Charlotte's lover might be.

He returned to his car, took his shotgun from the trunk, and waited for Ademus to return.

When Charlotte and Ademus heard the slamming car door, fear raced through them. Charlotte peeped out her bedroom window and saw her father sitting in his car.

She stayed glued to the window.

Then the sound of spinning tires on gravel sounded an alarm.

With a perplexed look on her face, Charlotte uttered, "He drove away. He just drove away. Do you think he could have been in the house and heard us?"

"Don't know."

"He heard us," Charlotte sighed. "I just know he did."

"This is bad." Dread rose within Ademus like the evening tide.

He put his pants on first. "Where's my shirt?" he barked. "Get dressed. No. Put on a cotton nightgown. Go ta bed and pretend ta be sleep. Ya shouldn't be up if he comes back t'night."

"Are you going home?" she whimpered.

"Might not be safe," Ademus said. "He might wanna lynch me."

"He wouldn't do that," she mumbled, wrapping a sheet around her body.

"Dat's whut ya say. Dis is the south and I'm a Negro. Ya, forbidden fruit." He turned his back to her.

"But..."

"Ya know whut that means. I been warned."

The atmosphere in the bedroom changed as if a bucket of water had been poured on an open fire, extinguishing the light of love and all flames of desire.

As Charlotte reached for her robe, the big house took on a cover of foreboding.

"Ya know ya Daddy said if he ever caught me wit ya again he'd lynch me, and that time we were jis lookin' at each other. He saw da look in ya eyes. Dat look was 'nuff for him ta threaten me. We can't do dis no more."

Ademus bolted from her room without looking back.

Running down the stairs, he grabbed his shirt and ran into the night. Drops of perspiration rolled down his forehead and small of his back. He heard the high-pitched mating calls of male crickets as they joined the shrilling cicada chorus under the cover of night. Fear made the insects' mating sounds seem louder than ever before.

He fled along the dark path, the clouds still covering the moon.

Huffing and puffing, he ran to his parents' cabin, thinking fast. He would have to tell his parents goodbye. His breathing grew louder but he pressed on in the darkness, certain of impending doom if he did not get out of Georgia quickly.

He found his father alone. His brothers were out attending a wedding reception at the community hall across the highway.

Bursting through the unlocked screen door with sweat dripping and fear in his voice, Ademus said, "Dad, where's Momma?"

"She caught da bus to Gainsville ta see her people with Hattie," Washington said. "Your Gramma Mae is sick. Might not make it. What's wrong wit you?"

"I've come to say goodbye," Ademus said. "I've gotta leave town fast."

"What's happened?" Washington demanded. "What ya talkin' 'bout boy?"

"I was wit Charlotte tonight in da big house. She sent for me. I was in her bedroom. Mr. Jackson came home early from his trip ta Atlanta. I think he heard us."

"Heard what?"

"You know, me pledjuhr'um. She thought no one could hear us. And if you and Momma did, well, you two would jis' mind your own business anyway."

"Boy, you weren't havin' no white woman in her own house, were ya? Ya couldn't be dat much of a fool."

"I think Jackson seen my shirt on da stairs when he came in. It dropped."

"He don't know ya got dat fancy shirt," Washington said. "Gimme that shirt." Washington snatched it. "Did he see ya?"

"Naw, but he know my voice. He came in da house and then left. Probably didn't wanna kill me in front of Charlotte. He won't mess up her wedding. Da need her to marry inta dat rich family to save dis place. No, Mr. Jackson won't mess dat up over me, but I know he plannin' what to do 'bout me. I gotta go."

"Naw. We gotta go. If they can't find ya, they jis' might hang us in ya place. Jackson mus' be mad as hell. No tellin' what he might do. Ya got any money?"

"I got 'bout thirty dollars and a hundred left from da money dat Mr. Adam's gave us. Dat should be 'nuf ta get us ta da relatives up North. We have ta take Hattie's car."

"What 'bout Leila?"

"We can't run wit da babies. Won't be 'nuf room in da car after we pick up my brothers. They'll need to lie down on the backseat 'til we out of da state. And Leila's pregnant again. If dey catch us, dey might kill her and da kids. Gotta leave 'em."

"Go git Hattie's car," Washington said. "I'll pack some things. We gotta move fast. I hate ta leave dis place. No place been bettuh for us. But what's done is done. We jis gotta do what we gotta do. Stayin' here after whut ya done is a sure rope. We gotta move quick."

Washington pulled a gun from under the sofa and gave it to his son.

Ademus took it and placed it in his back pocket.

"Papa, I'm sorry," he said, reaching for his father.

With a look of steel Washington said, "Go."

Ademus turned from his father and bolted out the door, running through the woods behind the big house toward Hattie's car. His eyes were focused on the blue car as he approached it.

He did not see Clayton in the shadows, waiting.

The sounds of running feet and dead branches crushing under Ademus's feet announced his approach. Clayton stepped into his path. Ademus stopped. Their eyes locked.

Clayton raised his shotgun, aiming at Ademus's heart.

"I'm gonna kill you, cut you up, and feed you to the pigs," Clayton said.

Ademus stood in mortal fear. *Did he have time to pull the gun?*

In that instant, a flash of lightening lit up the Georgia skies. Distracted, Clayton glanced over his shoulder toward the light. The sound of thunder vibrated through the air as if the heavens were witnessing a clash of titans.

Ademus pulled out the pistol. He aimed it at startled eyes, firing three rapid shots. Clayton fell without firing his weapon.

Ademus raced to the body and felt for a pulse. It was gone.

Ademus found his brothers at the wild wedding reception and pulled them outside. He spoke fast. "Mr. Jackson is dead. Ya gotta help me. I shot him."

"Where da body?" his brother Junnieboy asked with a slur.

Ademus told them.

"Can you see it from the road?"

"No, it's near da hiding spot. His car, parked not too far away. We'll have to use Hattie's car to get rid of the body."

"What you gonna do with da body?" Neeck, the older brother, whispered.

"I don't know," Ademus blurted out. "Mr. Jackson's body can't be found. Charlotte might not be able to take it. Seein' her old man dead might make her talk. After da reception over, meet me in da woods by da body."

"What ya want us to do?" Neeck asked. "I don't wanna go out ta da marsh t'night. No high tide ta carry da body ta sea."

Junnieboy said, "Whut 'bout da Ogeechee River? Jus' t'row em in."

"We haffuh cut da body up," Neeck said. "If yaw don't, it might float."

"I can't cut him up like a pig," Ademus said. "Too messy. We'd git his blood all over us. I know—we can put'um on the back of one of da sawmill trucks, put logs on top of him, then put'um in the boiler and burn da body up."

Neeck said, "Dat'll work. Nutt'n left but ashes. No mo' Mr. Jackson."

"I'll tek Hattie's car back ta pack up and park Mr. Jackson's car 'round bak of the big house like he always park," Ademus said. "I'll git the truck for da body. We'll tek'um to the sawmill when everybody's lights goes off. Nobody will come out 'til morn' if da smell smoke."

Junnieboy said, "Yeah, burnin' him up a lot bettur than cuttin' him up. I don't wan' his blood on my hands. Gonna take Hattie's car?"

"Got no choice."

"Anybody see ya in Hattie's car tonight?" Neeck asked.

"Not nobody I'm worried 'bout. I'll just come pick ya up in 'bout a hour. If we burn da body, ya won't have ta run wit me. Mr. Jackson jis be missin'. I'll tek his car. Leave Hattie's car here. When Hattie Mae come bak wit Mamma, tell'um what happened." With his escape plan hatched, Ademus said, "I gotta go tell Papa—ya'll don't need ta run. I'm the only one gotta go."

311

Where was Ademus?

Charlotte couldn't stay in her bed. She got up, glanced at the clock. 1:30 a.m.

She threw on her robe and went down the stairs to peek out of the kitchen window. As she gazed toward the Cobb family cabin, she saw a figure running toward their cabin. A few moments later, the lights popped on. Her heart pounded. Something must be wrong.

Who was running to his parents' cabin this late at night? Determined to find out, she dashed through the kitchen door, grabbing a walking stick from the corner.

She had to find out if her father had hurt him.

Charlotte stepped at a fast clip toward the Cobbs's cabin with a lantern and the walking stick at the ready. She stepped in a mud puddle, then she almost fell in a rut along the way. She slowed her pace , the lantern extended in front of her. Above, she heard the song of the kadydids: *katy-did... katy-didn't.* Crickets chirped at her feet. The wind picked up.

She needed to hurry. It felt like a storm was coming. She kept going until she reached the Cobb's front door where she heard his voice.

He was alive.

She steeled herself and knocked on the door.

Ademus and his father were startled. They froze, their eyes shouted, *Don't answer!*

Ademus moved silently toward the door. Adrenaline flooded his body, his muscles readied for flight. Spine-chilling demons danced in his head, blocking rational thought. Ademus did not plan on being taken like Hattie's father. He wasn't going to give himself up to be hung by an angry mob.

He was gonna kill'um.

He pointed the gun with his arm out as his father opened the door and backed away without a sound. Ademus started shooting before he saw the face of his victim.

Unjustified defense.

Blinded by fear.

Charlotte gazed at him with shocked eyes as she fell to the ground.

Ademus wailed like a wild animal when he realized what he had done.

"No! No!" Ademus repeated over and over again.

"Go get the truck," Washington barked. "There's room for both of them."

Ademus didn't move. Weeping, he fell to his knees beside Charlotte's body. A pool of red blood flowed from her breasts.

Washington headed for his pick-up truck, hustling with great speed.

He drove to the door of their cabin. Eyeing Ademus still on the floor, Washington dashed to his side. He yanked Ademus up before hitting him with his fist with all of his might.

Ademus fell back. Stunned.

"Get ya ass up now!" Washington shouted. "Ya caused all of dis damned trouble over her and now ya wanna sit down and cry. Get up! Park Hattie's car where it belongs and git back here. Now we got two bodies to git rid of by mornin' light."

"Charlotte's death changes everything," Washington said, after Ademus returned from parking the car. "But it gives us more time before people figure out they're missing. After we burn da bodies, ya need ta go home and tell Leila you're leavin' her. Just have a big fight with her. Storm out. Take da truck. We've gotta clean it to make sure ain't no blood in it."

"Not sure burnin' 'em in da sawmill gonna work," Ademus said. "The smell of two bodies burnin' in the middle of the night might smell like roastin' meat. People might talk. Don't know if da burning logs will cover da smell up."

"Da people sleep now," Washington said. "And with da burnin' oaks fuelin' da fire, people won't notice any difference in da smell. Set da fire 'round four-thirty. Be gone by five. If you don't burn 'em up then ya gotta cut'um up."

"No," Ademus said without emotion. "I'll take my chances with the boiler and da smoke. I'll be outta here by five, Lawd willin'."

As Ademus drove along the back roads out of Georgia before dawn, he remembered what had happened to them many years before, when he was just five years old. He remembered that dark night as if it were yesterday.

But this time, his father would stay behind to help raise his fatherless grandchildren.

Ademus would never return to Needle Pointe.

In the weeks that followed, Hattie suffered emotionally and physically. She went to have a talk with Judge Jackson, Clayton's older brother. She couldn't tell him everything, but she told him enough. Clayton and Charlotte had been missing for weeks. Bad things had happened on the Jackson Planation. She was sure of it. But the Sheriff found nothing.

With Clayton missing, Hattie was afraid to stay in Savannah alone with a baby on the way. She needed a blessing from the judge to survive and leave town.

Judge Jackson helped Hattie land a job at Harvard Law— because she was of his family.

Hattie changed her name and married in Boston, never contacting her family again.

Many years later, when the family left the graveyard in Georgia after the funeral of Hattie's real mother, the final key to

Hattie's past was left behind. Hattie wasn't there. No one in the family knew how to reach her. Hattie was lost to them.

Like Ademus, Hattie disappeared from Georgia in 1958 and was never seen there again.

Like Hattie, Ademus changed his name and birthed a new life.

He became Russell A. Cobb.

Ademus told the people he met to just call him AC.

Vivian L. Carpenter

Chapter Sixty-Three

The Ritz-Carlton Residences
Sunday, September 15

Katherine settled into her desk chair and fired up her computer before reaching for the pile of cert petitions that awaited her judgment. With pen in hand, she sped through the pile, signing denial after denial. Finally, her pace slowed when she read the name of the petitioner on the next cert: *Hilton Head Corporation.*

Would she have to recuse herself?

She had represented the Hilton Head Corporation in her first case before the Supreme Court, so her interest was primed. Her staff had made no recommendation on the *Hilton Head Corporation v. Old South Carolina Bank* petition. What was this about?

Katherine dug into the facts, some of which she already knew. The Gullahs were brought to America in the eighteenth century, forced to work as slaves on Sea Island plantations. After the Civil War ended, the Gullahs got legal ownership of the abandoned property they had lived on for generations. They were isolated, maintaining their own culture. Ignored by the world.

Twenty years ago, her father convinced a group of Gullah Sea Island property owners to put their land into a corporate entity— Hilton Head Corporation—to take advantage of the tax and corporate laws that gave preference to corporate property rights over individual rights. Her father had promised the Gullahs they could live on their

316

Sea Island land, even if the corporation changed ownership, so long as the corporation owned the land. There was a restriction in the corporate charter that prevented Hilton Head Corporation from ever selling the land.

That was the beauty of their incorporation.

But the Gullahs' right to incorporate in the State of Georgia had been challenged when a state employee processing their corporate renewal application discovered the Hilton Head Corporation shareholders had Black faces. They should have sent a white attorney like they always had done. That was a mistake. Their corporate status went dormant for years while their annual renewal applications were trashed. Jim Crow took another stand.

Katherine's father took the case all the way to the U.S. Supreme Court at his own expense. He decided not to mention race as a factor in their appeals. They would stand on the doctrine of corporate law alone. The State of Georgia argued that the Hilton Head Corporation simply did not exist, maintaining the South Carolina Gullahs had no corporate rights in Georgia.

Corporate rights trumped Jim Crow. The Supreme Court ruled the Hilton Head Corporation was a person with a constitutional right to renew its life. Case closed.

But four years ago the Gullahs had lost their land in court. Was Jim Crow back?

The facts were simple. Old South Carolina Bank had found Hilton Head Corporation's beachfront land listed on the delinquent property tax rolls. The bank offered Hilton Head Corporation a loan at a bargain rate to pay their taxes and other obligations, using their land as collateral. Then the bank didn't accept their loan payments. Hilton Head Corporation sent check after check to the bank. None were cashed. The bank said they never received any payments.

Hilton Head Corporation sued, claiming fraud, to protect their property rights.

The bank won.

After the Gullahs were evicted, Old South Carolina Bank fenced off the property with barbed wire. Numerous no trespass signs with camera images were posted, giving notice that trespassers would be shot. Roads that had been open to the public stopped at their property line. Armed sentries guarded all roads that led onto the Hilton Head Corporation's property. All of the sentries had Asian features. Massive building structures, wide roads, and shipping docks were under construction on the Gullah's ancestral land, rising at an alarming rate.

The United States filed an amicus brief, arguing that the Framers never intended to create constitutional rights for persons who were not U.S. citizens. Their brief pointed out that the Old South Carolina Bank, incorporated in 1901, was now owned by a group of Shanghai investors—none of them U.S. citizens. The Founding Fathers had not foreseen this.

Was the Supreme Court going to stay on autopilot? Would this be allowed to happen?

It was the same issue that had been challenged in the Hawaiian land rights case which had yet to receive the four votes needed to be heard, except that the foreign interests claiming corporate rights in the Hawaiian land rights case were British. Not a threatening foreign invader. Katherine held her vote on the Hawaiian cert, waiting on Galt. If Galt was in control, why was he holding back?

Katherine spun around and typed two disposition memos voting for the Hilton Head and Hawaii cases to be heard, signed them, and dropped the memos on the pile of processed petitions.

Reading on, she discovered Crowne Works Corporation originally had Gullah shareholders and owned beachfront Sea Island property in Needle Pointe. *Needle Pointe?* Something was going on here. Crowne Works' creditors forced it into bankruptcy proceedings. The Gullahs lost their ownership. Would Galt recuse himself in this one? No. Probably not.

The Crowne Works Corporation was purchased out of bankruptcy by the Old South Carolina Bank in a deal to satisfy all of its creditors. Katherine felt something wasn't right. The Gullah descendants also had a provision in their corporate charter that gave them and their descendants the right to live on their ancestral land forever. But Crowne Works had challenged the surviving Gullah descendants, requiring them to prove they were descendants by DNA. They couldn't prove it because DNA samples of the original shareholders didn't exist.

Nor did they have accurate birth records.

A lower court issued an order for the Gullahs to vacate their ancestral land.

As in the Hilton Head case, the Gullahs settled under duress with an agreement that all shareholder families would be relocated to a housing complex in Savannah with their expenses paid and a yearly stipend for life.

Were they creating an urban reservation for the disenfranchised?

The United States government was challenging the right of Crowne Works Corporation to create a private club on five miles of strategically located beachfront in the Sea Islands, citing national defense. *What?* The United States argued that the Framers never intended to create constitutional rights for persons who were not U.S. citizens. But she knew the U.S. Small Business Administration encouraged foreign nations to establish U.S. corporations under various state laws. She had always had concerns about that.

Did they know what they were doing?

Old South Carolina Bank owned at least two Sea Island properties. Not good.

Katherine banged out a disposition memo supporting review of *The United States v. Crowne Works Corporation* by the Court. She didn't believe the Founding Fathers considered corporations a part of "We the People." In her mind, these cases showed that corporations could become stronger than the individuals who had created them. Unintended consequences.

A constitutional crisis, too? It was time to set things right.

Next she picked up the *NAACP Legal Defense Fund v. Colored Investments Corporation*. Descendants of the Black Seminoles were driven out of Florida in 1948 in a trail of blood and tears, and forced to abandon land granted to them by the Freedman's Bureau in 1870. Their cert petition argued that the State of Florida had a moral obligation to pay reparations for the loss of ownership of their property, the violation of their constitutional rights, and mental anguish.

There was a shameful record in the press and public records of what had occurred. Their land was located at the northern tip of the Florida coast in the Sea Islands. The Colored Investments Corporation was incorporated in 1948 by whites—the same year Katherine's ancestors were forced to abandon their land in Dublin, Georgia. In 1952, title to these abandoned properties was deeded over to the Colored Investments Corporation.

Repose was an issue. But should they give the land back to the Black Seminoles?

Katherine had a hunch. She spun around and started hitting the keys on her computer. In a few moments she had the answer. The Colored Investments Corporation was owned indirectly by Old South Carolina Bank—through several corporate shells. It was clear to her. A group of Shanghai investors was buying up land in strategic positions in the Sea Islands, and covering their tracks with corporate shells. She tapped on a few more keys, checking the public records. Poor whites along the coast were losing their lands to the Old South Carolina Bank, too. But they had not filed any lawsuits. Were they too poor to file? Probably. Were they settled? Maybe.

The United States filed an amicus brief. Good, someone was paying attention.

This could be a very dangerous situation for America.

Chapter Sixty-Four

The wheels of Katherine's brain spun—then she heard her doorbell. She wasn't expecting anyone. She glanced at the clock. 5:30 p.m. Sitting up straight in her soft leather chair, she narrowed her eyes. Who could that be, unannounced? She reached for the phone, then remembered that her neighbor had said she would drop off tickets to an opera at Lincoln Center later that evening. So she got up to answer the door. A breech in her security protocol.

It must be Ann. If it were someone from outside the building, the concierge would have called.

Reaching the door, she opened it.

And blinked, as uninvited memories rushed back.

Suddenly caught in the winds of an emotional tornado, she didn't know if she would bend or break. She couldn't count the number of times she had dreamed this moment would materialize. And now he stood before her, at the wrong time.

"What do you want?" she asked, drawing back.

Skip Graham, dressed in a gray Adidas jogging suit with black stripes and a bright red tucked-in t-shirt, towered before her. He did not seem turned off by her cold reception.

"I love you," he said in an unmistakable expression of raw emotion. "I'm tired of being alone. I'm tired of pushing all of my feelings for you away. Look at me. I've thought of you every day since the first day we met and regret the day I decided to let you go. Forgive me. Give us a chance."

She avoided dangerous eye contact, letting his words play in her head. Her emotions swelled. Hope? Love? Anger?

Tears threatened.

She could not look at him, fighting to keep her composure.

"I love you," he said with tenderness. "There's nothing more I can say."

She stared at him, blocking his entrance. "You have a lot of nerve coming here."

"I know, but I've got to have you in my life again."

"Not on your terms."

"Then state your terms."

With a poker face, she calculated the terms of engagement. In his penetrating gaze, her heart was touched. Their souls met on an invisible plane. She felt tremors of hope, but her rational mind wouldn't let her forget their circumstances.

Her ego screamed, *No!* Thoughts, hopes, and fears raced through her head.

He waited.

At last, she spoke. "I accepted the fact a long time ago I might not know how to land a jet with the engines thrusting. Gliding through the air on autopilot with programming that had not taken into account the weather conditions along the way. Programmed for a destination we couldn't reach in the face of strong headwinds. So I just gave up on you."

With patience, he waited and pleaded with his eyes.

"I think that was the right decision," she whispered. "To put a shield around my heart and just let my love for you die. It can't work now. I think you know that."

Her door remained open with the knob in her hand. She made no effort to close it. Nor did she invite him to enter.

"When I held you in my arms the first time," he confessed, "I felt love for you."

He paused.

Her eyes shot accusations of disbelief.

He braved on, "But my heart was too wounded to just let my feelings flow. I told myself a lie. I thought I was just feeling the love I'd had for my wife and confusing that emotion with you. I knew my body was waking up after the shock of her death. I thought my heart should still be in a coma. I didn't want to mess over you. My head wasn't right. I knew I wasn't right."

"But you did," she said, her voice cracking. "You did mess over me."

"You were too nice to just use for my own physical needs. You deserved someone who deeply loved you, without all of the baggage I carried."

"That's no excuse for hurting me the way you did. Why didn't you call? You said you would—why should I believe you now?"

"I was depressed and I knew it. I couldn't distinguish my love from lust, so I decided to let you go. I just didn't believe I could be in love again so soon. But I know now. I never remarried because of you—you should know that."

She heard sincerity in his voice as her trained eyes searched his face for truth.

"Are you going to let me in?" he asked.

"I can't let you in."

"Can we go for a ride so we can talk?"

Her shoulders relaxed. "Let me put on some shades and a baseball cap. I'll meet you at the elevator. There's a bench there."

"So I'm being benched," he said.

"Let's call this a 'time out.'"

She closed the door leaving him standing in front of it.

Five minutes later, she appeared in a baseball wig hat with blonde bangs and a long ponytail hanging out the back. She sported black designer sunglasses with rhinestones in the corners. Her jacket was zipped up to her chin.

She strolled down the hallway, her rubber-soled shoes brushing the plush carpet.

The senator stood, waiting for her. She felt pulled toward him, smelling his cologne.

She spoke as he reached to press the elevator button. "We lost thirty years because you thought you couldn't love again and didn't want to try. Is that what you're telling me?"

He blinked and pursed his lips. "I didn't believe love could happen like that, so soon after the loss of a soul mate. I was trying to be rational."

"Love isn't rational," Katherine stated as her father's words from long ago drifted into her head. "It's irrational. And one can't be sure it's love unless it's tested. You failed my test. I want to believe you, but I don't believe you love me."

"If you loved me…"

"If you loved me," she said, "you wouldn't ask me to prove anything to you."

"Can't you feel it?" Emotion seeped through his eyes as the doors to the elevator opened. They stepped in. He reached for her. She stepped back before he could compromise her.

"Cameras," she mouthed.

"Can we go back to your place?" he whispered.

Their eyes locked in a passionate gaze.

His heart spoke.

Her heart spoke back.

As the elevator doors began to open, he pressed the close button and the one for her floor. With a squeal, the elevator began to rise.

"Not now," Katherine said.

"When?"

"When you do something irrational to show me you love me."

"Isn't my being here now irrational?"

The elevator doors opened.

"No," she said as she began her exit and turned to face him, blocking his advance again. "Not if you want to use me to get Galt."

She walked away without looking back.

Chapter Sixty-Five

Arlington, Virginia
Sunday, September 15

As the evening of their twenty-fifth wedding anniversary rolled to an end, the marriage between Jennie and John Galt was solid, bonded with strong moral values after years of bombardment by those who opposed them.

Private contributions to the Liberty Train Foundation which she organized and ran allowed Jennie to be home, at his side, whenever needed. With Galt in rehabilitation, learning to live as an amputee, she often served as his right hand.

The marriage worked for both of them.

Galt trusted her, and he had the authority to run his chambers as he saw fit. He worked from home and had his "signed" work ferried to and from his chambers by his wife. After all, she was a Harvard Law School attorney. He knew that rumors rumbled through the halls of the U.S. Supreme Court and Senate that his law clerks were taking their day-to-day direction from her.

He didn't care.

In their library, she had just denied the disposition memoranda for the Native Hawaiian land rights cert while Galt's attention was elsewhere. He didn't even look up.

Jennie placed it on a pile of certs and went on to the next one. "I just finished the disposition memorandum in the Humphries case. Who drafted that?"

"Nathan Butt," Galt responded.

"I thought it was his work," Jennie said. "Brilliant. I so enjoy working on the memos he drafts for you."

"He follows my instructions well," Galt said, returning his attention to the manuscript that Joshua had left on his desk. It rested on his prosthetic right forearm as he turned a page with his left hand.

"What are you reading?" Jennie asked.

"Draft chapters of a book by Justice Ross's mother," he replied.

"Really? It's time to go to bed."

"Joshua said I should read this. He was insistent."

Jennie arched her eyebrows. "Why?"

"I'm not sure. He said I needed to read it before I talk to Justice Ross again. The opening scene is in Dublin, Georgia—where my father was born. I hope that's just a coincidence."

"There must be a reason she asked Joshua to read it. What's it called?"

"*Hattie's Story.*"

Jennie reached for it. "Let me see it."

"When I finish."

"I can read it tomorrow during the day," she said.

"Don't you have to go to work tomorrow?"

"You're more important. You're my main concern."

"Don't you think you're being a bit over-protective of me? This is just another sad story that took place in the South a long time ago. Frankly, I don't know why her mother would want anybody to read this. It doesn't complement her refined image."

"Come on. Let me see it." Jennie reached for the manuscript again.

"I'm reading it first. It's not that long. I'll be upstairs in a little bit."

"Don't take too long. I might fall asleep."

"I might wake you up," he chuckled.

The more he read, the more he suspected who Mrs. Ross might be. Could she be Hattie?

The details were lining up.

One hour turned into two as he read and thought without leaving his seat.

Smoke rose from the pages. Smoke that only he could see. Smoke that he hoped Jennie would not be able to see if she got her hands on the *Angry Justice* chapters.

What would Jennie do if she knew?

His father's family history was no longer lost to him. There it sat *in* his lap. Unpublished details lined up. What was fact? How much was fiction?

Galt knew some of it was true.

His family nickname was JT. His birthday was right. His Cousin Hattie had disappeared without a trace when he was nine, like his father. Mrs. Ross was about the right age to be Hattie. He sighed. Jennie was not going to like this.

Galt decided to wake her up.

Jennie fumed, grabbing the manuscript. She thumbed it in a flash. Then left their bedroom to make a call to Paula Morris. This didn't need to get out.

She hoped it wasn't too late.

Could a blood relative influence him? Maybe. She knew his son was making progress.

The situation needed to be managed.

Paula would know what to do.

She always did.

Chapter Sixty-Six

Street Side Café
Monday, September 16

Seated across from Joshua Galt, Mrs. Ross nursed a cup of coffee in both hands. Steam vapors rose from the mug.

"So what did you think about my story?"

"I just don't see how *Angry Justice* could be the opening of a memoir for you," Joshua said. "It's an engaging opening, but you weren't really in it. I found that strange."

"Well I've been having a hard time finding the beginning of my story," Mrs. Ross said. "There were two events that changed the course of my life. The life-changing event with the better outcome is Chapter One of *Angry Justice*. That's where I'd really like to begin."

"Why?"

"Did you get the FedEx package with the rest of my manuscript?"

"Yes, got it Friday. I'll give it a good read when I have more time."

She stared down into her coffee cup. "I don't want to remember the sweltering heat of Dublin, the five mile walks to school or having to run away with my uncle and aunt—I don't want to start my memoir at that crisis point in my life. I'd rather start with the story of Ademus because what happens afterward is a great love story, while the story of Needle Pointe stays dark for too long."

"But if it's your story, you need to be the central character in the opening chapter. It's a good beginning for a book about Ademus, but it's not a good opening for a story about Hattie."

Mrs. Ross stirred her coffee without comment.

Joshua continued, sliding his marked-up draft across the table. "Your opening chapter should introduce you as the main character. What was the shaping event in your life? This is an opening chapter for a story about Ademus."

"It was a turning point for me," she whispered. "It changed the course of my adult life."

"Then maybe it's a prologue," he said, sipping his juice. "Why should I care about Ademus in your life story?"

Mrs. Ross stared at Joshua for a moment, feeling a pain. "I have trouble with backstory."

"If you're Hattie, how's Ademus related to you?"

"He's my first cousin, but we were raised as brother and sister on the Jackson Plantation as part of a cover-up." She stopped talking.

"And?" Joshua prodded.

She paused for a moment, realizing she had to say it. There was no other way.

"He's your grandfather," she blurted out in a cracked voice, shaking her head.

"What?"

Mrs. Ross slid Joshua's marked-up copy of her draft back across the table. "Ask your father to read the FedEx package I sent along with this and let him judge my story."

Joshua pushed the marked draft back across the table and rose. "I won't do that."

Mrs. Ross made eye contact with a familiar-looking man, two booths over. She darted her eyes back to focus on Joshua. "Sit back down," she said, feeling another quiver of pain. "You're drawing attention to us. Your father should know."

"Why?" Joshua gazed down at her.

Mrs. Ross knew this might be her last shot, deciding to warn them. "Clayton Jackson is Justice Ross's natural father and I'm going to give her this part of my story tonight. She doesn't know. Your father needs to know I'm going to tell her. He needs to talk to her."

Joshua lowered himself back into his seat.

Mrs. Ross noticed the man she had seen before paying his bill at the cash register. She returned her attention back to Joshua. "I've been keeping my daughter from issuing the fifth letter because we're family, but we can't let him be used. You know what's going on. I think he needs to resign. You probably do, too."

Joshua defended him. "There's no reason for him to resign. Your little story doesn't change anything. My grandfather is dead. What does it matter anyway?"

"Concealing evidence of a murder is bad behavior. The family cover-ups must stop now. The truth about who we are must be faced."

"If what you say is true, then you're the one guilty of bad behavior."

"I'm not a Supreme Court justice. But yes, I might be guilty of not reporting a crime. But I never knew where Ademus went after he stole my car that night. I could have been hung."

Joshua shot back. "You're the one who helped cover up the murders. My father was just a child when that happened. Now you want to use me to pressure him into resigning."

"If you say so," Mrs. Ross said. "But I'll also be guilty of finally telling the whole truth. Everybody knew a crime had been committed. They found blood, tire tracks in the mud—they just couldn't find the bodies. I heard the bodies were burned up in the sawmill. I think JT knows what happened that night. He should be willing to talk to me. We're family."

Joshua said nothing, protecting his dad.

"Okay. I withheld evidence. I had no choice but to run." Her voice cracked. "I was afraid of what might happen to me. I couldn't defend myself. We didn't have any rights back then. So I ran away. I kept my mouth shut to stay alive—just like your dad."

"How do you know what happened?" Joshua asked, narrowing his eyes.

"Washington told me when I got back," Hattie said in a soft voice. "He told me everything—that's why I left Savannah and moved to Boston."

Joshua stared at her with guarded eyes.

"Ademus found your father. I saw their picture in the paper during his confirmation. I grew up with your grandfather. We were close cousins—I'm sure Ademus told your father what he had to do to cover his tracks. Our vital records in Georgia have been erased from the public records and that's how Katherine got through the confirmation process without our relationship being revealed. I checked. All of the damning records are gone, as if we never existed."

"That means you can't prove anything."

"DNA can prove if we're cut from the same cloth. I know my family's history. Your father, I'm sure, knows his, and he should face the fact I'm his missin' Cuz'n Hattie. Tell him I want to see him. We're from the same family tree. Bet you know about *Uncle Remus*."

Chapter Sixty-Seven

September 16

Air Force One—flanked by fighter jets with hot missiles—cruised through clear skies over the South Carolina seacoast. The pilot announced, "We'll be hitting some air turbulence in about fifteen minutes, please fasten your seat belts."

President Abraham Canty wondered if they just wanted him to sit down.

It was unsettling to him when he learned the CIA and Secret Service had recommended against their flight because it posed an undue risk to his life. The reconnaissance pictures on the flat screen before him showed the buildup of alien complexes below. He had insisted on seeing this for himself—and on showing U.S. sea and land power to them. *How had we let this happen?*

A foreign threat on U.S. soil.

The President saw it with his own eyes—then turned away.

He sat speechless, reading a copy of a Letter of Marque and Reprisal issued by President James Madison on December 12, 1814. The document read:

Letter of Marque
PREAMBLE: This Letter of Marque is to be carried by the Captain or agent(s) on any vessel, craft or other transportation vehicle owned and operated by the privateer National Strategic

Services, Incorporated during periods when the United States is under threat of invasion by foreigners, whether by individual persons or foreign governments.

BE IT KNOWN, That in pursuance of an act of congress, passed on the twenty-fifth day of June one thousand eight hundred and twelve, I have Commissioned the private corporation National Strategic Services, Incorporated, and by these presents do commission, the private armed services of National Strategic Services to subdue, seize, and take any armed or unarmed vessel, public or private, which shall be found within the jurisdictional limits of the United States of America along any of its borders, or within the borders of the United States of America or elsewhere on the high seas, together with all persons acting on board any vessels or within United States territory identified as a threat to U.S. interests resulting in the declaration of a state of National Emergency by the President of the United States.

The rights under this Letter of Marque and Reprisal shall inure, in perpetuity, to National Strategic Services, Incorporated—A New York corporation. This commission shall remain in force, in perpetuity, at the pleasure of the President of the United States.

BY THE PRESIDENT James Madison
James Monroe, Secretary of State

Morris, with dark eyes and bushy eyebrows, had passed out photocopies of their *letter*. The President finished reading his copy and glanced up. He caught Morris's smug expression. They locked eyes. Was Morris a descendant of the privateers?

"Authenticate these signatures," President Canty said, handing the encased original letter to the Chairman of the Joint Chiefs of Staff. Canty knew the privateers had sunk more enemy ships during the American Revolutionary War and the War of 1812 than the U.S. Navy. In fact, privateers had been critical to winning the Revolution—but to some people, they were just legal pirates. Was it still possible to call them into service for defense of the country?

Seated with the President around his airborne conference table were the White House Legal Counsel, Chief of Staff, National Security Advisor, Secretary of State, Secretary of Defense, Secretary of Homeland Security—and Alexander Morris, CEO and Chairman of NSSI.

NSSI was a well-known defense contractor—but the President was just finding out an important fact about it: National Strategic Services, Incorporated was a subsidiary of NSSI. President Canty didn't know what to make of what they were reading.

He waited for the White House Counsel to finish reading. Ignoring the others still processing and taking notes, the President asked him, "Is this thing still in effect?"

"Might be," the White House Counsel said. "I'll have to check it."

"Please do," Morris said. "You'll find the words are very robust."

"Did any of my predecessors use your company's services?" the President asked.

"Yes," Morris said.

The White House Counsel said, "The Congress attempted to put an end to the use of privateers in 1899, but I don't think that law passes constitutional muster. If this Letter of Marque is authentic— National Strategic Services, Incorporated might still be able to serve the country under its authority, but I don't think we can pay them without the Congress."

"Wait a minute," the Secretary of Defense said, "I know NSSI was incorporated in 1899, but this Letter of Marque is dated 1814 to a New York corporation. I don't understand."

Morris explained. "Delaware adopted a general incorporation act in 1899 that provided better protection for corporations. The 1899 date is not a coincidence. When Congress decided to stop issuing Letters of Marque, we had to figure out how to protect our Letter of Marque while keeping people out of our business. We…"

"*We?*" the President asked with wide eyes.

"Yes, my family. NSSI is a family business—all of its shareholders are descendants of privateers. We simply created the NSSI corporate shell to protect our most valuable asset—National Strategic Services, Incorporated—because New York's corporate laws were so weak. NSSI owns all of National Strategic Services, Incorporated shares. Solved a lot of problems. If NSSI is the parent and gets in trouble, it can just pay its fines. It can't go to jail. As a child of NSSI, National Strategic Services, Incorporated can keep its hands clean and out of sight."

"I still don't understand how this survived so many years," the Secretary of State said.

"Corporations don't die when properly cared for. Our family has kept it alive."

The President straightened his back. Aware. "How often has your *letter* been used?"

"Many times. Of course, we used it in the War of 1812 against England. Then against France—in both World Wars—and recently in Iraq. We've operated secretly since 1899 on a number of missions. We can negotiate something in this case that properly compensates us."

"Like what?" the President asked.

"Like ownership of the assets we seize. Historically that's been the American way."

"Is that legal?" the President asked, turning to toward the White House Counsel.

"A court could give ownership to a privateer. Otherwise I'm not sure."

"We don't need the courts," Morris said. "Since 1899 we've been quietly compensated."

"If we don't go to the Congress or the courts, how do we legally compensate you?"

"Go on television and announce the predatory invasion of the Sea Islands by armed dissidents from China. Under the Alien Enemy Act of 1798, you can then detain or deport them. Give them time to wrap up their business affairs while they're in detention. We'll give them what they paid for their property. You can set up regulations for dealing with them as aliens—set up some hearing board to get it out of the Supreme Court's jurisdiction."

The White House Counsel spoke. "If you proclaim the events that give rise to the declaration of a national emergency, Morris is right. You have the authority to set up regulations to dispose of the seized property. We might be able to use NSSI in the Sea Islands."

"It's easy," Morris spoke fast. "You declare a state of national emergency, we secure and seize the Sea Islands property, and we detain them until they sign over their corporate rights in a fair value transaction. We'll pay the Chinese what they paid for the Old South Carolina Bank—then we'll develop the Sea Island property. We'll get our compensation."

"What about the Gullahs?"

"They've already lost the property and they'll be off the land by the time we go in. When you declare the national emergency, everybody who's left can be relocated under your authority. All you have to do is use your authority to compensate the weak and move them out of our way. We've done this before."

"I won't do that," President Canty said. "I don't think we'll be needing your services."

Unruffled Morris said, "You need us to control the situation down in the Sea Islands."

"The Gullahs could get their Sea Island land rights back," the White House Counsel said. "The United States is already involved with three Supreme Court cases, citing national security concerns. We can't say what's going to happen in those cases. Ross represented the Gullahs in one case years ago, so she might recuse. Galt never recuses, but one of the cases involves his hometown. For the first time, I think Galt might be a wildcard on a corporate rights case. The cases could be heard. Then what? A big mess."

Morris made his case. "We'll see a lot of blood if you try to handle this conventionally. You need our new stealth drones for this to avoid unnecessary casualties, but I don't see you getting budget approval from the Congress in time to manage the current situation— and that's what the Chinese are betting on. They're betting they can launch an attack before we can zap them. We've made a very fair offer to you. Don't make the weak your issue."

"I don't like your offer," President Canty said, his forehead wrinkling.

Morris said with ease in his voice, "Perhaps I wasn't clear. All you have to do is declare a state of national emergency. We eliminate or move them into detention camps. We'll have no problem looking like the Navy since we supply your uniforms. We're ready to deploy ten thousand well-trained men to protect the country's interests. And, of course, we have the state-of-the-art Navy ships that you've been unable to pay for because of your failed budget battles with the Congress."

"Let the Supreme Court rule. I won't give NSSI the people's land like that."

"If you won't—you might as well declare war."

Chapter Sixty-Eight

U.S. Supreme Court
Tuesday, September 17

Not wanting to be late, Julianne LaSalle arrived at the west side security entrance on the Court's plaza level at seven.

The security guard checked off her name and motioned for her to place her things on the electronic screening table. She put her purse, laptop computer and briefcase on the X-ray machine conveyor belt, then rushed through the metal detection scanner and turned toward the guard with her arms raised. He waved a wand across her body checking for concealed weapons, then motioned her on.

On the second floor, she strolled into Galt's chambers. The suite of offices was quiet. None of his staff had yet arrived. Justice Galt greeted her in the antechamber area in his wheelchair and motioned for her to proceed into his private space.

"Please take a seat." He moved toward his desk while she headed for a seat at the table facing the west window with a magnificent view of the Capitol Building.

There was no clutter in Galt's office. Not on his desk. Not on the conference table. No piles of papers in sight anywhere in his inner chambers.

It didn't look like anyone worked in this office. All for show.

She caught a whiff of spiced tea with an orange scent and turned toward Galt's desk. A small service cart held a stainless steel electric kettle and all the appropriate tea fixings: lemon, honey, artificial sweetener in yellow, pink and green packages, and brown raw sugar packages with an extra mug. Two Brew-In-Mug Infusers were also in plain view along with donuts. Good. She was hungry.

She watched Galt roll to an open space at the conference table, a navy blue mug in his hand. He placed it down with a tapping sound. He looked well rested; no bloodshot eyes. She heard a renewed strength in his voice. The oxygen tank was still strapped to his wheelchair, but the clear tubing rested around his neck, not in use.

He took a sip of his tea.

She perused the mixture of exotic teas in small clear containers and smelled Spice of Life White Tea, her favorite.

Galt spoke first before she could offer any small talk.

"We should get rid of Black History Month."

She heard his challenge to her beliefs and started a slow boil.

"As hard as we fought to get Black History Month—why?"

He leaned in her direction. "Because we should—Black History Month only allows them to ignore our history in their American and World History courses. We shouldn't celebrate the separation of our history from the history of everybody else."

"If we didn't have Black History Month," she said, slowing to make her point, "most Black children wouldn't know our history. Smart people know their history."

She reached for her notepad and searched for a pen in her purse. Ready to take notes, she turned her attention to him again. She knew he was trying to anger her. She had to keep cool.

Julianne continued, "The problem is white people don't think our accomplishments merit inclusion in their history books. I was an adult before I heard about Robert Smalls's contributions to American History. Are you aware of Robert Smalls?"

"Of course," Galt said. "He was a former slave who played a critical role in the Civil War. We've got Black History Month and most Blacks still don't know he was our first African American U.S. Congressman. Why do you think we don't know about him?"

"Because the whites don't want us to know much about Blacks who showed courage in the face of extreme racial injustice. We might still be in slavery if it wasn't for him."

"We have Black History Month and Smalls's accomplishments are still little known Black history facts," Galt persisted. "Do you know why Smalls doesn't get the credit he deserves?"

"His story has a sad ending," Julianne said. "We like hero stories. We don't like tragedies and the Robert Smalls story is an American tragedy."

"It's not wise to ignore the bad endings in history. Did you know he was jailed as a U.S. Congressman for a crime where there was no credible evidence? He made an appeal to the Supreme Court that was never acted on. It took a political deal to save Smalls."

"Had you been on the Court then, would you have voted to hear his case?"

"I don't know. That's a hypothetical question I can't answer."

"When are you going to return to work?"

"I'm at work now."

"I don't see any work or appeals on your desk."

"I have a system for getting the work of this office done whether I'm sitting here at my desk, sitting at my desk at home, or reading in a lounge chair on the beach."

"How many hours a week do you work here with your staff?"

"With technology, I work with my staff from home most days."

"Are you well enough to come here and interact with your colleagues when needed?"

"As you well know, the new term doesn't begin until the first Monday in October. So I'm not missing anything around here."

"Can you write with your left hand?"

"Who needs to write anymore? I can tap on an iPad with one finger."

Julianne scribbled. "Do you have a left-hand signature that others can recognize?"

"I have an authorized signature stamp."

"I was told your wife was signing for you. Is that true?"

"She's my right-hand when I need one." Galt put the oxygen tube back in his nostrils.

"Who controls your signature stamp? Do you take it home?"

"It stays here in my chambers where it's safe."

"Who controls it here?"

"Nathan Butts."

"How do you know he can be trusted?"

Galt chuckled. "We have enforcers. Like me, Nathan is an egoist. I know how he thinks. Nathan is my secretary and the highest-ranking law clerk in my chambers. Everything flows through him. He keeps the trains rolling around here."

"Does that mean he sees everything you see?"

"Nathan Butts decides what I see and what I don't see, like all executive secretaries."

"Do you realize what you just said?"

"I said what I wanted to say. Save it. Tuck it away. One day, you might be able to piece together an accurate story about me."

Julianne glanced at the grandfather clock in the corner. Soon it would chime. She leaned forward. "You haven't said anything from the bench in years. Why?"

"I listen," Galt replied. "If a lawyer's spent months preparing to make a one-hour argument before the Court, I think I should listen without interrupting. If he's done his homework, he will have anticipated my questions and answered them. A lawyer who hasn't written a quality brief will walk away from this Court a loser. I just don't think a one-hour argument matters."

The grandfather clock chimed on the hour.

"Your time is up today."

Chapter Sixty-Nine

The Russell Senate Building
Tuesday, September 17

"Can we have an off-the-record conversation?" Senator Graham asked Julianne LaSalle over the telephone. He whirled around in his chair to face the windows as he talked, returning her call from earlier in the day, but he had his own agenda.

"Sure," Julianne said. "If you'll answer three questions on the record."

"Okay, so long as they aren't of a personal nature."

"Deal."

"I need Justice Ross's cell or home phone number," he said. "I've been told she's drafted the fifth letter, but I haven't seen it yet. Time is running out."

"Why don't you just call her office?"

"That might create a public relations nightmare for us," Graham said. "I'm sure she won't take my call."

"But you're chair of the Senate Judiciary Committee."

"Doesn't matter to her."

"I can't ask a personal question?"

"No. Do you have her number?"

"I don't have her number, but I do have her mother's."

"Can I have it?"

"Do you have the votes lines up on the Judiciary Committee to take Galt to the floor?"

"Yes, if I get the fifth letter in time."

"Do you know her mother?"

"That's a personal question," he said.

"That's a question I need you to answer to see if I can help you."

"Off the record, she tried to get us together a few years ago."

"Might she try again?"

"I don't know."

"How about I give her mother your cell phone number and tell her you're trying to reach Katherine on a personal matter and don't want to call the office."

"I don't think that'll work."

Graham pulled a few more strings and got Katherine's number from Cheryl with a promise not to reveal his source. He reached Katherine just before eleven.

"Can I see you tonight?" he asked. "My uncle lives in your building and is out of the country. He left his keys with me to use in case of an emergency."

"So that's how you got in the building before."

"Yeah. I'm in your building now."

"It's too late."

"I didn't sleep last night thinking of you."

"It has to be right."

"What's wrong with love between adults?"

"Nothing, when it's love and not just lust."

"I know you feel the same way I do. Lust doesn't last this long."

She resisted his lure. He persisted.

Finally she said, "Yes."

In less than five minutes, Skip appeared at her door. When she closed it behind him and turned to face him, he kissed her and whispered in her ear, "I love you."

Katherine gazed into his eyes, then pulled away from his embrace. "I can't do this."

"Don't reject me."

"You rejected me."

"I'm sorry."

"Sorry can't bring back what we lost." Tears filled her eyes.

"We have now. Tell me what I have to do to prove my love."

"I want to believe you, but I can't. I can't help but think you're here, after all these years, because you want Galt. I can't believe you."

He reached out for her and held her in his arms until the tears subsided.

She spoke with her voice cracking. "We can't have a relationship unless you're willing to give up your chairmanship of the Senate Judiciary Committee. Do you love me that much?"

She pulled back, waiting for his response. He took too long.

"If you're just playing with me to get what you want, the game is over."

"But..."

Katherine moved past him and opened the door for him to exit.

"No buts," she said in a voice that was serious and demanding. Then in a lower tone she said, "It's over unless you propose marriage. I feel too strongly about you to just play. I'm in love with you." With her voice cracking, she said, "I never stopped."

"I told you—"

"And I told you what it would take to make me believe you. I know—I'm unreasonable. But that's the only way it can work for me."

Chapter Seventy

Tuesday, September 17
9:30 a.m.

After making her bed, Mrs. Ross checked her phone. No call from JT. She buckled her belt and gazed in the mirror. She was shrinking. She sat on the side of the bed and pushed her feet into a pair of low-heeled Italian pumps with matching buckles, a birthday gift from Katherine.

She lifted the telephone handle from its cradle and punched in the number to her daughter's chambers.

After a few rings, a secretary answered. "Chambers of Justice Katherine Ross."

"Yes, this is Justice Ross's mother."

"Oh, hello, Mrs. Ross. How are you this morning?"

"I'm doing very well. I was wondering if you could get me the home telephone number of Justice Galt? I'm in his son's yoga class and need to speak to him."

"I don't have it, but I can call down to his chambers to see if they'll release it to me."

"Thanks."

A couple of hours later, Mrs. Ross's phone rang.

In the kitchen, she dried her hands and grabbed the wall telephone on the third ring.

"Hello, Mrs. Ross, this is Officer Ball from the marshal's office. How are you today?"

"I'm fine, and you?"

"Just fine. Justice Galt's office got a request from your daughter's chambers for Justice Galt's home telephone number on your behalf. Did you make such a request?"

"Yes, I did. I'm in Joshua Galt's yoga class and I wanted to speak to him."

"I see," the marshal replied with professional coolness. "Your daughter has that number. We would prefer you get it from her. I hope you understand his chamber is on a heightened security alert."

"Yes, I do."

She replaced the receiver on its cradle, feeling another pain.

Katherine wouldn't stand for her meddling in Court affairs.

She couldn't ask her for the number.

Chapter Seventy-One

U.S. Supreme Court
Wednesday, September 18

Katherine heard the echoing of laughter from the Great Hall and observed the growing line of power brokers as she floated pass the registration tables on the way to the reception for the annual Supreme Court Historical Society dinner. East Room or West? It didn't matter.

The reception guests migrated between the Court's two public conference rooms at will.

At 7:20 p.m., Katherine entered the East Conference Room alone. She scanned across a sea of prominent faces and spotted two of her fellow justices huddled in conversation with glad-handers.

The black-tie event, normally held in June, had been delayed due to security concerns. Katherine knew Galt would not be present. He'd sent his regrets, but his wife was in attendance.

She glimpsed Jennie Galt enter the West Conference Room with Cheryl, her best friend, and her mother right behind her. Cheryl and her mother had ridden together.

They could talk later.

Formally dressed waiters passed hors d'oeuvres on silver trays. A waiter in a white jacket offered Katherine a shrimp cocktail. She declined and eyed food selections that included smoked salmon crisps and mushroom mini-quiches. She accepted a colorful melon skewer.

Her mood mellowed at the clear, cascading sounds of a harp.

Near the bar station, two justices and their wives posed for pictures as guests rotated past the Court's photographer.

A waiter took her soiled napkin and offered her a glass of champagne.

"Thank you." She lifted a flute from the tray.

Katherine had dressed in a formal two-piece navy blue satin dress which featured a curved neckline and hand-embroidered bodice with a dropped asymmetrical waistline, topped off with a matching bolero jacket with three-quarter length sleeves. Her hair was styled in an up-do, her ears accented with modest pearl drop earrings.

Suddenly attention in the room shifted toward the open double doors. The Chief had arrived with his wife. He stopped in the hallway with an instant crowd of admirers hovering at his every turn, just like a rock star. It looked like they had a sell-out crowd.

"Hi, Kathy," said Alexander Morris. "How's it been going in the Marble Palace?"

"It's been a roller coaster ride," Katherine replied. "Have we met before?"

"You don't remember me?" Morris picked grilled shrimp off a silver platter floating by. "We graduated from Duke together. I remember you. Guess I haven't aged well."

She glanced at his nametag, recalling his name. "What are you doing these days?"

"I'm CEO and Chairman of the Board for NSSI—we're defense contractors."

"So what brings you here?"

"My company is a strong supporter of Galt's and I just wanted you to know that. He's a valuable asset to this country. We were happy to support your nomination to the Court with our political weight." Then he leaned closer and said, "My friends want you to know we pulled you through your confirmation process because Al told us we could depend on you to protect our assets."

Katherine felt alarm at his comments but knew she couldn't show it. She gave him a look of pleasurable agreement. "Yes, you can be certain I'll make decisions that will protect the country's best interest. I appreciate your support. I'll let Al know we spoke."

Katherine spun on her heels, warmly greeting another approaching guest and ending the irritating conversation. She hoped Al hadn't made any commitments he couldn't keep.

Chapter Seventy-Two

In the Great Hall, busts of the present and former Chief Justices of the U.S. Supreme Court lined the marbled walls. Four rows of eight-top tables filled the hall. Each table was draped with a royal blue satin tablecloth, covered by silk-laced overlays interwoven with red and silver threads. In the center of each table, a tall glass vase stood filled with mixed white flowers cascading downwards. Place cards rested at each seat with the guest's name and the menu printed below the Seal of the United States of America glimmering in gold accent ink.

Husbands and wives were not seated together.

Seating assignments had been made, following background checks.

The justices sat at tables in the center of the room like queen bees, with the nation's legal elite and service staff buzzing around them like drone and worker bees in a hive. A small trio played soft music. Five rows of risers positioned at the front of the hall for seventy-five members of the Navy Band Sea Chanters who were scheduled to perform Mrs. Ross's favorite gospel, *Wade In The Water.*

Taking her seat, Katherine heard the song's words playing in her head.

God's gonna trouble the water...

With all seats in the room filled, the president of the Supreme Court Historical Society rose to welcome its honored guests while waiters hustled with salads held high in the air.

Katherine was seated with Al Carlton on her left and, to her mild surprise, Alexander Morris to her right. She did not recall his name being on the list of guests at her table. She would have recognized his name. *What had happened?*

Her mother sat across from her and busied herself in conversation with the revered attorney George Matson. Katherine knew Matson was a regular at the annual society events and turned out to be a neighbor of Mrs. Ross. And Katherine knew her mother could hold her own.

A waiter filled her glass with red wine. She turned to Al and asked, "Where's Sarah?"

"Her mother's ill," he said. "So I brought Morris—NSSI is a client."

"Oh, no wonder I didn't see his name on the guest list."

"Morris asked me to deliver a message to you. I told him I'd bring him to the dinner and he could deliver it himself."

Katherine turned to Morris. "I understand you have a message for me."

"Your mother is a very lovely person," he said.

She waited for him to say more. He didn't.

His face took on foreboding seriousness—sending a silent threat she could feel.

"Is that your message?"

"We've talked," he said, wiping his mouth with a red napkin. "I think you understand."

"You should assume that I don't." Her thoughts raced, trying to make sense of situation.

"Then I won't assume," Morris said.

She wondered if he was trying to intimidate her in her most secure surroundings. She had to show him that she was not unnerved.

She would keep the conversation going. "Did you attend the lecture this afternoon?"

"No," Morris said. "My plane was delayed getting in."

Seated next to him, Cheryl butted in. "It was great. The history about Revolutionary War financier Robert Morris and Chief Justice John Marshall was fascinating."

"I wish I could have attended," Katherine said. "Things just got too busy in my chambers. What did you learn?"

"That John Marshall and Robert Morris were related," Cheryl said with excitement. "John Marshall's brother was married to Robert Morris's daughter. They were all related."

"John Marshall was Robert Morris's advocate," Matson said. "That's an important point."

Cheryl continued, "As a Congressman, John Marshall pushed through the National Bankruptcy Act to get Morris out of jail."

"I'd forgotten Marshall was a Congressman before becoming Chief Justice," Mrs. Ross said. "I believe Marshall was a Federalist."

"Yes," Katherine said. "Robert Morris, Alexander Hamilton and John Adams were Federalists, too. Thomas Jefferson and James Madison opposed the pro-business policies of the Federalists. John Marshall's leadership influences the Court to this day."

Morris said, "John Marshall was probably the only person living at the time who had the persuasive skills needed to get a bill passed that could free Robert Morris from debtors' prison."

"A lot of people hated Morris," Matson said, "They were happy to see him in jail."

"Must be more to this Robert Morris story than what I know," Mrs. Ross said.

"A lot more," said New York attorney Michael Spade, seated to her left.

"Many people viewed Robert Morris as a blackguard," Matson said.

Cheryl turned toward Matson. "Are you a history buff?"

"As a matter of fact, yes. The Revolutionary War period is my primary area of interest."

"Didn't John Adams appoint Marshall Chief Justice?" Mrs. Ross asked.

"Yes," Katherine replied. "Adams viewed Marshall as his best appointment."

The Court Curator spoke to all. "By the way, the Fairfield Marriott sits on the land Chief Marshall struggled to pay for. Even though Morris's troubles forced Marshall to leave his legal practice and pursue public service, there's a historical consensus that Marshall's independence of thought and action were not diminished by his family ties nor by his service to Robert Morris."

"The Fairfield tidbit is a little known American history fact I didn't know," Michael Spade said. "No telling what you might learn at one of these dinners."

"Nor can you be sure whose descendant might be sitting next to you," Mr. Morris said.

Al looked tense.

"Might you be a descendant of Robert Morris?" Katherine asked, feeling her heartbeat.

"I can't say. My grandfather's name was Robert Morris, but I don't know if that proves anything. There have been thousands of Robert Morrises in the world. The financier Robert Morris died three million dollars in debt. That certainly is nothing to brag about."

Morris paused, then glanced at Justice Ross with a smirk on his face. "But then again, if I were a descendant of *the* Robert Morris I would likely know, because he was one of only two people to sign the Declaration of Independence, the Articles of Confederation and the U.S. Constitution—and that's something to pass on to your grandchildren's children with a warning not to be so quick to share their ancestry because people might say the Revolutionary War financier Robert Morris was a pirate—"

"A pirate!" Cheryl blurted out.

"Yes," Alexander Morris said in a deep baritone voice. "He was a privateer."

Now the entire table was paying attention to the conversation about Robert Morris.

"A legal pirate," Katherine said, placing her wine glass on the table.

She said to Morris, "Is it possible a naval defense contractor that builds warships for the Navy, like NSSI, could be a modern day privateer?"

Morris looked Katherine dead in the eyes with a revealing stare. "Of course. Article One, Section Eight of the U.S. Constitution permits it. Private channels to protect the country's assets have always existed. And they always will."

So she might be sitting next to a legal pirate. Could Morris be a member of one of the powerful families that President Greene had warned her about? Were they attempting to use Al to influence her? *Wouldn't work.* Did he think that he could?

She needed to have a powwow with Al.

Then she heard the first note of warning from the Navy Sea Chanters as her emotions churned like a stormy sea. She needed to find her sea legs. The warnings were clear.

Katherine needed to prepare for battle.

Could Al be trusted?

354

Chapter Seventy-Three

Thursday, September 19
7:20 a.m.

"What's the surprise?" Katherine arrived at her mother's door dressed for work in a black suit with a white ruffled blouse. Smelling the aroma of Maxwell House coffee, she headed to the kitchen for a caffeine fix.

Her mother followed behind her.

"I'm making a special breakfast for you."

Hattie put four strips of bacon in a large skillet then poured orange pancake batter onto a griddle. Eight pancakes began to sizzle. Next, she poured coffee and took it to the table.

"Smells good," Katherine said. "What is it?"

"Sweet potato pancakes. I was going to make sweet potato biscuits for you to take to work, but I forgot to boil the potato last night and didn't have enough time to make them."

Katherine went over to the stove. "They sure smell great."

She watched steam bubbles pop up through the warming batter. "Let me turn them for you. They're fluffy. I think they're going to need a quick turn."

"Good pancakes are flipped once," her mother said.

"I know that, Mom." Katherine checked the bottom of the first pancake flipped for doneness. It was perfect. "Give me two plates."

Once the pancakes were plated, Katherine poured maple syrup over her short stack. She bit in and wiggled back in her chair. "What did you think of the dinner last night?"

"The conversations were enlightening," Mrs. Ross said, taking her first bite. Stirring her coffee, she added, "A law professor from Duke talked about the impact of the Scottish Enlightenment on the founding of this country. He said Adam Smith was the most important of the Scottish scholars of his period. You know, I was all ears when he mentioned Adam Smith because of that first edition copy you bought in London."

"What did he say?"

"George Washington, Adams, Hamilton, and Jefferson all had copies of Adam Smith's work. We're all linked and the government is nothing more than one big wealth-transferring vehicle."

"Did I tell you whose first edition of *The Wealth of Nations* I purchased?"

"You might have, but I don't remember."

"The Revolutionary War financier Robert Morris," Katherine said with an English accent, while shaking her head as the rare bookstore shopkeeper had done.

"*The* Robert Morris we were talking about at the dinner?"

"Yes, one in the same."

"Why didn't you mention it last night?"

"I didn't want them to know I purchased something so expensive."

"Well, I may have made a mistake," her mother said, sinking back in her seat. "I mentioned to George Matson—in front of other people—that you have a first edition copy."

"I just hope they don't have a clue what it cost."

"Have you read any of it yet?"

"Of course not. I haven't had time for that. It's an investment."

"Baby, I think what you have might be more than just an investment. *The Wealth of Nations* that I read back in the fifties, in paperback, was maybe three hundred pages. I recall what you have is over nine hundred pages with comments and corrections. You have Adam Smith's original unedited words. Who knows what the editors have cut over the years, or changed and added to his work."

All of Katherine's pancakes were gone. She spied her mother's plate. *No. She couldn't.*

Her mother continued, "The professor said Karl Marx saw class struggle, while Adam Smith saw special interests being in conflict with the public good. If all men could reason and respect others, we would come to realize enlightened reason is better than brute force."

"That's a saying of George Washington." Katherine drank the rest of her orange juice.

"Maybe Washington got it from the enlightenment scholars," her well-read mother surmised. "I think he understood that forcing any group's will on the people would not make a lasting foundation for the country, and took their call for tolerance of differences seriously."

"We need compromise for the stability of the country."

"Think Robert Morris' copy of *Wealth of Nations* was sold during his bankruptcy?"

"Probably," Katherine said, glancing at her watch. "I bet John Marshall had a first edition copy, too, and that's why we operate the way we operate, listening to all viewpoints."

"Do you think it's possible families of the original privateers passed on any special property rights over the years?"

"Interesting question. I've wondered if that type of authority could have been passed on as a property right from generation to generation in corporate entities. I hope not—but Alexander Hamilton was very creative. I think I need to spruce up on admiralty law before something hits my desk."

"Admiralty law?"

"That's the area of law that addresses the property rights of pirates and privateers."

Later that evening, seated before her computer screen, Katherine wrote an email to her law clerk Ron Payne, asking that he prepare a review memo on the status of admiralty law and note any cases related to Article One, Section Eight of the Constitution that addressed property rights associated with letters of marque and the termination of their authority. In particular, she wanted to know if property rights associated with letters of marque issued by George Washington could be passed on to this day through corporate entities, and whether or not the congressional action to limit their use in the late 1800s, in his view, was constitutional.

Done.

Next, she pulled biographies on John Marshall, Benjamin Franklin, John Adams, Thomas Jefferson and George Washington from the built-in white wooden bookshelves in her home office. She spread the books out on her desk before settling back into her cushioned chair. One by one, she turned to the indexes in the back of the books and searched for references to Robert Morris, pirates and privateers. Scanning page after page, she formed an image of the history shaping her current circumstances. She swayed back in her seat when she discovered several of the Founding Fathers were privateers.

George Washington funded privateers, too. He had six armed ships. *Interesting.*

Turning to her computer screen again, she tapped into the Library of Congress database to access a typed version of George Washington's diary. Skimming the entries, she discovered that George Washington dined with Robert Morris almost every night during the 1787 Constitutional Convention, and wondered why she didn't know more about Robert Morris.

He was an important historical character.

As she pushed through the biographies before her and surfed websites, she told herself stories. Her level of anxiety increased with each new discovery. *This was ridiculous. Robert Morris was dead.* Nevertheless, Katherine was alarmed.

She perceived the growing presence of danger.
She felt it in her gut.

Chapter Seventy-Four

Friday, September 20

Sensing opportunity a few blocks away, Stratagem emerged from the McPherson Square Metro station at Fourteenth and I Streets and proceeded to Fifteenth Street en route to a meeting with a K Street lobbyist. The people's protest at McPherson Square, just a few blocks from the White House, had grown and gained energy.

Stratagem wore a suit and tie and polished shoes, in contrast to the many who had slept in the park for days in soiled clothes. The protestors sported budding Afros, flappy blonde hair tied back in ponytails, Statue of Liberty crowns sculpted from locks of hair gelled in place, bald heads, baseball caps, tattoos and eyebrow piercings.

Stratagem strolled, taking the temperature of the disenfranchised protestors.

He was scheming.

He spotted a clean cut young man in a Howard University hoodie camped on the corner. He knew that college grads were finding their place among the ranks of the uneducated and unemployed. Yes, it was almost time for the seeds of displacement to bloom into waves of violent protest. Once again, the economic cycle had replenished the ranks of the oppressed—creating a critical mass for revolutionary change.

These people meant to put a light on the government's failure to address their needs. Broken business people in rumpled suits were among those who slept in sleeping bags and tents to protest the lack of a safety net for those who'd lost in the musical-chairs game of corporate downsizing, lay-offs, and finding new jobs at lower pay. They, too, were homeless.

It started to rain.

On public display, the people provided compelling evidence that the government needed to take action. They also provided heart-warming evidence that the people could find meaning and purpose for their life—by advancing the cause for economic justice in America.

Stratagem picked up his pace moving down Fifteenth Street.

A man in a Guy Fawkes mask stood on a step stool and tried to rally the crowd. Stratagem could not make out his message above the street sounds, but still rated his effort as weak. He felt that the protest could be developed into much more. The people needed money to organize—and an articulate leader to paint a vision of what could be.

They needed unity of purpose.

A sea of signs marked positions in the park. The signs contained a ragbag of messages like, *The Time For Revolution Is Now!*, *JUSTICE For Poor People*, *THE 99% DEMAND EQUAL RIGHTS*, and *The End Of Capitalism Is Near.*

Stratagem surveyed the mostly white crowd of frustrated people and thought, Spade was right—time to add some color.

Then he spotted others in Guy Fawkes masks, claiming their right to protest in anonymity. One sign with bright red lettering caught his attention. It read, *Selfish John Galt Must Die!*

Another in bold blue lettering read, *CORPORATIONS HAVE NO NATURAL RIGHTS UNDER THE 14TH AMENDMENT.*

Observers from the National Legal Guild wore yellow hats and stood under a tree, holding a street conference with news reporters and cameramen around them. One of them took notes on a clipboard. The D.C. Metropolitan Police kept their distance.

Stratagem strolled through, observing. There was no leadership. This was a great opportunity.

The unemployed, unemployable, and close-to-unemployed had occupied McPherson Square for the last ten days. The protest was peaceful. But nothing had happened.

They needed a little help to create revolutionary change in America.

Stratagem liked the role of a polished recruit on the road to revolutionary change. An educated agitator with a socialist agenda to awaken the spirit of protest—funded with greenbacks for angry Black faces by invisible Asian hands from afar.

Guided and paid by a skilled hand to execute a disruption strategy in America.

By any means necessary.

He made his way to an office building near Fourteenth Street, located on a section of K Street known as Lawyer and Lobbyist Row. Many deals with the federal government were cut in this office building which was full of lawyers for the elite.

Stratagem checked the office directory for the Law Offices of Spade, Spark and Lightfoot, then he took the elevator to the fifteenth floor. He would be meeting with Michael Spade, a lobbyist who provided money to finance protests and special projects needed to push the political agendas of powerful corporate clients who wished to remain anonymous.

Michael Spade was in it for the cause: money. He could work for anybody.

Spade's office had no receptionist and was sparsely furnished with a computer, printer, file cabinets, and large desk. A coffee station and one medium-sized conference table for eight occupied the west side of the room. A white board was filled with red writing from an earlier strategy session. The blinds were closed.

Behind the desk sat Michael Spade, who had been seated next to Mrs. Ross at the Supreme Court Historical Society dinner. Along the wall to the side of his desk were fifteen columns of boxes stacked eight boxes high.

Spade leaned back in his seat as Stratagem ambled through the door, glancing at his watch with impatience. "You're late," he said, his eyes tightened by tense muscles.

In a tone that was not apologetic Stratagem said, "My meeting with the brothers ran late."

"I don't see any of your brothers in the park."

"That's what I'm here to talk about. We need to take over the protest. Form alliances with some other groups so I can shape a message that moves people."

"What other groups you looking at?" Spade asked. "Stop The Machine? Occupy Wall Street Soc—"

"Those aren't Black groups. The brothers understand it's a class struggle at the root. We need—"

"I know what needs to happen. You've got to stay focused on our agenda, if we're paying the bill."

"Then what do you want done?" Stratagem asked, sitting down.

"We've ordered 10,000 black masks. That's the first order over there. The park needs to be filled with demonstrators wearing black masks. The black protest mask represents wounded spirits trapped behind Black faces. The Black protesters should join hands with the Guy Fawkes protestors because they are one and the same energy, one and the same spirit, both about to explode from injustice."

"When we get a crowd, what are we going to do with them?"

"March to the U.S. Supreme Court and demand Galt's removal. Galt is a symbol of what's wrong in America. Raw selfishness. Big business. We'll protest for Ross to issue the fifth letter or resign her seat. We want a rowdy crowd. A crowd ready to turn into a mob."

"Is there a target?"

"Ross."

"Not Galt?"

"Not Galt," Spade said. "She's a better target. We don't want her to feel safe. Plan something for her mother. A warning. She needs to know we can get to her."

"You sure you want to mess with her?"

"Just follow your orders," Spade sneered. "Figure out how to get thousands of your people in black protest masks on the square. Give me your budget."

"I need ten million."

"That's too much."

"You want five thousand protestors. I'll have to fly-in folks to hit that number in a week. They'll have to be fed and trained. We'll need tents. Flyers. Recruiters. They'll need port-a-potties. We'll need staging and signs—and my personal fee has to be covered. Ten million is a bargain. Can't do it for less. You decide."

A few hours later, Michael Spade sat across the desk from Alexander Morris at the world headquarters of Naval Strategic Systems, Incorporated (NSSI) in Bethesda, Maryland.

Spade said, "It's all been arranged for ten million."

Morris leaned back in his chair. "The bigger the demonstration, the better I'd say. The Supreme Court has to be protected. When the protestors cross the concrete barriers and step onto the Court's plaza, we'll have the military cut them down on television—and that should be the end of protests for a while. Fear! We've got to put fear in the people to keep control."

"You really think you can get the President to use the military to slaughter them?"

"It's going to look like the President issued the order," Morris said. "But it will be a grand display of our control over the military chain of command to the President."

Chapter Seventy-Five

Saturday, September 21

With folded arms, Katherine waited for Al Carlton in her judicial robe with white lace dripping down her collar. Where was Al? She had asked him to meet her for a little talk that morning, and at ten she would be presiding at a Constitutional Law Moot Court student competition as the Chief Judge with two federal appeals court judges. *Why was he late?*

Katherine simmered. Al tromped into the Dean's Conference Room at George Washington University Law School shortly after nine-thirty. Ten minutes late. *Enough time.*

"This should be quite a debate," Al said, taking a seat next to her by the window.

"I agree," Katherine said. "I met the student advocates at breakfast. They're sharp."

"I didn't want to miss seeing you preside over your first moot court."

"The topic we have today is a tough one, and it's the cause of most of our split decisions. Original intent versus the Constitution as a living document."

"To keep the union together, the Framers put a dream on paper," Al said.

"A dream we must fulfill over time. I was up most of the night reading, weaving bits and pieces of our history together. I didn't know about Robert Morris, so I did a little research into our history of using privateers to beef up our national defense. I've been wondering if we might have First Families descended from Robert Morris that have influenced the Supreme Court throughout the years."

"That seems unlikely."

"Did you know Gouverneur Morris was the primary drafter of our Constitution, and Robert Morris's right hand assistant?"

"I knew Gouverneur Morris was a drafter, but I didn't know about his Robert Morris tie."

"I discovered another interesting point." Katherine paused. "The authority to legalize privateers wasn't in the August sixth draft of the Constitution, but it was included in the final draft presented to the states for ratification."

"I'm not sure what you're getting at." Al hunched forward in his seat. "We needed the privateers—they seized more British ships than the Continental Navy."

"That doesn't surprise me, since Robert Morris controlled the Continental Navy and had more armed ships than the Navy. He was the biggest legal pirate of all, and controlled the market for confiscated goods from the seas. His fingerprints are everywhere that deals with the dollar during the Revolutionary War period. Yet we rarely hear his name as one of the Founding Fathers. Isn't that strange?"

"Yeah."

"I found it interesting that Morris and Washington were thought to be best friends. If they were such great friends, why didn't Washington convince John Adams to pardon him?"

She saw Al look at her with concern. She wanted him to think she was out of control.

"Morris made millions on the backs of those who sold their confederation debt certificates to him for cents on the dollar, after he arranged for the federal government to assume the confederate debt and pay the full principal amount due to holders of the debt instruments. He made eighteen million dollars from the passage of the Assumption Act, but that wasn't enough." Katherine continued her planned remarks without pause. "I think it's possible Morris was the most powerful man in America during the Revolutionary War. Morris wanted to ordain George Washington King of America. When Washington wouldn't bite, he started plotting against Washington. You've heard of the Newburgh Conspiracy. Haven't you?"

"It's history," Al said. "You seem pretty worked up about this. What's going on?"

"Who is Alexander Morris?" Katherine asked. "Is he a descendant of *the* Robert Morris?"

"I don't know."

"How do you know him?"

"He's a client," he said. "I already told you that."

"How long?"

"Thanksgiving last year. He became a client of the firm just before your Senate hearing."

Ross boiled on the possible implication. "I also discovered the United States Minister to Hawaii at the time of the unauthorized 1783 overthrow was John L. Stevens, son of Captain John Stevens, a known privateer who had a Letter of Marque issued during the Revolutionary War. A Letter of Marque that perhaps could have been passed on to his descendants as property in corporate entities. The historical record notes that financiers and Stevens caused naval representatives of the United States to invade the Hawaiian nation with our armed naval forces without proper authorization for war. Who would dare do that?"

"Where are you going with this?"

"Wherever it leads... Why did you give me the Hawaiian case on the eve of my confirmation hearings?"

"Gee," Al said. "I hate to admit it but Morris told me a Hawaiian land case was on the way to the Supreme Court, and he wanted to know your thoughts about the last Hawaiian land rights opinion issued by the Court back in 2009. I didn't see any harm in that."

"Al, you've been a friend of my family for a long time, but you're standing on a thin line with me now. I believe denial of property rights is a denial of liberty."

She wasn't going to say what he wanted to hear.

"So for me, it's not original intent versus living constitution doctrine, it's the marriage of the two concepts that I seek to find in my interpretation of the Constitution. The original intent of the U.S. Constitution can't come from one person or group. The rights of all matter to me."

She stood up. "I reserve my right to consider everything relevant to arrive at justice. Gross historical injustice is something that I will consider when I make a decision."

The dean of the law school poked his head in through the door. "We're ready for you."

"Can we finish this discussion later?" Al asked.

"We're finished now. You can't influence me on anybody's behalf. Understand?"

"I think..."

"Understand?" Katherine asked again.

"Yes."

"It was subtle, but I think I've been threatened by *your* Mr. Morris."

"You—"

"Don't bring him around me again."

Chapter Seventy-Six

The Watergate Complex
Saturday, September 22

Senator Skip Graham had not slept well the night before. Thinking of *her*. Worried. He had tossed in his bed all night never losing consciousness, wondering what he could do. He knew Katherine's life was in danger.

He wished she wasn't so tough to deal with.

Was it too late for them? Had he waited too long?

Over drinks at an evening event at the Willard Hotel, Graham listened to new intelligence from George Matson, the orchestrator of an invisible fraternity that had survived since the founding of the country to protect the nation's interests when compromise failed. Evil forces could not be left unchecked. But its methods were questionable. The fraternity's membership was so closely guarded that meetings were held on a need-to-meet basis with only necessary members present. George Matson was the only person alive who knew all of its members. Matson had personally recruited Senator Graham into their invisible fraternity.

And it was *their* proposed constitutional amendment for the involuntary retirement of Supreme Court Justices that Graham shepherded through Congress.

Now they were ready to retire Justice John Galt.

That character had to go. They had given up all hopes of redeeming him.

Matson spoke to Graham in the noisy lobby bar. "Her relationship with Al Carlton is a problem. Al promised them he could deliver her vote. Now she's cut him off. They're pissed."

"She shouldn't have voted for the Native Hawaiian's petition," Graham said. "Somebody should have told her what she was up against if she dealt with that property rights issue."

"She was ambushed at the Supreme Court dinner. I was seated at her table next to her mother. Ross was between Al Carlton and Alexander Morris. With the pressure Al's under at his firm to make rain, he's turned into a snake. Everything about the evening, even the lecture topic, was meant to unnerve her. Michael Spade was at her table, too."

"I'll try to reach her again, but we need a backup plan."

"Let's meet at my place with the communications director," Matson said. "There must be a way to get her. You should have reestablished your relationship with Ross a long time ago."

"Still working on it. It's complicated. But I think we have the votes to get John Galt out if we can get her to issue the fifth letter by the end of the term. She'll come through for us."

"Well we'd better get her to do it fast—she might not last long."

Graham shuddered at the words and understood the stakes were high. He knew enough to know Morris was a real threat to her. He had to do something now or all would be lost.

He plotted their next move…

Chapter Seventy-Seven

The Watergate Complex
Sunday, September 23

"No. No. It's too long. Get to the point. She doesn't have time to read a book."

Senator Graham grabbed a pen—then he crossed out the following lines:

> *Look around you. Evil forces are arrayed on all sides ready to attack to take our rights away. They are driven by economic self-interest, hatred and ignorance.*
>
> *Some of the economic principles espoused by the renowned economist Adam Smith are misunderstood by the masses. The myth of an invisible hand making all acts of selfishness and greed work to the economic good of all is rubbish.*
>
> *Look at Book IV in* The Wealth of Nations.
>
> *We know you have an original copy.*
>
> *The invisible hand metaphor relates to global risk aversion.*
>
> *We must embrace enlightened self-interest and fight for our unity.*

They were almost out of time—desperate to find a way to influence Justice Ross without showing their hands. What they were doing was risky, but they had to take a chance. The implied threat would stand. She was in danger. Graham had told his colleagues he was sure he could get her to issue the fifth letter. But she had blocked him. Now they had to come up with a written appeal and played with its opening line for hours: *You must take action.*

Senator Graham, George Matson and their communications director worked feverishly on their appeal, writing and talking fast. The Supreme Court's term would end on October sixth. Just two weeks away. Nobody understood why she had failed to act.

Their letter needed the effect of a guided missile. Its goal: to ignite an involuntary removal process that would end the term of Justice John T. Galt.

What was the right message?

After five hours of searching for the right words, checking references and moving sentences around, Senator Graham reread the letter for the last time.

"It's good," he said to Matson, who lived in the Watergate complex on the floor just below Justice Ross's mother. "It gives us a cover. Slide it under her mother's door before you go work out in the morning. Be careful not to be seen. Do it early."

Across town at the Ritz Hotel, Alexander Morris, crown prince of the Descendants of the Privateers, shared drinks at the bar with his key political strategist, Michael Spade.

"Another Native Hawaiian property rights case hit the Supreme Court last week," Morris said. "Galt has to stay in place. We can motivate him. Cut the line now or she'll take us under."

"Stratagem's already working on a plan," Spade said. "She'll be dead in a week."

"Good. Her mother is a problem, too. Let's clean everything up. Now."

Chapter Seventy-Eight

"Kathy, what happened between you and Skip?" Cheryl asked. "I'm starting to feel like your refusal to issue the fifth letter is something personal between you and him. This isn't like you. Come on. Tell me what's really going on."

"I can't talk about it. I've got to go. Bye."

Katherine hung up the phone, grimacing and biting her lips. Skip had touched the inner most part of her being and she had not been able to forget it...

*****

They had gone to a movie, then to McDonald's for cheeseburgers and fries. They talked, sitting on hard plastic seats, until closing. Sharing their most precious life stories and hopes for the future. He shared his deepest regret. She shared her greatest hope. Then they shared their desires to have a family. He wanted four. She wanted two. She had thought three could work, but hadn't told him that. If it worked out, they could compromise. They laughed.

He revealed his vulnerabilities to her, while at the same time showing her his strength. She revealed her insecurities, while sharing her desire to get over them.

They opened up to one another on a deep level. They clicked, wanting the same things out of life. She felt like she had already known him for a lifetime.

In that hard seat at McDonald's, she fell in love with him. She knew this was a man who could love deeply.

She could wait for him to heal.

Love was patient.

This was the man of her dreams.

He escorted her home to her apartment on Forrest Street near Michigan's Law School. He kissed her goodnight on the cheek and turned away. She still remembered the warmth of his lips. She closed the door, not wanting to see him go. But she knew that was the right thing to do.

She got ready for bed, already in a dream world.

Then she heard a knock on the door.

Her heart jumped.

She peeped through the door. It was him—with moonlight and stars surrounding his silhouette. She opened the door and stepped back. He moved toward her and closed the door.

They were alone in her dimly lit living room.

His Old Spice cologne was intoxicating. He reached out and kissed her. She fell into his embrace. She didn't care. He could have her. She surrendered. They went into her bedroom. She wasn't prepared and neither was he, but she had let him in.

All of her insecurities ran away.

She loved him with her entire being.

The next morning he said, "I'll call you later."

She waited for that call. It had never come.

She waited for her monthly visitor. It never came.

She cried for the life that she wanted and could not have. She didn't understand how he could do that to her. She accepted the reality that he didn't love her—still not over what had happened that night—fearing she might never get over it.

Would God forgive her? She prayed for forgiveness every day.

They could never reclaim the life that was lost to pride and shame.

Could she forgive herself?

*****

Katherine called Cheryl back and confessed. "I've never told a soul about this."

"You need to tell him so both of you can heal," Cheryl said. "Especially since you obviously still love him. You need to forgive him—and he needs to forgive you—then maybe the two of you can find the love that you lost. But most of all, you need to forgive yourself."

Chapter Seventy-Nine

Monday, September 23
9:35 a.m.

At the end of yoga class, Joshua walked up to Mrs. Ross as she folded her mat.

"Ready for breakfast?" she asked.

"I can't this morning," Joshua replied. "I've got to go get the GPS installed in my tooth."

"You're just getting that done?"

"Yes, I didn't want it. But my dad finally convinced me. Just give me what you have and I'll try to arrange the meeting for you with him. I'm sure you understand he's guarded. He wants to read everything you have before agreeing to meet with you."

"Tell him I've already sent him everything by FedEx," she replied. "He should get it in the morning. I need to see him by the end of the week. We don't have much time."

A young Black man sat behind the wheel of a black Ford Expedition with its motor purring. He'd pulled up to a spot across the street from the yoga center at nine-thirty.

At nine-forty, Mrs. Ross exited the building for the walk home. The man in the Ford put the vehicle in drive and took off.

Mrs. Ross's security officer dropped in step behind her as she proceeded down K Street toward the Potomac River. Taking on the long strides of a person with intent to exercise, she made her way at a fast clip, passing a young mother pushing a stroller. She felt peace, ready to release her last secrets to the universe. Keeping secrets didn't matter to her anymore.

She stopped for a walk signal at K Street and Nineteenth Street.

Mrs. Ross was finally ready to tell her daughter.

Kathy should know they were related to Galt by blood.

They were just one mixed-up family with generations of dark family secrets.

Knowing the truth was freedom—maybe the family could find a path to reconciliation that would benefit the nation. Family unity was the first step to national unity.

National unity—the next step to global unity.

We were a nation of all world cultures.

Out of the many, one.

She heard a fire truck approaching and remained on the curb even though the little white man in a walking strut on the streetlight signaled to cross. After maneuvering around stopped traffic on K, the fire truck made a wide left turn onto Nineteenth Street.

The fire truck whizzed past, speeding into the distance.

Aware of her surroundings, she observed a black SUV in back of a stopped Hyundai waiting to make a left turn across her path onto Nineteenth Street. She made eye contact with Hyundai's driver. He waved her on.

She proceeded into the intersection with a bounce in her step.

Her security officer paused to tie his shoe, still on the curb.

Suddenly the black SUV gunned its motor. It swung around the Hyundai, making an illegal left turn from the wrong lane. Whirling toward the screeching sound, Mrs. Ross saw a black face behind the steering wheel.

She closed her eyes for the impact.

Her hands flew up.

Her mouth opened, but she had no time to scream.

Instinctively, she dived for the sidewalk as the black beast raced by. Breaking her fall with her hands, she rolled onto the curb.

Blood flowed from cuts to her head, hands and midsection.

Two hundred feet away, a gloved hand emerged from the Ford Expedition and released a cardboard sign. The homemade protest sign read *ROSS: ACT OR DIE!*

Two gleaming black masks that the driver and his passenger had been wearing also hit the pavement. The black SUV had no rear license tag.

The security guard knelt beside Mrs. Ross and checked her pulse, then yanked out his cell phone to call for help.

The young man in the Expedition sped away, Stratagem at his side.

Chapter Eighty

Monday, September 23
A Dentist's Office on Virginia Avenue

When Joshua returned to the waiting area of the dentist's office after his procedure, he was surprised to find he had company waiting. Galt had sent his personal security officer to drive his son home.

Joshua did not want to be handled. "I don't need a ride. I've got plans that don't include you. I've finally met someone who doesn't know who I am and I don't want you to scare her away. Okay?"

"Are you sure you're okay to drive?" Roy asked. "Your father's concerned about you. There's a lot going on…"

"There's always a lot going on. I'm fine. The dentist didn't use general anesthesia on me. I just went into a meditative state. I'm not drugged. I can drive."

"I still wish you would let me take you home. A car hit Mrs. Ross walking home after your class. It wasn't an accident. We're on high alert."

"What happened?"

"Don't know details. Your father just told me to get to you and make sure you got home safe."

"Well, I'm not going home." Joshua paused. "And I don't want you tailing me. If anything happens you can track me now, so you don't have to follow me everywhere. That's enough invasion of my privacy. I'm a grown man and I'm not going home tonight. I have special plans that don't include you."

"You know there's growing concern about the protestors over at McPherson Square? They're planning a march to the Supreme Court in the morning. Looks threatening."

"I'm not going over to McPherson Square or the Court tomorrow. My dad has his job to do in the face of threats and I have my life to live under the same burden, as John Galt's son."

"I still don't think this is the right time for you to ditch me."

"I have to have some time to pursue a lady. I'll see you when I get back."

Joshua left Roy sitting at the dentist's office.

Several blocks away, Joshua turned a corner and was alarmed to see his car, a new silver metallic Chrysler 200, being loaded onto a flatbed truck.

He sprinted toward it, hollering, "Hey! Hey—that's my car!"

The tow truck driver reached into his pocket, pulled out a card with an auto compound address, and handed it to Joshua before returning to his task.

Without looking up the white driver said, "You can pick up your car at the pound after ya pay yo parkin' tickets."

"I don't owe any tickets," Joshua bellowed with perfect dictation.

"The city says ya do." The driver continued to secure the vehicle on the ramp. "Jus' doin' my job."

"You can't just take my property like that."

"Yes, I can." The driver gave Joshua a copy of his paperwork. "Got legal papers."

Joshua inspected the paperwork, then snarled, "We'll see about this."

The truck driver shrugged.

Joshua headed back toward the dentist office. Roy could pick him up there.

He punched numbers into his cell phone as he marched down the street—he *didn't* have any unpaid violations and he didn't have time for this. With his phone to his ear, he approached a parked white van near a delivery entrance to a building, its motor humming.

Two soldiers of fortune sat inside, waiting for him.

As Joshua passed the vehicle, the men grabbed him and forced him into the van. They placed a white cloth over Joshua's mouth while ramming him into a corner of the vehicle.

Joshua was out as cold as a hibernating bear.

There were no witnesses.

Immediately, the van took off. Shawn made a call from the rear of the van on a new spectrum band phone with a secure connection.

"Yes, sir," he said. "We have him."

"She's down too," Stratagem replied. "That's the order—maximum chaos. We have an additional order to clean her apartment."

"That's challenging," Shawn said. "Streets are blocked. The Watergate's well-guarded."

Stratagem said, "I have a plan."

Chapter Eighty-One

U.S. Supreme Court
11:15 a.m.

In her chambers, Justice Ross sat at her secure computer screen and banged out succinct responses to the day's flood of electronic missives. After completing the last sentence of a decline to attend a UM Law School Reception honoring Senator Stephen "Skip" Graham and hitting the *RETURN* button, she turned around and glanced at the arrangement of blue roses that her secretary had placed on the edge of her desk. She had not wanted to deal with her emotions at the moment, so the sealed yellow envelope remained attached.

Turning back, she went on to the next email—with a serious-as-a-heart-attack demeanor. Focused. He was blocked. He wasn't going to get to her now.

She heard her secretary enter her sanctum again.

Katherine spun back around.

"There's been an accident," her secretary whispered. "Your mother's been hit by a car. They've taken her to Georgetown. Your ride is waiting in the basement to take you to the hospital. They want you to come now. It's serious."

After more than two hours in a small room just behind the double doors of the Georgetown Hospital Emergency Room,

Katherine still awaited word on her mother's condition while nursing a cup of coffee.

Hal was on guard, seated across the table from her. "Can I get you anything to eat?"

"No, I'm not hungry."

"You should eat something. Let me go find something for you."

"Just make it sweet," she said without looking up from her cup.

When Hal opened the door, she saw a hospital security guard and two Metro police officers posted. Glancing out the window, she saw that two black SUVs had been added to her regular security detail. She knew the marshals were wearing bulletproof vests and were heavily armed. Would she ever be able to walk along the streets of D.C. again? She watched the second hand move around the face of a large clock on the bare wall. *1:30 p.m. How much longer?*

She closed her eyes, praying for her mother.

Then she heard the door open and turned. A young doctor in blue scrubs who looked as if had been up all night entered the room and closed the door. He had the look of defeat.

"I'm sorry," the doctor said with sorrowful eyes.

Katherine felt her body tense, bracing for what she knew would be bad news.

"Her hip and wrists were broken. But we found a hard mass in her abdomen during her initial exam near a flesh wound, so I ordered a CT scan in addition to x-rays. We decided to open her up at the wound site to explore the mass—then we found stage four cancer throughout her lower abdomen and elected not to proceed to hip surgery. I didn't know it was your mother."

"What are you saying?" Katherine knew he might have made a different decision had he known his patient *had influence.*

"She needs to see an oncologist right away," he said. "I can't say how much time she might have, but I thought it best not to disturb her at this time."

Tears rolled down Katherine's face.

"When she comes around we'll give her pain medications to keep her comfortable. I'm sorry. There's nothing more we can do for her now."

"Please don't tell her about the cancer," Katherine pleaded. "Let me tell her."

"She might already know," the doctor said. "It's not uncommon for terminal cancer patients to conceal their illness from their family to spare them early grief."

"I'd be surprised if she didn't know. But in case she doesn't—I want to be there."

"Then I recommend you see her in recovery when she comes to, then go home and get a good night's sleep. Plan on being back here at six, before we start rounds."

As the doctor left, three suits entered the room. Hal carried a small bag of Oreo cookies and a white plastic bag with *PATIENT BELONGINGS* printed in bright blue.

Katherine recognized the two U.S. marshals in Hal's company. They had been standing at the door.

"These are your mother's belongings," Hal said. "We took a look. In her tote bag there's a sealed letter addressed to you and a package. We'd like to take a look at the letter. It might give us some clues."

Hal asked her a question with raised eyebrows. "Did you know your mother was enrolled in Galt's son's yoga class? That's where she was coming from when she was hit."

"No," Katherine answered. A barrage of questions exploded in her brain. "Where's her security officer? I want to talk to him now."

"He's in the waiting room," one of the marshals said. "We've already debriefed him."

"I want to debrief him, too."

Hal left the room to get him.

When Hal returned with the summoned officer, Katherine asked, "What happened?"

"I was a few steps behind her. A child dropped its bottle, I picked it up and saw my shoe needed tying. While I was tying my shoe, the light changed. She stepped into the street and the car at the traffic light gunned its engine—I can still hear the wheels squealing."

"How long has she been in Galt's son's class?"

"About four weeks," he replied. "We didn't see a problem."

"Do you know if Joshua gave my mother the sealed letter?"

"We've confirmed that he talked to her at the studio and she sent something FedEx to Galt," a marshal said. "We don't know where the sealed letter came from."

Katherine reached into her mother's bag and pulled out the sealed envelope.

She tore it open and pulled out a two page typed letter, her eyes raking over the words:

Justice Ross,

You must take action. You have a clear shot. Fire! We can't leave sleeping sentries at their posts. John T. Galt must be removed for the good of the country.

Greed and rational self-interest can no longer be allowed to rule in this country based on a work of fiction. There's nothing wrong with the wealthy having wealth, so long as they don't use their power to crush the underclasses.

George Washington said, "We can always trust in the Invisible Hand." We can trust in God to make things right in the end. But we, the people, must take brave action when we get the chance to make a difference.

Why are you protecting Galt?

The character of a perfect man, created by God, would have a heart.

The perfect man would fight injustice with his last breath.

Galt celebrates the making of money as a mission in life.

Our economy is in decline because of the ruthless pursuit of rational self-interest on Wall Street, Main Street and Union Street.

Our economic transformation must go forth on a platform of enlightened self-interest. Everyone must wake up and take action. Everyone matters.

We are a group of enlightened souls with passion in our hearts that drives us to fight for what is morally right—we share the spirit and passion of General George Washington. That spirit compels us to act in the face of great danger.

If you won't issue the fifth letter, you'll leave us with no choice. This is war. We are willing to sacrifice one to protect the masses.

The time has come to pick sides.

—The Enlightened Spirits of the United States of America

*****

Katherine issued an order one second after she completed reading the letter. "Take me to see Galt. Let him know I will be coming to his home after I see my mother in recovery. Nobody is to speak to my mother before I do, in the morning. No visitors should be allowed."

Placing the letter back into its envelope, she wondered where her mother had gotten this.

Chapter Eighty-Two

Somewhere in Arlington, Virginia

Katherine felt her armored vehicle roll to a stop. She heard the door locks pop and opened her eyes. She saw the miniature mansion of Justice John T. Galt. Two imposing black SUVs loaded with firepower were parked in plain view across the street from Galt's home—in addition to the two SUVs that accompanied her. Another signal to her that the Court was now beyond a red alert.

Her door opened and she rose, brushing a few Oreo cookie crumbs from her suit. That's all she'd had for lunch but she wasn't hungry. Her feet struck the winding red-brick path between manicured carpets of green. She noticed sections of holly bushes on each side of the front porch steps.

Katherine wondered if Galt knew who her mother was. He probably knew about the red clay brick *his grandfather* threw to save her. The holly bushes reminded her of all of the injustices her mother had endured in the South. Yet her mother had still managed to find happiness without letting her past define her. Could she do the same?

Katherine paused at the door and fought for control of her emotions.

She rang the doorbell.

Sambo, Galt's well-dressed Blackamoor personal assistant, opened the front door. Katherine composed herself in an instant.

"I'm sorry to hear about your mother," Sambo said, shaking his head in sympathy. Katherine noticed that he looked her over with suspicion.

"So am I," she said. She wasn't surprised to see Sambo open the door like a guard. She had heard he loved Galt like a son and would do anything for him.

"Is Justice Galt ready to see me?" Katherine waited for direction.

"Yes, ma'am, right this way," Sambo said, darting his eyes down the hall.

Katherine felt her energy draining. On instinct, she straightened her posture.

"He's waiting in the library." Sambo pointed to an opened double door.

Katherine entered an antechamber paneled in walnut. Over the mantel was hung a huge picture of an American bald eagle. There was no fire in the fireplace on that cool evening. Three-foot curved catwalks provided extra walnut bookshelves to store Galt's collection of rare books. She'd known he was a collector, too. Beneath the walnut-paneled underbelly of the catwalks, soft recessed lighting accented the room. There were fresh flowers in crystal vases.

Picture-perfect.

She smelled spiced tea and found Galt in a brown leather armchair with his feet up on a matching footrest, a white pillow at his right shoulder. He held a cup of tea in his left hand. Clear plastic tubing ran up to his nose.

He wore a fine bathrobe over bedclothes with bronze suede and leather slippers on his feet. A prosthesis matching the color of his flesh rested on the floor next to an oxygen caddy.

Katherine observed no stacks of cert petitions on his massive desk as she passed by it. Both his in and out boxes were empty. She realized that the Court's business was not being conducted from this space. There was no evidence.

"Have a seat." Galt motioned to an armchair. "Would you like some tea?"

"No." She unfolded the letter and placed it on his lap desk. "I brought this for you to read. They found this in my mother's purse."

"What's her condition?" he said, reaching for the first sheet of the letter.

"She's in recovery. We need to decide what to do."

Katherine watched Galt read the letter. His eyebrows rose.

Finally, he shrugged. "Well, you can't take me out in the face of a threat. If you did, that would be bad behavior on your part. We can't allow them to bully us."

"Is Jennie here?"

"No, she went shopping this morning, then she had meetings this afternoon on Capitol Hill. You can speak freely. Nobody's here but Sambo."

"I'm wondering if that letter was planted on my mother as a seed to remove both of us," Katherine said. "My mother would only take a sealed note to deliver to me from someone she knew and trusted. Your son was the last person she saw, other than her security officer, before she was run down. Where's your son?"

"He hasn't come home yet. Have the marshals seen this?"

"No." She reached for a butter cookie. "I told them I would discuss it with you and we would decide if anyone else should see it."

"Well, one thing's for sure," Galt said, glancing at the note again, "an enlightened spirit didn't write this because they made a threat. That's how evil forces often work. This message is from a highly intelligent group with an evil intent. You should give it to the marshals."

"I don't think I want to acknowledge I've been threatened. It's easier for me that way. I want to keep this between us."

"I don't think that's wise. But I'll honor your wishes."

"Did your son mention to you that my mother was enrolled in his yoga class?"

"Yes, I found out last week."

"From your son?"

"Yes." Galt reached for her hand and searched her eyes. "I know you're family."

Pulling back her head, Katherine asked, "Are you JT?"

"Yeah," Galt said. "That's a thing with our family. We're big with nicknames. My father's brothers were CL and DW. I had a sister who was just B. Don't know why I didn't recognize your mother as kin. She looks just like my Aunt Helen."

"So she read *Uncle Remus* to you?"

"Of course. The Walt Disney version. That's how I learned to read. I still have it. How is your mother, really?"

She struggled to speak without losing control. Finally, her emotions broke free as her shoulders shook and her breath quickened. Sobbing, she whispered, "She's not going to make it."

"I'm so sorry to hear that," Galt said, releasing her hand.

Katherine reached in her purse for a tissue and blew her nose.

Galt said, "When I read the first two chapters I immediately realized who she was. What happened to her was the big mystery in our family. Your grandfather knew what had to be done in the face of threats, and did it. He gave his life to save his family. He faced evil with no fear. That's how we have to be."

"It's just too much to deal with." Katherine pushed back waves of emotion.

"What can I do to help? You've been threatened and Hattie's been hurt. I think we should turn the note over to the marshals. We can't give in to threats."

"I can't keep on pretending nothing is happening."

"Yes, you can. The pressure on me has been building for some time. I've thought about resigning. My health is declining. I've lost my arm. My body aches all over from sitting in chairs for hours reading. And, I'm tired. But I can't quit like this."

"I was going to ask for your resignation," Katherine said. "But I think you answered."

"Are you asking me to make a sacrifice for Hattie?"

"It's not about her anymore. It's about us. I have to make a decision about your fate in the face of a threat." She paused. "Until we give up our seats, we have to decide what's best for the nation, irrespective of what happens to us as individuals. We have to put the nation first—what's best for *all* of us."

"That's our legacy. Your grandfather put the family first. He died. My Grandpa Wash saved your mother, then ran. He told me the story many times. I've always been able to see that red clay brick flying through the air like an arrow headed for the bullseye. But we can't run."

"I won't be intimidated," Katherine said with resolve. "They'll have to take me out."

"I could resign for the right reason. Turn myself in like Hattie's father did."

"We can't just give in to them. That would just encourage the bullies."

"It's not giving up, when a person leaves on their own terms. We could make a deal."

"Make a deal with who? We don't know who they are."

"Senator Graham," Galt said. "He's the symbol of my opposition."

"Why would he make a deal with you?"

"To get me off the bench. That's his mission. His resignation as Chairman of the Judiciary Committee for my resignation from the Court—a fair trade between two men who can't be forced from our positions. We could both walk away with our dignity. Does that make sense to you?"

"Do you really think he would give up his chairmanship to get you?"

"He might want me out that bad. The political process of removing me is unsure. He knows that. But on second thought, that might not work. If I resign first, he has no incentive to resign. He won't resign first because he won't believe I'll resign, and I wouldn't resign first for the same reason—won't work."

Katherine sat in deep thought for a few moments.

"I think I'm issuing the fifth letter," Katherine said. "Graham has the votes to get it out of committee—but it's not clear what will happen when the full Senate votes. It'll be close. But then again, maybe Jennie can cash in a few of her chips to save you from the full vote."

"I believe Graham has the votes to get it out of the Committee," Galt said. "That's why they're hitting you. If he got it out of committee, my supporters would work their magic on the Senate floor. My seat is safe. But your seat might not be, if you pulled the trigger on me by issuing the fifth letter. My supporters would fire back. I think you lose in a shootout."

"If I took a deal to Graham and got him to resign first, would you resign?"

"Yeah," Galt said. "I guess so. It would be the honorable thing to do. But my ego just won't allow me to be forced out, no matter what happens."

"Okay," Katherine said, rising from her seat. "I'm issuing the fifth letter. I can't be afraid to do what needs to be done."

Galt hunched up. "You won't survive if you issue it."

"I may not survive no matter what I do. You said you would resign if a deal could be cut with Graham. That's what I heard you say. Did you mean it?"

"I was just thinking out loud. Graham's not irrational. He'd never make the first move and neither would I—too much risk. That's a deal that can't happen."

"I think it could if we have a deal," Katherine said. "Are you a man of your word?"

"Of course," Galt said with a quizzical look.

*****

After Katherine left, Galt sat in his library facing the reality of his circumstances—remembering what they'd told him when he tried to give them notice of his plans to retire on the Fourth of July:

"We can control what happens to you. We think it's in your best interest to hold onto your seat. If the fifth letter is issued, a recommendation on your involuntary retirement will never get out of the Senate Judiciary Committee. A fifth letter should be of no concern to you. We helped you get a lifetime appointment for our benefit. You're still a valuable asset to us in your current capacity. Therefore you must understand, resigning is not an option for you.

"Death is your only way out."

Chapter Eighty-Three

Galt pulled the oxygen tubing from his nose and let it drop to the floor. He lifted his slippered feet off the footstool and onto an oriental rug, pushing himself to standing using his left hand with minimal effort. He moved to his desk and pressed a button, then eased over to the windows and parted the vertical wooden shades, watching Katherine's vehicles pull away from the curb.

The branches of the trees in his yard danced with the wind in unison. How long would he be able to resist the force of a strong wind? What would they do to keep him from resigning?

Moments later, Sambo appeared. "Did you ring for me?"

"My mail please," Galt said.

Sambo moved to the tea table, picking up the used service set, "Is there anything else?"

"No." He watched Sambo retreat.

Galt stayed at the window and watched the gathering storm. He felt a tinge of pain where his right arm had been. Phantom pain, the doctors called it. It wasn't real. Nevertheless, he felt it. *What was real?* He gazed up, but could not see the sun through the clouds. He felt troubled at the dark forces gaining power. He closed his eyes in silent prayer.

A few minutes later, Galt heard the squeak of the mail cart's wheels. Sambo entered the library with a basket of processed mail, a pile of magazines and journals, and two fresh flower arrangements in the center of the mail cart.

"We can't have any more flowers in here or it'll smell like a funeral parlor," Galt said.

"Shall I put the notecards on your desk?" Sambo plucked the cards from a dozen blue roses and a colorful arrangement of tulips.

"No," Galt said, holding out his hand. "I'd like to know who sent them."

Sambo tore open the sealed envelope attached to blue roses first and handed it to Galt.

Galt froze when he saw the stylized Blackletter typeset on the notecard.

Justice Galt:

> We have accomplished the impossible.
> We have your son under our control.
> We need you to stay in position.
> Important cargo is headed for your desk.

The Privateers

Galt fell back in his chair and wailed, "Noooo!"

"What's wrong?" Sambo cried.

Joshua would not want me to let the pirates bully me, Galt thought. *He would not want my love for him to be used as a weapon.* Galt handed his cell phone to Sambo. "Hold this."

He punched a text to Roy, his security officer, with one finger. The message was short:

Code Blue: Locate Josh with all arms.

Chapter Eighty-Four

The Ritz Condominiums
9:00 p.m.

In the privacy of her blue bedroom behind double doors, Katherine pulled Skip's card from her nightstand drawer. She finally had the courage and a need to call him.

She slid her finger across the face of her smartphone and tapped in his number, each touch creating its own unique sound in the backdrop of silence.

It rang four times before he answered.

"Hi, this is Kathy"

"How are you?" Graham asked with concern. "I heard—"

"Shaken," she muttered. "So much is happening."

"I heard about your mother. How is she?"

"She has a broken hip. She's been sedated."

"Are you crying?"

She said nothing, forcing the threatening tears back down.

"I wish I could come see you tonight," he said. "But I'm sure your security is tight."

"It is," she acknowledged. "You won't be sneaking into my building tonight. But we need to talk. Can you meet me at my mother's? I need to retrieve some things for her tonight."

"Sure. I can get into the Watergate without attracting too much attention. What's her unit number?"

"Nine Twelve."

"Okay, I'll see you at ten."

Sitting in her favorite armchair at her mother's apartment, Katherine poured the senator a glass of wine. The stress of the situation showed on her face as she searched for the right words to start the conversation. Topping off his glass with a slight twist of the wrist, she glanced at the lights of a single boat twinkling on the Potomac River.

Graham spoke first. "I want to protect you."

"I have to protect myself. I have to protect my heart."

"You don't have to protect yourself from me—I'm in love with you."

"You can't say that now." She struggled to hold back the tears. "How can I trust you?"

"Can you forgive me?"

"I don't know if I can forgive myself." The tears broke free.

"Forgive yourself for what? It was my fault."

"It was my fault I never told you we should have had a life together."

He stared at her, shocked—catching the unthinkable meaning. "Are you saying—?"

"I can't say it." She turned her head toward the window and noticed—yet could not clearly see—the brightening light in the distance through her tears.

Her brain was no longer processing; her raw emotions took charge.

He pulled her to her feet and embraced her. "I'm so sorry. I can't bear the thought."

She felt his body tremble. "Can you ever forgive me?"

"I want to."

"I wish I could take us back."

"But you can't." She wiped her tears and pulled away. "I have to deal with today as it is." She gazed at him. She didn't know what to do. But she had to do something. She dealt with the issue. "I need to decide what to do about Galt. This can't be personal. If I issue the fifth letter to remove Galt, you can't be a part of the process to remove him, too."

"What do you mean?"

"You can't act to retire him as Chair of the Judiciary Committee. And if you remain Chair of the Judiciary Committee after I issue the fifth letter, we'll never have a chance to recover from what happened. I'll never get over the pain of knowing that you took me and didn't love me. You have to decide if you really want me."

"I want you. I know that."

"Then you know what you have to do," she mumbled like a child.

"Are you going to issue it?"

"I'll do what's right," she whispered, turning her face to glance at the river. "I always try to do what's right." She turned away, her face twisted as she began to sob again. Reaching for a tissue to blow her nose, she sank back into the safety of her mother's chair.

"You drive a hard bargain. Come here. Let me hug you."

Katherine rose in a flash, responding to the touch of his hands. She marched toward the entrance door, brushing past him and, upon reaching the door, flung it open before announcing her most recent decision.

"You should leave now."

As Katherine reached the elevator alone with a small bag, one of the U.S. marshals guarding her emerged from the stairwell. She pressed the down button while he surveyed the hallway for the slightest sound or movement.

"We saw Senator Graham," the marshal said. "We assumed that was okay."

"Yes." She should have known a secret meeting with him was impossible now.

"Did you get everything you needed?" the marshal asked.

"No," she said. "Something wasn't where I expected it to be. I'll have to come back later when I have more time. My mother is great at hiding things. But I did find her favorite bed jacket. It was the last gift my father gave her before he died."

As the marshal opened his mouth to respond, the building shook and the sound of a blast pulsed through the hallway.

Immediately the marshal shoved Katherine toward the exit sign at the far end of the hallway, saying, "Let's take the stairwell."

They dashed for the exit door.

Speeding down nine flights, they were met midway by an armed SWAT team who surrounded them as they continued their descent to armored vehicles in the underground parking garage of the Watergate. The protectors stuffed Katherine into the backseat of a silver SUV with tinted windows.

"Where did the SWAT team come from?" she asked as they sped off.

"There are other officials in your mother's building who required heightened security," her security officer said. "A team has been housed here for weeks."

The marshal in the front seat of the vehicle with a clear plastic bug in his ear issued an order to their driver. "Roll with siren and lights."

Turning around to speak to Katherine, the driver said, "A small rocket went through a picture window in your mother's unit. It's on fire. We're lucky you didn't stay in there any longer."

Chapter Eighty-Five

At 10:00 p.m., Stratagem sat at a card table reading emails on the small screen of an iPad in a dimly lit apartment on J Street. The room smelled of incense. A wooden icon of a brown baby Jesus hung on the wall between two windows with drawn shades and flimsy flowered curtains. An assortment of knives lay on a small table, ready for use.

He glanced at Sambo shaking in the corner. Crying. Hunched over. They had snatched him from the parking lot of Costco at Pentagon City just before the superstore closed.

"Bring me a carving knife," Shawn said.

"Please, don't do this thing," Sambo said.

Shawn barked orders. "Shut up and bring me the knife."

Sambo picked up a stainless steel knife and shuffled toward him, sniffling with each step. His hands shook as he wiped his nose on his sleeve.

Joshua sat in the middle of the room, his hands tied behind his back.

"Give it to me now," Shawn said to Sambo, holding out his hand.

With a whimpering sound, Sambo handed over the blade.

Waving the knife under Joshua's nose, Shawn said, "Sambo takes orders from us now. Your father is no longer his master. We are. And you'll be takin' orders from Sambo if you want to stay around. Do you understand?"

"Oh, no!" Sambo squealed, folding over to his knees.

"I'm a free spirit," Joshua said. "I only take orders from my God."

"You're a spoiled brat," Shawn said, slapping Joshua in the face. "Your father may let you get away with doing nothing but sitting in silence for hours, writing your rags and teachin' da bitches and sissies how to 'bow down and just let it go.'"

Shawn waved his arms in a warrior pose, striking Joshua in the face again as he came out of the pose. Joshua recomposed himself in an instant.

"You'll do what we say or we'll just let go," Shawn said. "You tell your father what we tell you to or he might not survive the next explosion. Tell your old man Walter Rodney didn't commit suicide tryin' to kill him. Walter talked tough, but he was just a man of words. That's why he didn't make it. He wouldn't embrace the need to use violence to accomplish a mission. So we took him out to show your dad just how close we could get to him. Tell him that."

Shawn moved to where Joshua was sitting and squatted in front of him. "If you don't believe what we're sayin', wait and see what's gonna happen. We're movin' on Ross. Should be big news. Tell your father he needs to do what he's been doing. Then you'll be safe."

"You have no power over me," Joshua said.

"We can get to anyone." Shawn put his face nose-to-nose with Joshua and exhaled. "Are you aware Mrs. Ross had a terrible accident after she left your class today?"

"Shawn tell 'm what happened to the uppity old bitch," Stratagem said.

"The bitch stepped right in front of my brand new Ford Expedition and bounced to the ground like a rag doll. She got in my way."

Joshua closed his eyes to find the peace within himself.

Shawn slapped him again and said, "Come back! Class isn't over yet."

"Lord help us," Sambo said, hugging and rocking his upper body.

"We work for men of great power you should fear," Stratagem said. "You need to do as you're told to keep you and your Dad alive. You like livin', don't cha?"

"No earthly man can take my life unless I freely give it up," Joshua said in a calm voice.

"I can take your life now," Shawn sneered, pointing a knife at Joshua's heart.

Sambo cringed back into a corner and pleaded, "Josh, just do what they say."

Joshua faced Shawn, boring into his eyes, "I have no fear of you because I have conquered my demons within. You are the one in mortal danger."

Making a circle around Joshua's left ear with the blade of the knife, Shawn said, "Perhaps we should send an ear to your father. He may not share your foolish faith."

Stratagem turned to Sambo. "Come over here."

Sambo shuffled over, sniffing all the way.

"Give him the knife," Stratagem said to Shawn.

"Please." Sambo fell to his knees. "Please. Please."

"Please put Joshua's ear in this box to deliver to Justice Galt," Stratagem said.

Sambo inched toward Joshua from behind. Quivering. Surrendering to fear.

"Don't do this thing in ignorance," Joshua said. "You don't want my blood on your hands. Let them kill me, if I must die now."

"I love you like a son," Sambo said with tears flowing.

Shawn hazed Sambo. "Do it now or you're a dead man."

The knife trembled in Sambo's hands.

Joshua's shoulders dropped. His body relaxed according to his will.

"Have no fear Sambo," Joshua said in a calming voice. "I forgive you—I'm saved."

Joshua closed his eyes.

Sambo raised the knife. Then he froze.

"Do it!" Shawn hissed.

"Can I have a sharper knife?" Sambo petitioned. "Bigger. I want it to be over quickly."

"Give him the chef's blade," Stratagem said.

Shawn walked over to a table of shiny knives and selected a ten-inch Japanese chef's blade with a black pearl handle. "Here," he said, handing the blade to Sambo.

Standing behind Joshua, Sambo took the blade, raised it all the way up over his head and stabbed himself in the heart. Blood sprayed from his chest as he fell to the floor.

"What the *fuck?*" Shawn ran over and pulled out the knife. "How we gonna get Joshua back home now?"

"You'd better figure something out," Stratagem said. "You shouldn't have scared him to death. You knew he was weak."

"Lemme take a piss," Shawn said. "I'll figure somethin' out. Jus' give me a few."

Shawn joggled toward the bathroom, then paused as he caught muffled sounds coming from the hallway and turned his head toward the door.

He motioned for Stratagem to look out of the southwest window.

Joshua remained reposed.

Meditating.

Outside, D.C. Metro police cars and unmarked black SUVs were stationed around the corner, out of sight from all the corner apartment's windows. A SWAT team positioned itself on top of a vacant building across the street, taking aim at the shaded windows of the targeted apartment. Four U.S. marshals, heavily armed with helmets and bulletproof gear, entered the apartment building and made their way to the stairwell. They eased up the steps until they reached the third floor. A technician in a white van parked at the end of the street read a computer screen with a diagram of the building. Yellow, blue, green and red dots moved on the screen. Joshua's dot, transmitted from the chip implanted in his crown, was red and showed no movement on the screen.

A directional listening device that looked something like a bullhorn was pointed at the third floor window. The dire circumstances of Joshua's situation were recorded in the van. "It sounds like Sambo just killed himself and bought Joshua a little more time," the technician said transmitting to all members of the team. "Out of time. Enter at will—take the targets."

A red dot moved on the screen.

The technician spoke into a microphone. "Josh has been moved to a position near the southwest window. Fire no shots through the southwest window. Extraction team—your position is correct. He is clear of the door. Use fire power to blast in now."

With one accurate shot, the lock was blasted from its safeguarding position.

Shawn grabbed for his automatic weapon.

He was shot four times before he could clear his weapon.

Four marksmen stood with guns drawn, holding fire with no safe shots remaining.

Stratagem had jumped behind Joshua, kneeling, using his body as a shield. His gun was pointed at Joshua's temple. "Stalemate," he said. "Let me walk with him."

Joshua closed his eyes, a calm expression on his face.

"That's not—" One of the marksmen was saying as Joshua flung his body up, the chair coming with him, in a jump backward. Shots from Stratagem's gun flew past his ear.

Joshua's movements were lightning fast. Forceful, and with intention. Precisely executed by powerful legs. They landed on Sambo's body with Stratagem pinned down.

Stratagem's gun was still in his right hand. Bullets flew. Stratagem took two clean shots to the left temple before he could free his hand from under Joshua and his chair.

Joshua was freed.

During Joshua's debriefing, a crumpled piece of paper with Mrs. Ross's address and the word "clean" was found in a nearby trash can.

A U.S. marshal said, "Two cases closed."

Then they found army uniforms, automatic weapons and explosives with a document titled, *The Chaos Plan*.

The situation was not yet under control.

Chapter Eighty-Six

Just before Midnight

Galt grabbed his son with his single arm as soon as Joshua walked through the door. With a beaming face, tears of joy sprang from Galt's eyes. He held his son in a tight embrace.

"It's not over yet," Joshua said, pulling back. "We must go see the President. Now."

"The President?" Galt examined his son's bruised face.

"Yes. They're planning to massacre the protestors in front of the Supreme Court tomorrow. We must stop them."

"We can call him," Galt said. "They can handle it."

"We need to go to the White House for secure communications with the President," the U.S. marshal said. "That's the only way we can hope to get messages to and from the President without interception. We need you to make calls from your secure line."

"Who do you want me to call?"

"The Chief and Justice Ross," the marshal said. "Ask them to meet us at the White House. We must hurry to avoid chaos in the morning. Please make the calls now."

"Okay," Galt said. "Let's go to the library."

"Dad," Joshua said. "There's one more thing you should know before you make the calls." He paused, gazing into his father's eyes. "They kidnapped Sambo and he committed suicide. They plan to kill Justice Ross. The person who ran her mother down is dead, along with his boss, but we don't know if the threat against her life is still in effect."

In the White House Situation Room, Chief Justice Harlan Gaines, Ross, Galt, Joshua, the Secret Service and other appropriate staff, and President Abraham Canty listened to the report from the U.S. marshals.

"Let me summarize and tell you what we think we know," the National Security Advisor said. "Stratagem was a member of Delta Force and an explosives expert. After his official discharge from the Army, he enrolled in graduate school in London. That's where we believe he came in contact with unidentified Asian interests. We suspect he had an assignment to infiltrate the Black Activists Mobilization Network and was responsible for the blast that killed Walter Rodney and injured Justice Galt.

"In the end, Stratagem's only loyalty was to the U.S. dollar and he turned into a double agent—he might even have been a triple agent. He served all willing to pay his enormous fees."

The Head of the FBI weighed in. "We infiltrated BAMN as their organizing efforts took on the energy of a cyclone last month. What they're planning is unthinkable."

The National Security Advisor continued. "Stratagem accepted assignments with conflicting political objectives—an assignment to intimidate and/or assassinate Justice Ross from one group and an assignment from another group to keep Galt from resigning."

"We can't prove it, but we believe Alexander Morris is one of Stratagem's clients."

"Let's just stick with what you know for sure," the President said to the FBI Director.

"Stratagem assumed leadership of the McPherson Square protest," the U.S marshal said. "We found a plan to create chaos tomorrow in front of the Supreme Court. They're going to march from McPherson Square to the Supreme Court, inciting violence. Hired guns will be uniformed as our Army troops. We found uniforms, assault rifles, ammunition, and staging plans all along the planned route."

The U.S. marshal made the key point. "They're planning to fire on the marchers when they reach the Supreme Court plaza. Their plan suggests our military chain of command has been compromised."

"We can't let that happen in front of the Supreme Court," Chief Justice Gaines said. "This must be contained."

One of the Secret Service agents left the room.

"We should call General Pet...?"

"No," President Canty said. "We've got to call the Commanding General of the DC National Guard. He reports to me directly—nobody else. Get him on the secure phone now."

A staff aide jumped into action.

"We need someone who can keep the crowd from reaching the Supreme Court," the head of Secret Service suggested.

"Our reports indicate they have no other grassroots leadership," the National Security Advisor said. "There's no telling what will happen tomorrow."

"I think we continue to use the Metro police for crowd control," the Secretary of Homeland Security said. "The National Guard needs to ring the protest area perimeter."

The Secret Service officer reentered the room. "The crowd at McPherson Square is swelling." He clicked on the six flat panel display monitors with a remote. Images of the drama unfolding flooded the walls. "Busloads of people from the Temple of Mali are arriving now. They're setting up tents and porta-potties. Tables with free food and drinks. A stage with a speaker system."

"Jesus," President Canty said. "What's going on here?"

"A chaos strategy," the National Security Advisor said. "If one bullet is fired, we'll quickly lose control. We need to give the crowd something they want."

"Can we redirect the march from the Supreme Court to the White House?" the Secretary of Homeland Security asked.

"Why the White House?" the Chief of Staff asked.

"To protect the marchers," the Homeland Security Secretary replied. "We'll have better control of the situation here, better security, and a shorter marching distance from McPherson Square."

The National Security Advisor said, "We need to keep anyone wearing a regular Army uniform away from the protestors. If the National Guard has to fire against people in Army uniforms, with legitimate Army troops deployed, it would create chaos."

The FBI Director said, "Stratagem seemed certain of his ability to have a high level officer issue a command for our Army troops to enter the city."

"Then they've got to have a General. Maybe we can get some Marines in undercover."

"Gentlemen," the President said. "Are you suggesting we've lost control of the Army?"

"We don't know, sir."

"I'm the Commander-In-Chief," President Canty said. "If you don't know where there's a break in the chain of command, I'll have to assume leadership and direct this thing myself."

"We can't protect you in a crowd like that, sir," the director of the Secret Service said.

"You can't protect me in here if I don't have control of our military," the President said. "I'll issue an order to the Army that no uniformed troops are to be in the Capitol tomorrow, then I'll go to the square and lead the people to the White House for a—"

"Sir, we can't let you do that. We don't know where the breech is, if we have one."

"Sorry to make you uncomfortable, but this is what is going to happen in the morning—"

"That's not wise," the director of the Secret Service said. "We can't provide proper security on such short notice. Plus you can't solve their problems because you don't control the Congress or the Supreme Court. Your presence only makes things more volatile."

The White House Chief of Staff spoke to the President. "You're not the target."

They all looked at Galt.

"I'll not resign under mob pressure," Galt said.

"Justice Ross?" Chief Gaines glanced in her direction.

"Nor would I expect Galt to resign under pressure if he's fit to serve," Katherine replied. "None of us should act out of undue influence, but we must also not be afraid to act because of public perceptions. I've concluded the fifth letter must be issued now to protect the integrity of the Court. I don't think any of our chambers should run on an auto-pilot."

She glared at Galt.

He shrugged.

Katherine continued, "Maybe that's not happening in your chambers. But you must admit there is a basis for reasonable people to have strong doubts about your ability to serve."

Galt offered no defense.

She continued, addressing the group. "The people have given us a process to deal with the issue of an incapacitated justice and I now believe that process should be allowed to work in Galt's case. I'll go to the people in McPherson Square and give them my decision."

Chief Justice Gaines said, "It's not necessary for you to put yourself in danger."

Katherine faced the President. "The people will lose faith in the Supreme Court if we bow to threats and work from our homes like we're the Wizard of Oz. If I face death tomorrow, there would be no better way for me to die than in service to our country. I'm not afraid."

She turned to face Galt. "If you're not incapacitated, prove it to us. Defend yourself. Here. Now. Are you in control of your chambers, at this time, or is Nathan Butt keeping the trains running on time with your wife conducting with her *invisible hand*?"

Galt shrugged again, without comment.

"John, know this," Katherine said. "My decision to issue the fifth letter is being made without fear of what our intimidators might do."

Chapter Eighty-Seven

Tuesday, September 24

Katherine opened her eyes to darkness, awakened from a fitful sleep by the ringing of the phone on her bedside table. It was 4:30 a.m. She wasn't sure she had slept at all. It had been just two hours since she had pulled the covers over her head in an attempt to fall asleep.

Instinctively, she knew the call was not good news.

"Hello."

"May I speak to Katherine Ross," the woman on the telephone said.

"Speaking."

"This is Georgetown Hospital. Your mother has taken a turn for the worse. She asked that we call you. You should come in now."

"I'll be right there." Katherine hung up the phone.

She reached for her cell phone, scrolled to Pastor Adams's number, then pressed his name on the screen to dial.

She listened. No answer. She left a message. "This is Katherine Ross. My mother is near death. She's at Georgetown. I need someone to talk to. Please pray for her—and for me."

Katherine pressed the *END* button.

She went to the bathroom and turned on the tub water for a quick bath, then turned to brush her teeth. Gazing in the mirror, her mother's features were reflected in her own face as she confronted the reality that soon she would be alone in the world with no one who truly loved her. No children. No father. No mother. No husband. Nobody.

No love she could count on for sure.

Tears sprang forth. She sobbed out loud. Free to let all of her emotions out in the privacy of her bathroom. She slid to the cold marble floor, her body folding in despair. She felt as if her soul was being ripped out of her body.

The pain of loss emanated from every single cell. Suddenly, she knew she would be crushed and would never be strong, if she didn't get up from the floor at that moment.

Katherine rose.

The bathtub was close to overflowing before she turned off the faucet. She stared into the water, knowing this would be her mother's last day on earth. A calm came over her. She dried her eyes with her hands, then, on her knees—leaning on the edge of the tub—she prayed:

Dear God, If you cannot restore my mother's body in this life, I am ready to let her go into your arms. Take her soul into heaven so she can be united with thee. Help me to follow the right path to your door. Lift this pain from my heart. I surrender my will to you. Amen.

*****

Katherine moved down the hospital corridor to her mother's room feeling like she was walking to her own execution. Each moment seemed like a minute, each minute like an hour. Approaching her mother's room, she wondered if her mother was still there.

As she made the final steps to her mother's bedside, she found her mother awake.

Her eyes were wide open.

"Hi, baby," her mother said with a weak smile.

"Hey, Mom."

"It's getting hard to breath."

"I know. Don't talk."

"I must."

"Why? You can't have any more secrets. I finished reading your memoir."

"I have more secrets," her mother whispered.

"What now?" Katherine braced for the tears starting to race up stream. "What could be important now? You need to save your energy."

"There are other chapters I left out—they're beneath my mattress." Hattie struggled for breath. "Didn't finish—it needs work." She paused for labored breath. "You finish."

"It's gone, Mom," Katherine said with soft breath. "Maybe we should keep the family secrets. You said keeping secrets made it easier to get along in the world."

"Not gone. No more secrets. You must struggle. Easy, not best way."

"I love you, Mom." Katherine thought she would never know her mother's last secret—her condo having been destroyed. What knowledge had been lost in the fire? It didn't matter.

"I love you, baby." Hattie took another winded breath.

"Don't talk. Just stay with me for as long as you can. Save your breath."

"Don't give up on JT," she whispered. "What you do to him, you do to yourself."

"Stay with me."

Hattie smiled, nourishing Katherine's soul—passing on her strength. "Baby, I'm gonna be free from the burden of my body soon. No tears. I'm ready. Smile for me."

With sorrow in her eyes, Katherine put on her best smile—holding onto her mother's hand and feeling the warmth of her love through her wrinkled skin.

Hattie closed her eyes, fighting for another breath.

Her shoulders relaxed.

Katherine braced for the final breath.

A few moments later, Hattie opened her eyes. She strained to see, struggling to lift her head. Several images stood at the foot of her bed. The light behind the images was dazzling. The figures glowed. Bright light shone through the three figures, making their images translucent and difficult to distinguish from the light.

A comforting sight.

Hattie perceived the presence of her husband's spirit, her father's, and, finally, her mother's. Her mama. Her father. A vision? No, he was there.

"My father was white," Hattie said in a strained voice.

"Don't talk," Katherine said, knowing every word took critical breath.

"Not in my story." Hattie struggled to tell her last secret. "I was adopted by my mother's sister—'cause I couldn't pass for white."

Hattie took a loud breath that sounded like the roar of the ocean. "Last time I saw my mama—I was four. Hmm. My family's from Putnum County, Georgia. We're Thomases. Hmm. Find the relatives. Hmm. From Eatonton. Hmm. Somebody knows." After several haggard breaths, Hattie said, "Find dem. Thomas judge. Hmm. Family broken by color."

"I'll find them." Katherine wiped her cheeks with a disintegrating tissue. "I'll unite us."

"My mama's here," Hattie said with strained breath. "Dreamed 'bout her last night—said she was coming to get me at eight." In a barely auditable voice she said, "She's here."

Katherine looked around the room—then at her watch. 7:57 a.m.

Hattie stared at the foot of her bed with wide eyes. She saw the bright light. Her hand dropped to the bed. Other translucent bodies moved into the bright background. Hattie's gaze was fixed.

Katherine stared at the foot of her mother's bed, too.

415

Light from the rising sun shone through the window, shimmering at the foot of the bed.

Hattie heard her name being called from far away. *Hattie Mae.*

"Lord have mercy on me," Hattie said in a clear voice.

Katherine was astonished at the strength of her mother's voice. Hope rose that death would not arrive that sunny morning, in spite of the foreboding she now felt in the pit of her stomach. Her gaze fixed on her mother's timeworn face.

"Rest," Katherine whispered, hearing her mother wheeze with each struggled breath. "Don't talk anymore. I'm okay."

Katherine squeezed her mother's hand.

Her mother's gaze returned to the foot of the bed.

Katherine looked at the foot of the bed, too—but saw nothing. She glanced back at her mother. Her mother stared straight ahead, still tightly holding her hand.

"We're all one," her mother whispered, shifting her gaze back at Katherine.

Hattie's body relaxed—her eyes closed. Her last breath was a death rattle.

Katherine felt her mother's hand go limp.

Life support equipment alarms wailed.

Katherine's head hung in sorrow. Her eyes closed. Her shoulders slumped. Tearless.

She gazed at her mother's lifeless body, knowing that her mother's spirit no longer resided there. Yet she felt her mother's love all around her.

In her head, Katherine heard her mother's voice. *Baby, I'm okay.*

The Code Blue team rushed in. Katherine moved out of their way in silence, glancing at the large clock on the wall.

"She's gone," Katherine said. "No need to attempt resuscitation—it's her time."

It was 8:00 a.m. Exactly.

416

Chapter Eighty-Eight

"Let's go. She's gone."

At the nurses' station, Katherine said, "Please notify the hospital's public relations office, no press on my mother's death until I claim her body and that won't be for several hours. Please allow her body to stay in this room until I claim it later today."

Katherine put on sunglasses to hide the sorrow in her eyes.

Pastor Adams rushed through the hospital doors on a mission. Serious. Before he could reach the Information Desk, he bumped into Katherine and Roy on their way out. "Where is she?"

"Gone," Katherine whispered.

"Oh, no," Adams said. "She had them call me last night. I jumped on the first flight."

"I think she called you for me," Katherine said. "I left a message for you, too, early this morning when the hospital called. Can I talk to you alone? I only have a few moments."

"Of course. Let's go to the chapel."

Roy closed the door behind them after they entered the chapel. Katherine turned and motioned for him to wait outside. "I need privacy for a few moments," she whispered to Roy.

Roy left them alone.

Pastor Adams helped Katherine to a seat near the altar. She trembled but didn't breakdown. He sat beside her. She knew he was waiting for her emotions to burst. She took off her sunglasses and revealed her dry eyes, then said, "This is no time for tears." She reached into her purse and pulled out the note, handing it to Adams. "They found this unopened note for me in her purse."

As he read, Adams asked, "Has anyone else seen this?"

"Yes. Galt."

"Why him?"

"We're family."

"Family?"

"Yes. His father and my mother were first cousins."

"How long have you known this?"

"A few weeks. My mother kept it from me."

"Does Galt know?"

"Yes, she let him know."

"When?"

"A few days ago."

"Do you think Galt would know who wrote this?"

"If he does, he didn't share that information with me."

"You know he still can't be trusted to help us. Are you going to issue the fifth letter?"

"Yes. I looked him in the eye when I told him I was issuing it."

"What did he say?"

"Nothing. No defense."

"Typical John Galt behavior. Don't waste time explaining to lesser beings."

"Will you say the prayer of protection for me?"

Adams took her hand and knelt. "...And under his wings you shall take refuge. His truth shall be your shield and buckler... Amen."

"Thank you," Katherine said in a soft voice. "Meet me at McPherson Square at eleven. The people are protesting. So am I. We, the people, have to bring this situation back under control. What do you make of the note?"

"You'll need the full armor of God. You're in the line of fire."

Chapter Eighty-Nine

Hal had been waiting for Katherine outside of the chapel. Exiting the hospital, he offered his hand to her for support. She was relieved there was no press in sight as they approached her armored SUV. Stepping up to her seat, she turned and said to Hal, "Call Julianne LaSalle and tell her what's happening at McPherson Square."

"Got a call from Roy," Hal said, shifting the transmission into gear. "She knows. Galt called Julianne after we left the White House last night and told her to show up early at McPherson Square with a crowd if she wanted to get on top of a breaking Supreme Court story. He told her, for the record, he's not resigning. I understand she's already working the square."

Katherine gave a weak response. "I don't want anyone else to know that my mother just died. I can't deal with sympathy right now."

She closed her eyes for the ride back to her Georgetown condo.

At 8:35 a.m., Katherine and her security detail arrived at her building. Graham was waiting for her in the lobby, having been notified of the plans by the White House. He stood when she entered.

"Can we talk in private?" he asked. "It's important."

"Not now," she responded without slowing her pace.

He tried to stop her. "You don't have to do this. It's dangerous."

"*Not* doing my job is dangerous," she snapped. "You need to do your job when asked."

She turned her back and proceeded through the open elevator door, her security detail in close ranks behind her.

Graham called out to her. "I'll do what you ask."

The elevator doors closed.

Katherine entered her unit and called the girls. "This is Kathy. Check out the news. I'm speaking at McPherson Square this morning. Need your support, if you're not afraid. After London, you know the risks when you out hang out with me. Whatever you decide is okay. But if you can—meet me at K and Nineteenth in a half hour wearing black, ready to march to McPherson Square. This is important. I don't have time to say more. Bye."

She didn't tell them that her mother had just died. Unable to deal with that emotion, she buried it deep. She could pretend her mother was still alive for the next few hours.

By 9:15 a.m. Katherine was dressed for the protest. She wore a black cape with a black wide-brimmed hat. Her hair was pulled back into a small bun. Grabbing her sunglasses, she glanced in the mirror. Ready for the march.

She hadn't given up her right to protest against evil when she became a Supreme Court justice. This was the right day for her to give a fiery speech. She didn't care what happened. She was going to do and say what she thought was right.

She sat at her office desk and banged out the fifth letter in less than five minutes, put it in an envelope, sealed it, and tucked it into her purse.

She felt a strange sense of calmness. *She's still with me—I'm okay.*

Katherine straightened her back, lifted her head, and strolled down the hallway. The words she would say to the crowd began to play in her head. No weak thoughts were allowed. But she couldn't think rationally. She had to say what she felt was right.

This would not be a political speech. She would speak from her heart.

Her thoughts jumped to Skip. It wasn't his fault. It was her fault. She had put up a shield that no man had been able to penetrate—and now she faced life alone. She had seen love in Skip's eyes. Would she be able to give love a chance?

How could she have all of these mixed emotions and thoughts now?

"I'm surprised to see you on my detail this morning," Katherine said to Roy, settling in the back seat. "You're entitled to a day off after what you've been through."

"Naw," Roy said, "I couldn't let you face this without me. I know you missed President Canty's press conference this morning. He declared a state of national emergency due to an invasion of the Sea Islands by known Chinese dissidents acting without the support of their government. On live television, he ordered all uniformed Army personnel in the D.C. area to Andrews Air Force base for immediate deployment to the Sea Islands—with no delay. All uniformed Army personnel in the city were order to be picked up and transported by the DC National Guard to Andrews. Impostors are being arrested at this moment. The DC National Guard will be assisted by Navy SEALs. No uniformed Army personnel will be allowed on the streets of the District today."

"That's good news."

Roy pulled a black mask out of a bag. "I brought something for you to consider. I found these at a Halloween store. I thought they might help us keep you undercover until the last moment. The plain one is the one BAMN is distributing. Your mask has red heart teardrops on the right cheek. You can blend in with the crowd. All security personnel will have on masks with the red hearts." Roy added, "I bought all of the Guy Fawkes masks, too."

"Guy Fawkes?"

"You know, the Gun Powder Treason Rhyme guy— 'Remember, remember the Fifth of November should never be forgotten' or something like that. The Guy Fawkes mask is used by protesters who want to remain anonymous. You'll recognize them when you see them."

"I was about to say the masks are a great idea, but I think Guy Fawkes represents the use of violence to accomplish political objectives. It's my job to keep us from the path of violence."

"I thought about it a little bit differently," Roy responded. "I thought we needed to identify the Guy Fawkes energy in the crowd to make our job a little easier. I think we tag the radicals better with the Guy Fawkes masks. But Homeland Security will decide if they are to be used."

Roy's cell phone rang. "We're on our way." The SUV began to roll again. "Everybody's in position. One more thing—this sealed envelope was on the arrangement of blue roses sitting on your chambers desk and we don't have a record of the delivery. Don't want to invade your privacy, but could you open it now?"

"Let me have it," she said, holding her hand out.

She pulled out a yellow notecard and settled back into her seat. She read:

Justice Ross:

> **Your mother stepped in our path.**
> **Do not compromise our valuable asset.**
> **We think the Court is properly balanced as is.**
> **Watch your step.**

"It's very personal," Katherine said in a soft voice, stuffing the notecard and envelope in her purse. "We can talk about it after the march."

"You sure? Galt received a dozen blue roses with a note yesterday, too."

"I'm on overload," she snapped. "I can't deal with it now."

"Okay," Roy said.

"This mask is the ultimate poker face for a public official in distress," Katherine said in a half-joking manner, cocking her head. "I might not take it off when I speak." She pulled her hat off and slipped on her mask. "Do you have six extra masks?"

He chuckled. "I have hundreds."

The SUV slowed to a stop. She took in the high level of pedestrian activity on the street. Nineteenth was closed off in both directions. Dozens of police cruisers and motorcycles were ascending, preparing to close K Street. Uniformed U.S. Marines swarmed the streets of D.C.

She watched Debbie, Jolene, Ronnie, Merle, and Cheryl arrive one by one at the corner. All dressed in black. Jo in her baddest boots from London. Debbie in black jeans with thigh highs. Ronnie in a leather jacket over black scrubs and gym shoes. Merle in Timberlands, and Cheryl in UGGS.

"Those are my friends on the corner in black," Katherine said to Roy. "Go give them their masks and ask them to join me when the march begins. Tell them to come up on the stage with me when we get to the square."

Roy got out of the car and went to speak to the girls.

Katherine waited thirty-five minutes for the security arrangements on the street to be completed. She listened to radio news reports about the national emergency in the Sea Islands, the growing crowd at McPherson Square, and the distribution of thousands of masks to the protestors from an unknown source. News commentators were speculating that this was a well-planned event, in spite of previous reports of no known leadership for the protest.

She saw a uniformed Army soldier being questioned by two Marines. One Marine drew his weapon, then the other quickly handcuffed the soldier. They lead him to a mobile detention unit in the middle of the block, heavily guarded.

Could they catch all of the rogue soldiers?

Would the rogue soldiers act with no leadership to direct them? She could only pray.

At least they were easy to spot now.

At 10:40 a.m. her door opened and she stepped out of the car. Several masked security officers flanked her. Katherine turned to face K Street. The girls joined her protectors. Debbie jumped out front with her exercise trot, happy to be the leader. Cheryl and Merle assumed positions in the rear. They stepped at a vigorous pace while the masked crowd in front of them grew. Katherine marched down the middle of K Street with her emotions thundering.

An image of her mother's lifeless body pushed its way into her consciousness.

She focused on her path, one calculated step after another.

Ahead, she spotted a few others in masks with red hearts. Spontaneously people popped out of buildings, most with masks, joining the march of anonymous souls toward the square. Her strides commanded attention as the army of protestors and protectors grew behind and beside her, as if orchestrated for a movie scene.

Those around Katherine kept pace with her commanding strides.

In anonymity, she started a peaceful movement on K Street.

Crossing intersections closed to motor traffic, she felt her power to make a difference.

There were several thousand people around her by the time she reached McPherson Square. Curious people had emptied from their buildings. Many accepted the masks, not wanting to be caught on camera at a protest march. The availability of a massive quantity of masks allowed the crowd to mushroom into thousands without fear.

Katherine cut through the crowds, which gave way as if her arrival had been announced.

She spotted Julianne's red shoes. Julianne wore a black mask with red tears.

There were hundreds of black masks with red hearts along her path, mixed together with the Guy Fawkes protestors. Unified. Peaceful. Protesting for justice.

Although it appeared to be a picture-perfect event, there were no planners of the McPherson Square march present—because they were all dead. *But who had paid for all of this?*

Alexander Morris crossed her mind.

She wasn't out of danger yet.

And she knew it.

Chapter Ninety

A uniformed sentry allowed Katherine and her entourage to pass without challenge. Eight members of her security detail and her friends followed her onto the speaker's platform. Reaching the center of the stage, the justice stood, flanked by her guards and friends, before a crowd that had swelled into the thousands overnight. She saw white satellite trucks in the distance. The networks had carved out their space. Camera crews battled for position with their lenses trained on her. Peering out into the crowd, she felt numb.

Would she survive this day?

Across the street, Alexander Morris was seated at Sweet Georgia Brown's, sipping sweet tea in the outside seating area of the restaurant and watching everything from behind dark glasses. He felt the hunger of an eagle about to devour its prey rise up in him. He ordered fried chicken with greens and cornbread—a fitting meal. Morris wondered where Michael Spade was.

He glanced up toward the roof of his condo building at the far end of the park, knowing that he had company waiting. Julianne LaSalle had been told to be there by eleven to get a great shot of the rally from the living room window of Unit 1108. Julianne thought she had talked to John Galt's secretary and would be interviewing him there after Justice Ross spoke.

Earlier that morning, Jennie Galt told Paula Morris that Katherine was going to deliver the fifth letter after the rally in McPherson Square. Paula had given the bad news to her husband.

His response had been quick. He issued orders—Galt's seat would be protected by whatever means necessary, and Galt reeled back in. They couldn't let him get away. Morris decided that Galt's new mouthpiece needed to be silenced as the first step in his control strategy.

They had the perfect setup to make that happen.

The hunter would report that Julianne LaSalle had broken into Morris's condo and was taken out by his private security in self-defense.

Julianne carried a concealed weapon. But she would be no match for the hunter.

At 11:05 a.m., Morris's cell phone chirped with a text. It read: *She's in position. Ready.*

He punched a text to a second number, *Execute.*

On command, clad in black, the hunter climbed the stairwell in Morris's building.

Katherine watched Hal out of the corner of her eye. Finally he gave her the signal to start. She took a deep breath, squared her shoulders, and straightened her spine before approaching the microphone. She put on her emotional armor. A robe of steel.

Her image appeared on large video screens on each side of the stage. She gazed out at an ocean of masked faces, some with red hearts, most without. The brave wore no masks at all. She began in a calm voice. "I am here today to lead us in a march for justice."

The crowd grew silent.

"I'm speaking to you from my heart today, as an American who cares about protecting our freedoms. We are in a state of national emergency today because foreigners have a beachhead in the American Sea Islands—and we have been fenced out. Should we allow our constitutional rights to be bought by foreigners? That is a question that must be answered soon.

"So let's think about what brought us to this point today. We simply cannot allow our Constitution to be used as a weapon against us. We are facing a national emergency because we have embraced a lie and accepted compromises that have not been in the interests of the people."

She caught a glimpse of a uniformed Army soldier emerging from a porta-potty to her far left. *Was that an automatic rifle? They'll get him.* She couldn't show any fear. She resolved to continue, snapping her attention back to the crowd awaiting her next words.

"Even with our problems, this is a great nation. We must resist attempts to push us off balance and into anarchy. Today there are agitators among us who would like to see this crowd turn into a fighting frenzy, so that trigger-happy uniformed agents representing *we don't know who* can use us for target practice. We can't allow that to happen. So I'm asking you to remain calm and march with me in peaceful protest against our intimidators to the White House. We will act as if their threats are powerless because, in truth, they are. We will remain fearless and I will give voice to your concerns."

She paused. "Look at what history has shown us about peaceful protest. Through nonviolence, Mahatma Gandhi overcame British colonialism. Nelson Mandela demonstrated that regimes of self-interested rulers could be broken down by nonviolent means. I will face my intimidators today without fear," Katherine boomed into the microphone, taking her mask off and throwing it aside. "Are you ready to face yours with no fear?"

Mask after mask hit the ground. She felt her energy rise. "I am Associate Supreme Court Justice Katherine Helena Ross, and I join you today in defending our inalienable constitutional rights as people who are free. Know this—there is no need to march to the Supreme Court today for I have the fifth letter with me now."

She waited, finding strength to speak forcefully. Energized by the crowd's response.

Morris's meal was placed before him, the crowd roaring in his ear. *Good.* He attacked the greens first, with cornbread crumbs falling onto his plate. He savored a chicken wing as the sounds of protest danced in the air, and saved the breast for last. *Again. Where was Spade?*

The hunter forced the lock on Morris's condo door when the cheers of the crowd covered any noise he might make. He moved in silence and found Julianne peering out the window with a wide lens camera. One quiet bullet to the head and she went down. The red shoes matched her blood. He checked her pulse. Julianne was dead. Silenced. A message to Galt.

He pushed her body out of the way and took her position at the window, peering through his binoculars. The hunter spotted a Navy mate in the crowd. His old buddy surveyed the rooftops. The buddy monitored movements in the crowd with trained eyes. Working.

Katherine continued. "I share your righteous anger at the special interests. I share in your personal losses to evil forces." With her voice cracking she said, "For, this day I have lost my mother to violence defending the principles of our Constitution. And I want the bullies to know I have just begun to fight!

"I stand here in public protest of violence in America as a vehicle for change—and I will not be forced into a cage of fear. I hereby give my intimidators notice that their fear tactics will not work to create chaos across America. The evil forces arrayed around us will fail."

She noticed a military helicopter overhead and ignored it.

"You came here today to march against the U.S. Supreme Court, but the Court is not your oppressor. Often the Supreme Court rules against your oppressors but, you know, sometimes the Court does nothing in egregious cases, in the name of keeping the peace. Often a price is paid for unity in the family, unity in the country, and unity in the world. But there are times when the price of unity becomes too high, and we must fight those who would deny us our freedoms and rights as human beings. But how do we fight? Not with violence. We fight by resisting and speaking out. We fight by debating with the power of our words. We fight by changing unfair laws. We fight by doing what's right in our hearts without fear. We fight with public protest."

"You might not know this, but there is a long history of Supreme Court justices speaking out against oppression and intimidation. Today I join the ranks of those, like Justice William O. Douglas, who said: 'As nightfall does not come all at once, neither does oppression. In both instances, there is a twilight when everything remains seemingly unchanged. And it is in such twilight that we all must be most aware of change in the air, however slight, lest we become unwitting victims of the darkness.'

"I think we're in the twilight zone in America. A time when we must move toward unity by fighting selfishness that leads to darkness in our lives and darkness in the world. Each of us carries a light that can make a difference in the world—if we have the courage to use it."

In a forceful tone she said, "We are not powerless."

When the crowd quieted, she moved on. "I put on my marchin' boots this mornin' because violence only breeds more violence. Diplomacy with compromise and patience is the only path to lasting peace. We can't force our will on others. And we can't allow others to force their will on us."

The hunter reached into his bag and assembled a high-powered rifle. He rose to check on the crowd through his binoculars again. His old buddy raked the crowd over—searching with his eyes. He had an earpiece in place. His head turned toward Morris's building, surveying it with interest. The hunter pulled back from view, lowering the Hunter Douglass blinds. He peeped through the side of the blinds—he still had a clear shot. He heard a helicopter overhead.

The hunter decided to hold his shot.

"Our Constitution wasn't written in 1787 for people like me," Katherine continued. "It was created with a fiction that people like me were just three-fifths of a person. That wasn't right. And it took a long time for us to break down that socially constructed reality because the people let it be. In truth, we have the political power to force change."

She leaned into the microphone. "I think it's time for another fiction in our country to fall. But this fiction wasn't created in 1787. This fiction was created by the U.S. Supreme Court in 1817 and it is the cause of our state of national emergency today.

"This legal fiction is called: *The corporation is a person.*

"So what do I want you to do to fix this problem? I want 'We the People' to amend the United States Constitution to make it clear that 'We the People' are human beings. And I am calling on the Congress to pass a constitutional amendment to do just that. The corporation today is no more a human being than a slave in 1787 was three-fifths of a person.

"This doesn't mean we don't need corporations, but corporations should not have the same inalienable rights as human beings—and they certainly should not have super rights over our American citizens. I think the original intent of the Constitution is clear. The U.S. Constitution was written for the human people and I have a right to say that."

Roars from the crowd reached for the clouds in the sky.

Moving in, they covered the sun.

Morris watched a SWAT team enter his building.

Quickly, he punched out a text to a third number: *NOW!*

Morris put a one hundred dollar bill on the table. Got up and went to the men's room where he threw the stolen cell phone into the trash.

"We cannot allow foreigners to gain the rights of U.S. citizens by simply buying our U.S. corporations. But that is what we are allowing today. Can American citizenship rights be bought in the stock market by anyone with a U.S. dollar? That's why we need to make it clear that 'We the People' are not pieces of paper with super-human rights that benefit the moneyed interests of the world.

"We are facing a state of national emergency today in the Sea Islands along the coasts of Florida, Georgia and South Carolina because foreign interests have claimed corporate property rights to strategically important U.S. soil. I will not say more because the Supreme Court might have a case on this matter. But I will say, I think we need a simple constitutional amendment to make it clear that 'We the People' are human beings of the United States of America."

She drilled on. "Our freedoms will be reborn to us when we have 'government of the people, by the people, for the people.' We should have rules of law for *the* people, not laws shaped by the lobbyists for *their people.*"

Katherine felt her energy rise. "For the people who don't like what I'm saying: this is public notice to the bullies that I'm going to stand up for what's right. Even when I must stand alone in the face of threats. Even if I must die."

The crowd was hushed.

"When we learn how to work as one, like the individual molecules that make up a wave in the ocean, in sync with the will of the Creator, acting without rational thought or fear of crashing onto the shores of this life, we will become a nation that values all life, creates opportunity for all, and has no violence in its culture.

"That's what I believe America's destiny to be."

The cheers erupted again.

As Morris strolled down K Street, uniformed Navy SEALs surrounded him.

Michael Spade, a former Navy SEAL Team Six member, watched through his binoculars. He knew a couple of the SEALs on duty. They were under contract to him for information only, and had just warned him. Spade knew Morris would be arrested. Their plan was falling apart.

A search of his building was underway.

That information sealed Morris's fate.

There was no choice. *Paula Hale Morris would understand.* The descendants of the country's privateers all had tough skin and had learned to survive loss. She would get over it. He reached for his weapon. Spade took aim at Morris from an unoccupied office in his K Street building with a high-powered rifle.

He fired. The bullet hit the target in the head.

Can't let a big fish take us under—Morris's favorite line. *Cut the rope if you have to.*

Spade was in it for the cause.

"I will deliver the fifth letter to the Chair of the Senate Judiciary Committee at the White House today," Katherine said. "As you may know, the decision to issue the fifth letter has been a difficult one for me. After weighing all of the evidence, I have decided to trigger a process that should strengthen the Court. I trust the Senate will carry out its duties without undue influence from the lobbyists and others who see violence as a legitimate means to an end."

The hunter took aim at Katherine's head.

The door to Alexander Morris's condo flew open. The hunter spun around. Multiple rounds of silenced automatic bullets ripped through his body armor and vital organs.

The hunter's body fell to the floor with a thud next to Julianne's.

"Will you march with me to deliver the fifth letter this morning?" Katherine asked. "Join me, marching as a unified force—moving like a forceful wave—ultimately becoming a tsunami of change for the people of the United States of America. Follow me to

K Street to march down Lobbyists Row, then down Nineteenth Street to C Street for another peaceful demonstration in front of the White House. I think we're expected and we'll be well received. As we march today, be mindful of the fact that true power is immune to force."

Katherine stepped off the platform to reach the people who were one with her. Their masks were all on the ground, now trash being blown away by the winds of change. She felt the sunlight on her cheeks and saw the clouds rolling away. The people made way for her as she marched in a line to K Street. Katherine's friends surrounded her, with thousands falling in line behind them in peaceful and determined protest against the puppeteers who sought to render them powerless. With each step, more and more brave souls fell in line behind the justice until a critical mass for change made its way to the White House.

The weakened legal eagles for the moneyed interests on K Street peered through their windows at the unprecedented crowd. The people were making their demands known on national television. Katherine had made the people's demand for a constitutional amendment known: recognition of 'We the People' as human beings. Simple. Direct. Self-evident.

That day, Justice Katherine Helena Ross took her first step on the road of becoming a great Supreme Court justice, breaking down another socially constructed reality that had limited the power of the people in America for two hundred years.

ABOUT THE AUTHOR

Vivian L. Carpenter is a writer, motivational speaker, and teacher. She holds three degrees from the University of Michigan: a BSE in industrial engineering and operations research, an MBA and a Ph.D. in business administration. As an academic, she has won several awards and grants for her scholarly work in institutional theory from the National Science Foundation, Governmental Accounting Standards Board, Kellogg Foundation and Ford Foundation.

As a business professional, she was Director of Academic Programs at Florida A&M University's School of Business and Industry (SBI) and served as chairperson of the board of MotorCity Casino in Detroit, Michigan. She lives in Tallahassee, Florida and Birmingham, Michigan.

Acknowledgments

Over the seven years it took me to create *The Fifth Letter* I received help from a lot of people. I know there are at least a hundred people that made contributions to this work whom I have not mentioned below. Forgive me. Thanks to all.

A heartfelt thanks to William Martin, my main editor, who challenged me on every word and every page to take *The Fifth Letter* from the 758-page first draft to the finished work you are holding in your hands today. Then to Jean Jenkins, another editor, who helped me shape *The Fifth Letter* when I couldn't figure out how to do anymore cuts and was afraid to go back to Bill without the 200-page haircut he demanded while insisting I add the senate confirmation hearing scenes.

Next, I owe a big thanks to my class at the 2007 Maui Writer's Conference. I attended a retreat for beginning writers that was taught my Ann Hood. Nellie Williamson (Sara Stark) and Barbara Capell from my retreat class read countless early drafts. It was Ann Hood who taught me how to put emotion into the Hattie's Story scenes. Attending her classes was a blessing.

At a writer's retreat in Fiji, I attended Steve Berry's novel-writing classes. That's where Hattie's Story continued to mature. Steve made me cry, teaching me about the power of showing, rather than telling. Thanks, Steve. I got your point.

Thanks to Rev. Charles G. Adams, Pastor of Hartford Memorial Baptist Church. I used some of his sermon points. He provided spiritual energy and intellectual insights.

A dinner with Princeton University President Christopher Eisgruber led me to read his book, *The Next Justice*. This inspired a complete rewriting of Katherine's senate confirmation scenes. Thanks, President Eisgruber.

Thanks to Richard D. McLellan and Gregory Allen Howard for being advance readers and providing critical comments that significantly improved *The Fifth Letter*.

Thanks to all of my tenured friends who read multiple drafts along the way: Cheryl Hatton, Doreen Dudley, Jo Coleman, Marilyn Norwood, Emma Lockridge, Nancy Colah, Sibyl Chavis, Debbie Smith, Prof. Pamela Jones, Esq., and Dr. Veronica Wells Butler.

Last but not least, thanks to my family. My mother, Jennie Thomas, who agreed to allow me to use her name in *The Fifth Letter* before I realized the character's name needed to be Jennie Galt. Not Jennie Thomas.

To my uncle Hiram Thomas, the Thomas family historian, who said, "You don't know how much truth is in your story," after his first reading of Hattie's Story.

To my twin aunts, Doris Stroud and Dorothy Swann, who have encouraged and supported me in all of my life efforts.

To my daughter Carmen Strather, who challenged me to do more research to better understand the character John Galt. To my daughter Nikki Strather Middleton, who helped with development of TheFifthLetter.com website.

And finally, a special thanks to my husband, Jon Eric Barfield, who has read more drafts than anyone, and provided me with a constant stream of emotional support and legal insight during the creation of *The Fifth Letter*. It was nice to have a Harvard Law School graduate for pillow talk during the creation of *The Fifth Letter*.

Made in the USA
Middletown, DE
19 May 2015